*The Best*
# AMERICAN
# SHORT
# STORIES
# 2019

## GUEST EDITORS OF THE BEST AMERICAN SHORT STORIES

1978 TED SOLOTAROFF
1979 JOYCE CAROL OATES
1980 STANLEY ELKIN
1981 HORTENSE CALISHER
1982 JOHN GARDNER
1983 ANNE TYLER
1984 JOHN UPDIKE
1985 GAIL GODWIN
1986 RAYMOND CARVER
1987 ANN BEATTIE
1988 MARK HELPRIN
1989 MARGARET ATWOOD
1990 RICHARD FORD
1991 ALICE ADAMS
1992 ROBERT STONE
1993 LOUISE ERDRICH
1994 TOBIAS WOLFF
1995 JANE SMILEY
1996 JOHN EDGAR WIDEMAN
1997 E. ANNIE PROULX
1998 GARRISON KEILLOR
1999 AMY TAN
2000 E. L. DOCTOROW
2001 BARBARA KINGSOLVER
2002 SUE MILLER
2003 WALTER MOSLEY
2004 LORRIE MOORE
2005 MICHAEL CHABON
2006 ANN PATCHETT
2007 STEPHEN KING
2008 SALMAN RUSHDIE
2009 ALICE SEBOLD
2010 RICHARD RUSSO
2011 GERALDINE BROOKS
2012 TOM PERROTTA
2013 ELIZABETH STROUT
2014 JENNIFER EGAN
2015 T. C. BOYLE
2016 JUNOT DÍAZ
2017 MEG WOLITZER
2018 ROXANE GAY
2019 ANTHONY DOERR

# *The Best* AMERICAN SHORT STORIES® 2019

Selected from
U.S. and Canadian Magazines
by ANTHONY DOERR
with HEIDI PITLOR

*With an Introduction by Anthony Doerr*

MARINER BOOKS
HOUGHTON MIFFLIN HARCOURT
BOSTON • NEW YORK 2019

hmhbooks.com

ISSN 0067-6233 (print)
ISSN 2573-4784 (ebook)
ISBN 978-1-328-46582-5 (hardcover)
ISBN 978-1-328-48424-6 (paperback)
ISBN 978-1-328-46712-6 (ebook)
ISBN 978-0-358-17210-9 (audio)

Printed in the United States of America
DOC 10 9 8 7 6 5 4 3 2 1

# Contents

# Foreword

MY KIDS, TWELVE-YEAR-OLD TWINS, both love books. At least they do for now. I say this not with immodesty but awe. They also love YouTube, as well as my phone (we are holding out as long as possible before getting them their own phones), certain movies that are streaming, and TV shows and video games. But they prefer their fiction and other long-form reading between covers and on pages made of paper. The fact that they choose to read anything long-form that is not required for school gives me hope. According to a Pew Research poll, in 2000, 48 percent of Americans did not use the internet; in 2018, only 11 percent were nonusers. This is my thirteenth foreword to *The Best American Short Stories*, and I wonder if there has ever been a more change-filled thirteen years in the way that we spend our day-to-day lives. Our phones can alert us to upcoming traffic, accidents, and even roadkill. Amazon Alexa can order your refrigerator to turn on its icemaker. I don't need to recount all of the methods by which we now stay in touch, fall in love, champion causes, shame others. And read.

Early on in his reading for this book, guest editor Anthony Doerr described to me his challenge in reorienting to each new short story sent to him—120 distinct voices, plots, sets of characters—and frankly, I was relieved to hear that I was not alone. I confess that in the past few years, I have found my own attention span fractured. We are now, many of us, moving so quickly from task to task, from texting to life to work to social media, that it has grown a little difficult to engage in something that requires our minds to slow down for an extended period of time.

In my house, we do impose screen limits and constantly urge our children to be more in the world, to have physical experiences, but also to get comfortable with being bored. *It's OK to just sit still and be blank,* I tell my kids. *Look out the window sometimes. Think, imagine, let your minds wander—and see where your mind lands.* Of course, moments of stillness and blankness have become rarer for most of us. I too am not all that comfortable with boredom anymore. And so I find my children's engagement with books these days almost miraculous. I will not lie: given the choice between a book and a computer, they will usually choose a computer. But I have seen them fall into certain books—and it does look like they have in fact landed somewhere they want to be. During a quiet afternoon or before bed, I have watched them turn pages, oblivious to me and the dog and everything else, and I am reminded of what a story can do. A good narrative can slow a mind that's moving too quickly. A great story is its own kind of meditation, and at the risk of sounding even more woo-woo, its own kind of out-of-body experience. A ceding of one's heartbeat and focus to another place and time. What a gift this is, especially now.

I truly enjoyed working with Anthony Doerr, who, as he describes in the following pages, arrived at this gig with his analytical mind prepared and ready. When he began, he pointed out to me the plot holes in certain stories, the inconsistencies and implausibilities. Here's a secret: every year, in some way, I find myself telling the guest editor that there are not twenty perfect stories. There is not even one perfect story. There is, to my knowledge, no such thing to all people. What one person sees as implausible, another sees as imaginative. You have to keep your eyes on something other than the authors' missteps to do this work, although of course, too many missteps can sink any story. But in general, you learn to keep your gaze on something bigger and broader, the horizon of a story, say, rather than the potholes. The horizon —the place where voice, mood, plot, characterization, language, and perspective coalesce and expand—the horizon is where you'll find, as Anthony calls it in his introduction, the "magic."

Lately I am drawn to bold stories, stories that without any equivocation go somewhere. Sentences that set something simple and clear on the table. To be bold in one's writing right now seems to me an act of tremendous courage. The legendary Ursula K. Le Guin never shied away from fearless thinking, and her astonishing story of a woman nursing a wounded mine inspector does not disappoint. Ella Martinsen Gorham's story, "Protozoa," rings with poetic assurance: "With crazy eyes she pretended she was about to jump off the edge of an overlook, like the ocean was a trampoline she could bounce on." In the first sentence of his searing story, Manuel Muñoz does not waste words: "Her immediate concern was money."

The stories in this volume are bold, some are transgressive, and all are relevant to this moment in time. Some eschew conventions of plot. Anthony and I discussed the diffuseness of this year's stories, how wonderfully unfocused and digressive so many were. I have a kneejerk tendency to play armchair psychologist when it comes to trends in short fiction, and I do wonder if because there are so many gripping plots coursing through our country—just read the news any day of the week—story writers are filling their pages with a different kind of thinking now, one more meditative or sprawling as respite from the deluge of conflicts in the real world. I have zero data to back this up, of course, simply my own gut feeling and a very regular diet of short stories. But in this time of so much bad news about our climate, intolerance, corruption, and violence, I'm grateful for these stories and the way they slowed my mind, transported me, and reminded me of the power of language.

This year we say goodbye to two magazines that have been beacons for writers and readers over the years. Farewell, *Glimmer Train* and *Tin House*, and thank you for the enormous amount of beauty that you brought to readers over the years. I also want to thank April Eberhardt, Jenny Xu, and Nicole Angeloro for their invaluable help with this book.

The stories chosen for this anthology were originally published between January 2018 and January 2019. The qualifications for selection are (1) original publication in nationally distributed American or Canadian periodicals; (2) publication in English by writers who have made the United States or Canada their home; (3) original publication as short stories (excerpts of novels are not considered). A list of magazines consulted for this volume appears at the back of the book. Editors who wish their short fiction to be considered for next year's edition should send their publications or hard copies of online publications to Heidi Pitlor, c/o The Best American Short Stories, 125 High Street, Boston, MA 02110, or files to thebestamericanshortstories@gmail.com as attachments.

HEIDI PITLOR

# *Introduction*

As a boy I dreamed of becoming a writer, though this was an aspiration I articulated to no one, partially because I lived in rural Ohio and had never met or even glimpsed a writer, and partially because the writers I brought home from the library were all superworldly like Paul Bowles or superfamous like Gabriel García Márquez or superdead like Sarah Orne Jewett, and I was not worldly or famous or dead. Writers seemed a rare and exalted species; I figured I had as much of a chance of growing up to be one as I did of growing up to be a blue whale.

Yet I wrote. I wrote a nine-page book about snails titled *Mollusks* (riveting) and typed stories about my Playmobil pirates on my mother's typewriter, primarily for the pleasure of typing swear words, then frantically covering them up with gobs of Wite-Out. In my teens I scribbled short stories into spiral notebooks, most of which featured a boy who walked out of school in the middle of the day and never returned, because to a kid with a science-teacher mom and a perfect attendance record for four years running, walking out of school in the middle of the day and never returning was the most epic beginning to a story imaginable.

I didn't show these stories to anyone. Someday, maybe, long after I was dead, a beautiful and intrepid researcher might unearth my notebooks, decipher my microscopic handwriting, and be overcome by my brilliance. For now the magic of using black marks on a white page to conjure people and places out of nothingness was reward enough.

Or at least it was enough until our junior-year English teacher announced a forthcoming short story contest. I was not good at basketball, growing facial hair, or talking to girls, but maybe, I thought, maybe I could be good at this. Maybe I could win.

My current story-in-progress was "Avalanche," about a boy who strolls out of a trigonometry test, steals a delivery van containing thousands of chocolate bars, and drives to the Yukon only to become caught in (surprise!) an avalanche. I had loads of fun describing the snow whooshing and tumbling and grinding around the van, then switched to the point of view of a nearby dog who, out of the goodness of his dog-heart, begins searching for the buried kid. Then I jumped into some backstory on the dog (nice farm-girl, mean farmer, a misunderstanding involving chickens) and I described how the dog smells all that chocolate through six feet of snow and digs out the boy and they eat frozen Twix bars and the boy never studies trigonometry again.

Guaranteed victory, right?

I wasn't sure. A drip-drip of uncertainty sent me to the library, where I discovered a paperback titled *Writing in General and the Short Story in Particular*, which claimed to reveal "the secrets of the craft." Though the author, Rust Hills, sounded more like a South Dakota land feature than a short story expert, the jacket copy explained that Mr. Hills worked at *Esquire* and had discovered all sorts of famous writers, and so it was with a mix of excitement and terror that I toted the book to my attic bedroom.

"Everyone knows what a short story is anyway," Mr. Hills began, and I thought, *Hmm, everyone?* Then he said that "the successful contemporary short story will demonstrate a more harmonious relationship of all its aspects than will any other literary art form" and I thought, *Hmm, what's an aspect?*

With each passing paragraph my anxiety compounded. "The story writer will not usually elaborate secondary characters," Mr. Hills declared on page 3, "won't usually mess much with subplots . . ." Was my runaway dog a secondary character? Maybe he was a subplot?

"Where the novelist may bounce around in point of view," Mr. Hills went on, "the short story writer will usually maintain a single point of view . . ."

Wait, dog point of view wasn't allowed?

On page 4 Mr. Hills hurried back to his harmony thing, declaring that in a successful story "everything enhances everything else, interrelates with everything else, is inseparable from everything else—and all this is done with a necessary and perfect economy," but by then my drip-drip of uncertainty had swelled into a torrent. Rust Hills had published E. Annie Proulx, he had published John Cheever, whose bright-red tome of collected stories my mom kept face-out on the shelf downstairs, he knew *the secrets of the craft*, and here he was saying that the moves that brought me the most joy —introducing new characters midstream, hopping into the minds of farm animals, and chasing digressions—were exactly the moves I shouldn't be making.

I felt like the boy at the end of "Araby," alone in the darkening bazaar, my eyes burning with anguish. I wanted to make big sprawling jungles but Mr. Hills was saying I ought to be growing little bonsai trees.

I scrapped "Avalanche" and wrote a new story for the contest, most of which I have blocked from memory, except that it stayed in a single point of view, included zero subplots, contained zero secondary characters, and was zero fun to write. I titled it "Caesura," despite not really knowing what a caesura was, and handed it in, and did not win the short story contest. My friend Gabe won, for a three-page story in which he told me, laughing, nothing meant anything.

Years passed before I risked showing a story to anyone again. Any time I started careening around in time machines, introducing talking goats, or hot-wiring vans full of chocolate bars, my pleasures got all tangled up with insecurities. I worried I was breaking rules that I didn't properly comprehend, that nothing I was making was harmonious enough, and that my "economy" was unnecessary and imperfect.

In my twenties I encountered many more rules for writing short stories—I'm guessing you probably have, too. Don't start with a character waking up. Jump right into the action. Exposition is boring. Backstory slows you down. Stick with a single protagonist. Make sure he or she is likable. Don't break up chronology. Don't digress. Don't overwrite. Don't tell a story inside the story. Don't take a moral stance. Don't have a character wake up at the end of a story and discover that everything was a dream. Etcetera.

Although I could see where the rule makers were coming from —backstory risks slowing down frontstory, it's true, and time-jumping risks confusing the reader, and stories with moral stances risk becoming preachy—I always felt a bristling aversion to rules, because the stories I loved usually broke two or three of them in the first five pages. Indeed, whenever I came across a list of rules like the one above, what I really wanted to do was write a story that was all backstory, in which multiple protagonists, none of whom are exactly likable, wake up, tell lots of different stories inside the story, argue significant moral points, then wake up a second time and realize the whole thing was a dream.

Last fall, when the indefatigable Heidi Pitlor sent me a first batch of forty stories, I dove right in. I had been reading lots of (very) dead writers—Sophocles, Homer, Ovid—and it was a delight to read stories involving Tinder and Lyft and underage Irish cabbies and Jamaican grandmothers and John Updike's sneakers in an oven.

Each time I'd start a new story, I'd get about two paragraphs in and see why Heidi selected it: it had a magnetic rhythm or an explosive opening or a spare beauty or a fabulous rain motif or a hobo-chic-transient-stalker-creep who looked vaguely like Brad Pitt. The hooks would go in: Manhattan was flooding, astronauts were falling from the sky, a woman was headed to a wake pretending to be her neighbor, and the golden drug of narrative would flash through my nervous system.

By Thanksgiving I felt as though I had lucked into the best gig ever. I had a gifted, generous, and Herculean reader examining every short story published in North America and mailing me tear sheets of her favorites; I was discovering brilliant similes everywhere; I was meeting adulterous Alaskan moms and White House switchboard operators and nuns buying beehives. I kept thinking: There are so many brave voices singing out there!

It was mid-December when I remembered, Shit. I'm supposed to decide why some of these stories are better than the others. I panicked. I spent an entire morning constructing a spreadsheet; I built fields to score and summarize and evaluate, and in about fourteen seconds all the pleasure ribboned away.

Evaluating is a very different experience than enjoying, and I suppose this is true when it comes to parenting, traveling, eating, having sex, and reading short stories. Evaluating sucks. Evaluating turns eating a delicious piece of pie into homework.

By Christmas my spreadsheet had grown gigantic. I synopsized every story, rated it on a scale of 1 to 10 by how much joy it gave me, how many risks it took, and how much literary merit it had (whatever that meant); I handed out 9s, 10s, and a few 11s, and my "What I Loved" fields became long and passionate, and my "What I Didn't Love" fields became short and painful, and I decided I was giving too many 10s and summarily demoted all pre-existing 10s to 9s, and by January my office resembled a Ministry of the Short Story run by drunken bureaucrats. Stacks of stories loomed on the file cabinet, on shelves, in drifts across the carpet, my *these-are-definitely-the-best* pile draped over the arm of the sofa, my *I-ranked-these-as-8s-but-was-I-being-fair?* pile next to the dog bowl, my *this-prose-is-dense-so-I-need-to-be-well-rested* stack on the desk, my *did-I-rank-these-too-low-because-they-were-about-cancer?* stack on my desk chair.

It was around then that I realized that I was having a familiar experience. I was doing what everybody who has ever tried to make a list of rules about short stories does: I was trying to bind the unbindable, circumscribe the uncircumscribable—to catch magic in my hands, measure it, and decree: This is how it should be done.

But the amazing and beautiful thing about the short story is the elasticity of the form. As soon as you complete a description of what a good story must be, a new example flutters through an open window, lands on your sleeve, and proves your description wrong. With every new artist, we simultaneously refine and expand our understanding of what the form can be.

At some point around mid-January, maybe ninety stories in, I gave up on trying to quantify everything and went back to reading for the pleasure of reading. My spreadsheet became a little less "Caesura" and a little more "Avalanche," and I aimed for a less rigid kind of rubric: Did the story last in my memory? Two days later, would pieces of the story come spiraling up during some quiet moment?

What I was looking for were fictions that walked the tightrope between control and exuberance, that exhibited not so much the flawless consonance that Rust Hills (and Poe before him) admired as, to borrow a phrase from Edmund White's *The Beautiful Room Is Empty,* a "cat's cradle of tensions." I wanted sentences that pulled me in multiple directions at once, structures that unsettled preexisting patterns, and techniques that took some previously ratified rule and poked it. The stories that lingered in my memory, I was learning, were at once the bonsai and the anti-bonsai; if they were a bonsai tree, they were a bonsai tree with a trash can full of moths dumped on top of it.

Rust Hills suggested that a short story writer stick with a single point of view, but Deborah Eisenberg, in her dystopic paean to the imagination, "The Third Tower," leaps into a doctor's mind in two of its thirteen sections. Without those leaps away from her protagonist's point of view, her story would collapse.

Wendell Berry waits until the last seven paragraphs of "The Great Interruption" to introduce a first-person narrator—a character you didn't even know was part of the story until you meet him. Berry also wraps a story within a story and accelerates wildly through time, and it is these contraventions that make you feel the story's moral heft: this isn't about a humorous old anecdote, it's about *now*, about a nation "dismemoried and without landmarks," about the destruction of local-ness and what it costs us. If Berry doesn't break these rules, his story doesn't work.

Hills said a story writer shouldn't mess much with subplots, but from a certain angle, Nicole Krauss constructs her gorgeous "Seeing Ershadi" entirely around subplots—three of her first five paragraphs, for example, are spent summarizing an Iranian film. Yet her story utterly wrecked me. The prose in Kathleen Alcott's haunting "Natural Light" is always trending away from straightforward clarity toward something more interesting; the central narrative hangs just out of reach as you pursue meaning down through the thickets of her sentences. And Jenn Alandy Trahan's "They Told Us Not to Say This," narrated by a collective "we" of NoCal girls, transforms the familiar expectations of rising and falling action into something newer: an anthem of independence.

Hills argued that in a story "everything's bound together tightly," but Julia Elliott's "Hellion," which contains kids racing yard carts, a gator named Dragon, and a Swamp Ape that eats Slim Jims, embraces exuberance with a courage I wish I possessed when I was a young writer. For decades writing teachers have been warning students not to open stories with too much exposition, yet Saïd Sayrafiezadeh opens "Audition" with seven long paragraphs of fluid, funny exposition before settling you into a proper scene, and I think you'll be grateful for it.

Sigrid Nunez, in "The Plan," smashes the "make your protagonist likable" dictum into splinters, then grinds those splinters into dust: her narrator, Roden Jones, is one of the most despicable actors you'll find in fiction, yet "The Plan" sucks you down into its whirlpool just the same. Or maybe you've heard the injunction that a short story is too small to sustain multiple protagonists? In this book two masters, Jeffrey Eugenides and Ursula K. Le Guin, contribute pieces that embrace dual protagonists as well as any short stories I can remember reading. Jim Shepard's epistolary "Our Day of Grace," about Confederate soldiers on their way to the 1864 Battle of Franklin, presents *four* protagonists, all while shining a light on our current hour, "when we consider how much corruption runs riot in high places, & that it may be that our country's day of grace is passed."

Speaking of which, anyone who thinks short stories can't or shouldn't ask moral questions about our political moment should turn to Weike Wang's "Omakase," a story as meticulously structured as any *omakase* dinner and which will wake you up to the minute-by-minute realities of white privilege as well as anything you'll read this year. "Black Corfu" by Karen Russell presents an Ovidian parable about xenophobia, racism, and the wealth gap—a zombie story set in 1620 that seems entirely about 2019. "They are neighbors," Russell writes, "and yet their breath barely overlaps."

In "Letter of Apology," Maria Reva presents a hilarious and heartrending glimpse of life under a regime where it is illegal to criticize or even joke about political leaders; Nana Kwame Adjei-Brenyah imagines a freaky postnuclear future of genetic modification and pharmaceutical addiction in "The Era"; Alexis Schaitkin's "Natural Disasters" explores profound questions about authenticity along America's urban/rural divide; Ella Martinsen Gorham's "Protozoa" demonstrates, in alarming detail, how difficult it is for its teenage protagonist to live both online and "in the actual world"; and Manuel Muñoz's moving "Anyone Can Do It," about a woman whose husband has been rounded up by immigration police, might be set in the 1980s but could not be more timely.

Empathy might be the most-talked-about value attached to fiction writing nowadays, but even that precept gets tested here. As you start Jamel Brinkley's "No More Than a Bubble," you wonder: Am I being asked to empathize with two young men who think of girls as "snacks"? Gradually, though, because another, wiser voice (the author's) populates the world around the narrator, the texture of your understanding deepens.

And Mona Simpson's "Wrong Object" pushes the reader to a different frontier of empathy—pedophilia—but by the end of her story, you might be surprised to find yourself asking: Who among us can't relate to trying to repel our own unbidden desires?

I started reading these stories as Christine Blasey Ford finished testifying during the Senate confirmation hearings for Brett Kavanaugh, and I finished these stories as the president's former lawyer Michael Cohen testified before the House Oversight Committee. All winter, questions about the truth and who gets to control it rippled through my thoughts. The stories we chose for this volume don't all focus on these questions, and they don't all violate the so-called rules to the same degree, but they do each stray far enough from the familiar to feel new and strange and true. They're about people severed from their places or their histories, about girls being told they "weren't worth much, not as much as sons" (Trahan, "They Told Us Not to Say This"), about an overdependence on pharmaceutical solutions to unhappiness, and about the insidious ways racism and classism can silence voices and distort memory. They are provocative, weird, dazzling, dark, bright, serious, and hilarious, and as a group they demonstrate the incredible possibilities implicit in the form.

Are these all the voices that Heidi and I should have discovered, all the voices that warrant inclusion, all the voices that need to be heard? Not even close. They're merely twenty stories that found us at the right intersection of interest and fatigue and experience and joy and longing. What I can promise is that, depending on whatever intersection of interest and fatigue and experience and joy and longing at which these stories find you, they will put their hooks into you.

Flip to a story at random, blink your eyes, and then it comes —"The first time I smoked crack cocaine was the spring I worked construction for my father on his new subdivision in Moonlight Heights" (Sayrafiezadeh, "Audition")—and your attention slips through the walls of your skull and lands in the hands of someone generous, someone you want to go examine the world with.

It's a kind of love: you fall in love.

Storytelling is the first and oldest spell, cast around lamps and fires since before there were cities, alphabets, and domesticated herbivores. The lives we live through stories intermix with our own memories, and because of stories our experiences multiply; our apprehension of the humanity of others is broadened, improved, and complicated, and each voice we hear becomes a small part of our own experience on this earth.

Inside the boards of this book are twenty different voices singing in twenty different registers to twenty different tunes from twenty different corners of *right now*, composed at a time when we worry about the future habitability of our planet; need to work harder to understand the lives of people who don't look, love, act, or vote like us; and continue to fight to allow marginalized stories to be told as publicly as any other. These stories push back against tradition even as they simultaneously embrace it, and help us remember that in art, so long as we humans manage to keep having children, and our children keep growing up and looking around at the stories their forebears have told and deciding they can tell them better (which is to say faster, or slower, or greener, or longer, or with more monsters, or fewer verbs, or more stolen vans full of chocolate bars), the resistance is always happening.

ANTHONY DOERR

*The Best*
AMERICAN
SHORT
STORIES
2019

# The Era

FROM *Guernica*

"SUCK ONE AND DIE," says Scotty, a tall, mostly true, kid. "I'm aggressive 'cause I think you don't know shit."

We're in HowItWas class.

"Well," Mr. Harper says, twisting his ugly body toward us. "You should shut your mouth because you're a youth-teen who doesn't know shit about shit and I'm a full-middler who's been teaching this stuff for more years than I'm proud of."

"Understood," says Scotty.

Then Mr. Harper went back to talking about the time before the Turn, which came after the Big Quick War, which came after the Long Big War. I was thinking about going to the nurse for some prelunch Good. I do bad at school because sometimes I think when I should be learning.

"So after the Big Quick," Mr. Harper continues in his bored voice, "science and philosopher guys realized that people had been living wrong the whole time before. Sacrificing themselves, their efficiency, and their wants. This made a world of distrust and misfortune, which led to the Big Wars.

"Back then, everyone was a liar. It was so bad that it would not have been uncommon for people to tell Samantha"—Mr. Harper points a finger at Samantha, who sits next to me—"that she was beautiful even though, obviously, she is hideous." Samantha nods her ugly head to show she understands. Her face is squished so bad she's always looking in two different directions. Sometimes, kids who get prebirth optiselected come out all messed up. Samantha is "unoptimal." That's the official name for people like her, whose optimization screwed up and made their bodies horrible. I don't have any gene corrections. I wasn't optimized at all. I am not optimal or ideal. But I'm also not unoptimal, so I wasn't going to look like Samantha, which is good. It's not all good, though, since no optiselect means no chance of being perfect either. I don't care. I'm true. I'm proud, still. Looking over, being nosy 'cause sometimes I do that, I see Samantha log in to her class pad: *I would have been pretty/beautiful.*

"Or"—and now Mr. Harper is looking at me; I can feel him thinking me into an example—"back then a teacher might've told Ben, who we know is a dummy, that he was smart or that if he would just apply himself he'd do better." The class laughs 'cause they think a world where I'm smart is hee-haw. In my head I think, *Mr. Harper, do you think that back then students would think you were something other than a fat, ugly skin sack?* Then I say, "Mr. Harper, do you think back then students would think you were something other than a fat, ugly skin sack?"

"I don't know what they'd say about me," Mr. Harper says. "Probably that it was a great thing that I was a teacher and that my life wasn't trash. Anything else, Ben?" I start to say something else about how they must have really, really liked lying to say Mr. Harper was a good teacher, but I don't say that out loud because, even though I'm being true, they'd say I was being emotional and it was clouding my truth.

"I understand," I say.

Being emotional isn't prideful, and being truthful, prideful, and intelligent are the best things. I'm truthful and prideful as best as I can be. Emotional truth-clouding was the main thing that led to the Long Big War and the Big Quick War.

They're called the Water Wars because of how the Old Federation lied to its own people about how the Amalgamation of Allies had poisoned the water reservoirs. The result was catastrophic/horrific. Then, since the people of the Old Federation were mad because of their own truth-clouding, they kept on warring for years and years, and the Old Federation became the New Federation that stands proudly today. Later on, when the Amalgamation of Allies suspected a key reservoir had been poisoned, they asked the New Federation if they'd done it. In a stunning act of graciousness and honesty, my New Federation ancestors told the truth, said, "Yeah, we did poison that reservoir," and, in doing so, saved many,

many lives that were later more honorably destroyed via nuclear. The wars going on now, Valid Storm Alpha and the True Freedom Campaign, are valid/true wars because we know we aren't being emotional fighting them.

"Class, please scroll to chapter forty-one and take it in," Mr. Harper says. The class touches their note-screens. The chapter is thirty-eight pages. I don't even try to read it. I look at some chapter videos of people doing things they used to do: a man throws three balls into the air, a woman in a dress spins on one leg. After three minutes, the class is done reading the chapter. Their Speed-Read™ chips make reading easy/quick for them. SpeedRead™ lets optimized people take in words faster than I can hardly see them. Since I'm a clear-born, I look while they read. I will read the chapters on my own later. But even staring at the videos and pictures is better than some can do. Samantha can't hardly look at her screen. And then there's Nick and Raphy, who are the class shoelookers. All they do is cry and moan. They were both optimized and still became shoelookers. Being emotional is all they are, and it means they aren't good for anything. I'm glad Samantha and Nick and Raphy are in the class. Because of them, I'm not bottom/last in learning, and I don't wanna be overall bottom/last at all.

After the others have read the chapter, Mr. Harper goes back to talking about how untrue the lives people used to live were. We've all heard about the times before the Turn, but hearing Mr. Harper, who is a teacher and, hopefully, not a complete ass/idiot, talk about all the untruths people used to think were regular makes me proud to be from now and not then. Still, I mostly only half-listen 'cause I'm thinking.

When the horn goes off and it's time for rotation, I hang back so I can speak truth to Mr. Harper.

"Mr. Harper," I say.

"What, Ben?"

"Today, during a lot of your session, I was thinking about beating you to death with a rock."

"Hmm, why?"

"I don't know. I'm not a brain-healer."

"If you don't know, how would I? Go to the nurse if you want."

I walk toward the nurse's office. On the way there, I see three shoelookers together in front of one of our school's war monuments: a glass case holding a wall with the nuclear shadows of our dead enemies on it. Two of the shoelookers cry, and the third paces between the other two, biting his nails. Marlene is near them. Marlene is my sibling. She is five cycles older than I am and training to be a NumbersPlusTaxes teacher.

Marlene is also the reason I was not given a prebirth optiselection. When Marlene was optiselected, all her personality points attached to only one personality paradigm and made her a paraone, a person who's only about one thing. There are all kinds of paradigms, like intelligence, conscientiousness, or extraversion. OptiLife™ releases different personality packages people can pay for. My parents were successful enough to get a standard package of seven points to spread across a few paradigms. That's what they wanted for Marlene: a balanced, successful person. But all seven of the points that could have gone toward her being a bunch of different stuff all went to one paradigm. Ambition. And that much of anything makes you a freak/the worst. But some companies like Learning Inc. prefer people like Marlene. She is a good worker. She is good at getting things she wants. It's all she does. Get things.

When Marlene was six and I was still a crying bag of poop, my parents had to convince her that having a younger brother would actually help her to be a good teacher because she could practice information transfer on me. They also told her that I, as a clearborn, could never be in competition with her in life or their hearts after they caught her trying to smother me with a pillow. They tell that story and laugh about it now.

After Marlene, my parents decided optimizing me wasn't worth the risk. When I was younger, she used to force me to read books for hours. She tried to make me remember things, and when I couldn't, she would slap me or pull my hair or twist my fingers. When I cheated and she didn't notice, she would hug me and squeeze so tight I couldn't breathe. She'd kiss my forehead. When I got old enough to really be in school and didn't do well there either, Marlene gave up on me. "No one can make a diamond out of a turd," she said.

"Got it, Marlene," I said.

"Diamonds are actually made from—"

"I don't care, Marlene."

I'm proof she isn't the perfect teacher, and she hates me for it.

How I feel about Marlene: she could keel over plus die and I'd be happy plus ecstatic.

She has two cups of water in her hands. She looks at me quickly, then pours a cup of water onto the heads of each of the crying shoelookers. Wet the Wetter is a game people play with shoelookers sometimes. People like to trip them or pour water on the heads of criers 'cause they won't do anything back and it's humorous. The two shoelookers are crying harder than ever now but not moving. Water drips, drips from their heads and clothes.

"Ben," Marlene says. "Isn't it your lunch section?"

"Yes," I say.

"This isn't the food sector."

"I understand."

"I am inquiring because your ability to move effectively through an academic space reflects upon my own person," Marlene says. I look at the empty cups in her hands.

"I am me and you are you. I don't care what reflects on you," I say.

"You know this school will be mine in the future," she says. "Even you should understand that." Marlene always talks about how she will take the school over, how she'll be such a good teacher that everything will be hers.

"OK. Don't talk to me," I say loudly. "Para-one," I say much more softly because she's scary. Marlene comes close to me. The shoelookers drip. The dry one paces back and forth.

"What'd you say?" Marlene asks. I don't say anything. I look at her eyes that always look the same, always searching for something to push over and stomp. Marlene backs off and lets me go. She walks away laughing at the wet shoelookers, and at me, I guess.

Shoelookers don't really do anything to anybody except make them proud to be themselves and not a no-good shoelooker. People say that if you tell a lot of lies you eventually start being all depressed and weepy like them. The shoelookers don't feel anything but sad. They feel it so much you can see it in everything they do. They're always looking at the ground.

I walk to the nurse in big steps. Everybody gets their mandatory Good in the mornings with breakfast at school, but they have extra at the nurse's. I go to the nurse because Good makes me feel good. When I have Good, it's easy to be proud and truthful, and ignore the things that cloud my truth, like Marlene, or being made into an example, or knowing I'll never be perfect.

The nurse, Ms. Higgins, is shaped like an old pear. Her body type is not attractive. She isn't in a union and doesn't have any kids because she's ugly and works as a school nurse. Today her face looks tired plus more tired. I prefer Ms. Higgins. Ms. Higgins looks at me, pulls her injector from her desk. There are vials of fresh Good on a shelf behind her.

It's quiet, so I talk. "Why don't you quit if you hate it here so much?" I ask as she screws the Good into the injector gun.

"Because I need credits," she says. She steps to me. I stretch my neck out for her and close my eyes. She puts one hand on one side of my neck. Her hand is warm plus strong. She stabs the injector needle in. My head feels the way an orange tastes. I open my eyes and look at her. She waits. I look at her more. She frowns, then gives me another shot. And then I feel the Good.

"Bye," I say to Ms. Higgins. She sweeps the air with her fingers, like, *Be gone.*

On the way to my usual foodbreak table, I walk past a table of shoelookers whispering to themselves. A few are crying. Shoelookers—if they're good for anything, it's crying. I laugh 'cause the Good is going full blast and it's funny how the shoelookers just don't have a chance. How they're so down that even Good doesn't help them much.

At my table, Scotty, John, and some others are laughing, but I don't know why, so I feel mildly frustrated.

"Oh, hey, Ben. We were so worried. Please have a seat," says John. I sit down next to him. "How are you feeling today?" Scotty asks, and I feel even more frustrated 'cause I think they're using me for humor because I needed extra Good instead of just the mandatory breakfast Good. "We care," Scotty says, making his voice like a bird. The table laughs. I look around, then I relax 'cause I catch on to things, and I can see that they're making fun of how things used to be, not me.

"Why, thank you for asking," I say. "I'm doing great." They laugh more, and it feels great. All the laughing at the table.

"Please take my drink because you look thirsty and 'cause you're a really smart guy," Scotty says, and everybody laughs even harder. "Catch, Ben," Scotty says as he tosses a box drink. I don't move to catch it fast enough 'cause I'm thinking, *I just got Good from the nurse, and already I'm feeling things other than good, which isn't how it works.*

The drink box goes over my hand and smacks Leslie McStowe right in the head.

She drops her tray and her food. Leslie frowns. I laugh with everybody else. Leslie was a twin, then her brother, Jimmy, died. Jimmy was a shoelooker who cooked his head in a food zapper. Leslie is always telling lies about how great things are or how nice everyone looks and how everybody is special. Leslie McStowe is one of the least truthful people around, which is frustrating because she and I scanned high for compatibility on our genetic compatibility charts. Probably because we're both clear-borns. Leslie's parents have protested against OptiLife™. They don't believe in perfect. I believe in it—I just hate it.

Leslie stands there looking lost and stupid. I want more laughs, so I stand up and make my mouth a big huge smile, and say, "Sorry about that, Leslie, let me use my credits to get you a new lunch." The table goes crazy. I have a lot of credits because my mother and father are successful, which I benefit from. Leslie's face goes from *Ow* to all smiles as she looks at me. Then she says, "That's so nice of you." It's a surprising thing to hear 'cause no one has said it to me before. The table is wild/crazy, which makes me proud. I keep it going. "C'mon, let's get you another lunch," I say in a voice I imagine would have been regular a long time ago.

Leslie McStowe follows me into the food part of the cafeteria. "Those people are idiots," my mother said once. She wasn't talking about the McStowes specifically, but about a bunch of people who were giving away candy and flowers to strangers on the newscast. The McStowes and the people my mother called idiots are part of the Anti. They're anti-Good, anti–prebirth science, anti-progress. At my school I can count the number of Anti families on my hands. But there are a lot of them in worse parts of the New Federation.

"Get whatever you want," I say, even though the guys at the table can't hear me over here.

"Thanks so much!" Leslie says. When she smiles, it looks like somebody scooped holes in her cheeks 'cause of her dimples. She grabs a juice and a greens bowl, and that's it. I register my credit code into the machine for her, and she smiles at the lunch man, who doesn't say anything. "Have a great day," I say to him because I'm still doing the thing I was doing. He stares. When we come back to the main part of the cafeteria, I'm expecting a bunch of laughs. No one at the table notices. They're eating now. I feel frustrated.

"Thanks, Benny, you're such a sweetie," Leslie says. I want to let her know the whole thing was for laughs, but then I don't, because I'm thinking. I sit down, and Leslie goes to sit with the shoelookers though she herself is not a shoelooker. I think, *Maybe I should have been truthful and reminded her about the fact that her face is arranged nicely, so she would remember we scanned as compatible and might eventually be part of a workable, functional familial unit with me.*

Everybody has their own room in our housing unit. I have a mother and a father, and there's Marlene. In my room I do physical maintenance like push-ups and leg pushes, and then I read the chapters from school until I smell food. I go downstairs where my mother and father and sibling are all at a table chewing.

"What are you looking at me for?" I ask.

"I received a message saying you've been taking extra Good," my father says.

I take a bowl from the washer, and I push the button that makes the cooker front slide open. I put a spoon in. I feel the hot inside the cooker box. I fill the bowl with meat and grains from the cooker. "Sometimes I need it. And why aren't you being truthful?" I say. "Marlene told you that." Marlene, since she's training at the school, knows stuff about me and what I do there.

"Don't accuse anyone of not being truthful," my mother says.

"I obscured the full truth because you have a tendency to respond emotionally, like some kind of neck-crane," says my father. Standing and staring at them, I dive my spoon into my bowl. I take a bite and chew. The grains and meat taste like grains and meat.

"I only pay attention because people still associate me with you," Marlene says. "Once I'm certified, I won't be interested. Until then, you are still a periphery reflection of my person."

Sometimes I imagine Marlene drowning in a tank of clear water.

"OK, I've listened to you and now I'm frustrated," I say.

"We are also frustrated because people still associate you with us even though we are our own successful individuals," my mother says.

"Not to mention the fact that your clear-birth was a mistake and that you are alive only due to your mother's irrationality brought about by maternity," my father says. My mother looks at me, then my father, and then nods her head. "It's true; it's true," she says.

I drop my food on the floor and walk away. The bowl doesn't break. The food splats on the floor.

"Have some pride, Ben," my father says.

"You always say the same things. It's frustrating," I say from the hall so they can't see me. I squeeze my eyes shut so no water can come from them. I try to have some pride. "I know I was a mistake already, so I don't know why you mention it so often."

"It's because the fact that we didn't select genes during your prebirth period almost certainly correlates to your being so slow and disappointing," my father calls. "And we're frustrated with you and tangentially with ourselves as a result."

"I know all that," I say. I go to the bathroom. I grab the house injector from behind the mirror. I go to grab a vial of Good. There is none. I spin around like it will be in the air somewhere. Then I take a breath and close my eyes and close the mirror. I open it again slowly, hoping it will be different. It isn't. There is an injector but no Good. I want to scream but don't. Instead, I go to my room. I sit on the bed.

I try to sleep. All I do is sweat and feel hurt all around my body and in my head. It gets dark. By then, I feel like death/poop. Deep into the night, my mother comes into the room.

"You've been screaming," she says.

"I don't care if I've been disturbing you; I'm frustrated you hid our Good," I say from under the covers. I hear her step to me; she rips the covers away. She is frowning in the dark. She puts a hand on my face and turns it. Then she uses the injector in her hand and stabs it into my neck. She gives me three shots, and the Good makes my teeth rattle. My mother's hand sits on my head for a while. Then she turns and leaves. And then everything feels so right and so fine that I fall asleep smiling.

At school I get my usual morning Good. And in HowItWas class we talk about before again.

"So even though people said all these things and acted like everyone else was important, there were still wars and hurting, which proves it was a time of lies," Mr. Harper says.

"But yesterday you said some frog crap about how some things were better and how it was easier in the old days," Scotty says.

"This is why you'll be a midlevel tasker at best," Mr. Harper says. "I said some people still believe that the old way was better. Some people still live the old way because they prefer it."

"I think those people are assjerks," Scotty says.

"No one cares what you think," Mr. Harper says. "Though I agree with you."

"H-how dow know?" says Samantha in her deep, broken voice. She is normally quiet. "Mahbe OK."

"Shut up, screw-face," Scotty says. He takes off his shoe and throws it at Samantha. It hits her and makes a thunk sound and then bounces off her head onto my desk. The class laughs. Mr. Harper laughs. Samantha tries to laugh. I stare at the shoe.

"See, here we have a teachable moment," Mr. Harper says. "Back before the Turn, Scotty might not have been honest about how he expressed himself, and Samantha would go on thinking he thought what she said was smart."

I go straight to Ms. Higgins after class. When I get there, she looks at me like I'm broken.

"You've been put on a Good restriction by your legal guardians," she says. I can see the vials behind her. I can almost feel them. Almost but definitely not.

"I only need two," I say. "Even one shot, please."

"A formal restriction has—"

"I know," I yell. I turn around and leave.

The floors of the school are tan and white. I walk to lunch. It is hard to keep my head up 'cause I don't feel proud or good at all.

When I get to the cafeteria, I hear someone say, "Happy birthday." When I look up, I see Leslie McStowe looking at me. She's sitting at a table with a bunch of sorry shoelookers. Then she stands and wraps her arms around me. "Happy birthday," she says again. I used to hide in my room and try to remember everything from whatever Marlene had given me to read so I could get a hug like that after her tests. But this is the first one I've had in many cycles. I'm standing there thinking of how Leslie McStowe is strong plus soft. I can feel her breathing on my neck a little.

"It's your birthday," Leslie says. She is smiling at me. Her eyes seem excited/electronic.

"Oh," I say. I have seen fifteen cycles now.

"We scanned compatible, you know. It's in your charts," she says quickly, answering the question I was thinking.

"Oh."

"If you want, my parents would love to have you over to celebrate." She looks down at the floor, not like a shoelooker, but like she's ashamed. "They like celebrating things."

"I don't celebrate like that or associate with you. Also, everyone thinks your parents are strange," I say.

"I know, but it would make us all really happy," she says. This, I realize, is exactly what Mr. Harper was speaking of. Leslie McStowe wants me to make her happy for no reason. I look at her and am lost in something that doesn't feel like pride or intellect or what truth should feel like. "Please," she says, and she hands me a paper that is an invitation for later in the day. I take the invitation, and then I walk to the table where I normally sit with the people I usually associate with.

At home, my familial unit says things to me.

"Hello," my father says.

"You seem agitated," my mother says.

"You are now on the Good restriction list," Marlene says.

I don't say anything to anyone. Without any Good in me, everything looks like a different kind of bad. And all I can imagine are the worst things about everyone and everything. And I can't tell if my stomach is aching or whether I'm imagining how bad a really bad stomachache might be if I had one right then. Either way it hurts. Ideas that scare me run around in my head. I go to the bathroom. I pull the mirror back. There is an injector, but there is still no Good. None. Only a shaver and fluoride paste and a small medical kit. I look in the medical kit just in case. No Good. I take the empty injector and bring it to my neck. I hit the trigger and stab and hope maybe I'll get something. I hit the trigger again. Again. I close the mirror, and a small crack appears in a corner of the glass. I go outside. I'm afraid of how bad I feel. No one asks where I am going.

The McStowes live in a complex on the outer part of the section. In our section the poor people all live on the outer parts so those of us on the inner parts don't have to come in contact with them all the time. They live cramped together in small spaces that are cheaper and, as a result, not as nice in looks or housing capabilities: keeping warm/dry, being absent of animals, etc.

I haven't had any Good since breakfast. I can feel the no-Good pressing on me. Pulling me down. It is getting dark outside. Out at the edge of the section, there are so many shoelookers slowly moving through the walk-streets. They've been abandoned by the people who used to be their families. That's what happens to most shoelookers. There are a bunch of soon-deads, and there are a few kid-youths and also every other age there is. Once in a while, one of the shoelookers will snap her head up and her eyes will be wild like she just remembered something important. Then, after a few seconds of wild looking and head turning, she'll drop her head back down.

It's worse than frustrating. Being around all those downed heads makes me want to close my eyes forever. I follow the grid-walks toward where the McStowes live. I focus on the ground because it doesn't make me want to disappear as much. The ground on the way there is gray and gray and gray. My shoes are black and gray. Good in its vial is clean/clear.

Long fingernails bite my shoulders. I look up and see a shoe-looker my mother's age. Her hands are near my neck. She screams, "Where are we going?" and shakes me like she's trying to get me to wake up. Her voice is screechy like she's been yelling for a long time. I shove her, then I run because I'm very disturbed.

I make sure I'm looking up as I run. I'm sweaty when I reach Leslie's housing complex. Inside it is not nice. A bunch of cats and a raccoon race and fight in the lobby area. The walls are dirty and the paint is peeling. I walk up a stairwell that smells like a toilet. When I find the McStowe door, I knock on it. I can hear people rustling inside. I imagine myself falling into a jar of needles over and over again. I haven't had any Good. The door opens. It's bright inside.

"Happy birthday" comes out of several mouths. The voices together make my heart beat harder.

"Hello," I say.

"Come in, come in," says Leslie. There's a tall man with a skinny neck and gray hair. He wears an ugly shirt with bright flowers on it.

"Great to see you; really great to see you," Father McStowe says. I'm wondering if in the McStowes' home people say everything twice.

The food sector is a small space to the left. It smells like something good. In the main sector are Leslie McStowe, her mother, her father, and three fidgeting shoelookers about my age. They have the usual sad/dirty look. They might be from the school. I don't know. I don't look at shoelookers.

"Come in," Mother McStowe says even though I'm already inside. She is a thin woman with a short haircut. There are folds of loose skin under her neck. I come in farther. Everyone is looking at me.

"How was your walk over?" Leslie says. Her face is smiling.

"Bad," I say. "This part of the section is worse than where my unit lives."

"Well, I'm sorry to hear that," Father McStowe says. "Let's have some cake now that the man of the hour is here in one piece!" *Man of the hour.* He is talking about me.

There are two beds in the main section. There are sheets and plates on one bed so it can be a table. There are pillows arranged on the other to make it a place to sit.

"I've never had cake," I say. I haven't. It isn't something proud people eat. It makes people fat, my mother says, just like the candy the Antis hand out in the streets.

"Well, isn't that a shame," Mother McStowe says even though she is smiling. She has dimples like her daughter. "In this house we eat cake every chance we get, seems like." She laughs. And so does Father McStowe. Leslie laughs. Even one of the three shoelookers laughs a little. I can tell by how the shoelooker's shoulders jump while she stares at the floor.

"You shouldn't feel sorry for me," I say. "My housing unit is much nicer than this." It gets quiet, then the house starts laughing some more. Even though I don't know exactly why they are laughing, I'm not too frustrated.

"This one!" says Father McStowe. "A true comedian."

"What's a true comedian?" I ask.

"Joke-tellers, humor-makers," says Father McStowe. "Back in the old world, it was a life profession to make laughter. One of many interesting old-world lives."

"I don't believe that," I say, 'cause I don't.

"That's OK," says Mother McStowe, still giggling. "Let's eat some cake."

"Sounds sweet to me," says Father McStowe. He laughs, and so does his family.

We move over to the table/bed. The main sector of the housing unit has walls covered in sheets of paper with too many colors on them.

"Cake," Mother McStowe says as she walks to the food sector, "was a delicacy in the old world used to celebrate events like union-making, the lunar cycle, battle-victory, and, of course, birthdays." Mother McStowe looks for some utensil in the food sector. I look at Father McStowe and ask, "Is that the food sector your son killed himself in?" There's a clang/clack sound from Mother McStowe dropping something on the floor.

Father McStowe looks at me. He touches my shoulder. His hand is large/heavy. "You know something"—he speaks low so only I can hear him—"one of the things we like to do in this home is be careful of what we say. What you said didn't have to be said. And now you've hurt my wife. She'll be fine but—"

"Lying for others is what caused the Big Quick and the Long Big," I say.

"Maybe. Or maybe it was something else. I'm talking about thinking about the other person, ya know?" Father McStowe whispers to me. "I'm sure you have a lot of ideas about this, but it's something we try around here." He smiles and touches my shoulder again. "Let's eat some cake," he says in a big voice, a voice for everybody.

I haven't had any Good since breakfast. And here I am. In Leslie McStowe's house. Because she invited me and because she makes me think of things that aren't Marlene or optimization or being forever dumb/slow.

Mother McStowe comes back. She smiles at me as she hands me a knife big enough to cut a bunch of things. "It was tradition for birthday boys to cut the cake after the singing of the traditional birthday hymn," Mother McStowe says. She looks around quickly with wide eyes, then begins to sing. The rest of her family joins in. The shoelookers look down and up, and down and up, trying to decide what to be, and even they mumble along with the Mc-Stowes.

*Happy birthday to ya, happy birthday to ya*
*Happy birthday, happy birthday to ya*
*Happy birthday, it's your day, yeah*
*Happy birthday to ya, happy birthday, yeah!*

When they finish, Mother McStowe tells me, with her eyes, to cut the cake. The knife cuts through easily. "I forgot that, traditionally, you are supposed to make a wish before you cut into the cake," says Mother McStowe. "But after is fine, I suppose. You can wish for anything."

Of course, I wish for Good. I put one more cut into the cake, then Mother McStowe takes the knife from me, and I see she cuts into the middle of it instead of off the side like I did. She cuts pieces for everybody. Father McStowe and Leslie and I sit on the bed made for sitting. The rest stand and chew. The cake is the sweetest thing I've ever eaten.

"Do you like it?" asks Mother McStowe.

"It's good 'cause it's so sweet," I say. It makes my tongue and teeth feel more alive.

"And it's an authentic old-time recipe you can't get anywhere else," Mother McStowe says.

When half my cake is gone, I turn to Father McStowe. "Do you have any extra Good?" I ask somewhat discreetly, since taking too much Good is not a proud thing. Father McStowe looks at me with cheeks full of cake.

"We like to think of our home as a throwback to an era before industrial Good," he says. He swallows, then puts a hand on my shoulder, then removes it.

"I need Good."

"You're thinking now; this is then." Father McStowe does something with his hands. "Think of our home as a place where no one needs industrial Good."

"Is it because you're poor that you don't have any Good?" I ask. Father McStowe laughs so hard he spits wet cake onto the floor. Quickly, Mother McStowe cleans it up. He looks to his daughter, and says, "This one is funny. A real comedian."

"I'm not telling jokes," I say.

"That's why you're so good," Father McStowe says. "When I want to be funny, I usually tell an old-time joke, like this one." He clears his throat. "Have you heard the one about the deaf man?"

"What?"

"That's what he said!" Father McStowe says. "If you would have said no, I would have said neither has he. Get it?" He touches me on the shoulder and chuckles. Leslie and the shoelookers giggle with him. "Truly, we like to think we, as you've seen, have created a space that is really a throwback to a time before the Big Quick or even before the Long Big. My family and I re-create that decent era for people who might want or need it."

"I'm frustrated because you don't have any Good. I'm leaving," I say.

"What we—hey, Linda, could you grab some of our literature? —offer here is a way to feel and be happy without Good. We can feel good just by being together, and you can join us a few times a week depending on the package that works for you." Leslie is smiling, and the shoelookers are eating cake, switching between weak smiles and lost frowns.

"I'm going home," I say.

"Take some literature," he says. With her face smiling, Mother McStowe hands me a pamphlet. On it are smiling faces and words and different prices. Different amounts of time are trailed by different credit values on each row of information.

"There are lots of choices," Leslie says.

"Think it over. If any package feels right for you, let Leslie know. We recommend starting off with at least three days a week here with us in the Era. You'll feel brand-new. Just look at these guests." Mother McStowe points to the shoelookers, who are still munching cake. They look at me and they all try to smile.

I get up. "I'm frustrated because I thought this was something different," I yell. I haven't had any Good. I feel the pamphlet crushing in my fist. On the front, it says LIFE IN THE ERA in curly letters. "Also, your daughter doesn't frustrate me, so that's why I came."

"Look over the literature," Father McStowe says when I'm at the door.

"I haven't had any Good since the morning, that's why I'm emotional," I scream before I slam the door and run back to my own housing unit. I get tired, so I have to walk. Plus, there is no Good at my housing unit anyway. The night is black. The gridwalk is gray and gray and gray. There's some sweet left on my teeth, and even after the sweet is gone, thinking about it helps keep me walking.

At breakfast the next day, the Good makes me feel better for a few minutes but not even through to the last sip of my milk. My neck aches. My brain throbs. The floor of the school is mostly tan, and the patterns against the tan are at least easy to drown in. In Mr. Harper's class, we are talking about the Long Big and how it led to the Big Quick, like always. I think of cake during class.

At lunch I go to sit with my usuals. At the table Scotty says, "Back off, we don't want to associate with a shoelooker like you." Somebody else says, "Go sit with the downs over there." I just stand there looking at the ground because I'm not a shoelooker even though, with my head down, and the feeling in my head, and the tears almost in my eyes, I probably look like one.

I try to be proud and look up. I feel a boom and a hurt under my eye. I fall. The table laughs. I see that John has punched me to say I am officially not welcome. My face hurts. I want to lie there, but I get up because I'm pulled up. It is Leslie McStowe who pulls me. She is frowning. When I'm standing, I pick my head up, and she walks with me to the nurse's office. "It's OK," Leslie says, lying like they used to, like she does. And I am happy to hear her do it.

In the nurse's office Ms. Higgins stares at the two of us. Samantha is sitting in a chair. Samantha is not healthy, ever, but she looks at me, like, *Welcome,* and does her happier moaning sound. Ms. Higgins pulls a cold pack out of a cold box. I put the cold over my eye. It makes the hurt less. I sit in a chair next to Samantha. Leslie sits in one next to me.

"He got hit," Leslie says.

"Yah ohkay?" Samantha groans.

"You got hit," Ms. Higgins says.

"Yes," I say. Ms. Higgins says nothing. Then she stands up and opens the drawer that holds her injector. Hearing the drawer slide open makes my skin tingle. She turns her back to us so she can feed some fresh new Good into the injector.

Then, at the office door, I see my sibling. "I heard," says Marlene, "you've become a real shoelooker." Leslie touches my not-cold hand. Her fingers are warm on mine. "Ben is on a Good restriction, Higgins," Marlene says. With one eye, I look at Leslie

McStowe, then at Samantha, then at Marlene, and then at Ms. Higgins. Ms. Higgins screws a vial of Good into the injector. "I'll report you," Marlene says.

Ms. Higgins continues screwing the vial into the injector and does not look at Marlene. Marlene stands at the office door. She's holding a cup of water. All I want is Good. Ms. Higgins looks at me with her loaded injector. Leslie squeezes my hand. I look at Ms. Higgins. I shake my head. Ms. Higgins drops her injector on her desk then sits down in her chair. She turns her head and looks at the wall. We are quiet. It's quiet for a long time. Leslie looks at me. She wants to smile, but she can't, so with my head down, one hand warm, one hand cold, one eye bruising and the other looking at her, I say, "Have you heard the one about the deaf man?"

KATHLEEN ALCOTT

# *Natural Light*

FROM *Zoetrope: All-Story*

I WON'T TELL YOU what my mother was doing in the photograph —or rather, what was being done to her—just that when I saw it for the first time, in the museum crowded with tourists, she'd been dead five years. It broke an explicit promise, the only we keep with the deceased, which is that there will be no more contact, no new information. In fact, my mother, who was generally kind and reliable in the time she was living, had already broken this promise. Her two email accounts were frequently in touch. The comfort I took in seeing her name appear, anew in bold, almost outweighed the embarrassment of the messages that followed. She wanted me to know that a small penis size was not an indictment against my future happiness. She hoped I would reconsider a restaurant I might have believed to be out of my budget, given a deal it made her pleased to share. She needed some money for an emergency that had unfolded, totally beyond her control, somewhere at an airport in Nigeria. Though these transmissions alarmed me, it was nice to be able to say what I did, when an acquaintance or administrator at the college where I teach saw my eyes on my phone and asked, Something important? It was nice to be able to say, Oh, it's just an email from my mother. Given how frequently we had written while she lived—the minute logistics of a renovation, my cheerful taxonomies of backyard weeds—she avoided the spam filter after her death, and I could not bring myself to flag her.

She had not *died as she lived*. Does anyone? Though my mother had not been vain in a daily sense, she often made me, in the weeks of her dying, rub foundation onto the jaundice of her skin. This was something she could have done alone—she never lost power in her hands, as far as I knew—but one of the dying's imperatives is to make the living see them. This is nobody's fault, but it is everybody's burden. That sounds like something my father would say, half-eating, in the general direction of the television: Nobody's fault, everybody's burden. Perhaps he did, and this thinking made its way into mine. I don't always know well where I've left a window open.

The photo was part of a multi-artist retrospective, curated less to discuss a school or approach than to cater to nostalgia for a certain era in New York. Shows like these are a dime a dozen here, and they are not of the sort I seek out, having lost most interest I might have had in the type of lives and rooms they always feature. Bare mattresses on the floor, curtains that are not curtains, enormous telephones off the hook, the bodies always thin but never healthy. Eyes shadowed in lilac, men in nylon nighties pour liquor from brown paper bags into their mouths. A woman with a black eye laughs, her splayed thigh printed with menstrual blood. These photographs are in color, the light strictly natural. There is always some museumgoer finding her imprimatur there, looking affirmed and clarified about the ragged way she'd arrived feeling.

That day I had come to the museum for a show of paintings, landscapes of Maine refashioned with a particular pink glow the painter must have felt when he saw what inspired them. I was wearing a shirt that buttoned high on my neck, and my rose-gold watch, vintage, which I had just repaired. The wedding ring remained. It wasn't that I had any hopes for reconciliation, but its persistence on my finger was a way of matching inside to out. I needed to be reminded, when I caught myself deep in a years-old argument with my husband, alone and furious on the mostly empty midday subway, that he had been real—that my unhappiness was not only some chemical dysfunction of mine.

I decided to take the stairs, and then to pass through the exhibit in question: I had an hour to spare, and I thought it might be an interesting metric. How little I related could be the proof of a transformation I had undergone, a maturation evident in how I saw and felt. When my husband met me, twenty-two to his forty, he saw a girl with a rough kind of potential, and he tended to me as one might a garden, offering certain benefits and taking others away. He did not wish me to grow in just any direction. That I allowed him this speaks just as poorly of me. I was once a girl with an exquisite collection of impractical dresses—ruched chiffon, Mondrian prints—and a social smoking habit, a violent way with doors and windows. I left him in taupes, my arches well supported, my thinking framed in apology. It is true there were parts of me that must have been difficult to live with, namely an obsessive thought pattern concerning various ways I might bring about my own death, but also clear that I rose to the occasion of this malady with rosy dedication, running miles every day and recording the impact of this on my mind, conceiving of elaborate meals, the hedonistic pleasures of which I believed spoke to my commitment to life. Could a person who roasted three different kinds of apples for an autumn soup really be capable of suicide? I asked him this question laughing, wooden spoon aloft, during an argument about a drug I did not want to take. Doesn't the one cancel out the other, leaving you with a basically normal wife? They could delight me, my obsidian jokes, but he saw them hanging from me like statement jewelry, heavy, aggressive, things that could not be forgotten even as I spoke, quietly and practically, about the empirical world. He began not to trust me on issues I saw as unrelated: what a neighbor had said about a vine that grew up our shared fence, a letter from the electric company that I claimed to have left on his desk.

I passed through the contiguous rooms, high-ceilinged and white, as briskly as could be called civilized. Whatever my feelings about the work, I never want to be one of those people rushing through a museum, intent on immunity—I was here, their bodies say, and that was it. It is true I sometimes court discomfort, that I will deny my headache an antidote, and that I don't expect to feel the same way from one hour to the next. This was a quality my husband feared, then hated. That's the usual trajectory, it might be said. If we don't talk to the thing we are afraid of, it becomes the thing we hope to kill.

All the people in the room were young women, and I felt tenderly toward them, their damaged wool and winged eyeliner and overstuffed shoulder bags. They interested me more than the photos. What could I tell them, from just the other side of thirty, except that things did not seem to exist on the continuum we needed them to—so little of life was a rejoinder to something said or done earlier, the opportunity to, as school had often demanded, show what you had learned. Your real self was mostly revealed in negotiation with the unforeseen element. How did you behave when the emergency room bill arrived, triple the estimate? When someone you loved was suffering, how long did it take for you to wonder about a life that didn't include her? I had saddled up to one of them, the girls, whose face intrigued me particularly, a saturation of peachy freckles she had made no attempt to cover up. Hanging there, the object over which she was pouring her young mind, was my mother.

As far as I knew, my mother had lived in New York City for only six unfortunate months. The image I associate with them is not a photo of her looking bewildered by the Rockefeller tree or exposed on the steps of the Met—they don't exist—but rather a gesture she would make, at her suburban dining table, if ever asked to describe her time there: a low hook of the hand, swiped an inch or two to the left. Total dismissal. Sometimes, on the rare occasions she'd had more than her characteristic half-a-glass with dinner, a blush and a remark. I had no idea what I was doing there, she would say, and pat the hand of my father, the ostensible representative of a life she found a year later and understood quite a bit better.

About the photo in the museum, I will tell you this: my mother looks like someone who knows exactly what she is doing.

Seeing her like that, I started to cough and I could not stop. There is very little ambiguity about what has gone on in the pictured bedroom that contains her, shot from just outside it so that the leftmost third is a slice of peeling door, paint riddled with thumbtacks. There is the characteristic mattress, right on the floor, the open window and fire escape. There is some rubber tubing, knotted in places, elevated above the usual detritus on a milk crate. The inner sleeves of records, the cellophane casings of cigarette packs, a battered silk tie one must assume, from its crippled shape, has been used otherwise. That time passed for me, there in front of the photo, was a separate cruelty, for it came with no palliative or normalizing effect, and so the third minute I took it in elided with the ninth and the twelfth. A German tourist, the kind of spokesperson for a concerned and patient group of them, touched a finger to the back of my elbow. It was clear, from the damp focus of their faces on mine, that it was not the first time he had spoken the word in my direction. "Please," he said. "Please," I replied, stepping back so that they could see her.

Though all identifiable marks were in place, the mole I had liked to press at the base of her jaw, the gap in her eyebrow from a childhood accident with the Girl Scouts, there was nothing about my mother's facial expression I recognized. It had not come up in her rare flirtations with anger, episodes about which she felt embarrassment for days. A faulty appliance without a warranty, a time I had, at fifteen, responded rudely to an elderly neighbor's offer of homemade rice pudding—Ev, whose teeth looked to me like towns devastated by hurricanes. Young lady, my mother had said, that the cruelest thing she could think to call me, your days aren't any bigger than hers. Even before she was ill my mother was a diminishing creature, eliminating distinctive or inconvenient parts of herself by the year. At fifty she stopped wearing the perfume she had for decades, her one luxury, thinking an insistence on a certain scent was an affectation of the young. What do people need to smell me for, she said, with a horsey puff of air out the side of her mouth. Once, from the passenger seat during a trip home, I watched her wait patiently while the man driving the car in front of us, by all observations asleep at the otherwise empty intersection, leaned farther across the wheel. Honk, I said, but my mother would not honk. Honey, have you considered he might need the sleep? Choose a radio station, for God's sake. There are some good ones around here, you know.

The Germans had formed a barrier around my mother, talking and gesturing, so I exited the museum, taking the stairs as my husband had always insisted. *A little bit of exercise* was a phrase he kept spring-loaded. The gap in our ages was hardly noticeable to others, and I had often imagined the point when the stunning preservation of his youth would overtake the rapid deterioration of mine. Growing up his beliefs as their rigidity dictated, I was something like an espalier, the distance between the vine and the thing that trained it almost imperceptible. I wanted to call him, to wash his reasonable pragmatism all over the issue of the illicit photo, but our terms would not allow it. I can't deal with another crisis, my husband would say, the last year we were together, in response to vexes I saw as relatively small, a mix-up at the pharmacy over the drug I agreed to take, some passive-aggressive email from a student I read out loud in the kitchen, hoping to parse. I can tell you're in a state, he would say, hands raised like an outdated television preacher. Rather than responding to my speaking, he took to waving at it, scenery to be considered later with the right amount of rest and reflection.

I can't imagine the man, he said more than once, who would have an easy time living with you. This hurt particularly, for he had a fabulous imagination—a jaunty talent with a colored pencil, a habit of coming up with a song on the spot, a fond feeling for the absurdity of animals. I began keeping a tally of my behavior, days I had been so anxious at the incursion of these thoughts that I wept or went sleepless, others when my charm had been big and flexible. On a New Year's we hosted, I built fantastical hats of construction paper and balloons, things that looked like cities of the future. On his forty-fifth birthday, in the park near our house, I hid his ten favorite people behind his ten favorite trees, and guided him on the snowy walk to discover them. I always scanned his face, on occasions like these, for a look of recognition, one that would say, Here, here you are.

Contact between us now consisted mainly of three words, even the contraction never parted into its constituents. *Hope you're well,* he wrote. *Hope you're well,* I wrote. Hope you're well! Hope you're well! The statement never altered into a question, and with time it began to read to me as a kind of threat, beveled, ingenious. To his last *hope you're well,* six weeks before, I had not replied, and I believed that was the end he had in mind. Pills in a blender with strawberry ice cream, I thought. An email scheduled a day ahead of time with very clear instructions. We had been separated a year.

On the outdoor patio of the museum the tourists were unhappy, scratching their fat ankles, saying how far is it, how far, how much. It was midsummer, a time in New York I have always loved and dreaded for how it keeps no secrets, all smells and feelings arriving fully formed, unavoidable. I called my father. Since the separation from my husband he has been unsure of how to relate to me, in part because the small knots and amusements of domestic partnership were the only aspect of my life that mirrored any part of his. He had sometimes liked hearing what I was cooking, and always about the expensive and malfunctioning alarm system my husband had purchased. What, did it go off in the middle of the night again? my father asked once, excited enough that he was a little short of breath.

"Hey, it's me," I said.

"It's you."

"Do you know about this photo of Mom?" I referred to this without any introduction, I suppose because I felt I had been deprived of one and so wouldn't be offering such consideration to him.

"What's that?"

"There's this photo of Mom in a museum here."

I had to repeat myself several times, and when the point had been made and I had told him I was sure, he paused, the way he always did to gesture that my mother pick up the other phone in the hall. He could not kill the habit. I had seen this a million times, his left hand scooping the air up, the other pointer raised. She would stop whatever she was doing, leave the sentence unread, the sandwich half-assembled, so that they could hear together what it was the mechanic had to say, the second cousin with the coupon obsession. Visiting meant listening to the conversation of theirs that never ended, mundane talk that went on until they'd shut off their bedside lamps and sometimes after. Passing their room in the middle of the night once, I heard my father say, it must have been in his sleep, It's the damn compressor, and my mother reply, without missing a beat, You bet your ass it is.

"She was a looker, wasn't she? What is it, some kind of—do they call it street photography?"

"No," I said. I described in euphemism what was occurring in the photo.

"There's been some mistake," my father answered, finally, resolutely. "That's your eyes playing tricks on you."

It was one of a thousand precooked phrases he had on hand: canary in a coal mine, teach a man to fish, taste of your own medicine. Language to him was the same set of formations and markers, certain maxims always leading the way to others. After you pulled up your bootstraps, you reaped what you sowed. It was something he had adopted in recovery, I thought, the beginnings of which took place a decade before I was born. For my whole life, he had referred to himself that way: in recovery. It seemed cruel to me one had to adopt that title for the duration of living, but for my father it became a helpful boundary, a gate he could close on any conversation he wanted. As a child I had found the overheard expression comforting, repeated it to myself on anxious walks home from school. Thinking of a game whose rules I had failed to understand, the nubbly red Spalding that had flown past me, I would say, with mimicked weariness, You know, I'm in recovery.

He started to talk about television, a corner to which he often retreated when uncomfortable. It was a reliable tactic for how it bored and frustrated me, and ensured I'd be off the phone sooner than otherwise. "Well, there's a show you wouldn't believe," he said. "It's called *Naked and Afraid*. Well, they drop these people off on an island somewhere, and they don't give them any clothes." He always used that interjection, *well*, when describing something he was happy to have no part in. Shortly thereafter I said goodbye.

By the next morning I had decided to email the photographer, but thought first I needed to return to the museum and take a photo of the photo. In the afternoon I taught, a creative writing workshop for people of nineteen and twenty, a task I could keep myself alive to only by pacing the rectangular formation of tables—as if by directing my voice from different corners of the room I had better chance at some diplomatic pluralism in my thinking. We were talking about figurative language, and I wondered aloud how close a simile should get to the character's actual life and circumstances: in comparing her inner sadness to the color of her dress, weren't we depriving the reader of some useful speculative distance?

"No," said an opera singer with four names who despised me. "I literally love that."

There was always one student who hated me. This was a problem I could solve more easily with young men, pretending to lessen my authority while I sharpened my argument. But with girls it was never clear, for their hatred was much more original, multifaceted, and they clung to it even while enjoying whichever dialectic I'd introduced to distract them. They could entertain my line of reasoning while deriding the person beneath it. The opera singer had a habit, raising her hand against my litany of leading questions, of pointing out some aspect of my appearance. There's a hair on your jacket, your top button undone, that lace about to untie, a little something on your face. She made me wish I was only a voice, piped into the room and delivered by speakers placed along its windows.

On my way off campus, feeling comforted by the architecture and landscape, the Doric columns and rectilinear hedges, I called my father again, prepared to meet somewhere closer in feeling to him, accept his denial and negotiate with it. No one answered the home number he'd kept, and when he picked up his cell phone he did so with an exaggerated element of surprise. It was clear just from the way he said hello that he was not going to acknowledge the conversation we'd had, that he'd hoped to forgive me it as he might anyone's spike in emotion, something attributable to hunger or fatigue.

"Honey, you ever wake up and want a hamburger so bad you believe you could will it into being? I finally gave up. I'm at the grocery store now, my poor soul."

"I want to apologize for yesterday," I said. "I hope I didn't upset you."

"Ants at a picnic," he replied. "You went with your gut." There was a slight delay to his speech, like he was trying to describe something moving to someone who couldn't see it, hoping to determine a pattern before he put it into words. When I began to continue he cut me off, telling me it was time for him to get in line.

In the last hour the museum was open, the exhibition was even more crowded, and I waited politely while a young couple holding hands observed the warped circle of my mother's mouth. The thoughts had not totally ceased since leaving my husband, but because there was no one else to assign them any importance, they were less of a source of alarm. I have a friend who lives in an apartment where the door can be opened only with a wrench, but it doesn't keep her from leaving. Anything can be lived around, so long as it's only you who has to do it. The betrayal of my mind, when we were together, had seemed to my husband like a betrayal of him, of the life that looked like a happy one. A hotel suite uptown, I thought, a maid you'd somehow apologize to beforehand.

My husband had met my mother just once before she was ill, a lunch where he had paid and she had been impressed, and then he knew her for the five weeks she was vanishing. Despite her embarrassment at having to die, she was generous about allowing him into it, often saying how nice it was to be spending so much time with him, and he was saintly with her, crushing her pills into water when he saw swallowing was an issue, making sure she heard her name spoken lightly. These were the sorts of problems he took to with alacrity, ailments and logistics, a crooked angle or a smudged glass. To this day I cannot look at a man who is looking at a map, for it recalls him so totally, how happily he believed in things reduced to their signifiers. At first he delighted in my missing sense of direction, asking me with wide eyes where I thought I might be going, but in the end it infuriated him, the time I might take for just any left. That's not teaching you anything, he would say, when I raised the map on my phone to pull up a list of directions. Did he believe a certain native impracticality of mine was part of the same looseness in the world that made me want to leave it? During trips he'd spread a brittle map on the trunk of the rental car and say, Just take a minute alone with this. Tell me what you think the best way is. Perhaps he thought the problem was margins, that if I could better plan A to B in the physical world, avoiding tolls and traffic, then in my mind, too, I could ignore the periphery. A downtown six you might leap toward like a deer, I thought, pliant, ready for what it would do to you.

That I had never "tried anything"—this was the phrase that he used—seemed to me to be an obvious point of credit, a spotless record that pointed to more of the same. Of course, the thoughts had disturbed me enough that I had confessed to having them, about a year after my mother died, in the dark after sex in the middle of the night. This was the time he wanted me the most, calling me in from where sleep had taken me, his body my reintroduction to the living world.

I had hoped that if I let the thoughts into the room they would lose some of their power, a kind of blackmail in the way they were invisible to others but kept my life on a leash. I would have two drinks but never three, accept a compliment but never believe it. Though he was warm and soft when I first confided, the separative effect I had wished for, some congratulations I might receive for naming the thing that hunted me, did not take shape. Instead, my husband began looking for cohesion, seeing any dip in my feeling as proof of the roots the thoughts had taken in me. If I was quiet at a dinner somewhere, despite the light being good and the weather lucky, my forehead might as well have been a strip of celluloid projecting the ghastly imperative: k i l l y o u r s e l f. What is it, he would say, his mouth firming up and his eyes losing a little color. For God's sake, what are you thinking right now. Once, because I had only been remembering a college friend and her peculiar party trick, a dancer who had smoked cigarettes with her toes, I snapped. Strictly of your happiness, I said, holding up my empty wineglass as if to toast.

I was able to contact the photographer only through a friend of mine who taught at the university where she sometimes lectured, and he warned me Sam Baldwin was moody and unlikely to reply. She conducted famous seminars on her own work, performances I'd heard described once as a whole childhood, meaning every possible emotion, meaning each pared to its loudest part. People said she'd lost her wire-frame bifocals sometime in the mid-eighties and since wore her prescription sunglasses, which she removed just to shoot. *Good luck,* he wrote, and concluded his email with a typo of omission, the question *Are you feeling?* to which I responded only *Yes.*

My note to her was brief and included the photo, which had not otherwise been catalogued and was scarce and low resolution online. I explained the situation and asked if she'd mind telling me anything she remembered, about that day or my mother. My phone rang within the hour, while I was observing a pickup game of basketball at West Fourth Street, my fingers threaded through the diamonds of the fence. I like watching the minor parts of the body during moments of leaps and stretches, acts we think of as the jobs of legs and arms. The cut of an ankle as the foot rolls, ball to toes, upward, or the hip bone exposed to sun for the instant, mid-dunk, when the shirt rises up the ribs. I like to be inside the shouting but silent to it. This was something I did that I told no one about, a whole hour unaccounted for, and it was one of the great pleasures I'd experienced since leaving my husband, a certain thought ringing like a bell calling me in: *Nobody knows where I am, nobody knows where I am, nobody knows where I am.*

After clearing her throat excessively, as if alone in a room, and unwrapping what sounded like three small candies, the photographer asked if I'd like to come by sometime that week. She lived a few blocks from where I stood then, a fact I decided not to mention. It seemed a step had been skipped in resolving the distance between us, but I agreed, my mind still half-tied to a swiveling calf I saw through the fence.

The day came to see her and I could not decide on the appropriate clothes to wear. Finally I decided on a jumpsuit, sienna, linen, which made little about who I was easy to imagine. The building, once industrial, was air-conditioned in the way of a car dealership. She opened the door coughing, rolling her eyes at her body and gesturing with the hand not covering her mouth for me to come in. The apartment was cluttered but not unclean, the feeling being that the stray books in stacks were often removed and referenced. Pointing at my shoes and the straw mat where I should place them, she walked toward two cracked-leather egg chairs that faced one another under a skylight, and I followed. She was not wearing any glasses. She was speaking through the middle of a thought she had begun without me.

"And of course I was so glad it was included in the retrospective," she was saying. "You know, the pieces of mine that gain some valence, the ones the most reproduced, often aren't the same I would have chosen. Funny that it wasn't for so long. I guess a woman taking the thing she wanted, a man doing something for her, was never as interesting as the alternative. Funny that was your mother. I liked her."

She didn't hesitate in the transition from the talk of the photo to its subject. The way that she poured the tea, a minor flourish of her wrist, into two Japanese mugs without handles, made me feel vaguely guilty about the way I'd dismissed her work. As it was steeping she got up—distracted by a memory, I believed, ready to pull out some arcana that would help her comment—but then she was drawing something around my shoulders, a knit blue afghan, imperfect, smelling of smoke.

"You're supposed to ask people if they want to be taken care of, isn't that right? I'm sorry." She rolled her eyes again, this time at her instincts. "She came the first time it showed, wearing a pantsuit and pearls. We all loved that. Irony was not valid for her. She thought, Well I've got my picture up at a gallery, I better look like a taxpayer."

Something in my face must have changed, because she put a hand on my knee.

"Did I?" she said. "Is there?"

"I didn't know she knew."

The photographer watched me figuring out why this mattered. It was clear she had a way of encouraging a person's natural state, even becoming a part of it, by goading on any reaction, turning the room to its expression. On the table between us she set a ceramic Kleenex holder, and then she moved about opening the windows to the noise from the street, bringing the heat in and making the throw around my shoulders irrelevant. I couldn't help believing she was the reason for every feeling I had, the comfort but also the anger. A bay you found lovely to begin with, I thought, a bridge in the afternoon. The color changing with your view of it, the depth uncertain.

Why did it matter? I had wanted to believe the photo was taken not of my mother but from her, a thing she would not have given freely. I had wanted to see it as an exception. I asked the questions I did next without totally asking them, maybe so I could convince myself later that the photographer had told me things I never needed to know. Sitting back in the chair with her tea held halfway up her body, the photographer mentioned that my mother had been the girlfriend of a friend of a friend.

"I remember loving the way her face and body reacted separately. It was like the body would tell the face what was happening and the face would say, Are you sure? She had her days-of-the-week underwear soaking in the bathroom sink, which broke my fucking heart."

When she said this, what came to mind immediately was another photo of hers, one of the most famous. The soiled pale pink, the shallow basin of water the hue of disintegrating leaves, the elastic losing its threading. W E D N E S D A Y. On the mirror above are phone numbers in eyeliner, a long-antennaed cockroach crawling over fives and sevens. I was waiting for her to expand upon this, to attach her memory to the abbreviated public record of it, but it never came. It was as if she had seen as much as I had, could speculate about the lives behind the torn faces in her work no better than anyone else. If she knew she was not sharing an anecdote but referencing a canonized image, she gave no indication.

The silence that ensued was like a change in weather, something that rendered us powerless in a way it was hard to take personally. I would ask nothing further about the woman in the photo, the splay of her knees, the delicate bloom of a bruise on her inner elbow, just visible in the way she gripped the man's hair, and the photographer would ask nothing at all about the rest of my mother's life, not even her name. "I'd love to shoot you sometime," she said, after the disappointing moment had turned over, and I said only, "Thank you," a response as vague as it was insincere.

When she closed the door behind me it was easy to believe that it had never opened, that the apartment was unknown to me. In the jerking elevator down I sent my father two texts, one the photo of my mother, and the next a part of it I had zoomed in on and cropped, the distinctive split of her left eyebrow. I understood how the conversation would go, and I was using a tack I knew would aggrieve him, preempting his protest. I walked along Sixth Avenue and into the first movie I found, an Australian art-house thriller. A middle-aged couple wearing the colors of hard candy had kidnapped a teenage girl, a blonde in shorts that crossed her ass at a mean diagonal. The camera loved the wet line of her teeth, wanted to move all the way down them and into her throat. It was scoreless, the sounds of her torture offscreen the subdued soundtrack to what happened on-, where the husband or wife persisted with the domestic, pouring budget cereal into plastic bowls, filling the water trays of their twin Dobermans. In scenes across town we saw the pale back of a mother's neck, the fallen elbows, while she looked through her daughter's possessions for a sign of what had driven her away. The handheld shots suggested a state of watching from another room, without the desire to enter or the resources to leave.

When the movie let out I saw that my father hadn't responded to my texts, so I sent two more, words this time, *What do you think?* and then, *Well???* They did not show up as delivered. The evening was dark enough that it felt physical, a deepening of color that came with a smell and a taste. I had never known my father to turn his phone off, and in fact would have imagined he did not know how. He spent most of his truant feeling on it, revisiting the photos of cracks in the wall to be caulked, tapping at the weather icons of cities he'd visited once a long time ago.

An email from the photographer appeared as I stood in front of the theater, in view of the basketball courts that were empty now. Devoid of people they looked liquid, interruptions of pure space that did and wanted nothing. The email referenced neither the minimal conversation we'd had nor the complicated one we'd avoided. *I'd like to shoot you sometime,* she had written. *When can I?* A gun shop, I thought, where you bantered a little outside your politics with the owner, some bald man with ideas about a woman's instincts for self-preservation, who congratulated your investment in personal safety.

I could tell by the way my skin felt, inadequate for the task of holding in everything it had to, that I was going to call my husband. Like anybody about to break a law, I felt a thrill at the decision I'd made—that, however briefly, the rules did not apply, that I was free from the forces that had circumscribed me. With each ring of the phone I imagined the different places he might be, at the counter of our neighborhood Italian restaurant with the long, mirrored bar, in bed with a girl who laughed at everything, on line at the airport with his rolling titanium suitcase. That he did not pick up did not surprise me, but that there was no response to my transgression saddened me. I wanted to hear his voice snap at the line I had crossed, to know what he thought was selfish about the thing I needed. I called him once more that evening, and sent my father three more question marks. I did not respond to the email from the photographer. My mother wrote at eight thirty, asking if I was feeling alone. There were many people nearby, young, single, possibly naked.

In bed at night I thought of the last hour of my marriage, which had unspooled, in predictable irony, the morning after a wedding. I had arrived to the breakfast first, at the Hudson Valley farmhouse turned rustic inn, to the row of carefully distressed tables along the porch. My husband had stayed in the room to shower and shave. Waiting for him with another couple, acquaintances who coordinated their clothing and spoke one another's names so often it seemed part of a prenuptial agreement, I looked out at the spread of hills, a green that was nearly uniform. When he appeared I watched him walk toward and then past me, forsaking the seat on my left for one at the empty table next to it. Embarrassed for me before I became embarrassed for myself, the couple exchanged a look. They straightened their silverware. They spoke one another's names.

A half an hour later, on the unmade bed that looked like an envelope torn open, I mentioned the chair I had saved. I used the word *divorce*. My husband accused me of looking for symbols where there were none, and then I was blithe, as I'd rarely been in our time together, packing up my weekend bag, checking in the morning light for what might have been forgotten.

In the studio apartment where I'd moved to be alone, I woke the next morning to a call from my father, the fourth in a row. In the background there was the sound of wind or water, in his voice a kind of directness that would have frightened me as a child. He asked if I'd had my coffee yet, and said he would wait while I made it, asking nothing after that, none of the little questions that buttoned our conversations together: hot enough for you, how's the city so nice they named it twice. I told him I'd need to put the phone down a minute, and if he'd rather I could call him back, but he said he was happy to stay on the line. As I boiled water and dumped yesterday's grounds from the French press, I kept looking at the phone where I'd set it on my small, high table, in the shadow of a copper bowl where I'd floated white carnations in water, worried that whatever he had to say would change given how long he had to wait.

When I finally settled on the stool I put him on speaker, wanting, in some childish way, for his voice to fill the room. I could imagine his exculpations: that she had been one in a million, full of surprises, and this was just another, bitter a pill as it was to swallow. So long as he accepted the most critical fact of it, I was prepared to give him every sympathy. I would offer never to bring it up again.

"First, I want to apologize," he said. "I never expected this to come up, and I guess I thought I might be able to push it back down."

"Of course you didn't," I said. "How could you have expected it?"

That I had spoken did not seem to matter. I had the sense, for the first time in my life, of what my father was like alone, fearful because he was brittle, unhappy because he was fearful, determined because he was unhappy.

"She never told you about that time in her life, and I believed that was her choice and her right."

I looked for his voice on the petals in the water, in the crystals of salt I kept in a low ceramic platter.

"Are you saying you knew about the photo?"

"I didn't know specifically about the photo, but I knew about the circumstances surrounding it. When I met your mother she was nine months clean and I was six, and she still had some New York on her. Crosswalks were invisible. If somebody said how are you, her shoulders went up. She'd done it cold turkey, no program, no rehab, nothing. That impressed the hell out of me."

"But she drank," I said. "What about the sauvignon blanc at dinner? Aren't addicts supposed to—"

This question, as with all others I asked in the brief remainder of the phone call, my father answered in as few words as possible, denying me any real information. My voice spiked and flew and his refused to meet it. In dismissing my catechism, he was returning her to the place where dead people live, her mysteries as irrelevant now as her peanut allergy or pilled lilac robe. I wanted to believe that another conversation was happening inside the one I could hear, that maybe, in allowing my mother her life, protecting it from my revisionist inquiries, he was reminding me of the rights I had, the questions about who I was or how I suffered for which there were no categorical answers. By the time my father said goodbye, the noise had grown around him, busy, total, and I said, vaguely irritated, "Where are you going, anyway?"

"I'm going to the goddamn game," he answered, knit so deep into his living that he did not think to tell me which.

I responded to the photographer sometime in the surreal afternoon that followed, a time in which all my thoughts felt half-lit, things that had belonged to someone else and which I held up to test for an emotion I'd know when I found it. There were certain memories of my husband I had never revisited, a night I had let a moth into the bedroom and he had been viciously annoyed. I had been reading, but he insisted we turn out all the lights and reopen all the windows, tempt it with the glow of the street, and while we lay waiting for the thing to fly out of the room I could feel his palms pressing on the mattress, taut against sleep or comfort. I did not cry out in satisfaction at its exit, as he did, and I could tell my silence bothered him, even though the sheets were clean and soft, even though the smell in our home was of spring. *I'm open to being photographed,* I wrote to the photographer, *so long as I'm asleep.*

A field, I thought then. A yellow caned chair. A room up some stairs that was empty.

WENDELL BERRY

# The Great Interruption: The Story of a Famous Story of Old Port William and How It Ceased To Be Told (1935–1978)

FROM *Threepenny Review*

BILLY GIBBS WAS as lively a boy, no doubt, as he could have been made by a strong body, excellent health, an active mind, and an alert sense of humor much like that of his father, Grover Gibbs. Like about all the Port William boys of his time, his life was not as leisurely as he wished it to be. From the time he grew from the intelligence of a coonhound to that of a fairly biddable border collie, his parents, who were often in need of help, found work for him to do. This occasioned his next significant intellectual advance: recognition of the advantages of making himself hard to find. For the next several years, however, his parents, Beulah and Grover, were better at finding him than he was at hiding. From the time of their marriage in 1920 until Beulah inherited her parents' little farm in 1948, they were tenant farmers, and Billy was always under some pressure to earn his keep. Needing to work, for a boy of sound faculties, naturally increases the attractiveness of not working, and Billy's mind was perfectly sound.

His life would have been simple if he had been only lazy—or, as he himself might have said if he had thought to say it, only a lover of freedom. But along with the wish to avoid work, his mental development brought him also to the wish to be useful to his parents and to work well, especially if an adult dignity attached to the work. And so he was a two-minded boy.

And so he grew up into usefulness and a growing and lasting pride in being useful, but also into a more or less parallel love of adventure and a talent for shirking. Throughout his youth he remained, with approximate willingness, under the governance of his father, a man famously humorous and much smarter than he allowed his children to know. He managed Billy by demand, by challenge, and by pretending not to know what he knew he could not prevent.

If there were times when Grover kept Billy pretty steadily busy, there were also times when he did not. When Billy was not at work, he would be out of sight and free, as Grover expected and more or less intended. And so Billy got around. He hunted and fished and trapped mostly by himself, and with his friends he roamed about. There were few acres within a walk of his house that Billy had not put his foot on by the time he was twelve years old. His mind was free and alert in those days. He saw many things then that education and ambition would teach him to overlook. By the time he was fourteen he knew familiarly every aspect, prospect, and place in the neighborhood of Port William.

He knew, for example, that the Birds Branch road curves down the hill past the old Levers place, where his family were tenants for many years, and goes on down and becomes fairly level and straight where the bottomland along the branch begins to widen and open into the river valley. In the summer of 1935, the year Billy would become fourteen at the end of September, an extremely brushy fencerow ran along the side of the road, and in this fencerow there was a gate, never shut, that led into a pasture abandoned just long enough to be covered with tall weeds and blackberry briars and so far just a scattering of seedling trees. If a gentleman from down at Hargrave wanted to conduct some business strictly private, he could turn his car through that gate, drive a hundred or so feet parallel to the *inside* of that fencerow, and become almost magically invisible to anybody driving a car or a team and wagon or even walking along the road on the outside.

He could be somewhat less invisible to a boy who would be across the road, fishing in the Blue Hole on Birds Branch, would hear the car slow down, turn in at the gate, and presently stop.

Now who could have a reason to drive into that forsaken place in a car? And what might be the reason? And, to boot, in the middle of a Sunday afternoon. Billy of course wanted to know. He stuck the end of his fishing pole firmly into the ground and ventured across the road and through the gate. From there he could see the top of the car shining between the lowest leaves of the trees in the fencerow and the tops of the tallest weeds. He thought he could hear voices, perhaps a laugh, but a breeze was stirring the foliage and he was not sure. His feet were itching to creep up close enough to become informed. But the same itch made him cautious, even a little afraid. The business at hand, whatever it was, was strictly for grownups. And William Franklin Gibbs, among the several other things he was, was a mannerly boy, accustomed to granting respect, not invariably sincere, to grownups. The place, moreover, did not belong to him, nor he to it, a matter that concerned him only after he had become cautious. And he was enough of a hunter by then to know that he could not make his way secretly through the hard-stemmed weeds of the old pasture in broad daylight.

When he got back to the Blue Hole he saw from the bobbing and darting about of his cork that he had come into good fortune. Presently he drew out a nice sunfish, and for a good while after that his attention was entirely diverted from the mysterious car to the mysterious undersurface of the Blue Hole where sunfish the size of his hand and bigger were expressing their approval of his worms. But when the car's engine started, quietly enough but loud enough to hear, of course he heard it.

This time he went no farther than the sort of hedge of leafy bushes and weeds along the roadside. As the car, a nice, new-looking blue car with a long hood, paused before pulling out onto the road, Billy could see the driver plainly through the windshield and then more plainly through the open side window. The man was important-looking, and intentionally so. He wore a dark jacket, white shirt and tie, a perfectly adjusted gray felt hat, eyeglasses, and a neat little mustache. Beside him but well away there was a lady, perhaps also important-looking, whom Billy could see even better. She too was well-dressed. She wore a nice little straw hat and a pair of dark-lensed glasses such as Billy had never seen worn by any woman he knew.

Billy did not then, nor did he ever, know who the woman was. But he instantly recognized the man as Mr. Forrest La Vere of the

Hargrave upper crust, then running for public office. To make
sure, as he really did not need to do, Billy waited until the car
was well out of sight and then walked not many steps up the road
to look at Mr. La Vere's picture on his campaign poster that was
tacked to a big sycamore.

Billy Gibbs, who did not know what a cynic was, was not a cynic.
But he had lived almost fourteen years within the farm life, social
life, conversation, influence, and atmosphere of the Port William
neighborhood, and he did not know when he had not known, and
always a little more, of the ways of the world.

And so it happened, maybe as a mere coincidence but maybe
not, that on the next Sunday afternoon he was again fishing in the
Blue Hole. Again he heard the big, quiet car turn in at the open
gate into the abandoned field, and this time he did not get up
to look.

Or he did not go to look until the car had again spent its interval behind the bushy fencerow and driven away. And then, having
again planted his fishing pole firmly in the earth of the creek bank,
he followed the car's two tracks along the inside of the fencerow
to the place where he could see that it had stopped before, and
several times more than twice. He saw furthermore that just at the
place where the car always stopped there was a stout tree, a box elder, that had grown leaning away from the fencerow into the open
sunlight of the old pasture, as such trees do. It was a tree climbable
enough, at least for Billy, who aspired to heights and was, if not yet
avian as he would become in seven years, at least arboreal.

Toward the middle of the following Sunday afternoon, and certainly now by no coincidence, the young Mr. Gibbs — Billy Frank
to his mother, of whom at the moment he was not thinking — was
perched somewhat comfortably on a branch above the lowest
branches of the box elder, which would position him, screened by
the wider-spreading branch below, just about exactly over the roof
of the big blue car. And when it came time for the car to arrive,
here it came, and it stopped where it always had stopped before.

Mr. La Vere stepped out, took off his jacket and placed it, neatly
folded, on the hood of the car. He then went around and removed
the back seat, placing it with some care on the ground and within
the car's shadow. He and the lady sat down side by side upon it.

What followed Billy had seen enacted by cattle, horses, sheep, goats, hogs, dogs, housecats, chickens, turkeys, guineas, ducks, geese, pigeons, sparrows, and, by great good fortune he was sure, a pair of snakes. And so he was not surprised but only astonished to be confirmed in his suspicion that the same ceremony could be performed by humans.

And he certainly was getting his eyes full, except that the roof of the car was a little in the way, and there was yet a detail or two that he needed to study in case he might himself some day be called upon to assume the role of Mr. La Vere. He ooched therefore several more inches out along the limb and leaned ever so carefully a few more inches still farther out. And then he heard a crack that entirely distracted his attention from the drama below.

It was not a warning crack. The box elder being a brittle, humorless, unforgiving tree, the branch Billy was sitting on had no sooner cracked than it broke off near the trunk. Billy redoubled his hold on the branch above, which, with utter indifference to his great need and with a crack of its own, came loose in his hands, letting him down with some force upon the branch below, which, with the loudest and most eloquent of the three cracks, also broke and went down. To the Honorable Forrest La Vere, thus rudely interrupted in his devotion, it must have seemed that he had been assaulted by a flying brushpile, fully leafed and unwilted, with a boy inside it in a hurry to get out.

Billy came down perhaps a dozen feet in more or less the posture of an airborne flying squirrel, and landed squarely on top of Mr. La Vere. He lost no time in disentangling himself from the various limbs, and he was on his feet, running hard, no doubt before Mr. La Vere could complete the necessary change of mind.

But the force of Billy's descent had been considerably mitigated by the intervening small branches and foliage. The damage suffered by Mr. La Vere having thus been about entirely limited to his dignity and peace of mind, he too was very soon up and running. Although he had reached the far side of midlife, Mr. La Vere was lean, evidently in good condition, well warmed up, clearly unresigned to second place, and his legs were longer by several inches than those of Billy Gibbs, who was after all still a growing boy.

Never before had Billy been obliged to think while running. But he thought then, surprised that he could do it, and he thought well. Like a hard-pressed rabbit, he had at first run for the nearest cover, heading up the hill toward the woods, but then, like a clever fox, he turned along the slope toward a thriving blackberry patch that had laid its tangles across the old pasture from one side to the other. This decision was costly to Billy, for without much damaging his clothes the barbed thorns, that snatched at his sleeves and pant legs only momentarily, clawed long bloody scratches onto his skin, but they touched Mr. La Vere's imagination several seconds before he reached them. He was not dressed for briars. Taking care never to look back, Billy sped freely out of sight.

For three whole years, while Billy grew into wholehearted envy, not of Mr. La Vere's ladyfriend, but of his automobile, and while he watched the tops of young cedars and walnuts and wild plums and redbuds emerge from the weeds and briars of the abandoned field, he alone of all the people in Port William and the country round about knew the story which, after Wheeler Catlett came to know it, would be known as The Great interruption. And likewise no doubt, of all in the urbs and suburbs of Hargrave, the only people who knew that story were the Honorable Forrest la Vere and the Unknown Lady.

The story must have laid on Billy Gibbs's mind with some weight, the more as he grew into the sophistication truly to appreciate it. He came to see it, or to imagine it, both as himself involved and as himself watching as from a higher limb. As it became more coherently a story in his mind, sometimes when he was at work alone he would tell it over to himself, beginning with the leaning box elder and how he climbed it and took his seat, and he would laugh out loud, and would laugh more as he elaborated the details and again made them visible to himself.

One mind, and a boy's mind at that, finally could not contain such a story. But such a story, a story of such high excellence and so rare, could be turned loose in Port William only with some caution beforehand, as one might release an especially exuberant big dog. Billy found that he was not able to tell the story to anybody unworthy of it, which eliminated forthwith all the boys more or less of his own generation.

A part of the culture of Port William in those days was a curious division between the men and the boys. The men in their talk of sexual matters were fairly unguarded in the presence at least of the bigger boys. Their conversation did not as a rule *include* the bigger boys, but it went on without regard or respect to them, leaving them to understand what and as they could. But the boys never talked of what *they* knew in the presence of the men, though all of them knew the same things. Port William big boys and young men did not want to be caught presuming to be more grown up than they were. It would have been extremely irregular for a boy under twenty, or even twenty-five, to offer a sexual joke or a bit of sexual gossip to an older man. This was, in short, a boundary trespassed by the men regardlessly and often, but never by the boys except by accident, as when Orvie Galingale and Worth Berlew crawled under the hootchy-kootchy tent at the county fair to confront, not, as expected, the intimate revelations of the lady known as Bubbles, but their own fathers, who had paid already, as they thought, to get in.

Billy was balked also by the fastidiousness of a true critic. The boys he knew were just about uniformly no good as storytellers, which suggested that they would not know a really good story from a pretty good one, and Billy knew he had a really good one. He wanted to tell it to a real storyteller who would recognize its worth. And so he told it to Burley Coulter.

Burley was a good friend and an old running mate of Billy's father. Burley and Grover Gibbs were not exactly like-minded, but they knew a lot of the same things, understood each other, and in essential ways depended on each other. And so Burley was in all but blood an uncle to Billy Gibbs. Since before Billy could remember, they had been on good terms. They trusted each other. And so if it should happen one winter night, as it did happen, that just the two of them, Burley Coulter and Billy Gibbs, should be coon hunting on the bluffs along Katy's Branch, that would be merely in the order of things.

As a coon hunter, Burley was easily pleased. If it was a good night for hunting and the dogs hunted well, he would be delighted to spend the necessary energy. If for whatever reason the hunting was poor, he would be about equally content to build a fire, sit staring at the blaze, and talk the unhurried talk possible at such times.

He and Billy had passed maybe an hour, now and again adding a stick or two to a fire large enough to give them its cheerful light and warmth but not too demanding of fuel. They had made the fire beside a large pile of rocks at the edge of a long overgrown tobacco patch. The ground was damp, and the rock pile offered a dry place to sit. They sat somewhat apart so as to face each other. Their talk had lapsed comfortably into silence and revived again two or three times, and finally Billy's silence was overpowered by the need to tell his story.

He said, "I'll tell you something." And then he said, "But now I don't want you to tell this to anybody else."

"Well," Burley said, "maybe I won't."

Billy in fact had not expected a better reply. If Burley had been another boy, Billy might have made him swear never to tell. But Burley was a man forty-three years old and Billy only a boy of seventeen. It may have been that Billy didn't mind much one way or the other. He was after all a two-minded boy.

Anyhow, he started into his story. Burley listened with what might have been respectful attention until Billy got to the part where he climbed into the box elder and took his seat on the second from the bottom limb and steadied himself by holding to the limb above, and then the big blue car followed its own tracks in from the road and stopped just where it had before, and then Mr. La Vere removed the back seat and situated it on the ground. And that was when Burley leaned back onto the rock pile with his fingers laced behind his head. "Oh good lord!" he said and started laughing.

If Billy told his story well, and he did tell it very well, that may have owed a good deal to the excellence of his audience. As Billy laid out the details just as he had done when he told the story to himself, and as the details accumulated, Burley's delight increased and he stopped laughing quietly only to laugh out loud.

When the story had been told, Burley sat up, thought a while, gazing into the fire, and from time to time laughing again to himself.

And then he said, "Well!"

In another little while he said, "Well, you knew the great man by face and name. Did he know you?"

"I never showed him my face. I had *some* sense."

"A little, I reckon. But you had as much as you needed, and you used it."

"Maybe I had even a little bit more than I used."

Burley ignored that. He said, "Hang on a minute. If I've figured this right, I'm now the fourth person in all creation that knows this story."

"Well, till I told you, I never told it, and I doubt if they ever did. Now don't you tell anybody else."

"You ain't got a thing to worry about. I ain't going to tell a soul but your daddy."

They both laughed then, for they knew equally that to tell Grover would be to tell Port William. He could have held such a story just about as long as he could hold his breath. And Billy was comfortable enough with that. He was too happy with Burley's pleasure in the story to want to deny it to others. He was a two-minded boy but purely and truly generous.

Billy never told the story again. He never needed to. It would be told from then on mainly by Grover and Burley. They were acknowledged storytellers, long practiced, and as they told it they adhered to the outline of Billy's recital to Burley in the nighttime woods, but they added ever more artistry to the details.

"He done it, she done it, *they* done it," said Grover, who loved grammar mainly for its comedy. "They got entirely incorporated. Yes in-deedy."

"They never even shook hands," Burley said. "They got right into business with their hats on."

"*Aw* yeah," Grover said, "they went straight to the hemale and the shemale, conjugating that old verb to who'd a thought it."

"When that misfortunate lady heard them branches crack and saw that young brushpile coming down," Burley said, "her eyes popped out to where they looked at each other with some concern."

For a while after he told Burley and Burley told Grover, every time Billy heard the men laughing, he fairly reliably would know why. His story was again being brought to mind, either by being told or by being alluded to. For of course the story belonged richly and complexly to Port William, pertaining about equally to its geography and its history. It was a part of its self-knowledge. It meant in Port William what it could not mean, and far more than it could mean, in any other place on earth. The ones who told it and the ones who heard it knew the abandoned field and the brushy fencerow at the lower end of Birds Branch. They knew the Blue Hole and the big briar patch. They knew Billy Gibbs, the boy he had been and was. They knew the nature and character of box elders. They had kept the stories of a greedy and miserly, eccentric and amusing family known around Port William as Leverses, who down at Hargrave were a family of greedy aristocrats

know as La Veres. The tellers and hearers of the story understood
in an ever-renewing instant the entire signification of their vision
of the august Forrest La Vere conjugating the commonplace old
verb upon an extracted back seat in a weedfield. Thus, for the
men, the story was a way of knowing what they knew, and a way
of teaching the boys. And of course the story made its way from
the gathering places of the men into the kitchens and bedrooms
round about and came to belong also to the Port William house-
wives and big girls.

From the night in the winter of 1938 when Billy set it free, his
story was one of Port William's ways of knowing itself, but only for
a few years. And then came the great tearing apart of the war and
what followed. A new time came, different from any that had been
before. Then, as the elders made their way one by one to their settled places in the graveyard, too many of the young became known
to Port William mainly by their absence. Tom Coulter and Virgil
Feltner and others perished in the war. The war promoted Billy
Gibbs from tree climbing to flying. He went into the air as a member of the crew of a B-17, and flew at last safely back to the ground
with maybe a story or two he was not so eager to tell. And then he
went to college, and from there, as his mother put it, "into a suit
and into business." *That* was the defining story then, of Port William and thousands of places like it. It was the story of the young
people, changed by the change of times, who by the war's end or
the midcentury had found their way to city jobs and salaries or
high wages, and who returned after that only to visit a bedside in a
nursing home, at a loss for something to say, or to bury the dead.

I heard the story of The Great Interruption only a few times in
the years after the war. It was becoming less and less a property
of its old community in time and place. Grover Gibbs and Burley
Coulter, remarkably, had ceased to tell it. I think it had begun to
make them sad. Port William by then was losing its own stories,
which were being replaced by the entertainment industry, and so
it was coming to know itself only as a "no-place" adrift with every
place in a country dismemoried and without landmarks.

Finally, if Billy's old story were to be told, it would have to stand
alone, bereft of the old knowing-in-common that once enriched
it. It would be heard then as little more than a joke on the subject
of what we have learned to call "sex," a biologic function disassoci-

ated from everything but itself. If one of the professionally successful descendants of the place as it once was were to tell it, say, at a
cocktail party, it would be understood as an exhibit of the behavior
of rural Kentuckians, laughable in all their ways, from which the
teller had earned much credit by escaping.

Of the five children of Grover and Beulah Gibbs—Billy, Althie,
Nance, Sissy, and Stanley—only Althie stayed close enough to accompany her parents and watch over them and share her life with
them as long as they lived.

One day in the year or so between Burley's death and his own,
Grover and I were sitting and talking on the tailgate of his old
pickup truck. Grover had been kind to me ever since I was little.
He was one of my own dwindling small company of elders, and
I loved to talk with him. We were talking, as we often did, of the
changes that even I, younger than Grover by nearly forty years, had
witnessed in Port William and the country around. We were telling
of course the story, clearly ongoing and with no foreseeable end,
of the departure of the people and the coming of the machines.

I said, "And the poor old ground is going to suffer for it."

Grover faced things by preference with a grin or a laugh that
was honest enough, for he had faithfully observed and relished
the funniness of the world. But he could give you a straight look
sometimes that would make you shiver.

"Andy," he said. "Honey, I know you know. The hurts ain't all
just only to the ground."

JAMEL BRINKLEY

# No More Than a Bubble

FROM *LitMag*

IT WAS BACK in those days. Claudius Van Clyde and I stood on the edge of the dancing crowd, each of us already three bottles into one brand of miracle brew, blasted by the music that throbbed from the speakers. But we weren't listening to the songs. I'd been speaking into the open shell of his ear since we'd gotten to the party, shouting a bunch of mopey stuff about my father. Sometime around the witching hour, he stopped his perfunctory nodding and pointed toward the staircase of the house. "Check out *these* biddies," he said. Past the heads of the dancers and would-be seducers I saw the two girls he meant. They kept reaching for each other's waists and drawing their hands quickly away, as if testing the heat of a fire. After a minute of this game the girls laughed and walked off. We weaved through the crowd and followed them, away from the deejay's setup in front of the night-slicked bay windows, and into the kitchen where we took stock of the situation. One of the girls was lanky and thin-armed, but notably rounded at the hips. She wore a white tank top, which gave her face and painted fingernails a sheen in the dimmed light. A neat ladylike Afro bloomed from her head, and she was a lighter shade of brown than her friend with the buzz cut, a thick snack of a girl whose shape made you work your jaws.

The party, thrown by a couple of Harvard grads, happened just weeks before the Day of Atonement, in late September of 1995. Claudius had overheard some seniors talking about it earlier that Saturday after the football game, as they all smoked next to the pale-blue lion statue up at Baker Field. Later he dragged me from my dorm room. We slipped out of the university's gates and took the subway down to Brooklyn, determined to crash. The party had been described as an affair for singles, so when you arrived you had to fill out a sticker that read "Hi, my name is . . ." and affix it to your body. The taller girl in the tank top had placed hers on her upper arm, like a service stripe. Her friend wore the sticker on her rump, and this was both a convenience and a joke meant to shame us. Neither of their stickers bore a name.

"Dizzy chicks," Claudius said to me, and we gave each other goofy grins. The main difference between a house party in Brooklyn and a college party uptown was that on campus you were just practicing. You could half-ass it or go extra hard at a campus party, either play the wall or go balls-out booty hound, and there would be no actual stakes, no real edge to the consequences. Nothing sharp to press your chest against, no precipice to leap from, nothing to brave. You might get dissed, or you might get some play. You would almost certainly get cheaply looped. But at the end of the night, no matter what, you would drift off to sleep in the narrows of a dorm bed surrounded by cinderblock walls, swaddled in twin extralong sheets purchased by someone's mom.

We approached the girls, pointed to our stickers to introduce ourselves, and asked for their names. The tall one with the Afro said her name was Iris and did so with her nose, putting unusually strong emphasis on the *I*. True to this utterance, she seemed the more insistent and lunatic of the two. She vibrated. We asked where they were from. Most of Iris's family came from Belize. Her friend with the buzz cut, Sybil, was Dominican. Claudius and I liked to know these kinds of things.

"You enjoying the party?" I asked. Iris didn't respond. Her attention flew all over the place. The house we were in was old— you felt its floorboards giving, perceived its aches being drowned out by the music and conversations that swelled with everyone's full-bellied bloats of laughter. In hushed moments, you heard the creaking of wood, followed by the tinkle of glass, the crunch of plastic, or the throaty rise of the hum. Iris seemed attuned to all of it, to every detail of the party house and its subtle geographies. She stared now through the glass doors leading to the backyard, where torches showed little groups of smokers breathing into the air.

I tapped her on the shoulder.

"Oh, hello again," she said and then looked at her friend.

"Yep, they're still here," Sybil said.

"Enjoying the party?" I repeated.

"We're bubbling," Iris said. From the living room the deejay began to play a new song. "What is this?" she said. "I know this."

"That new shit," said a guy standing near us. He had a patchy beard and double-fisted red cups of foamy beer. Maybe he was a Harvard man. "Newest latest," he said. "'Brooklyn Zoo.' Ol' Dirty Bastard."

Claudius and the girls nodded in recognition but to me it all sounded like code.

"Why's he called that?" I asked.

The guy laughed. "Because there's no father to his style."

The girls turned to each other and began a kind of stomping dance. "Damn damn damn," Iris said, "this song is so bubble!"

They seemed to understand the good life according to the image and logic of this word—simultaneously noun, verb, and adjective—its glistening surface wet with potential meaning. As they danced, their faces became masks of tension, nostrils and mouths flexed open. Iris kept her arms pinned to her sides while Sybil jabbed the air with her elbows. Claudius jerked his chin at Sybil and told me, "I call dibs."

"Nah, man."

"Already called it."

We both preferred girls of a certain plumpness, with curves—in part, I think, because that's what black guys are supposed to like, because liking it felt like a confirmation of possessing black blood, a way to stamp ourselves with authenticity—but he had made his claim. I was left to deal with Iris, the prophetess of the bubble. Fine, no big deal. Claudius could have his pick. This was all his idea anyway. We wouldn't be here if it weren't for him. He knew I needed a good distraction.

A few weeks earlier, late one August morning in Philadelphia, shortly before the start of sophomore year, I sat with my father, Leo, at the kitchen table and got drunk with him for the first time. He told me to beware of crazy women, angry women, passionate women. He told me they would ruin me. "But they are also the best women," he said, "the best lovers, with a jungle between their legs and such wildness in bed that every man should experience." I knew the kinds of women he meant. I also knew he was talking about my mother, but I didn't give a damn. She had left us, left him, a few years earlier, and recently she'd announced she was getting remarried. I saw how this news affected my father. He had stalked around our house all summer and appeared smaller and more frantic by the week. He searched as though the answer to the question of how his life had gone so wrong was hidden in one of the rooms. All but undone by this effort, my father regarded me that morning through his heavy eyelids and long Mediterranean lashes. He'd inherited bad teeth from his own father and before he turned sixty had had a bunch of them yanked out. He wore a dental partial but didn't have it in as we drank. The bottom of his face was collapsed like a rotten piece of fruit. "The best," he repeated. "And so." His Italian accent deepened the more he drank. His tongue peeked out of his broken grin. "And so every man should experience this, Ben," he said. "Once." He held a chewed fingernail up by his high nose and then reached into his pocket for something. It was a condom, wrapped in silver foil. "Use this with the most delicious woman you can find, *una pazza*. Let her screw your brains out, once and never again. Then marry a nice, boring, fat girl with hands and thighs like old milk. Making a dull life is the only way to be happy." He gave me the condom. It was an ill-timed ritual—I'd already gone out into the world—but he believed in it, just as he believed there was a way to be happy. Since I was his disciple, and quite drunk that morning, I believed in it too.

At the house party, Claudius and I slid in behind the girls and danced with them right there in the kitchen. Iris moved well but with aggression. She spun around, hooked her fingers into my belt loops, and slammed her pelvis into mine. She grinded herself against me for a while and then backed away to show her perfect teeth and claw the air between us. She was a kitten on its hind legs, fiercely swiping at a ball on a string.

I leaned in and asked if she'd gone to Harvard too. I tried to sound older, like I'd already graduated and was fully a man.

"We're Hawks," Iris said in her nasal voice, and then she spread her arms like wings. Claudius had a theory about girls with nasal voices that I now appreciated anew. The theory was that girls who spoke this way, cutting their voices off from their lungs and guts, did so as a kind of defense, a noisy insistence meant to distract men from the flesh.

"Hawks?"

"Hunter College, '94. Hey, why don't you get me and my girl some whiskey bubbles?"

"That's whiskey and . . . ?"

"Magic."

"Huh?"

"Just whiskey," she whined, with a disappointed shake of her head. "Be a good boy."

Passing Claudius and Sybil as they danced, I nodded to let him know we were in. The sensation of Iris's moving hips ghosted against me. Floating there in the face of the kitchen cabinet were her pretty smile and dark eyes, flecked with a color close to gold.

After making four healthy pours of Jack, I carried the cups back over. Sybil sniffed the whiskey and let her eyes cross with pleasure. Iris lifted her cup and with a dignified tone and expression said she was thankful for the universe and all of its moments.

"And for whiskey and music and madness and love," she added.

"And for the sky," Sybil said. "Have you seen the fucking sky tonight?"

The words were meaningless. It was a toast to nonsense.

"And for your tits," Iris said. She reached out and squeezed Sybil's right breast. "Doesn't she have great tits?"

"She does," Claudius said, staring at them. "She really does."

Claudius had come to Columbia from West Oakland with certain notions regarding life in New York, that the city's summer heat and dust, its soot-caked winter ice, were those of the cultural comet, which he ached to witness if not ride. Because of these notions, he manipulated gestures and disguises, pushed the very core of himself outward so that you could see in his face and in the flare of his broad nostrils the hard radiance of the soul-stuff that some people chatter on about. Though not quite handsome, he was appealing. He could convince you he was beautiful. For this trickery his implements included a collection of Eastern-style conical hats and retro four-finger rings. His choice for tonight: a fez, tilted forward on his head so that we, both of us, felt emboldened by the obscene probing swing of the tassel.

He and I knew what *we* were toasting: the next phase of life. At parties like this the crowd was older, college seniors who already had New York apartments, graduates who were starting to make their way, and folks who were far enough into their youth to start questioning it. The booze was better and the weed was sticky good. The girls were incredible, of course, especially here. You could taste a prevalent Caribbean flavor in the air, as if the parade through Brooklyn's thoroughfares on Labor Day had never stopped and this had been its destination all along. If not Caribbean like Sybil, then the girls were something else distinct and of the globe. These girls each had her own atmosphere. We were convinced they wore better, tinier underwear than the girls we knew, convinced they were mad geniuses of their own bodies.

"So where'd you two escape from?" Iris asked, though her gaze drifted out to the backyard again.

"Uptown," Claudius said. "Columbia."

*"Roar, Lion, Roar,"* Sybil said, mocking us.

"We graduated in May," I lied.

"Mazel tov," Iris said.

Sybil shook her head.

Iris's attention snapped all the way back now. "What? I can totally say that."

Sybil made a popping sound with her mouth, and the two of them laughed.

Claudius and I laughed too, though neither of us knew what was funny. Before we could pick up the thread of the conversation, the girls left us without saying a word.

We slid up the stairs after them and wound past the partygoers perched there gossiping or flirting or losing themselves in the privacies of thought. On the second floor, a group of people stood shoulder to shoulder in the doorway of one room, as though to block something illicit from view. Claudius and I pushed past them and found ourselves in an immense bathroom, where voices echoed off the tiles. Two girls stood fully clothed in a Jacuzzi painted a tacky shade of powder blue, their heads framed by a backlit square of stained glass over the tub, but they weren't our girls. Back in the hallway, we caught Iris and Sybil coming out of a bedroom, trailed by the skunky sweet odor of marijuana. We pursued them downstairs.

Claudius took a step toward them and said, "So let's play a game."

For a moment the girls acted as though they had never seen us before, then Sybil's eyes widened. "Wow," she said.

Claudius announced that we should all trade confessions.

"Shameful stories," he said. "Secrets. The worse they are, the better."

They seemed amused but unwilling.

He went on anyway. "Who wants to go first?" he said, and waited. But it was just a sham. Of course Claudius would be the one to start.

He and I knew exactly what we were aiming to achieve in these moments. It involved patience and strategic silences and then, when we did speak, a distinct lowering of our voices—even in loud places, so that we would have to lean in—and eye contact that was both firm and soft, not a stare, that broke occasionally to let our gazes trickle down the full lengths of their bodies. Less wolfish than a leer, more a sly undressing. The total effect would be a kind of hypnosis, a gradual giving of the self. As we developed it, this method had worked with the girls on campus, but we knew that this was nothing to be proud of. College is nothing if not four years of people throwing themselves wildly at each other.

In his affected murmur, Claudius told us a story I had heard before. The story may or may not have been true, but it shocked people, or aroused them, or made them feel vulnerable and sad. Claudius wasn't what you would call a patient guy. He needed to know as soon as possible where people stood, especially girls. Here is the story: When he was in high school, he discovered that the old lady who lived alone next door was watching him from her window. He would exercise in his room, wearing only his briefs, every morning and night. He locked the door to keep his alcoholic mother out. Furiously blinking, Claudius continued: "Calf-raises, push-ups, chin-ups, and crunches till I dropped. And there she was, this old biddy, looking dead at me with her old biddy glasses like it was the most natural thing in the world, like I was putting on a show. So that's just what I did. At first I stood at the window and stared right back at her, rubbing my chest and abs. Then, after a week or so of this, I started rubbing baby oil on myself. I took it up a notch by walking around naked, and when that didn't faze her, I tried to get my girlfriend to put on a sex show with me. Well, she wasn't having it. Too innocent, I guess, so get this: I masturbated instead, right in front of the window. The old biddy watched this too, but the next night she wasn't there. Wasn't there the next night either. That was the last night she watched me. I guess she got to see what she'd been waiting for all along."

In unison the girls let out a shriek, which spilled into rapid chatter that was like another language. Even in the dim party lights, their darting eyes stood out, fine russet and amber stones. The flurry of motion seemed to release scent from them: ripe sweat and vanilla and almond. Iris's body shook with laughter as she slapped her thigh and rocked her head back. Her perfect Afro eclipsed broad sections of the room in its orbit. Other girls had either been repulsed or aroused by the story, unambiguously so. None had ever reacted like this. And something else was off. Iris's wild mouth and eyes moved independently of the rest of her face. She resembled a hard plastic doll.

"What the fuck?" Sybil said finally. "This one thinks he's a freak," she said and sent his tassel spinning with a flick of her finger.

"Shame is the name of the game," Claudius said, with a flare of his nostrils. "Shame is the nonsense of every age." He was speaking a little too grandly now, even for him. "Let's get on with the nonsense of *this* age."

The girls whispered to each other, blew soft gibberish onto each other's necks.

"Well," Claudius said, "who's next?"

"Him," Iris said. "What's he got to say?"

All three of them stared at me, waiting. There were a million ways I could go, but every corridor of my mind led to the same place.

"My dad," I began, saying the first and only words that came to me. I explained that he was a white man, born and raised in Italy. He would always call my mother his *cioccolata*. Whenever she was angry with him, yelling for one reason or another, he would laugh and pet her cheek. In those moments he would tell her she was *agrodulce*, always retaining some of her sweetness.

Claudius smiled when I said this. He liked when I used Italian words on girls.

I told them my father loved my mother and her family. He especially liked when her younger sisters would visit. This was when I was a boy. Before they arrived I would sit on the rim of the tub and run my finger along the edge of the shower curtain, watching as he beautified himself. He put on cologne and decided whether to leave one or two buttons open at the neck of his finest shirts. He would make sure his cheeks were perfectly stubbled. During the visits he charmed as he mixed drinks, kissed the backs of hands, and admired new hairstyles. He ladled praise over my pretty aunts in easy pours. And I always adored him.

Claudius had stopped smiling. I wasn't telling a shameful story. I wasn't sure what I was doing, but I kept on.

Things like this would frustrate my mother, I told them; she accused him of flirting, loudly complained about his lack of respect for her. One day, when I was twelve, something else really brought out her fury. She came home from work hours before I was expecting her, and found me at the kitchen table looking through my father's collection of nudes. I had seen my father's dirty magazines before, and had avoided detection previously by taking only quick peeks, but this time I discovered, or could no longer ignore, that my father had specific preferences. I was riveted by the curves of the women's buttocks, their dark nipples, and the dense blackness displayed between their thighs. My mother picked through the pile—I hadn't realized until then how many were there—and from time to time, between glances at me, she would touch a finger to the mute faces of the women in the pictures, strained into expressions of pleasure. Her deeply brown skin against the images of theirs. My mother's silence unnerved me. I desperately wanted her to say something, anything at all, but she didn't. She simply took the entire stack from the table and gestured for me to go to my room.

When my father got home, he and my mother argued in the living room. I crept out and watched from the hallway.

"Leo, he's twelve," she said to him. It was as if my father had sat me down to show me the magazines himself, or worse, as if he had taken me to a whorehouse. Why would she blame him for what I did? I couldn't understand it.

"Benito's curious, almost a grown boy," my father replied. He thought it was no big deal, nothing to fuss about, and I agreed. "And isn't it good that he learns such women are beautiful? That his mamma is beautiful?"

"That's not what he's learning!" my mother screamed, and in that moment she looked hideous to me. "Don't you realize what you're teaching him? Don't you *see* what you're doing?"

At this, he took her into his arms and kissed her on the neck. She struggled against him for a little while, infuriated even more by his words. But he kept kissing her neck, and biting it. He snuffed out her anger with his embrace, and between laughs he murmured his pet names for her: *cioccolata, agrodulce*. I raised myself a little, still observing them from the hallway, filled with a distinct feeling of pride.

I stopped the story there, unable to go on, unsure how. For a while no one said anything. Iris took a sip of her Jack. Sybil looked around, as though she'd left something in another room. The music blared on. Finally Claudius grabbed the back of my head and laughed.

"This dude's a psychopathic thinker," he said. "A sensitive soul, a killjoy. He wears his heart *and* his mind on his sleeve."

The girls appeared unconvinced.

"OK, ladies," Claudius said, "your turn now."

"We haven't had nearly enough to drink for all that, boys," Iris said. "Not really feeling your game."

Sybil nodded. "Plus, you know what they say. Women and their secrets."

"And bubbles," Iris added with a wink.

Then they turned away, and just like that sealed us off from them. I marveled for a moment at this female power. From the corner of his eye, Claudius watched Sybil's ass, continuing to make a claim on her, the only one he could still make in this moment of rejection. "*That's* a goddamn bubble," he whispered to me. It was held up for scrutiny by the tightness of her jeans and the heels of her boots. He glanced at me and went on and on about the miracle of tight jeans—he recognized these as Brazilian, he said, nodding slowly as he uttered the word with reverence. Looking again at Sybil, the long and deep curve of her that communicated with something ancient in him, he moved his lips as if trying to remember the old language. But the girls were lost to us. Though Claudius didn't say anything to me about it, I couldn't help weighing our two stories in my mind. I was clearly the one to blame.

Claudius and I spent the next two hours or so chatting, smoking, and drinking out in the backyard, where the torches flattened everyone's faces and made them gleam. Eventually we went in. I munched on cookies and a sopping square of rum cake in the kitchen, intent on some sweetness, despite my own troublesome teeth, as we approached the end of the night. Claudius had gathered himself again and was scrambling around the emptying party, looking to see if there were any other girls worthy of our attention.

I couldn't stop thinking about my own shameful story. Not long after the incident with the magazines, my mother left us, and later she divorced my father. She claimed he loved her with his eyes instead of his heart. She said a woman couldn't spend her whole life with a man like that. But she was wrong about my father's feelings. Sure of this, arrogant in my knowledge, I ranted it to myself. My father worshipped my mother, every fact and feature of her. All he'd ever done was shower her with devotion. After she left, he complained to me one day that she wasn't gone at all, that she was too wicked for such a mercy. She was still there, he said, her flavor stuck in him: a froth in the veins, a disease of the blood. That's how I began to think of her too then, as a sickness, as a betrayal on the cellular level. My choice to stay with him became a badge of loyalty, and I brandished it in her face as often as I could, until she stopped trying to talk sense to me. She did write on my seventeenth birthday though, asking me to come to Newark to see her, to meet her new man and his kids. She also called my dorm room at the end of freshman year, right before final exams, to tell me about her engagement and to let me know how much it would mean to her to have me attend the wedding.

"What makes you think I would *ever* do that?" I asked.

She was quiet for a moment, and even this interval of thought enraged me, primed me to pounce on anything she said. I stared at the naked lamp on my desk and forced my gaze into the bulb's hot center.

"What makes you think you wouldn't?" she said. "At some point, baby, you have to give up the idea fixed in your head and say enough is enough."

I cursed at her and hung up the phone, shaking, purblind with anger, completely closed to her. I was still convinced she was a coward, unable to withstand the force of my father's affections, as if there were such a thing as too much love.

My father. The old version of him would have enjoyed this party. I walked into the living room smiling at this thought. There was a time when he would have hosted such an event, casting invitations far and wide to young, magnificent, colorful people, people he referred to as the essence of the earth. For these parties, he'd let me stay up, all night if I could manage it. So I could imagine him kissing the cheeks of the four girls who were now heading toward the door, whose brown feet were tantalizing in their heels and sandals, wearing jeans smoothed on like blue oil, and summer dresses like saintly robes. My father would hold their hands and beg them not to go yet. He'd tell them about a special bottle, some vintage he'd been saving for the right moment, and offer the promise of a home-cooked breakfast at the first peek of sunrise. He'd say almost anything he could think of to make them stay, to keep the party going as long as possible, to get a smile to flash across one of their faces.

But my father was wasting away in Philly, not here, the man he used to be long gone, and so the four girls were allowed to pass out of the house without ceremony. Many more guys than girls were left now, and most of them had these hangdog looks made more pathetic by the dreary music the deejay played at a lowered volume.

Iris and Sybil were standing by a makeshift bookcase, giving three lames the same treatment they had given me and Claudius. Now, drunk or high, maybe both, they lifted their feet and flailed their arms, swimming in a thick sea of hilarity. Then one of the lames clung to Sybil's arm as he begged her to stay, to give him her phone number, to go home with him. The guy looked older—old, frankly—and he and his buddies had probably crashed the party, though not the way we had. They seemed to come from someplace else entirely, another time, another dimension, and the stink of it emanated from them. That was it: something I couldn't name festered in their horniness, and it made their solicitations coarse, mean, and frightening. I could have interfered, played the gallant hero like my father would have, but Iris was able to drag her friend away and out of the house.

Claudius came into the room holding his fez upside down like a little bucket. He resembled certain homeless folks you'd see begging on the subway, crackling with foul energy, offended and beseeching. His hair was matted and kinked. He stormed ahead and almost walked through me.

"No luck?"

"Fucking sausage fest," he called back.

I followed him outside. He put the fez back on and its tassel flopped in the breeze. I had seen him this way before, agitated. He was terrible at idleness, much worse than I was, and the map of his life had no significance or shape without some destination to plunge his way into. He could quickly lose his way. We stood together, surrounded by the high-pitched barking of a neighbor's dog, the buzz of a faulty streetlight, a faint clinking of metal. I clapped him on the shoulder and said we should head back up to campus. He took out his pager. The greenish glow of its display told us it was just past three o'clock in the morning. Subway service would be awful.

Just then, on the sidewalk, Iris and Sybil teetered by on bicycles, their front wheels doing a spastic dance. They rode a little past us before Sybil swerved and crashed into the side of Iris's bike. She caught herself, but Iris fell. We rushed through the house's gate, and I helped Iris up. There were tears in her eyes, but she was making a noise that eventually revealed itself as a laugh. Sybil was laughing too.

"We're messed up," Iris admitted. Without apology she belched into her fist and then examined her arm. A wide cut ran from her elbow halfway to her wrist. It filled with blood and was rimmed with dirt. She dipped her finger into the thick line of blood. The way she did it made me want to dip my finger too.

As she stared at the reddened tip of her finger, I suggested we walk them home. I jumped back when she tried to mark me with the spot of blood.

"A couple of goddamned gentlemen," she said. "Chivalry is undead."

We walked with their bikes while the girls, holding hands, staggered ahead of us, their very movements synced in drunken exaggeration, suggesting a new rhythm to prolong the night. It was like the records my father would play in the wee hours of his parties, after the delicate guests had already gone home and the skeptics who remained sat and considered the hands of the clock. He had a selection of special vinyl, mostly bop, that made things jump into life again, nothing like the bleak music the deejay played back at the house. My father's music persuaded you that nothing ever had to end. Claudius and I, feeling good again, stared at the girls. Iris's calves and thighs were shapely for such a thin girl. Sybil's ass was like two warm, fat jewels on garish display.

Eyeing it, I said, "That's a goddamn onion."

"Make a grown man cry," Claudius answered to my call. But

then he looked doubtfully at me. "You wouldn't even know what to do with that though. I called dibs, remember?" He jutted his chin at Iris and said, "That's more your speed, B. Two sticks make fire."

With a laugh he picked up his pace so that he was walking next to Sybil, and I was back with Iris. Another gash split the skin near her wrist. Every once in a while, when the wound grew rich with blood, she sucked at it like an injured child.

We walked for a long time, deeper into Brooklyn, and it did feel as though we were actually sinking. Wooden boards slanted across the windows of the apartments above a corner store and lines of stiff weeds punched through cracks in the sidewalk. We passed a place called Salt, a bar that looked like it hadn't been open for business in years. Around the corner was a series of names tagged on a brick wall. Each of the names had three letters—SER, EVE, RON, REL, MED—and the drips of paint made murky icicles of color. The ground became more densely littered with crushed paper bags, empty bottles of malt liquor, and other shapeless hunks of trash. I guided Iris's bike around inexplicable puddles layered with scum. It hadn't rained in weeks, and it wouldn't tonight. Men sat on the edges of ramshackle stoops or stood in front of shuttered bodegas. They leered at us, but their looks were less threatening than mysterious.

Iris talked incessantly, invoking the bubble, picking her words with drunk deliberation. "It's not about being all profound and shit," she said, "it's not even about that. It's like, can you tiptoe over every surface? Can you go anywhere and be open to every little thing?"

Gazing at her, I was careful to appear interested in what she had to say. I wasn't going to screw up our chances a second time. I softened my tone and asked, "What's all this business with the bubble?"

Sybil's laugh drifted ahead of us.

"It's Japanese: *mono no aware*," she said. "A sensitivity to things. An awareness. Everything lacks permanence. A way of understanding beauty. I studied world philosophies, in college, and did a year abroad." To illustrate the idea, she started talking about *sakura*, the cherry blossom tree.

At first all this sounded like more pothead gibberish. Then the notion of *abroad*, and the mysterious worldliness it suggested, began to excite me as much as her hips did. Iris was black, Central

American, maybe Jewish somehow, and who knew what else. She was even more exotic than I had thought.

She talked about a dream she'd had about the cherry blossoms, a vision: the pink buds flowering, paling, and drifting down in bunches, left there like soft skirts on the grass. "I asked my mom about it," she said. "She can read dreams. She cried a tear from her left eye. Then she said life is exactly like that."

Iris was holding something out to me, something real, but I couldn't quite grasp whatever it was. "Here's what I want to know," I said, and then blurted, "Have you ever made love in the grass?"

She frowned and opened her mouth to reply. But before she could speak, a thin, straw-colored dog appeared from between two parked cars. Claudius, startled, let Sybil's bike fall to the ground. When the dog began to growl and bark, we tried to get around it. It didn't move very well, but managed to stay in front of us. It may have been rabid. Some of its pink skin showed through its patches of fur, and in the glow of the streetlight it looked like a mix of hyena and pig. Its rheumy eyes gleamed, the sound of its growling nearly subliminal. I kept my eyes fixed on it. Though the night air had cooled, waves of heat pounded my head. My teeth clenched, and my chest tightened.

The dog edged closer, ready, at any moment, to spring at us as we backed away. Claudius cradled the fez against his chest and cursed under his breath. He slipped behind the rest of us and used us as his shield. I lifted Iris's bike, ready to throw it, but then Sybil rushed at the dog and kicked its snout. The dog listed for a moment, whined in a way that almost seemed grateful, and then fell over. Iris joined her and they gave several more solid kicks, aimed at the dog's head and shriveled belly. The animal didn't move and it wasn't breathing. All of its wildness had been extinguished. I turned my back even though the violence was done, but odd little murmurs from the girls, disturbing sounds, still reached my ears. Someone's arms wrapped around me—my own arms, I realized. Not far from where I stood, Claudius's mouth gaped wider and wider.

The girls got quiet. Sybil walked her bike to us. She was breathing heavily through her nostrils, skin shining from her brief exertions. She went right up to Claudius, grabbed the back of his head, and pulled him down to her for a rough, hungry kiss. His fez crumpled in their embrace.

Unsteadily, I made my way to Iris. As she stood over the unmoving dog, her shoulders rose and fell. She turned to me and ran the palm of her hand down my forehead, smoothing it. "Stop being so . . . *astonished* all the time," she said. "It makes you seem old."

Just then, a man began to shout from behind the bars of a window across the street. "Goddamn!" he said. "Y'all bitches fucked that motherfucker *up!*"

We laughed, first the girls and then me along with them. Claudius, holding his ruined hat, didn't join in. I laughed with the girls and all of a sudden it seemed OK—what the two of them had done and how they had done it, that they had been the ones who were brave. It wasn't just OK; it was exciting, and more.

As we walked on, Iris stared ahead, in a dream state, and asked, "What was the dog offering us? What did its choice of death release into the world?"

I didn't, *couldn't,* reply. It wasn't clear at all whether her question was even meant for me.

We approached a station for a subway line I'd never even taken before, and Claudius looked back at me. A question formed on his tired, wary face, and I knew what he meant. I shook my head, and he knew what I meant. When I nodded, that was understood too: wherever this night led, we were following it all the way.

The girls' building was set back from the street and constructed in two moods, with clean brick on the first floor and gray vinyl siding on the second. A single window peeked out from the siding like a jaundiced eye. The girls skipped through the gate, up to the door, and stood in the threshold, waiting for us.

"Where *are* we?" Claudius muttered.

"Doesn't matter."

"We got them home safe. Like they even fucking needed it."

"And now they want to thank us," I said. "A couple of god-damned gentlemen."

"Man, I don't even know where the hell we are."

I placed a hand on his shoulder. "Who cares? The whole world is ours tonight, baby."

Iris asked if we were coming up or what, said to hurry up, she had to pee. I gave Claudius our habitual goofy grin. He stared at me. Finally, in a low voice, he said OK, but he didn't grin back. We carried their bikes inside.

Other than two Elizabeth Catlett prints on the walls, the living room was barely decorated, as if the girls didn't actually live here. Did anyone live here? The suggestion was thrilling, that the place was available to anyone in the know who wanted, or who was fated for, a crazy night.

The girls dropped some tablets into our palms—"love drugs," they said—and I swallowed mine down with a swig of overproof rum. Claudius followed my lead. The girls told us to sit tight and went to take a bath, together. We sank into the softness of their couch and let their voices caress us through the slightly opened door. The girls talked solemnly in the tub, like two sages.

"Does it hurt?" Sybil was saying.

"It does," Iris said.

I joked, knowing it was lame, that the girls must be taking a bubble bath. Claudius didn't say a word. Sweat ran from under his warped hat into his eyes. As the girls' voices floated on and time got fat and lazy, my heart pummeled my rib cage. Drunk and high and nervous, I was ready nevertheless.

They emerged at what felt like the edge of forever, at first wearing only the thinning steam from the bathroom, then essentially nothing, just some stray suds. Iris had strips of bandage on her arm. They stood in front of us and began to pose, slowly turning their bodies so we could admire them from every angle. Their wet feet stained the hardwood floor. I'd never seen such blatant female nudity in person before. Whenever I reached for them, eager to move things along, the girls took a step back. They wouldn't let me touch them. "Just watch," Iris said, and I did, we did, until Sybil went into one of the bedrooms and gestured for Claudius to follow.

In the other room Iris, still out of reach, told me to sit on the bed. As she approached, the door opened and Sybil burst into the room. Claudius, fully clothed, shuffled along behind her. "I got lonely," Sybil said. "I missed you." Iris said she missed her too. The girls kissed each other in skittish candlelight. I may have imagined it, but from time to time, Sybil's darker breasts touched Iris's. They kept smiling at each other until Sybil asked if we wanted in on the action. I said yes and they laughed at how quickly I said it. Sybil told us to take off our clothes. Quickly again, I began to undress but Claudius just stood there, gazing around the room. It seemed like he was trying to remember everything there—the large bed, the flickering light, the heavy curtains—as the setting he might use for an entirely different story. He was remembering everything, it appeared, except the people in it, ignoring us and therefore omitting us. Maybe he was even omitting himself.

While Sybil urged us on, saying she wanted to see what we were working with, Claudius forced his attention through the opening in the curtains, into the darkness outside, in denial of her voice. But then I called his name, scolding in my tone, and pulled his attention back into the room. What was it? The amount of booze we'd had, the drugs, the crazy talk, the vision of that animal dead in the streets, or just the girls themselves? All of it, in combination, made glorious sense to me. We had reached the proper destination of this night. Obviously Claudius and I had never been undressed in each other's presence—but so what? The girls we'd wanted from the start were offering their fragrant brown flesh to us, and all we had to do was get naked too, together. Why should shyness, if that's what it was, or fear, or a bit of further strangeness, a little kink in the first blush of day, stop us now? Why shouldn't this, all of us collected in one room, be our path? I stared at Claudius until he understood I wanted him to do it. He could have said no, to the girls, to me, to that part of himself that also wanted to keep going, and for a second, when he opened his mouth, I expected him to say just that, to shout his refusal. All he did was stand there and tamely nod in assent.

He took off his clothes, as I did, watching the girls as they watched us. When Claudius and I were naked, they didn't do anything. They weren't satisfied yet.

"Well," Sybil said, "look at him."

I wondered for a second who she meant, but it was a command meant for both of us.

"You have to be fully present," Iris said, her first words in a long time.

"Look at him."

"He's your friend."

"Don't pretend he's not there."

"There's always more to what you want than what you wanted." It was Iris again. "You have to take that too."

I turned to Claudius, standing there with his hands clasped in front of his genitals. Sybil went to him and moved his hands aside. His calves were thin in comparison to his muscular thighs. He had a well-developed chest but a bulging stomach, which was bisected by a vertical stripe of fuzzy hair. His penis was half-erect. Sybil placed the crushed fez back on his head to complete the description of his nudity.

The girls told us to keep looking at one another, through the embarrassment and curiosity, all the way through the entire exposure. They wouldn't let us pretend otherwise: four naked bodies on the verge of sex together in one room had to be exactly that. We did manage to arrive at sex, Iris with me and Sybil with Claudius, in that room as light began to slip through the gaps in the curtains. I didn't get to enjoy Iris's body, not really, because I was too concerned with keeping matters organized, under some semblance of control, fending off the orgiastic. I was much too aware of the other bodies in the room, much too aware of my own. I did, however, get to use my father's condom. I'd intended to use it, had become fanatical about using it and finally did, just as Claudius—perhaps another true son of another confused father—got to use the condom he carried around in *his* pocket. We had found our so-called wild and crazy women, and they slept with us. But first they made us look, for a very long time.

In a way, I'm glad I lived such a night before my father died, or completed his long process of dying. On the day of his funeral, watching his rigid, almost smiling face, I was flanked by my mother and her new family. I had kept my distance over the past decade or so, estranging myself, and therefore hadn't seen her in what felt like ages. At one point, she squeezed my arm and nodded. She didn't force me to speak to her, and everything she had to say was expressed in those gestures. In her black blazer and dress, with her gray-streaked hair pinned under a slanted hat, she remained a striking woman. What struck me even more than the elegance and dignity with which she was growing older was the presence of her husband and his, *their,* adult children. They didn't have to be there. Later, unable to settle my stomach or my mind, I stood alone, just as I had arrived, and my mother and her family talked together on the other side of the room. Other than me, I realized, they were the only black people in attendance. Together the four of them formed a portrait of calmness and grace that made me feel even more sick. I thought about the last public event my father and I attended together, a celebration of his long and successful career. There was desperation in the way he walked around with me, leading me by the arm from guest to guest. To anyone I didn't already know, he said, "This is my boy. This is my boy." He showed me off like a prize, as if to eliminate any doubt that I belonged to him. He'd done this kind of thing ever since I was a child. The day of his celebration was the very first time it didn't make me proud.

What did he mean back on that August morning before I returned to college? Did he believe what he was telling me about happiness? Could he have meant it? Or was he just heartbroken, bitter, drunk? Maybe he knew he was talking to a young fool. Or maybe watching what I did with my life would be his way of figuring everything out. I don't know, but I keep imagining what it would be like, to be a father to a boy who loves me and believes in me and, despite all our differences, wants nothing more than to be a man in my image. I see that spectral boy, my son, vividly, and feel frightened when he is with me. I have no idea what to say.

Sometimes I feel all I'd have to offer, other than questions, are my memories of that time in Brooklyn and that terrible apartment I had driven us to, obsessed. It sounds ridiculous, even to me, yet it's true. Among the strangest touches I felt there was my friend's hand gripping my shoulder, long after Iris and Sybil had left us alone in the room. I gasped when Claudius first touched me. I didn't look back at him and I didn't move his hand. I just lay there on my side with my eyes closed and tried not to be awake anymore. When I finally rose it was past noon. My head throbbed, and the faraway sound of the girls' voices rang in my ears. Claudius was sitting up in the bed, staring at me. At once an acute ugliness shuddered into being, a face revealed within his face, and he must have seen it within mine too. It has been that way with people in my life, with people I have loved: a fine dispersal, a rupture as quiet as two lips parting, a change so sudden one morning, so slight, you wonder if they had ever been beautiful at all.

# *The Third Tower*

FROM *Ploughshares*

## *Therese*

Julia found it in a pile of old stuff. She didn't want it, so she said she would give it to Therese.

What was she supposed to do with that? Therese said—a beaten up old book with nothing in it but blank paper.

Well, you like to do handwriting, Julia said.

Therese looked at the thing her friend was holding. Then she reached for it.

Julia laughed and her black curls bounced.

That night, Therese puts it away, under her socks—her dear, neatly folded socks. And the next night when she remembers and takes it out, it seems she has come to love it in her sleep, and through the long day at work. Maybe she'll even take it with her on her trip.

It looks like an ancient thing, with its soft, red cover. It looks like it has some tales to tell, hidden in those blank pages. She runs her fingers over the thick, rough paper, as if to awaken it . . .

## *Train*

*Back in the day, railroad tracks crisscrossed the entire country and trains sped morning and night to every corner of the great expanse.*

That's what Therese has heard. She thinks she's heard that. Or maybe it's a scrap from a dream—or maybe it's just an error of her brain; maybe there were no trains at all.

Who knows. But what's sure is there's one train now—and it goes through the town where she lives, all the way to the City, where the hospital complex is—lucky!

Felix has hired a temp to cover for her. He's promised to keep her on when she gets back, one way or another. She's a good little worker, he says. But for now, the spells have gotten so bad they're slowing her down.

When he arranged for her to go for the cure, he looked sad, she told Julia.

Hm, Julia had said noncommittally.

And it's true that Felix always has the same expression—pretty much all the old people do—of vague helplessness, as though they've just entered a day full of the troubles they've spent the night dreaming about.

But in any case, Therese is going to see the City!

Of course, they've all seen it a million times in movies and magazines—the brilliant air, the glistening towers and monuments, sailboats gliding from the serene harbor out toward the endless horizon—the gorgeous, gorgeously dressed men and women, the broad white boulevards, banks of flowers, grand restaurants, magnificent shop windows—great, heavy strands of gems twinkling away on velvet . . .

None of the girls from housing has ever gotten to go there until now, and the others are all jealous.

Really? Therese asks; do they want to go pitching over at random moments like she does? She'd trade any day. (Though, maybe she wouldn't, actually.)

But she'll be their eyes and ears, she promises.

The seats are so comfortable, even here in community class. There's a slight, thrilling jolt, and her heart lifts up as the wheels begin to purr against the tracks.

This morning, Julia knocked on the door of her room and gave her a cardboard box containing a sandwich and an apple so she won't go hungry on the trip.

Actually, she's already hungry, even though she's just settled onto the train. But she won't open the box yet.

Box! The word is starting to glow and shimmer—

Therese reaches into her satchel for her book and the pen she stole from laundry when Kyra wasn't looking—but she's too late to do whatever it was she meant to; the word has already exploded and now what's left of it is just a hard, dry little wad: box. OK, box. But she's sort of exhausted, as if she has awakened too abruptly from a profound sleep.

Now there's just darkness—a tunnel, it must be.

Now it's bright and her town is gone!

She plays a brand-new game on the seat screen, featuring zooming blobs that look like candy. Glossy! You shoot the blobs, and if you hit one just right, it emits a shower of gold coins, and then new blobs zoom in to try to eat the coins before you shoot them too.

The rays of the sun slant at the sooty windows, moving this way and that as the train crosses over a shining river of thick, rainbow-colored mud.

But where on earth *are* they? Therese has never seen places like *this* in movies or magazine pictures—these towns! Where no person is to be seen, where the windows are broken or covered over with boards and plastic, everywhere heaps of rusted, rotted trash with here and there a chair leg or part of an antiquated vehicle or a torn, filthy doll, sticking up from it . . .

The desolation spreads out and out, as if someone had tipped over a colossal container of wreckage by mistake.

A tiny train moves through the wreckage, carrying a minuscule speck called Therese. The train clacks slowly over another bridge —a rickety little thing spanning a cleft in the earth—and stirs up a swarm of children, who run along below, trying to keep up. Their faces are streaked with paint, or dirt. They scamper and tumble like wicked little demons, but the rocks and bottles they throw just bounce off the train's metal shell, and zoom—now they're just tiny, squiggling specks themselves.

It's cold, Therese realizes. And her speck self is speeding farther and farther from her friends . . . She holds the box Julia gave her tightly and looks around at the other passengers, but they're inseparably focused on their screens or devices and their faces are closed . . .

The sights stream by out the window, wavering, not quite solid, like pictures unfurling on a bolt of printed silk. Now there are woods. And raked-over fires, it looks like. More trash . . . an old boot? A ragged shirt . . .

A few weeks ago at supper, one of the girls said she'd heard that a bunch of criminals had escaped from the prison complexes. Could Therese be traveling through that part of the country?

*Fugitives*—the word erupts from its casing, flaring up like a rocket, fanning out, fracturing the air into prisms and splintered mirror. Therese snatches up her book and pen, and rapidly writes something down.

She's sweating. She closes her eyes and takes a few deep breaths before she looks at what the book says: *Uniforms—teams, prisoners and guards, shouting, clanging—blood and weapons. Two civil guards stumbling through trees, they trip on twisted roots, they carry a heavy pole, one of the guards at each end, a man hangs from it, roped to it by bleeding wrists and ankles* . . .

She stares at the words in the book. Horrible!

A good thing she's heading toward the hospital—maybe the excitement of travel is bad for her.

She glances out the window and takes a few more deep breaths.

No, she's OK—the glass-dust is settling, and the air is coming back together . . .

Good, and the woods are behind them now.

Oh, funny!—the pen has a tag on it that says RETURN TO LAUNDRY.

She watches a whole series of cartoons about a cheerful creature they call a platypus. And anyhow, her town is normal—a normal, busy town. The malls are filled with people shopping.

Besides, those men in the woods—that was just a picture.

The sandwich and apple are eaten, and they have arrived. Therese brushes some crumbs off the empty box, folds it flat, and tucks it into her satchel along with her good dress—she's brought her good dress!—and her book, of course.

## Doctor

Patient T716-05: Female, 17 yrs., 8 mos. Worker, intelligence average, height/weight/appearance ditto. Word-stabilization reflex far *below average.* Mental "crowding" or "smearing," excess liquidity of intellection. Fainting occasional but rare. Complaint suggests aberrant cortical activity, diagnosis as yet uncertain. It is to be hoped that a course of repetition modification in conjunction with indicated elaboration-suppressants ("fuzz-offs," as the kids call them) can be devised to alleviate symptoms.

## Assessment

Tree, the doctor says.

Tests make her so nervous! *Tree*—how is she supposed to keep that under control? It's already threatening to break apart! She looks at the doctor, but he's studying the ridiculous-looking contraption she's hooked up to.

Tree please, he says.

Leaf, she guesses.

The doctor, watching some dials, frowns.

She tries again: shade.

Just whatever comes to mind, the doctor says.

Trunk? Therese says.

Trunk? The doctor says. He sighs and takes off his goggles. It's important for you to say exactly what's in your mind, Therese, not what you think I want you to say. If I could wave a magic wand and make your symptoms disappear, I would not hesitate. Unfortunately, the process is more complicated than that, and we need your full commitment. There is no "right answer." What I want to hear is your spontaneous response, the one that comes immediately to mind when I say the cue word. Deception has no place here with us, nor does shame—the machine registers your sincerity. Any truthful response whatsoever is acceptable.

His smile illustrates patience and forbearance. Or probably that's a smile. His face is basically a broad stack of thick, rather squashy-looking layers, so it's hard to tell exactly.

So, he says. Do we understand one another?

Therese nods solemnly.

All right, then, he resumes: tree.

*Any truthful response whatsoever* . . . She's pretty dizzy, actually, and now the word is really taking over, glowing, and shimmering wildly, as the air breaks up and a breeze sends light and shadows tumbling through the garden. Inside the old-fashioned house there, a child deliberates over the instrument's keys, searching for the notes signified by graceful markings on the page. Released by the child's touch, the notes detach, wavering off the page and out the open French doors, one or two or three at a time, landing awkwardly on the leaves of the magnificent oak, where they teeter for a moment before evaporating into the diaphanous air. A delicate strain of music floats in their wake, like a fragrance.

Piano! Therese says loudly.

Excuse me? The doctor says. He peers at the dials, then thumps the machine, and frowns at the dials again. Excuse me—he turns to her—you said . . . ?

The music is evaporating now too, leaving only a phantom imprint on her senses, like the warm imprint left on a sheet by a sleeper recently arisen.

Piano—was that your response, Therese? The doctor's voice paints rough black streaks over what's left of the melody. Do you play the piano, Therese?

Does she play the piano? Huh? How could she *play* the *piano*? She's never even *seen* a piano, not a real one, anyhow! Oh—goodbye garden, goodbye marvelous tree, goodbye child, whoever you are . . . Up the sleeper goes, rising into the day, this particular day, which assembles around Therese into the gray, somewhat dingy consulting room, where the doctor, sitting across from her, waits for an answer.

## Room

She has been assigned a room (614). It has a window, and a cot made up with sheets and a blanket, and a little table with a drawer in it where she puts her things.

Nothing extra. They explain: it's important for her to have as little *sensory stimulation* as possible.

In other words, she understands, nothing to set her off. There's no mirror, there are no curtains on the window, just metal shutters that are kept closed to shield her from the glittering sound of the city, from the sunlight, from the mysterious moon.

*

Her teachers said she'd grow out of it, but it's only gotten worse since school—words heating up, expanding, exploding into pictures of things, shooting off in all directions, then flaming out, leaving behind cinders and husks, a litter of tiny, empty, winged corpses, like scorched gnats or angels.

It's too bad about the shutters though. Especially because the train arrived here through a tunnel, just the way it had departed from her town—as though the journey between tunnels was nothing more than a soap bubble—and then, in the station, she had stood on a moving strip of something or other that took her straight into the walled hospital complex. So she still hasn't had a look at the City.

For that matter, since the train arrived, she's hardly seen the sky.


## Forms

They sit her at a screen and she fills out scrolls and scrolls of forms. Hundreds of questions.

Her eyes and ears work fine. She's never broken a bone. Once at an Independence Day party in housing, there were some strawberries, and a few of the girls, including her, broke out in a rash that bled. But strawberries are her only allergy, as far as she knows.

She doesn't take any medications. No alcohol, no tobacco, no recreational drugs. Yes, she gets her periods. They're normal (she supposes). They started about four years ago. No, she has never had a child. (Obviously. In housing? What, are they kidding, these people here? How do they think that sort of thing happens!)

Any family history of heart problems, as far as she knows? Cancer? Diabetes? Crohn's disease? Bright's disease? Kefauver's disease? Degenerative diseases of the spine or the nervous system? Malformations of the limbs or of other parts? Disorders of the lungs, liver, gallbladder?

On a scale of one to one hundred how well does she cope with stress? On a scale of one to one hundred how anxious does she feel? Is she willing to let the clinic divulge information about her to the registry? (Treatment is contingent on acceptance.) Who should they call in case of emergency? (Yes, who? Felix? Julia?

Housing?) Does she give the clinic permission to perform X sort of test, Y sort of test, Z sort of test?

Of course she does—why is she there, if not for X, Y, and Z sorts of tests?

Then initial here, please—initial here, initial here.

She waits in a room, and after a while she's led into another room to see the doctor again.

He sits at his large desk and calls up on his screen the questionnaire she spent the morning filling out. He explains that although of course he is already familiar with her answers, he wants to scroll quickly through, reviewing.

Ah, he says, yes—what does she mean, precisely, by this sensation of confusion she refers to? Would she please describe it as exactly as she can?

He swivels the screen so she can see it.

*Confusion*—right, that's what she herself typed in, but now the word looks stark. Like a . . . warrant. A *warrant*?

Just give it a try, he says.

She's very thirsty, but she is taking up so much of the busy doctor's time! If she were at work, she would ask Felix to let her pause for a drink of water, and of course he would.

You see pictures, I believe, the doctor prompts. I believe you noted that on the forms?

*Sort* of see, actually.

What are these pictures of?

Just normal things, she says.

But then—for an instant she sees the two sweating, stumbling guards and the man swinging from the pole between them, trailing blood. Or of things that could be, she clarifies, things that could be happening. Or that could happen sometime, did happen maybe. Or maybe not. Something in the woods. Or a garden . . . just anything, anywhere . . .

The doctor waits, but that's the best she can do.

*And words sometimes seem* . . . he reads from the form—*sometimes seem like*—what does it say here? Twins? He looks at her, eyebrows raised.

She feels herself blushing. Maybe not *twins,* exactly, she says. It's like a word has the same word inside it, but the one inside's a lot bigger, and with better colors and more parts. And the inside word is sort of vibrating, jostling around, trying to get out of its wrapper? So there's sort of a halo. Or a floppy margin.

The doctor clears his throat.

All right, he says after a moment. And when do these episodes occur? What precipitates them?

Back home they thought it was something in the air. Particulate matter, she says, pleased with the nice sound. But the mask didn't seem to help, even when they changed me from the plant to the warehouse.

Not what *causes* them, he says—that's what we're here to find out. I meant, how do these episodes begin?

Well, they don't actually . . . *begin*, exactly. It's more as if they're just sort of happening . . .

Porous outline? He asks.

Porous outline? She says.

She glances back at the forms on the screen for some help, but it's just the forms, the way she filled them out, with the answers she checked and a few little notes where she keyed in extra information they asked for. "Dizzy," it says. "Confusion."

And there are her initials too, her initials on all the forms. It's as if she's in a mirror, staring back at herself—the initials seem more real than she does.

Well, sure. She brought those initials here, but now those initials have got her hooked up to a machine!

The doctor looks down at his folded hands, waiting.


## Tests

The hours at the clinic pass slowly, they do. The smells of antiseptics and filth. They have Therese ingest a dye, so they can observe its route as it slithers through the nooks and crannies of her brain. Needles draw fluids from her into tubes, nurses seal the tubes and put the sealed tubes into a special cupboard with flashing red lights. Other needles inject fluids into her. She waits in a waiting room. She waits in another waiting room.

Has she ever had hallucinations?

No, never.

But she sees pictures, she told the doctor, didn't she?

It's just sort of . . . pictures—not hallucinations! she's already said. Over and over.

They roll her into a metal cylinder that explores things beneath her skin. In other rooms, technicians monitor screens. A message is transmitted to her every five minutes: you're doing fine, the electronic voice says.

## Consultation

The doctor paces as he explains. His hands are behind his back: We have not yet fully ascertained the etiology of your affliction, nor have we been entirely successful thus far in isolating the full play of its tendencies. The likelihood of a culpable pathogen has almost certainly been eliminated. There is, however, a consistent constellation of characteristics—a profile, if you will—to which the manifestations of this hyperassociative state can be said to conform, though I'm happy to say that our readings indicate a low correlation with the worrisome Malfeasance Index that is frequently one of its most striking features.

Naturally, the overwhelming bulk of the literature on the subject treats the syndrome—this susceptibility to irrelevant, excess, or ambiguous substance—as an imbalance of some sort, a deficiency. It has been thought, variously, to be hormonal in origin, to disclose a congenital flaw in circuitry, to reflect a failure of character, to suggest a proto-psychotic vulnerability, to indicate a degradation of autoimmune-system defenses, to express the curse of Satan or conversely to express the gift of holiness, to result from a regional diet stripped of certain nutrients or from any of a number of viruses contracted in childhood.

We at the clinic regard it strictly as a physiological phenomenon, a sort of synaptic leakage, so to speak, and thus pristine, free of the moral stigma it otherwise often carries.

Our primary objective here, in addition to research, of course, is to help to relieve the patient. This entails, as you and I have discussed, a strong motivation on the patient's part to pursue the goal of restored health, which in turn rests on the degree of the subject's willingness to participate in his or her own cure.

The doctor returns to his desk as he talks and shuffles through some papers.

How long do you think I'll need to stay? She asks after a few moments.

He looks up, apparently surprised to see her sitting there.

Well, as I say, young lady, that depends largely on you.


## Rest

It's a bit chilly, and the blanket isn't really warm enough. She wraps herself up in it. She's tired from her day of tests, and they've told her to sleep, because there will be more tomorrow, bright and early. But instead, she takes her book from the drawer, where it's been sitting, next to the box that once held the sandwich and apple, under her soft, folded satchel and her good dress.

She probably isn't supposed to have it? But they haven't said that, exactly—there's no rule. And she didn't ask. Though they did say that, for her own sake, she should try to refrain from brooding on things. Not only is it tiring, it could adversely skew the test results as well.

She opens the book, just to admire again the lovely, thick, rough-edged paper, but then the air starts to shimmer, and it splinters, splashing words and pictures everywhere, all whirling and glittering.

She grabs up her pen: *wooden table dim cozy place. Funny song about mouse, hands clapping in time. Leaves dripping, fresh!—horse and buggy?? Bugy?? Blossoms, hooves. Glass mountain, meadow mountain tiny white flowers tiny yellow star-flowers tiny pearl moon. Clothes whisper night fields moon whispers—sailing moon, sorcerer moon, watchman moon. Marching band—shiny octopus-instruments—light or swords? Long robes little outdoor tables little glass cups, stars, moon . . .*

The pictures flow by, sparkling, dissolving, blending in their disorder, like the landscape outside the window of the train, fading finally.

She blinks, and looks around at the stillness of the room, the mute shutters.

Right. Back in the drawer goes the book. Maybe these pictures are memories that somehow became detached from other people and stray through the universe, slipping through rips in the fabric and clinging to whatever living beings they can, faulty beings like her . . .

She draws the blanket more tightly around herself and snuggles into the thin pillow.

Noisy outside tonight though. All that loud banging!

## Clinic Life

They fit a metal helmet onto her, and the procedure room darkens for a moment. Or that's what Therese thinks when she wakes up with a dull ache in her head. In fact, they tell her, it's hours later.

They work with her, one on one. A kind tech has been trying hard to help her with word-stabilization. Did you ever collect butterflies when you were a child, Therese? The tech asks.

Butterflies? Therese says.

With pins? the tech says. And chloroform?

After certain tests or procedures, she's wheeled out into a darkened room. Sometimes there are a few other patients lying on gurneys, swaddled in white like her, and she comes back to herself in a sort of forest of soft groans and murmurs, faint, senseless fragments of speech.

The other day, she turned out to be one of the people she was hearing. Funny! Except she was saying she wanted to go home. She hopes that didn't hurt anyone's feelings!

They pretty much keep the patients apart, but she begins to recognize a few of the others, just flickering past in the corner of her eye—in the corridors or a waiting room, or even sitting in the canteen. Sometimes in the woozy twilight of one of the recovery rooms.

There's a skinny, stringy girl about her age, with chopped-off dirty-blond hair, who sends off a blizzard of quiet curses as she wakes, and a very large, very old woman, maybe fifty or so, who twists and flops on the gurney under her little sheet. Once, she gets up and totters around like a big crazy giant, shrieking until she's subdued.

Therese comes face-to-face with her in a waiting room. They're both wearing the white paper robes that make them look, frankly, like lab rats. The woman stares at her with vacant, blazing eyes. *You!* she says, and *you* sears a path through the air, trailing ash, before a nurse appears to lead the woman away.

## Treatment

The drugs have started—she's doing better on the tests!

Tree, the doctor says.

She shuts her eyes and breathes deeply.

Take your time, the doctor says soothingly. Tree . . .

She gathers all her powers of concentration. Tree . . . , she says, hesitantly.

Good! the doctor says, looking up from the dials, excellent. He pats her shoulder. Tired? You've been working hard.

His approval emboldens Therese to speak. She *has* been working hard, she concedes. And all that loud banging at night keeps her up sometimes.

Ah, yes, the fireworks, the doctor says. He smiles—she's sure of it—and she's ashamed to have complained.

National holiday season, he adds, and pats her shoulder again.

## The Doctor Reflects

A taxing week, but one with its rewards. Patient T716-05 is showing great improvement. She's a touching little thing—limited comprehension, but eager to cooperate.

It's gratifying to think of the strides she's made with the help of treatment—he's looking forward to writing this up! It was only about a month ago, after all, that her responses in the Verbal Identification tests indicated apparently almost hopeless ideation-capacity. He shakes his head, recalling: "Piano" for "Tree"!

Any answer is valid, of course. In fact, there is a certain proportion of the population with very slight surplus-associative disorders who will respond quite spontaneously to "tree" with "leaf" or "branch." Even "bark"—*even* "trunk"—yes, even trunk. But such responses are considered to be within the periphery; such individuals are generally classified as "normal."

"Piano," however—clearly extrapolated from wood (itself an outer-sphere coordinate: tree>wood>piano)—is far beyond the scope of what can be regarded as healthy.

Failure to recognize the confines of words (*words, the building blocks of achievement,* to quote from his recent article on the subject in *Neural Function Today*) indicates an underlying degradation of those node clusters that enable the brain to comprehend the world in which its proprietor organism finds itself, and puts that organism at risk of potentially dangerous misinterpretation of data.

What if—for example—an organism were to identify a large obstacle in front of it as (for example) the "foot" of an immense tree rather than, correctly, as the *foot* of a giant prehistoric animal? Consider the possible consequences!

There is, however, a strain of current thinking in the field that categorizes those rare individuals subject to pronounced hyperassociative disorders as in some way viable: Visionaries of the Banal, as one pretentious colleague's paper on the subject styled it. (The fellow won some sort of prize for that bit of foolishness, the doctor recalls.)

In any event, it has been demonstrated that productive work can often be found for such individuals—for instance, in the field of branding.

The doctor, alone in his office, chuckles (somewhat self-consciously) at the thought of a former patient, whose bizarre (though, fortunately, curable) conviction that thousands of people were being shot as they returned to their homes at night and stood fiddling with their keys at their doors, turned out to be linked to his extraordinary (and ultimately very well-remunerated) ability to think up names for paint colors.

(Giant prehistoric animal possibly poor example, unconvincing, revise? Ha ha, maybe he should take a couple of those fuzz-offs himself!)


*Sunday*


Therese wakes just before dawn, gasping for breath in the gray glass-dust mist between sleeping and waking, surrounded by a static of phantoms. Can she manage to put some of them into her book? She starts to open the drawer where it is, but the whispering and flimmering is already winking out around her.

Just as well—she has been making high scores on the tests; she daren't risk a relapse. She closes the drawer firmly and walks back and forth in her room to shake off the phantom remnants.

The noise of the night's fireworks is still in her ears. The moon is there or not there, behind the metal shutters.

They've *strongly suggested* that she rest today. And that's just what she plans to do. She's calm enough now to fall back asleep, she thinks, and when she wakes up in the true day, she'll be careful to take it easy. Maybe just lie around and play some games.

She still hasn't seen any of the City though—*what* will she tell her friends at home?

Oh, but she knows how it looks out there, they all know how it looks, beyond the hospital complex, out on the broad avenues . . .

The pealing of the bells comes faintly through the metal shutters, and when she closes her eyes, she sees the sun shining, shining, a gold veil in the air, and gold reflecting over the entire glorious city from the Tower at its summit.

Streams of people, their arms laden with aromatic leaves and sprays of flowers, are coming from all the great houses; processions pour through the boulevards to worship. The women are so beautiful—their wrists flash with jewels, and their legs gleam. Their long, pale hair flows down their backs.

At home, her friends bow their heads and kneel. Julia has put a pretty Sunday ribbon in her black curls. Therese thinks: we are grateful.

Later today, the others will take their weekly salaries to the Mall, as they do every Sunday. Earrings, nail polish, maybe a new game, a T-shirt, some candy . . . what would she get if she could be with them?

Tomorrow, a new week will begin, with more tests. And they say they'll be able to measure exactly how well the drugs are working.

Therese opens the drawer in her table and surveys the tidy stack of her possessions. She tucks her book away on the bottom.

A little dry crumb clings to the cardboard box. Do her friends at home still remember her?

She unfolds her good dress, smoothing the soft fabric and admiring the sweet flowers printed on it. She puts it on and lies down again, falling toward sleep.

Yes, she can hear the doctor's voice. Tree, he says.

Tree, she says, and a peaceful sensation radiates through her, as the word locks down.

But then for a moment she feels her unruly heart, her skin, her neurons—the secret language of her body—sending evidence of treachery to the sensors and dials. All around her, behind the wall of locked words, hums the vast, intractable, concealed conversation.

Coin, the doctor says.

She closes her ears and strains to shut out the noise.

Coin, she says. Tears of effort cloud her eyes.

Good, says the doctor—mirror. His voice is growing softer and more insistent.

Mirror, she says—and her voice, too, is low and urgent.

Tower, the doctor says.

She takes a deep breath. Tower, she says.

Fireworks, the doctor says.

In her sleep, she struggles to scream, but she cannot make a sound.

Let's try that one again, please, the doctor says: fireworks.

Fireworks, she says . . .

Moon, the doctor says . . .

JULIA ELLIOTT

# *Hellion*

FROM *The Georgia Review*

"Y'ALL PUT THAT GATOR right back where you found him or I'll pepper your asses with 177s."

I aimed my Daisy right at Butch, the more chickenshit of the pair.

Mitch held Dragon by the jaws while Butch tried to steady his lashing tail.

"Feeding him Atomic Fireballs again, I see, which might could kill him. Why you want to mess with an innocent beast?"

"Come on, Butter, we just wanna see him fart fire," said Mitch.

"Y'all idiots and cruel. Now go on and lower him into his tub."

They couldn't grab their rifles with Dragon all thrashing and ready to bite, so they eased him down into his number-two tub, which was getting right snug now that he'd grown.

"Put that chicken wire over the top and get them latch-action toggles clamped."

Mitch kept Dragon's jaws shut while his little brother Butch crouched with the cover, slammed it down fast as soon as Mitch let go. Then Dragon went ape-shit, snapping at the wire, so mad I knew I wouldn't be able to hold him for a week.

"Was a dumb thing to do but we did it," said Butch, lighting a cig butt to play it cool. He leaned on his Beeman like John Wayne.

I lowered my gun.

"You do it again and I'll sick the Swamp Ape on you. I'll get Miss Ruby to put a hex on your entrails. You'll wake up at midnight with wasps in your belly, stinging you from the inside."

"What's entrails?" asked Mitch.

"Guts, idget. Now promise you won't mess with Dragon again."

"Promise," they said.

"Let's spit on it."

We spit into our palms and did some funky hand jives.

"You heard about the citified pansy at Miss Edna's house?" asked Butch.

"Who?"

"Your third cousin from Aiken, Butter, according to our mama. They got a mall there and a nuke reactor."

"Something tells me he's gonna be achin' real soon." Mitch laughed so hard he upped a lump of snot. He spit the loogie in the dirt and slid astride their Yamaha Midget X-7. Butch hopped on back, holding the sport fender as they sped off.

Miss Edna, postmistress of Davis Station and widowed a decade, didn't take crap. She allowed me use of her library, told me I could be a career girl if I'd apply myself. Tried to get me in a dress now and then and said my towhead was too pretty for a pixie cut, especially since I was almost thirteen.

Hands and face fresh-washed, I stood on her spotless porch, waiting for her to answer my knock. Saw a skink skitter over the steps and longed for my Daisy—an easy dollar down the drain. Suffering some phobia that went back to her childhood before the Civil War, Miss Edna paid me one buck for every lizard I shot. I'd present them in a shoebox, do a body count while she cringed, then bury them out back her shed.

"Well hello there, Butter." Miss Edna stood behind her screen door, aproned, the boy lurking in her shadow, a pale freckled scrap of male humanity who looked like he'd strain to lift an ice-cream spoon. "Come on in and meet Alex. He's just a few months older than you."

I'd never heard of a boy named Alex who wasn't on TV. He nodded, led me back to the den where he had his Atari hooked up to Miss Edna's console Panasonic. Sat right down to play Q*bert. Kept his eyes on that creepy head with feet, jumping it around on a pyramid of cubes, avoiding bouncing snakes and balls—an exercise in mindless stupidity.

"Come all this way to play Q*bert?" I asked him.

"Nothing much to do," he said.

"You stuck your head out the door since you came?"

"Why bother?"

"Why don't you let me show you a thing or two?"

When Alex pulled away from the screen, I noticed he was long in the neck, with big eyes the color of my mama's olive-fire agate beads. A cowlick ruined his strawberry-blond New Wave bangs, preventing them from cascading over his right eye. And his lips pouted like Simon Le Bon's.

"What you got to show?" He looked me over.

"A whole 'nother universe. Teach you how to drive a go-cart, for one, how to shoot an air rifle, plus several techniques for handling a live gator. How to creep up on the Swamp Ape without making him bellow and coax him out with a fistful of Slim Jims. Show you flesh-eating plants and deer dens, the Plat Eye demon floating over black water, forest fairies swooping up to mooch from Miss Ruby's hummingbird feeder."

The bragging spewed out like I was hexed. I would've kept going if Miss Edna hadn't called me back to the kitchen.

"Butter," she said. "You got to promise me you'll watch out for Alex, the boys around here being mostly hellions."

"I'm a hellion, too, Miss Edna."

"No, Butter, not like the rest. You're my great-niece, after all."

She drew me close so she could whisper, suffocating me with her White Shoulders perfume.

"Alex's mama just had a premature baby boy. Know what that means?"

"Came out before he was cooked."

"That's right. A poor three-pound thing struggling to breathe in an oxygen tank. Alex, being tenderhearted, is taking it right hard. So, you got to keep that in mind and be gentle with him. You can be a lady when you want to."

Ladies sat still and tormented themselves with stiff dresses and torture-chamber shoes. Ladies held their tongues when men walked among them and fixed them food and drinks. As my mama, who worked the night shift at Clarendon Memorial, said, "I don't have time to be a lady."

"I won't never be a lady," I said. "But I won't let the boys mess with Alex."

The next day was one of those blazing summer mornings: sky blue as a pilot light and birds going full throttle, opening their golden beaks and warbling, *Glory Be.* I had Alex riding shotgun in my Hell-cat KT100, a right decent yard cart upgraded by my daddy with thirteen-inch tires and a Titan engine. Wind in my hair, Dr Pepper between my thighs, one hand on the wheel while the other handled a fresh-lit cig butt: pure-tee heaven on a stick, except for Alex gripping the side rail like he didn't trust my driving. Had a mind to race the Hellcat that day, with Alex there to witness my triumph, and we were headed over to the Cliffs.

The boys were already there, brown and shirtless, popping wheelies and jumping gullies, flying ass-over-teacup around that eroded moonscape where a feller buncher had plucked pines out of the earth like they were dandelions. Second we arrived, Butch and Mitch did donuts around us, spitting loogies and slurs, calling Alex *poontang, gerbil balls, city flower,* and *fagmeat.*

"Your mama's got sweet tits," screamed Butch, who was all of ten. "Ask me how I know."

I eased into a clump of upstart pines and cut the motor. Sat in the prickly shade for a spell, sipping my Dr Pepper.

"Look," I told Alex, "first thing you got to learn is ignore their insults, save your wrath for what matters. Remember that nuclear radiation has endowed you with a Hulk-like condition where you might, any minute, pop out into a raging, muscular mutant."

"What?" Alex smirked.

"Well, that's what I told them, since you live near that nuke plant. Also said you could mind-read, tell futures, and levitate."

"Why would you say that?"

"For one, pardon me, you're weird. And two, they would've already snatched you off the cart and whupped you if I hadn't, or peppered you with BBs. We got to keep up the mystery. Now, if Mitch or Butch mess with you, mention that their mama's got webbed toes. They don't know I know, so that'll spook them. Tell Kenny Walker, a big fool who flunked three grades, that he *will* realize his dream and become a professional wrestler. As for Dinky Watts, the little redheaded spazz whose freckles run together, tell him redheads are mind-readers by nature and you'll teach him this art like Merlin did King Arthur. Don't even talk to Cag Stukes, the one in the Gamecock jersey, 'cause he speaks the language of fists."

Alex went bluish-pale like skim milk.

"I should go back to Meemaw's house."

"They'll track you there. They'll climb through your window at night and dump fire ants in your bed. Tough this one out and you're home free. Think about it like a video game. Get to the next level."

I drove straight into an orange cloud of clay dust that hovered like a nuke mushroom, came out the other side, jumped two gullies, hugged the outer wall of a U-turn, and fishtailed right up to the action. Though it almost killed him, Alex loosened his grip on the side rail, keeping up a half-assed appearance of cool. The boys went crazy strutting their stuff: Cag circling with a two-wheeled donut on his Rambler X10; Butch standing on the seat of their Midget while Mitch popped a wheelie; Dinky hopping the hind wheel of his Hornet while Kenny zipped higgledy-piggledy on his Scorpion 5. I realized how stoked they were to blow this city-boy away. They finished their daredevilry, circled us twice, and then stood idling, staring at Alex, half-hoping my tales were real—that the boy would float up out of his seat. Instead, Alex staggered from the cart, fell to his knees, and wallowed on the ground like a bass gasping for water.

"Aw, shit," I said. "Looks like he's about to turn."

Clutching his head, Alex stood up.

"I can-not al-low it to hap-pen a-gain," he said. "Too ma-ny in-no-cents slaugh-tered."

Alex twitched as though shaking a winged demon from his back. He tottered like an exhausted old man and then stared up at the sky, croaked out gibberish, pausing between bouts as though taking dictation from God.

"Your mother has mermaid blood." He pointed at Mitch and Butch. "Hence her webbed toes. She swims in Lake Marion on full-moon nights."

The brothers' jaws dropped at the exact same time, and I pictured them creeping around their den at night, their mama crashed on the couch, her feet freed from the Reeboks she wore to waitress, toes moist and pale in the spooky light of their television.

"And you." He turned to Kenny. "Blessed with giant's blood. One day you will know the glory of kayfabe, your name joining the ranks of Hulk Hogan and Ric Flair."

"Last but not least," Alex said, pointing solemnly at Dinky. "Red-headed elf of rare blood, small of stature but vast of mind, I will teach you the telepathic arts."

With his word-magic, Alex struck the boy-beasts dumb. They

stood, dreamy-eyed in the balmy morning air—all except Cag, who fidgeted, eyes goggling, waiting to hear his fortune. But Alex paid him no mind, sank into my Hellcat as though exhausted from divining. And we sped off, cackling at our stunt.

After lunch I fetched Alex from Miss Edna's porch, blood thrilling when I saw him smile. The boy was bored with his video games, revved up for real adventure, and I spirited him off into the afternoon. We zipped through three backyards to mine, scooted round the shed, and rolled up to Dragon's den. When I cut my motor, cicadas blared like summer's engine. We scrambled from the cart, hunkered down by Dragon's hole, dug deep by my daddy back in April when I'd found the baby gator moping motherless in the swamp. I'd fed him peepers and silver minnows, brought green life back into his yellowing scales. Now Dragon pressed against the chicken wire, flaring his nostrils and smacking his chops. He could smell the ripe chicken giblets and fresh bream I'd brought, his food bucket bungeed to my Hellcat's rear frame.

"Easy there, Dragon," I cooed, fetching his dinner. I swung the bucket over his head to let him catch the scent of meat. "Hungry, buddy?"

The reptile snapped at the wire, his tub spattered with liquid shit. I prayed those Atomic Fireballs hadn't torn him up too bad.

"Damn fools," I hissed.

"Who?" asked Alex.

"Nothing."

I unclamped the chicken wire.

"He won't bite you or try to run?" Alex backed away from the cage.

"Got him trained," I said, relieved to see Dragon creep halfway out the water onto his rock. He used to perch like an anole there, little and jaunty. Now, hemmed in by tub walls, he slithered, covering the mass of the rock with his body, tail whisking the tainted water. He stared up at me, gold-eyed, jaws cracked, waiting for the first giblet to dangle in his range.

Alex squawked when the gator jumped to snap the meat from its loose-tied noose. But by the third chicken gizzard, the fear had left him. When I lowered the baby bluegill, Alex inched up behind me, crouched hands-on-knees to peer. I could feel his body heat. Maybe that's what flustered me. Maybe that's what caused me to lean in too close and get snagged by a tooth—a jagged red rip right through the meat of my lower thumb. I didn't scream, but Alex did. I had to shush him, tiptoe to secure the chicken wire while Dragon chewed in a trance, savoring the taste of fish splashed with his adoptive mother's blood. Hot tears burned my eyes, but I didn't let them spill. I grabbed my first-aid box from the cart and doused the wound with peroxide. Watched pink froth sizzle in the cut. Wiped it clean with fresh gauze and covered the ugliness with a Revco jumbo strip.

"Sure you don't need stitches?" Alex asked that evening, after I'd whisked him off for fresh adventures.

"Just a scratch. Cleaned it again at home and put some anti-biotic ointment on it. My mama works at the hospital, so we got medicine galore."

We lazed in a cypress grove at the edge of the swamp, right where the woods got eerie. Frogs bellowed from the deep of it, down in the dark wet where the Swamp Ape lurked and pitcher plants opened their blooms to tempt insects into their acid bel-lies. When darkness came on, along with the glitter of bugs and stars, I taught Alex frog language: the twitter of wood frogs, the bark of tree frogs, the donk-donk of green frogs. Frogs bleated like sheep and rattled like woodpeckers, droned like power saws and bellowed like bulls. Peeper season was over, but I tried to imitate their high warble, like something from beyond the moon.

We stared up at the sky, didn't look at each other, and shared secrets about our lives. I told Alex my mama was a vampire, accord-ing to my daddy. A pale woman who drew blood on the hospital night shift, she slept through most of the day. I told him about my father's slipped disc, his failed soybeans and blighted corn, how he'd tried to stay busy after both cash crops failed. But his back was busted, and summer had broken him, driving him to drink when dusk came on. He tended to sit alone in our empty house.

"My parents' clocks are out of sync," I said. "And their moods never mesh. My mama sleeps in a mask in a darkened room, sun flicking around the edges of blackout blinds, while my daddy lurks through the house like a man held captive by silence."

Alex spoke of his own dad, an engineer who worked the nuke plant, a giant fortress gated off from the world. Alex imagined it glowing on a hill, surrounded by forest, contaminated animals creeping radiant in the night. He feared his father brought radiation home in his clothes, that it mixed in the washing machine and poisoned them all. Maybe that was why his mom had birthed a preemie, a three-pound frog-eyed baby that struggled to breathe in his incubator.

"His eyes are dark silver like a shark's," said Alex, "and you can almost see right through his skin. If they keep him in oxygen too long, he'll get brain damage. But if they stop the flow, he might die of asphyxiation."

"Terrible," I said.

But there were other babies even smaller than Matthew. One of them, a girl called Amy, just disappeared one day. Alex saw a grease spot on her sheet. And then the nurse pulled the sheet off the mini-mattress and gave him a weird look, wadded it up and threw it into a big rolling hamper. Made him wonder how many hospital sheets had been leaked on by the dead. Made him think about all the death mixed up in the washing machines and streaming from the HVAC vents.

We fell silent and listened to the frogs, with cricket-chirr shimmering over the lower calls. An owl hooted. A chuck-will's-widow cawed its own name. And through this delicate symphony came the bellow of the Swamp Ape, mournful and longing, as though epochs of human misery had been mixed together into this one voice, ringing out from the deepest dark. I knew where the creature's hovel was, a shack so mossy it looked like a bear's den, part and parcel of the wood. I'd seen pieces of the creature in the circle of my flashlight: a crazed red eye, a roaring maw, a hairy arm reaching out to snatch the Slim Jims I fed him from time to time.

"What the hell is that?" asked Alex.

"It's the Swamp Ape," I said. "Monster of the forest who only comes out at night. Some people say he's a throwback to ape times, a variety of Bigfoot that's half-aquatic. Others think he escaped from Clemson University, a lab-made creature half-human, half-ape. Another faction believes he's a regular man, gone feral from drink and craziness, second cousin and once-lover of Sadie Morrison, an ancient lunatic who lives in a mansion that's half-sunk into black water. Alligators, they say, creep right through her living room, and possums suckle litters on her velvet couch. Birds nest in her moss-festooned chandeliers. Open any closet and moths spew out."

Though I'd never been able to find her house, I saw Miss Sadie at the Piggly Wiggly sometimes: gray beehive like a crooked wasp nest, polyester dress from the 1960s, and tattered panty hose. She always filled her buggy with Saltine crackers and cans of oyster stew.

"But you've seen this Swamp Ape thing?" asked Alex.

"I have. And I can take you to him." I pulled a bundle of Slim Jims from my rucksack. "He won't hurt you if you bring him a treat."

We set off down a foot-trail, flashlight flickering over cypress knees that looked like Druids kneeled in prayer. The vines thickened. The trees were smothered with Spanish moss. Mosquitoes swarmed around our force field of *Deep Woods OFF!*

I felt something damp and knuckly brush against my wrist. It was Alex's hand, reaching for mine, half-scared, half-longing. We twined our fingers together and walked deeper in. I felt a sweet twist of nausea in my gut, and the ground went mushy under my feet.

"This is it," I whispered. "The Swamp Ape lives just beyond the border between wet and dry ground."

We let go of each other. I flickered my light through the trees and spotted the collapsing hovel. Out came a bellow so long and low, so misery-packed and wistful, that I longed to join in, to howl my own torments in the muggy dark.

"Mr. Swamp Ape," I said. "Got a treat for you."

I placed the Slim Jims on an ancient stump. And then we backed away and stepped onto solid land. I could hear the man-beast creeping out, the squelch of feet in mud, low grunts and thick breathing. I flashed my light just in time to see a red-frizzed hand take the Slim Jims. I caught a glimpse of shaggy potbelly. A bulging, baggy eye. And then the creature was gone, retreated into his den, tearing into shrink-wrapped meat with his claws.

"Did you see him?" I whispered.

"Yes," Alex rasped, his voice ghostly, light as a dandelion seed in wind.

The next morning Alex looked freaked, pale with bluish streaks under his eyes.

"What's the matter with you?"

"Nightmares. Dreamed I was lost in the hospital, looking for the preemie ward. Finally found it and peered through the glass, saw a bullfrog with vampire teeth grinning in my brother's incubator. Dreamed that the Swamp Ape crept outside my window. I kept waking up, relieved that it was only a dream, and there he leered, the ape-man, reaching in with yellow claws."

"Dreams within dreams," I said. "I get those too. And then I know I'm dreaming and start rigging the dream."

"Me too," said Alex. "It's called lucid dreaming. Makes me wonder if we're dreaming right now."

"Could be."

"You think the Swamp Ape's a real monster or just a crazy person?"

"A person can be a real monster too."

Alex chewed on that for a minute, then slipped into my go-cart, and off we drove toward Eb Richburg's farm shed. Eb was laid up at Clarendon Memorial, getting his sinuses drained. Since he'd let me drive his tractor before, I figured he wouldn't mind if I took a city boy for a trip to Ruby's Whatnots. I took the back way, so Miss Videl wouldn't spot us, and parked behind their propane tank.

Mr. Eb's shed, a glorified carport, smelled of diesel and peppery pesticides. His 4040S, pride and glory, was parked between a riding mower and a no-till corn planter. I smirked when I saw he'd left in the key, climbed up, and waited for Alex.

"Swear you've got permission for this."

"Sorta kinda," I said.

"I don't know." He made a fish face, but climbed up anyway, wedging himself beside me into the big bucket seat.

"Trust me," I said, slipping my brown hand onto his pale knee. I sat for a spell, relishing the warmth that flowed between us. I pulled a Camel butt from the pocket of my cutoffs, lit it with a Bic, took three tokes, and tossed it onto gasoline-spotted concrete, where a small puddle flared into flame. I laughed as I watched the fire wane. Alex winced, but didn't groan. When I cranked the 4040S, it shuddered to life like a T-Rex.

We lurched toward the sunny doorway, veered to avoid a nest of scampering kittens, and rolled into a bare-dirt lot. After shifting to second, we chugged around a pond and pulled out onto Moses Dingle Road. It felt good to shift to third, drive with my left hand while lighting another cig butt with my right, nicotine buzz coming on just as I upped it to fourth. And then we were cruising, passing the post office, Uncle Henry's store with its stack of watermelons, and Hog Heaven BBQ. We passed stray houses and mobile homes, crumbling barns and prefab sheds. The sky was cloud-crammed, light streaming through holes in the mass.

"I love to drive," I said. "Calms me down."

"Got to admit," said Alex, coughing up a chuckle, "that this particular experience is having the opposite effect on me."

We passed a neighborhood of sun-bleached shacks and trailers, what Butch and Mitch cruelly called Brown Town, and I eased into the lot of Ruby's Whatnots. We parked the tractor and went into the cinderblock building. Miss Ruby was a tall, striking woman who'd been to college and had traced her lineage back to Nigeria. She taught history at Manning High School.

Miss Ruby's parents ran the shop during the school year, but she worked it in the summer, the only hippie in Davis Station. She sold carved wood sculptures, a variety of cosmetics and hair products, incense, handmade macramé bags, her daddy's garden produce, and homegrown herbal remedies she mixed herself, along with fishing tackle, fresh worms, ice, chips, snack cakes, candy, sodas, and beer. I'd tried one of her headache powders and it really worked, but most of the whites and some of the blacks around here figured Ruby dabbled in African hippie voodoo. Miss Edna, however, who knew a thing or two about the world outside Clarendon County, purchased Ruby's stress-relief tea on the regular.

"Hey there, Butter," said Miss Ruby. "I see you've got a pal today."

"His name's Alex. A city boy from Aiken."

"Aiken!" She widened her eyes in mock awe.

"It's not that big." Alex shrugged.

"Well, glad to meet you, city boy. You here for the usual, Butter?"

"Yes, ma'am, except double on both."

I pulled out my lizard-hunting money and paid for two Kit Kats and two Dr Peppers, both a better price than my great-uncle Henry charged down the road. Just a few pennies made all the difference, if you knew how to scrimp and save. Once I got my Daisy and my Hellcat, I always asked for money on birthdays and at Christmas. Add in lizard money, chore money, Tooth Fairy, and Easter Bunny, and I had a right decent savings account at First Palmetto. Top Secret Escape Plan A, I called it, though I didn't dare let on that I plotted to bolt this backwater when the right time came. Maybe I'd move to Aiken, go to the USC branch they had up there, even though Alex scoffed at the school and said he was aiming for Duke.

We drove home in silence, watching storm clouds scud along the horizon. Alex almost sobbed with relief when I pulled that tractor into its shed, and then we scrambled out into the thunder-charged air.

When the storm broke, we ducked under a rusted jut of tin, the porch for Mr. Rufus Brock's rundown toolshed. We sat on the stoop to revel in our Kit Kats while staring out at the rain. And then I caught a blunt whiff of molten tar—the smell of flat-roof exploration, new roads winding off into the green distance, amusement-park blacktop gone soft in July sun. I jumped up.

"Smell that?"

"Stinks," said Alex.

"I love the smell of pitch."

We ducked into the shed, where a half-barrel of molten tar stood cooling, and I dipped a finger in.

"Still warm." I scooped up a glob of the black stuff and lobbed it at Alex, plopping his left cheek. At first he stood stunned, but then he flashed a grin, grabbed a fistful of dark mash, and pressed it against my throat. I felt his heart thudding as I smeared thick grime over his bony chest. And then we went at it, shoveling filth with our hands and smirching each other's bodies. We tussled on the concrete floor of the shed, wrestled and kicked our way out into the drizzle. Like puppies, we rolled and nipped in the wet grass.

We both spotted her at the exact same time: Miss Edna, her wash-and-set hairdo ruined by rain, her bulldog face scrunched with wrath under a broken paisley umbrella.

"Got a phone call from Mr. Rufus," she hissed. "Said y'all'd gotten into his tar. This about takes the cake."

She snatched our skinny arms, marched us to her carport, ordered us to strip down to our underwear. We waited with bowed heads, avoiding each other's eyes as Miss Edna fetched her gas can, a bucket of moldy rags, and a mean-looking scouring brush.

As the drizzle waned and sunlight gushed, lighting every pore of our bare flesh, Miss Edna rubbed us down with gasoline, pulled a thousand hairs from their follicles as she brushed bits of clotted tar from our screaming skin. I felt dizzy from gas fumes, flayed raw, streaked with chemical burns.

"Hellions," she hissed, and kept on scrubbing long after she needed to. Then she hosed us down, sudded us up with Octagon soap, and rinsed us off again. At last, she left us, goose-bumped and hunched in shame, our underwear transparent. We each faked interest in opposite corners of the carport—Alex absorbed with a dead geranium, me lost in a spider's web.

"Your meemaw's a bitch," I finally said, straining to break the silence.

When I turned to meet his gaze, hands cupped over my no-count titties, Alex stared at my wet underwear, and I wondered if he could see the puckered slit between my legs. I made out the shape of his thing, curled like a beetle grub in his sodden briefs.

When Miss Edna returned with a pile of towels, we turned away from each other again.

"I called your mama," she told me. "Said for you to get home right this minute."

Though I pretended to run home, I slipped behind her azaleas to spy.

"Pick your switch," she said to Alex.

"What do you mean by that, Meemaw?"

Miss Edna pointed at a hickory sapling, instructed him to tear off a flexible young branch, stood behind him as he chose his torture rod, and then ordered him to strip it of leaves. As Alex leaned facedown against the brick wall, his granny lashed at his poor, skinny legs, stinging those tender zones on the backs of his knees and thighs, silk-soft skin that had never known such torture. Mitch and Butch, who had a nose for misery, crept up behind a clump of forsythia to jeer.

"You rinky-dink piece of fagmeat," they called. "Our mama said she ain't no damn mermaid."

I closed my eyes, couldn't bear to watch Alex—green to switching—scream and flinch and jump. Couldn't stomach the sight of Mitch and Butch laughing so hard they staggered like drunks.

"City poon," they screamed. "Dork."

Running home, I looked back once, saw poor Alex hugging his knees and sniveling as his grandmother swept the carport in fury.

"Get home, hellion," Miss Edna hollered after me, lifting her broom in the air.

I slipped into the house, which was cold and dark as a tomb, and got dressed. I hoped my mama had gone back to bed, but there she waited on the couch, vampire-pale and smelling of hospital disinfectant. My daddy sat stiffly in his La-Z-Boy, in the non-recline setting, so I knew I was in for some shit.

"Butterbean." Daddy moaned my baby name, the name they'd called me when I was born six pounds with jaundice. And I pictured myself the size of a lima, curled in the warm wet dark of my mama, dreaming myself into being.

"Why'd you want to get into that tar?" Daddy said, his eyes red from drinking, and it not hardly noon. "And put your cousin up to mischief too, him on the honor roll and all?"

"It was a dumb thing to do, but we did it," I said. "Go ahead and whip me."

"Reckon I'll have to," Daddy said sadly. I knew he couldn't bear to beat me.

"She's too old to whip," said Mama. "How about you take her go-cart or her gun."

"But Mama," I said. "Can't survive without a ride and a weapon, not with these hellion boys."

"Stay inside, then. Read one of those books Miss Edna lent you."

I pictured myself shut up in the air-conditioning, sealed off from summer in this twilight house of whispers and swallowed words.

"Go ahead and take my Daisy," I said.

Then Mama's eyes went wide.

"What's that on your hand?" she said.

I looked down, saw that my Band-Aid hadn't survived Miss Edna's scouring, that my wound was puckered purple, but at least the Neosporin had kept off the pus.

"Tore it on a catbrier thorn," I said. "But I cleaned it and put on antibiotic. It's not oozing nothing."

"Elizabeth Ann." Mama shot across the room, picked up my hand, and turned it in the lamplight. "It's not infected, but it could've been. You ought've got stitches and an oral antibiotic. Tell me right now how you got this thing."

"Dragon nipped me."

I couldn't think of a reasonable fib. If I said dog bite, they might make me get twenty-one rabies shots in the belly, like Kenny Dennis suffered when that field rat bit him.

"But it was an accident. I had my hand too close to his dinner."

Mama gnawed her lip, doing math in her head. She'd forgot all about Dragon, and now she imagined how much he'd grown.

"God damn it," she hissed. A tremble worked its way through her.

I bowed my head, waiting for the tornado of her fury to bluster over me.

"I slave all day at the hospital, and you drown your worthlessness in drink," she screamed at Daddy. "The least you could do is keep an eye on things around here. How the hell you let that gator get so big?"

"What do you know?" squalled Daddy. "You're never here. And when you are, you're like a vampire sleeping, with us on pins and needles."

And then they went at it, screeching accusations, excuses, and insults, dragging up ancient shit from the deep latrine of their marriage, circling the room like professional wrestlers who'd never take the leap to strangle each other.

I sat on the couch and let their words lapse into noise, until Daddy went stone-cold silent. He stomped to his gun case, unlocked it, and grabbed his .22. I thought for sure he'd shoot Mama, that I'd be haunted for life by the sight of her spattered brains. But then, crook-backed and grabbing at the waistline of his pitiful too-big shorts, Daddy stomped out the back door.

"Don't you worry, Miss Dracula," he yelled. "I'll take care of it."

I followed him out into the afternoon glare, where hellions filled the air with thunder, go-carts and dirt bikes kicking up dust. When they saw Daddy bumbling like the Swamp Ape, mad-eyed with his gun, they idled after him. Trying to catch up, I sprinted under the high summer sun, my nose running with the snot of grief.

"Don't do it," I cried, but nobody heard me. A half-dozen engines revved.

Daddy stooped over Dragon's cage, unclamped the chicken wire, and flung the cover away. The hellions cut their motors and inched up for a better look. As cicadas chanted in the mystic heat, Dragon crawled out onto the grass and stretched to his full length, nearly three feet long, his spiked back slicked with water. The glorious prehistoric creature opened his mouth in a fanged grin.

"Please Daddy," I said gently. "Just let him run off. He'll smell swamp and head right for it."

"He might come back for food and bite somebody. Never should've let you keep him in the first place."

Still, Daddy seemed to consider my wish. Sat there thinking and cradling his gun.

"Shoot him," yelled Dinky Watts. "He looks big enough to eat a baby."

"Fools," I snapped. "None of your damn business."

"Call somebody a fool," Mitch and Butch chanted, "you in danger of hell's fire."

Daddy shook his head as though rousing from a dream, took aim, and fired, catching Dragon in the flank. The gator let out a gurgling hiss and rolled onto his side. The boys cheered. Daddy fired again at a closer range, kicked the poor beast onto his back, and blasted another bullet into his pale belly.

Daddy picked up the limp reptile by the tail, swung his gory trophy in the air, and staggered around the shed toward Mama.

"You happy now, Miss Dracula?" he shrieked.

Mama stood on the back stoop, fists clenched, her skin so white she glowed.

"Idgets all," I hissed, and ran off into the woods.

It was almost dusk, light tipping toward pink. I was in the swamp, bawling my miseries to the throb of frogs—my baby gator dead, Alex shamed and switched on my account, my house a tomb of silent wrath, vampire and ogre cramming it roof to cellar with what Miss Ruby called *bad vibes*. I was a hellion, for sure, who deserved to slip back into the swamp from which the first land creatures crawled: those fish with legs, skinks or whatever, primitive pining things. I had four hundred and thirty-six dollars in my savings account. Weren't enough lizards in Davis Station to shoot for college tuition. Plus, Miss Edna had banished me from her porch. Hellions like me never got scholarships, so why bother striving in school?

I was lost, doomed to attend Central Carolina Tech, master some bleak medical procedure, and turn into a vampire like my mama. I'd prick human bodies a hundred times a day at Clarendon Memorial, fill those little feedbags with sugar water, or worse: wash diseased feet, rub salve on bedsores, drain abscesses as big as tennis balls. I saw myself, pale and moving in a dream through a hive of the sick and dying, a one-week vacation the only thing to look forward to. Alex had said he wanted to build rockets, and I pictured him zipping off into the twinkling black of space, leaving the likes of me to rot on our ruined planet. I imagined humans crammed cheek to jowl, mutated by nukes, resorting to cannibalism after they'd devoured every last animal alive. I saw plant life stamped out by solid blacktop, the globe turned to a ball of tar.

Alex, fated to zoom through universes unknown, was right to keep his distance from both me and planet Earth, a thought that made me bawl the harder. When I finally stopped crying, the bellowing went on, as though the spirit of my grief had haunted the forest. But it was the Swamp Ape, I realized, roaring along with me. Now he, too, stilled his song. We'd twined our grief together, which had drained the poison from me. I was grateful to the man-beast for that.

Exhausted, I leaned against a cypress, watching lightning bugs sway out from whatever holes they slept in during the day.

I noticed a circle of light spotting the trees—the Plat Eye, I thought, sniffing my weakness, come out of his demonic dimension to hound me until I lost my marbles. But it was only a flashlight, my daddy come to fetch me, no doubt.

"Butter," said a voice high and boyish, not yet croaky from change.

Alex sat down beside me.

"Where you been?" I asked.

"Meemaw kept me locked in all day. But as soon as she dozed off, I put a fake person in my bed, towels and blankets, and slipped out the window to find you."

"You're not mad at me about the switching?"

"Not your fault. Got a will of my own and so do you."

"I guess we all do," I said, thinking it over. "Though some people got more room to move than others."

"Sorry about Dragon," he whispered, slipping his hand into mine. "Butch told me all about it."

"Daddy might've been right," I said. "That gator would've probably come back for food and bit somebody."

We sat there, sweaty hands fastened in a funny position.

"Little Matthew's coming home next week," said Alex.

They'd cut the oxygen in his brother's tank, and though the baby had struggled, he'd gotten the hang of breathing. I tried to think of something to say. I was happy for Alex but also sad: summer would suck when he was gone, the dog days coming on, me left with nobody to play with but hellion boys.

"Good," I said. "When do they come get you?"

"A week or so. We could be pen pals, you know."

I pictured myself trying to write a decent letter, struggling to impress, straining for the right words. I pictured Alex sniggering every time I misspelled something or got carried away with Miss Edna's thesaurus. And what would I have to tell him? About my vampire mama and drunken daddy? About go-cart races and BB-gun fights? About the King Arthur novels Miss Edna lent me? Or the Swamp Ape's preference for Slim Jims over beef jerky?

"Maybe," I said. "I've never been one to write letters."

We sat in silence for a spell, listening to night music—insect, amphibian, and bird. The Swamp Ape started up again, gentle and wistful, more soft-grunted song than howl. When Alex flicked on his flashlight to catch him in action, the creature lurched off into deeper swamp.

"What the hell?" said Alex.

Now big-eyed creatures glided through his circle of light—two, three, four—their limbs splayed, furry membranes stretched wide.

"Fairies," I whispered, though I knew they were only flying squirrels, come to feed on pawpaw fruit.

They landed on a branch and shimmied down to the heavy clusters, the fruit bruised and rotten-looking on the outside. But inside was soft yellow pulp like banana custard.

"Fairies," Alex repeated, as though to hypnotize himself into believing, and I strained hard to believe too, pictured the creatures twittering real language and working magic spells.

I could see the future of summer. Ravaged cornfields and soybean chaff. Cicadas buzzing like broken toys in parched grass. Muscadines past ripeness, fermenting on the ground, the woods smelling like wine. School would be here in a blink, and then I'd be in prison for a solid nine months.

But now, summer was at its height, offering its sweetest fruits, full of furry fairies and glowing bugs. Alex leaned against me, humming with warm blood, his brain like a different universe.

# Bronze

FROM *The New Yorker*

THE COLLEGE FRESHMAN, being high, was also a little para-noid. Therefore, as he boarded the Amtrak Colonial he had the impression that people could tell. Why was everyone staring? Some smiling, some raising eyebrows, a few shaking their heads. Do I reek? Eugene thought. I *used* Binaca.

Then he remembered what he was wearing. The white fur coat. The pink sunglasses. The striped collegiate scarf knotted at his neck. Sort of a new look for him, part glam, part New Wave.

Eugene's little secret? He wanted to be beautiful. If that didn't work, noticeable would do.

He unzipped his coat and fanned himself, hot from running down the platform.

It was a late-November afternoon, in the confusing year of 1978, and Eugene was headed back to school after a wild weekend exploring the demimonde. Eugene knew that was a French word associated with women of dubious morals, but in his mind it in-cluded the teen runaways at that chicken-hawk bar Stigwood had taken him to, Saturday night; plus Stigwood himself, who was rich and debauched. The main thing about the demimonde was that nobody back at the dorm had a clue about it. Only Eugene.

As he started down the aisle, he watched passengers' reactions through his sunglasses. One lady poked her husband, as if to say, *Only in New York!* An old guy with a mean red face and a Teamster's haircut scowled and said something that sounded like "Fruitcake." That was fine. Scandalizing the sensibilities of the masses was part of the vocation. Better get used to it, Eugene told himself.

He was so caught up in the act of scandalizing sensibilities that it took him a while to notice something. The train was packed. Should have got here earlier.

Raphael had made him late. They were up in Stigwood's bedroom, Eugene packing his duffel, when Raphael said, "Want to play a game with me? *Please.* It's fun."

Raphael was Stigwood's boyfriend from Venezuela. He was lying across the bed, dressed in tight salmon flares, a Qiana shirt, and platform shoes, his black hair cut in a wedge, like Dorothy Hamill's. Raphael was about Eugene's age, but he didn't go to college; he worked at a hair salon, sweeping up hair. The rest of the time he lounged around the town house.

Eugene felt sorry for Raphael. He hadn't known there were male concubines. Also, Raphael had just lit a joint. So Eugene said, "OK, I'll play for a minute."

Raphael passed the doobie and picked up a deck of cards. "Everybody has a word map," he explained. "Your word map is how you feel, inside, as a person. Here. I show you."

Raphael laid three cards on the bedspread. Each bore a word. *Sensitivity. Ardor. Celebration.*

"Pick a card," Raphael said. "How you feel, *inside.*"

Eugene took a hit and thought about it. His mom always called him sensitive. But not in a way he liked. You had to be sensitive to be a poet, of course, but Eugene's mom meant more like that time at swimming lessons, when he'd refused to get into the pool.

You do something once and your family never stops talking about it.

So: no to *Sensitivity.*

*Ardor* was like armpit plus odor.

*Celebration,* on the other hand, had appeal. First of all, it was Latinate, and Eugene had been taking Latin since seventh grade. *Celebration* was also a Broadway musical by the creators of *The Fantasticks,* the longest-running musical in the history of Off-Broadway theater. Eugene's high school had staged *Celebration* his sophomore year, and Mr. Baxter, the drama teacher, had cast Eugene as Orphan, one of the leads.

Plus, Eugene *did* like to party.

"Celebration," he told Raphael. "Definitely."

Raphael was dealing more cards when Stigwood burst in. Stigwood was a friend of Mr. Baxter's, from his New York acting days.

Having been alerted by Eugene that he was coming East for college, Stigwood had invited him to stay if he were ever in New York, so that was what Eugene had been doing. This was his third visit. Stigwood had a girlfriend, too. Her name was Sally. Eugene wasn't sure if she knew about Raphael. Probably not. "Gay, straight," Stigwood said, "it's all a bunch of bullshit." Right now, Stigwood had his Caligula face on, eyes dead, tongue lolling. That didn't usually happen until later at night. Ignoring Eugene's presence, he crossed the bedroom and tackled Raphael from behind. Then mounted him and sucked on his face. Raphael didn't resist at first. But when Stigwood stuck his hand down Raphael's pants he shoved him onto the floor. "You know what, Jerry? You treat me like a slut," he shouted. "Well, let me tell you something. I am not your slut!"

While this was going on, Eugene had retreated to the corner of the room. Seemed only polite. Plus, if he remained inconspicuous he could watch what happened next. But then he remembered his train. "See you guys! Thanks for everything, Mr. Stigwood!" he said, and booked. Got to Penn Station with two minutes to spare.

Which was why, now, no seats.

He kept going down the aisle, searching. This train was in better condition than the subways, at least. They were totally trashed. All weekend, Eugene had had "Shattered" stuck in his head, Mick singing, *Don't you know the crime rate is going up, up, up, up, up / To live in this town you must be tough, tough, tough, tough, tough!*

Hold on. Did he just sing that out loud? Now people were really staring.

Stigwood always had the strongest dope!

New York was dying. But that was OK. It was in dying empires that the greatest poets appeared. Virgil in Rome. Dante in Florence. Baudelaire in Paris. *Decadence.* Eugene liked that word. It was like "decay" and "hence." Things falling apart over time. A sweet smell like that of rotten bananas, or of bodies ripe from iniquitous exertion, could pervade an entire age, at which point someone came along to give voice to how messed up things were and, in so doing, made them beautiful again.

That was what Eugene wanted to do. First, though, he had to learn prosody.

Up ahead, he spotted an empty seat. Headed for it only to find an overnight bag there, its owner hiding behind a newspaper. Two rows later, same thing, only this time the seat-hogger was pretending to nap. People were such fakers.

Take the ballerina, for instance. Hadn't she promised to meet Eugene at the movies last week? And when he'd suggested bringing granola bars, so they wouldn't have to pay for candy, hadn't she said, "Good idea! Can you bring some for me?" But then he'd waited under the marquee, with a whole box of Oats 'n Honey, and she never showed up, and later he heard she'd been in the common room, drinking Asti with Rob, the RA with the beard.

Now he reached the end of the train car. On the door a blue button said PRESS. "See this button?" Eugene said to himself. "This is Rob's face," and he punched it, hard. To his surprise, the doors opened with a *whoosh*, like an airlock on a spaceship. Wow. Cool. Now he was *between* cars. Daredevil-like. He looked down, expecting to see tracks below—the train had started moving—but the area was an enclosed, accordion-like sleeve that bent gracefully as the train pulled out of the station.

Peering into the next car, Eugene saw more faces. It was like that poem from his imagism seminar. "In a Station of the Metro," by Ezra Pound. Since no one could hear him in this little space, Eugene recited the poem. It wasn't long, just this:

> The apparition of these faces in the crowd:
> Petals on a wet black bough.

Eugene's friend Mike always made fun of him when he read out loud. He said Eugene had a "poetry voice." But what could he do? He didn't like his regular voice. Too nasal.

Anyway, the reciting helped. He felt better already. To enter the next car, Eugene just pressed the button gently.

Same story, though. Totally packed. He wasn't going to have to stand the whole way to Providence, was he? He had homework to do!

He went into the next car. And the next. Each one stuffier and more crowded. As he was entering yet another car, he caught sight of his reflection and turned back to study it after the door closed. The curly Lou Reed hair, the Warhol sunglasses. Those were new. He'd seen the frames in an optometrist's window and gone straight in and bought them. Then decided to tint the lenses, and had picked dark rose, which maybe had been a bit much.

Something told Eugene not to wear the sunglasses around campus. Why not try them out in New York? So many storefront windows in which to look at yourself and decide.

While he examined his reflection, deciding, Eugene heard a mellow-toned voice.

"This seat's free," the voice said.

Eugene turned. Didn't see anyone. Then lifted his sunglasses.

Five rows deep, a man beckoned. He had a yellow cable-knit sweater tied around his shoulders. Blond hair that looked straightened, or dyed, or both.

Not *again*, Eugene thought. Man. Everywhere I go!

On the other hand, there was no place else to sit.

Fifteen minutes earlier, as he limped onto the train, Kent Jeffries had been in no mood for company. He was too wrecked. God, what a weekend! *Outrageous!* What was the joke Mickey had made? At that bathhouse? Oh, yeah: *Can I borrow an orifice you're not using?*

The last thing Kent needed now was some turkey talking his ear off. Accordingly, he'd taken a seat by the window, setting his bag beside him. Then he'd spread his Pierre Cardin blazer—the rust, not the kelly green—on top. That should do it. While people boarded, he leafed through *Variety*. As seats grew scarce, he started to worry, and laid his head back, pretending to sleep.

No sooner had his eyes closed than images of the past two days flickered in his mind.

Friday night: That after-hours place in the Village. Cable spools for tables. Rough trade in the back room. More Mickey's thing than his.

Saturday: They climbed into a refrigerator truck in the meat-packing district. Pitch-black inside. Smelled like a stable. Three dozen men creating a vortex, a flesh whirlpool, that sucked you in and around and out again.

Climbing down afterward, Kent said, "I felt a little overdressed. How about you?"

Next thing he knew he was taking a leak at someplace called the Dungeon. The urinal was open at the bottom. As Kent stared down into the bowels of the earth, a face appeared. A dignified, older gentleman, trembling with anticipation. Definitely Mickey's thing.

Finally, they went to that disco everyone was raving about, the Ice Palace. They were on the dance floor, doing poppers, when from out of the neon-lit, fog-machine fog a small Puerto Rican queen strutted past, wearing nothing but Christmas lights.

"Where do you keep the batteries?" Mickey called.

"In the shape of a dildo up my ass!"

Sassy! But still not Kent's thing.

Then it was Sunday and he woke up in Mickey's basement apartment on Cornelia Street. People's ankles going past the dirty windows. Already noon.

Mickey entered with a tube of Preparation H. "Dab in each nostril," he said. "Home remedy."

"I'm *never* drinking again," Kent groaned.

But at brunch, when Mickey ordered a Bloody, Kent said, "Oh, *all right*."

One led to three, by which point they'd developed a rationale. They were fortifying themselves. Had a difficult day ahead of them. At two, they were going to clean out Jasper's digs, now that Jas was sick and had moved back to Texas. Revisiting the scene of all their revels wasn't going to be easy. Not for any of them, and least of all for Kent, whose name used to be on the lease.

It also meant seeing Ron, who'd lived in the apartment recently. Ron was a purely stopgap measure, in Kent's opinion. Skinny. Bucktoothed. Taller than Tommy Tune.

"I suppose he's handy when you need something from the top shelf," Kent had said to Jasper once, on the phone.

"Don't be bitchy," Jasper said.

Ron still had keys. By the time Kent and Mickey arrived, he'd aired the place out and prepared a pitcher of mimosas. Louie and Ed were already going through Jasper's stuff.

The apartment looked unchanged. Still the familiar mélange, the Chinese trunk next to the Victorian love seat next to the bust of Jasper done by that sculptor in Key West. Jas's record collection—the ragtime, the Lotte Lehmann. His Roman trinkets, his colored-glass bottles. But, despite Jasper's flair for decorating, the spirit had gone out of the place. It looked rundown. Mouse droppings. Old-cigarette smell.

They drank mimosas while they dickered.

Ed wanted Jasper's secretary with the broken leg.

Louie had dibs on the framed poster for the Living Theatre, signed by Julian Beck.

Jasper's books, his annotated scripts, his correspondence with theater bigwigs (Brustein, Foreman, Grotowski) were to be boxed up and sent to Rice University.

What did Kent want? The leather pig footstool from England? The very tiny Miró?

Nothing was in the right drawers anymore. He couldn't find any scissors to cut the packing tape.

Finally, he went into the bedroom, stood on the brass bed, and reached up under the lighting fixture—and there it was. His old stash, from 1971.

Jasper didn't approve of grass. Kent had always had to sneak out to the fire escape.

When he exited the bedroom, Ron was on the phone with Jasper at the hospital. He held the phone toward the stereo and said, "Jas, we're playing Bobby Short in your honor."

Everyone who got on the phone with Jas screamed with laughter at something he told them. Jas's old chestnuts.

*In bed by twelve, home by three.*

*He's very butch. He gets it from his mother.*

*Look, he was dead. How can you be jealous?*

Then it was Kent's turn.

He tried to sound upbeat. Festive.

Good thing he was an actor.

"Last chance to change your mind and come back, Jas," he said. "We'll just unpack everything."

"What the fuck's the matter with Ron?" Jasper said. "Siccing all these well-wishers on me. I'm in no condition."

Jasper sounded mad. That made Kent happy. Ron was getting on his nerves, too, presiding over everything, auditioning for the role of widow.

"What do you expect from an understudy?" Kent said.

Jas laughed. Started coughing. Fought down the cough enough to say, "That's exactly what he is! Only good enough for the matinée!" As he paused to catch his breath, the receiver filled with noise. Phone calls to Jasper were party lines now, three people on at once: Kent, Jasper, and Jasper's emphysema, wheezing in the background.

Kent's voice was softer as he said, "How are you doing down there, Jas? Really."

"Oh, well. Back in the bosom of my family. You know how I've always felt about bosoms."

And now Kent managed it: the scream of hilarity.

"I'm tired," Jas said. "Hanging up."

It was Ron who ended up bawling. He crumpled onto the floor, crying out, "It's so fucking unfair! God!" Louie and Ed knelt down, patting and stroking him.

Kent went to the window and lit a cigarette. At drama school, they'd done an exercise where you had to pretend to be on an iceberg. The other students had shivered and hugged themselves, hopping around. Kent had had a different idea. He'd gone to the edge of the stage, alone, and let the coldness seep into his skin. Squinted his eyes. Tightened his sphincter. Retracted his scrotum. Just became *ice*. Frozen. Feeling nothing. *That* was how you played cold. It worked for a shivering peasant in Chekhov or a naked Fool on the heath.

Now Kent did it at other times as well.

Disconnected his phone, turned off the lights. People rang his bell, shouted at his window, "Answer the door, Kent! We *know* you're there!"

Sitting in the dark, frozen, the person Kent was at those times didn't answer to the name on his Equity card. He was still Peter J. Belknap, Liz and Roger's boy, from Buffalo. Good-looking kid. Class president. Girls all crazy about him.

Liz was gone now. That was another reason Kent shut himself in for days at a time. To think about her. Liz coming down the stairs, fixing a diamond earring, on her way out to dinner with Roger. Kent/Peter, ten years old, in charge of making cocktails. The way Liz smiled when he brought her drink, and said to Roger, "Darling, where did you find this new bartender? He's terribly good."

Behind closed eyelids, shamming sleep on the train, Kent Jeffries thought about Liz, his dear sweet mother. His eyes were welling. He shifted in the seat, turning his head toward the window, and slipped off his Gucci loafers. He'd bought a new pair at Bergdorf's, stupidly wore them out of the store, and now had blisters on both feet. That was why he was limping.

Finally, the train pulled out of the station. Kent figured it was safe to open his eyes.

That was when he saw the boy. In the Eskimo coat. And the Elton John sunglasses. Staring into the door window behind him like Narcissus into his pool.

Kent knew who the kid reminded him of. Himself, twenty years ago. Grow up queer in the sticks and it's like hearing a broadcast in the distance. You can make out the frequency all right, but the words get garbled along the way. So, when you finally run away to New York, you end up dressing like this kid, in some wild approximation of flamboyant.

Kent had taken a bus from Buffalo to Port Authority and then the subway to Christopher Street. Found a wall to lean against.

White tank top. Cutoffs so short the pockets showed.

Jasper, on his way from teaching at HB Studios, picked him up. Took Kent straight home, but only to feed him and let him use the shower. Made him sleep on the couch. The next day, he took him to a dermatologist to clear up his acne.

Kent was seventeen. Jasper thirty-eight. About the age Kent was now.

It was sympathy that made him call out to the boy. He knew how hard it could be.

When the kid lifted his sunglasses, his eyes looked just as pink. Stoned out of his mind.

If that was an advantage, Kent tried not to acknowledge it.

He didn't speak to the boy until they were out of the tunnel.

"I hope no polar bears died for that," Kent said.

"What?" the boy said, coming out of his stupor. "Oh. This coat? No. It's fake."

With a wiggle of its hips, the train shifted to a new track.

They still had a four-hour ride ahead of them.

Kent reached across the seat and touched the fur.

"Could have fooled me," he said.

He was getting used to this by now. Attention from men. Certain kind of men.

Last night, for instance, Stigwood took Eugene and Raphael out to eat. They were drinking Kir Royales when a friend of Stigwood's came up and, without even asking, started playing with Eugene's curls. As if Eugene were there for that purpose alone.

Which, Eugene realized, he was.

He let himself be fondled. It felt nice, to be honest, and it wasn't like any girls were offering. Also, it meant he could flag a waiter for another Kir Royale.

*Celebration!*

Most of the time it wasn't so overt. Eugene would be hitchhiking and some married guy would pick him up, then touch his leg one too many times. Or at a party, instead of passing a joint, some stranger would hold it to his lips and watch him inhale.

On the street men stared, their eyes aggressive, desperate, and frightened all at once. In some neighborhoods they came from all directions, like Space Invaders.

It was like being a pretty girl. The pluses and minuses of that.

Did Eugene give off some kind of signal? Was it his earring?

He'd forgotten about that. He'd pierced his ear himself, in his dorm room, using a needle and an ice cube. As soon as it healed he was going to wear a hoop, but for now he had a gold stud from the ladies' section.

But here was the thing about the men who pestered Eugene. They talked about interesting subjects. Existentialism. The New York School. Bertolt Brecht. Eugene loved the way girls looked and smelled, and how their voices sounded, but they didn't know much more about the world than he did. Often less. Sometimes a lot less.

You had to keep it under control, though. Otherwise, things could get hairy.

As soon as he sat down on the train, Eugene made clear he didn't have time for conversation. He lowered his tray table, hauled out his Loeb edition of Horace's *Odes and Epodes,* and opened to Ode XXX.

He'd never translated Latin stoned before. Maybe it would be excellent.

Didn't seem like it.

Just seemed harder.

Peeking at the English translation on the opposite page was cheating.

The train had come out of the tunnel. They were on an elevated track, passing close to slummy-looking apartment buildings. Bedsheets for curtains. Naked light bulbs on cords.

Eugene stared at the Latin. Chewed his fountain pen. Regarded the ode from a different angle. Gazed out the window again. And, in his notebook, wrote this instead:

Each window I see into
contains a slice of life
sliced by the train I'm in
two kids watching TV on the floor
an old man reading the paper
and just a couch, all alone
like me

The man tapped his leg.

Uh-oh.

But he just needed to get out. Eugene raised the tray and swiveled his knees. Then went back to translating.

At first, Eugene had taken Latin because it was required. But in ninth grade, when you could switch to a living language, he didn't. He *liked* that Latin was dead. He liked that only smart kids took it. He liked his idiosyncratic Latin teachers, Dr. Fletcher, who played "Shoo-Fly Pie" on his guitar to teach them dactylic hexameter, and Miss McNally, who described their grammar book as "gruel-colored."

*Gruel* was like "gray" and "cruel."

Which was like Latin grammar! Most kids couldn't take it. They flailed. Not Eugene. When he opened his Latin grammar book, he felt close to invincible.

*Exegi monumentum aere perennius.*

"I have made . . . a monument . . . in the air."

No, not "air," dummy. *Aere,* from *aereus,* meaning "bronze."

"I have made a monument more lasting than bronze."

Horace meant his odes. This whole book.

Jeez. Talk about conceited.

The thing was, though? Horace had written this ode two thousand years ago, and here was Eugene, on Amtrak, translating it.

He looked up to see his seatmate returning down the aisle, carrying something. Eugene looked away. He was wondering a couple of things. First, if it was even possible, at this point in history, to imagine people reading your stuff two millennia from now. Second, what could you do to increase your chances?

The man stepped over Eugene's legs and reclaimed his seat.

"I got you a libation," he said.

A what? Oh. Beers. In a cardboard tray. Looked pretty good. Eugene had the worst cotton mouth.

\*

They drank the first six-pack in silence, the kid writing in his note-book. The train crossed into Connecticut as the sky darkened. Al-most 5 p.m. At New Haven, they got hitched to a different engine, and then were on their way again. Past New London. Mystic.

An hour outside Providence, the boy got up, presumably to go to the bathroom. Kent Jeffries pulled out a twenty and said, "How about another round?"

The boy hesitated. "Will you watch my stuff?" he said. As if someone might steal the Latin book. Or the Liberace coat.

"It's safe with me," Kent Jeffries said.

By the time they started on the second six-pack, the atmosphere was different. The boy had finished his homework and become chatty. He was less stoned, more drunk. They talked about acting—the boy was excited to meet a professional actor. He'd done theater himself, in high school. Now he wanted to be a poet and was study-ing English literature and classics. He held up his Latin translation.

"Read it to me," Kent said.

"Really? OK. But only if you critique my delivery. I'm going to have to give readings someday. My friend says I use this fake voice when I read out loud."

"I'll be the judge," Kent said.

Holding the notebook like a hymnal, the boy intoned:

I have made a monument more lasting than bronze
And higher than the royal site of the pyramids
which neither harsh rains nor the wild North wind can erode
Nor the countless succession of years, and the flight of the seasons.
I will not entirely die! And a large part of me will avoid the grave.

Kent paid half attention. His mind was elsewhere, full of light. Moving at the same speed as the train, which was whistling along now, moonlit coves flashing by, the ocean out there somewhere, gravid in its depths. The boy wore a secondhand shirt, its celluloid collar missing, and black suspenders. So pale and thin inside these coverings, like a flower stalk. A reed.

Look who's getting poetic now?

The kid's reading voice was affected. He sounded like an ama-teur doing Shakespeare. Had no idea who he was yet, but it was touching to see how fervently he dreamed of being *something*.

That's what Jas never understands. How I actually *feel* about them. He always wants to reduce it to—

The boy had stopped. He was looking at Kent expectantly.

"Read it again," Kent said. "*This* time pretend you're talking to somebody you *care* about."

"Like who?"

Onstage, Kent always imagined Liz. Liz, out in the house, her head to one side, playing with her bracelet, and listening.

"Is there anybody you'd like to impress? This poem's sort of show-offy."

The boy said, "There's this girl. At school. I don't know her very well. But I could use her."

"Try it. Again."

The boy complied.

A girl. Hmm. Didn't mean anything, necessarily.

Kent waited until the boy had finished.

"Better," he said.

"Really? It sounded worse to me."

"You have to use the instrument you have," Kent said. "Any good voice coach will tell you that. You can *work* on your instrument. But you can't replace it."

"I'm going to remember that," the boy said. "Thanks!" He seemed genuinely grateful. "It would be easier reading my own stuff. But with Horace—"

"Heavy lifting, I know."

After that, they were silent. The train rumbled into Rhode Island. The sky was black. Twenty minutes later, the conductor called out Providence.

As they pulled into the station, they said nothing. As if embarrassed by their previous intimacy. The boy gathered his things and, without a goodbye, strode unsteadily down the aisle and onto the dark train platform.

That was for the best. It really was.

Kent put on his blazer and limped out of the train.

Colder out. No moon anymore.

Even darker in the parking lot. He was in his car, pulling onto Waterman Street, when a shape lurched into his path.

Kent rolled down his window. "Need a ride?"

The boy said nothing. Just swayed, gazing in the direction of College Hill.

Then they were both in the car, the heater blowing cold air, the radio on. Kent too bombed to drive but doing so.

The boy fiddled with the radio.

"I think a nightcap is in order," Kent said.

"I'm totally wasted already," said the boy.

Kent made a left, away from campus. "Is that a yes?" he said.

It was one of those historic houses on Benefit Street. No front yard. Plaque that said EBENEZER SWAMPSCOTT, WHALER, 1764.

Where Eugene was from, nothing was that old. In fifth grade he'd gone on a field trip to Fort Dearborn, but he'd had to blur his vision to erase the skyscrapers and car factories so that he could imagine the days when Indian canoes, laden with pelts, plied the river.

*Plied* was like "plunge," "fly," and "try," all at once.

The man had a hard time with the key, even though it was his house. To compensate, when he got the door open he went all English butler, bowing and scraping. "After you, My Lord." The low-ceilinged room they entered was full of old-fashioned furniture and oil paintings. The only modern thing was the stereo, which the man headed straight for.

It felt different, being alone with him. More tense.

Maybe Eugene should leave.

"Have you ever heard Mabel Mercer?" the man said, putting on a record.

"Who?"

"If you're going to be a poet, you have to know Mabel Mercer." He lowered the needle, scratching issued through the speakers, and then a piano tinkled and this voice came out. Low. Deep. Not singing, exactly. More like talking with extreme precision. Hard to tell if it was a man or a woman.

The man stood straight now, index finger raised. "Listen to her phrasing," he said.

Eugene listened. He was glad to have an assignment. Meanwhile, the man disappeared. He returned one song later to hand Eugene a drink. Something fizzy. Tasted like Sprite.

Didn't mix with beer so well.

All of a sudden, Eugene's mouth filled with saliva. He swallowed, but it refilled. Since opening his mouth didn't seem like a good idea, he put down his glass and hurried out of the room. He found the guest bathroom and spit into the sink.

Was he going to hurl? He couldn't tell. Mouth filling again.

Eugene closed the door. The lock was a hook-and-eye thingy —wouldn't keep anybody out. He hooked it, nonetheless.

The kid wasn't getting sick in there, was he? That would crimp things.

Kent Jeffries had come into the hall to listen.

Silence from the bathroom. No sound of retching.

Vodka tonic had probably been a bad idea.

Speaking of which, his glass was empty.

He returned to the kitchen. As he got a lime from the refrigerator, his eyes fell on the postcard from Jasper. A few years old now. A sepia-tone image of Jas in a fringed vest, his Wild Bill Hickok goatee graying, and the message "I'm back in NYC, and, for the nonce, this is what I'm doing."

That had been Jas's last stand. His Alamo. Had to lug that oxygen tank everywhere. Called it Trigger.

It pained Kent not to be able to take care of Jasper in his time of need. When Kent had hepatitis, he was in the hospital for a month, his eyes the color of blood oranges. Shivered all the time. Couldn't get warm. So Jasper had crawled into his hospital bed and held him. All night long. Nurses didn't like that. They kept saying, "Sir? Visitors aren't allowed in the beds."

Jasper hissed back, "Haven't you ever been in love?"

1969. Stonewall still months away. Took guts.

I could have died. Didn't realize it. Too young to realize. Jas knew how serious it was. He found Liz's number in my address book and called to prepare her. Didn't tell me until later.

So Liz had known. Jasper had said he was a "friend." But that voice of his. She knew.

Never said a word about it. Nor Roger.

What was that line? In the poem the kid had read?

*I will not entirely die!*

No, not entirely. Just piece by piece.

Kent took his drink back to the living room. Tried to light a cigarette but fumbled it onto his lap. Picked it up. Stuck it in his mouth. Tried the lighter.

Once. Twice.

Why won't this fucker—?

Oh, wrong end.

He lit the cigarette and took a long drag. Exhaled. Just as the record ended, he heard the bathroom door open.

It was clear from the beginning where the night would lead. So why hadn't Eugene seen it? The thing was, he had seen, yet somehow remained blind. Which was like so many things in his life. Like why he wore the white fur coat. And the pink sunglasses. And had an earring. All these things had adhered to him, as though he'd played no part in acquiring them, but who else had acquired them if not him? He'd gone off to college to read the great works of literature and philosophy and to understand himself better, but in the few months he'd been there it was as though some other self had taken residence inside Eugene and was making decisions for him.

He was still bent over the sink. You were supposed to puke in the toilet, but sinks were easier. Just rinse afterward. If stuff got stuck around the drain, take out the plug.

Eugene had experience with situations like this. One time, up at Mr. Baxter's cabin, he'd drunk white wine from a half-empty bottle in the fridge. Tasted sour. He got a killer headache and collapsed on the couch, his gorge rising. R.J. and Mr. Baxter outside somewhere, snowshoeing.

*Should* he use the toilet? The angle would be better. Before he could decide, though, his body spasmed.

Dry heaves. Hurt like a bitch.

Mr. Baxter's cottage wasn't winterized. They could heat only one bedroom, using a space heater. For that reason, the three of them slept in the same bed, R.J. and Mr. Baxter on each side and Eugene, who was the youngest, in the middle.

Another dry heave convulsed him. Then nothing. Was that it? Huh. Surprisingly, he felt somewhat better now. Turned on the tap and splashed water on his face.

And there it was in the mirror: that inscrutable factor. As much time as Eugene spent staring in mirrors, you'd think he'd know what he looked like. But he didn't. It depended. From certain angles he was actually good-looking. But if he adjusted the panels of his parents' three-way mirror to see his profile it was as if this other, commedia dell'arte face leaped out. Scaramouche, the clown.

Was that what he looked like?

It would explain a lot.

For instance, why the ballerina had stood him up. How could a creature like her, so small and perfect, go out with someone partially deformed like Eugene? If Disney made an animated film about them, the animators would render the ballerina as a pretty, long-lashed sea otter, sleekly twirling in the waves, whereas Eugene would be—he didn't know—a South American tapir. How could two such divergent animals ever consort? (The otter lived in the sea, so even if the tapir pursued her he would only drown.) No, the tapir would just be there for comic relief. A sidekick. A sub-plot. He'd get one song, tops.

The first time Eugene had noticed the ballerina was at fresh-man orientation. She was standing apart from everyone else, press-ing her back against the wall, wearing maroon Danskins and pink leg warmers. At the center of the room, Rob, the RA, was dispens-ing info on birth-control availability. While he spoke, the balle-rina kept stretching and limbering up, as though preparing to go onstage.

Other girls thought she put on airs. Well, maybe she did. But so did Eugene. That was a nice way to think about the stuff he did.

He'd attended a dance recital where the ballerina performed. The other dancers were larger and thicker than she was. Better for modern. The ballerina had looked so tiny in comparison—she was like a ballerina on top of a music box.

It was amazing that leotards were legal. The ballerina's nipples were distinctly visible. This was OK, because she was engaged in Art. In the audience, paying close attention, Eugene noticed that the ballerina, for all her delicacy, was perspiring. Probably even smelling a little. She had superdefined muscles in her shoulders and thighs.

Three days later, he saw her crossing the green and got up the courage to tell her how great she'd been. "Thanks!" she said, smiling.

That was when he'd asked her to the movies.

He'd waited outside the theater until the coming attrac-tions started.

But you know what? The ballerina's not showing had done something to Eugene that he must have liked. It didn't feel *good*, exactly, but it was familiar. It felt as if there were a drain inside him, as in a bathtub, and being stood up by the ballerina had pulled the rubber stopper out, so that Eugene's blood drained away. It drained out from a spot right under his armpit and above his ribs—the place of ardor.

Maybe that was his word all along.

Ardor sort of hurt.

The next day, Eugene had put on his fur coat and his new sunglasses and taken the train to New York to spend the weekend at Stigwood's. While there, he'd managed to get trashed enough to put the ballerina out of his mind. But now that he was back in Providence he was thinking about her again. Hoping he wouldn't run into her on campus. Hoping he would.

He stared into the bathroom mirror. His earring glinted; the skin around it looked inflamed.

When he squeezed his lobe, pus ran out.

*That* was attractive.

He clamped a hand towel to his ear. Now that his nausea had subsided, he was just drunk.

He tossed the towel. Didn't even bother to hang it up. Unhooked the hook and lurched out of the bathroom. Back in the living room, he saw his drink. The man sitting in the shadows, smoking, waiting.

Eugene picked up his drink and downed it. Four gulps. Throat-heat immediate. Dizziness.

He lay down on the floor. Right where he was.

There was no use.

No hope.

Something was impelling him. He didn't understand what.

So he lay. And waited.


Kent was about to change the record when the boy came in. Didn't say a word. Just snatched up his drink and dispatched it, before lying on the floor and closing his eyes.

As if following orders.

A voice in Kent's head said, "Put a blanket over him. Let him sleep." Whose voice? Not his. He was in a region beyond words by now. The place he set out to find whenever he was drinking. A land where he could be his true, appetitive self and everything was permitted. He rose unsteadily out of his chair. Crossed to the boy and knelt. With quick fingers, suddenly sure of himself, he undid the boy's belt buckle.

Next his fly. The kid was wearing boxer shorts. Easy off.

And would you look at that! Kid was ready for him. Had wanted this all along.

*Carpe diem*, Horace, honey.

Kent swooped down. No thinking involved. No person, even. No *actor*. Only a headlong descent, as if on prey. But that wasn't right, either. He felt too much tenderness for that. Was it tenderness? Well, he wanted it to be *good*. Wanted the boy to enjoy it and come back for more.

Kent Jeffries was surprised, therefore, when in the middle of his efforts the boy stood up. Got to his feet, coldly, and readjusted his clothes. Didn't so much as look at Kent. Just grabbed his coat and his bag, and strode, with determination, out the front door.

The pain of ardor was duller as he walked uphill. It was cold out. He was sobering up fast. Everything made sense suddenly. He'd been lying on the floor, with his eyes shut, feeling what the man was doing to him while also not feeling it. Not feeling it because (1) he wasn't in his body anymore, and (2) he was in his fourteen-year-old body, while Mr. Baxter was doing the same thing to him. They were alone at the cabin, just the two of them. R.J. had been demoted. Mr. Baxter had demoted him. And Eugene was so happy about that.

It was cold that night, too. Space heater going. Eugene had gone to sleep but, in the middle of the night, felt Mr. Baxter's hand on him, which meant that he must have been awake. Next, Mr. Baxter's head disappeared under the covers. Eugene had expected the usual thing, with his hand, but then he felt the wetness of a mouth. Since Mr. Baxter couldn't see him, Eugene opened his eyes. He made the face he and his friends made whenever something really wild happened. The face he would have made if a girl were doing what Mr. Baxter was doing and he wanted to say, "You guys won't believe what is happening to me right now!"

The memory of that moment filled Eugene's mind, as the man toiled over him. This wasn't at all what Eugene wanted. If he had arrived at the Ebenezer Swampscott house unsure of that, he was unsure no longer. The part of himself that Eugene didn't control had led him here, but now it was as though he could say to that part of himself, "Get out of here! Who put you in charge!" He didn't like his fur coat all that much. He didn't want to mislead people with his earring. He still wanted to write poetry, but that was about it.

Down Benefit Street to Waterman, then up Waterman and through the parking lot, back to his dorm. He was so tired. He wanted to go to bed.

But when he reached his room a surprise greeted him. On his whiteboard was a note from the ballerina. It said, "I'm still up if you want to come by."

When had she written that? What time was it now? Was she still awake?

Difficult to know what had happened. The boy had got scared, or felt guilty. Was it something I? Oh, well. Maybe he had a quiz in the morning.

Nothing to be done but freshen his drink. He banged into the kitchen to effectuate that, then brought his drink back to the living room, where he lit a cigarette, put the phone in his lap, and dialed the number to Jasper's hospital room.

"Hello?"

"Jas!"

"It's almost midnight. I told you not to call after nine."

"I wanted to tell you about a change in my life. A resolution."

"You're drunk," Jasper said.

"I'm not *that* drunk," Kent said. "And, anyway, pot calling the kettle."

"I'm completely sober," Jasper said.

If Jasper had been thirty-eight when they met, that made him fifty-nine now. "Age isn't kind to our kind," he always said. But he didn't mean this. Not death.

"Don't you want to hear my resolution?"

"I'd like to get some sleep. It's impossible in these places."

"I met a boy on the train tonight. Coming back from the city. Brought him back here. He left a few minutes ago."

"You can do whatever you like," Jasper said wearily. "I've got other things to deal with now."

"I didn't touch him, Jas. It was purely platonic. I wanted to tell you that."

"At midnight. You needed to tell me that at midnight."

"Not only that. Also that I was thinking of flying down to see you. When this show's over."

"I'm not ready for my closeup," Jasper said.

"I miss you, Jas." What was this? Tears? He was crying. Oh, God.

Jasper wheezed on the other end. When he spoke, his voice was gentle. "Let's *do*. Let's think about your coming down. When I'm feeling better. I'll have to get a lighting designer in here, so you won't reel back in horror."

"Jas?"

"No more. It's late. Good night, darling."

Kent hung up. Switched off the light. Sat unmoving. What was that sound? Something scratching to be let in. Oh, the record. He needed to lift the needle.

When he got up, he didn't go to the stereo, however. He went back to the kitchen. There was the vodka bottle. There was Jas's postcard. *For the nonce.*

That was all there was. The nonce. And then, Curtain.

Play ice, Kent Jeffries told himself, pouring. Become ice.


The ballerina opened the door.

"My roommate's away," she said.

She didn't mean it like that. She was just explaining why she was up so late playing music.

Erik Satie. Eugene recognized it.

About 1 a.m. at this point.

He stood outside her door, listing to the right. He still had his earring in but had left his coat in his room.

"I've been drinking copious amounts," Eugene said.

"I know. I can smell it."

She invited him in.

A poster for *The Turning Point* hung above her bed. Photos of the ballerina dancing were taped to the wall, along with a framed one on her dresser where she stood beside an old, twisted-up woman in a wheelchair. Her grandmother, maybe.

"Erik Satie," Eugene said. "I love this."

"You know it? Me, too! It's so beautiful!"

Should he sit on her bed? Or was that too suggestive? He didn't want to screw things up. Maybe better just to lean against her roommate's desk.

He was waiting for the ballerina's excuse for not meeting him at the movies. But she seemed to have forgotten. She asked if he wanted tea.

Why had she told him to come by?

Oh, good. He was still drunk enough to ask.

"Why?" the ballerina said. "I felt like talking to you. I can't figure you out. You're strange, but in a good way."

"I've decided to be more normal," Eugene said. "From now on."

"I don't know if you should," the ballerina said.

On second glimpse, the woman in the wheelchair wasn't that old.

The ballerina saw him looking, and said, "That's my mom."

He didn't ask what was wrong. One of those muscle diseases.

No wonder Erik Satie. So beautiful, so sad.

He looked at the other photos. The ballerina at various ages, leaping, pirouetting.

She held up two tea boxes, asking his preference. He chose the box without flowers.

She went out to fill the teakettle. While she was gone, Eugene went over to the photos to scope out her body in detail. He was back in place by the time she returned and plugged the teakettle in.

Say you were a little girl and you took ballet. Maybe your mother forced you. Maybe you thought it was part of being pretty. Or because ballet was a realm that girls dominated. A sport that was also an art, so way better than tennis, or gymnastics. Didn't ballerinas get deformed feet? Wasn't the discipline cruel and unusual? If so, the ballerina was just as brave-hearted as Eugene sensed she was.

"This is weird, but can I see your feet?" he said.

"Excuse me?"

"I want to see if they're all messed up. From dancing."

"They are!" the ballerina said. She seemed excited to show him. She lay down on her bed. Eugene came over to look.

"Pretty ugly," he said. (Not true.)

Then, brave himself, he sat on the bed and started massaging her feet.

"That feels good," the ballerina said. She closed her eyes.

For the next minute they were silent. Eugene started on her other foot.

"Can I ask you something?" the ballerina said. "Are you gay?"

"No," Eugene said.

"Because I was wondering."

"No!" he repeated.

"I wouldn't care," she said.

"I asked you out on a date!" Eugene said.

"That was a date? At the movies?"

"Not a very good one."

"I'm so sorry!" she said. "I thought it was like a bunch of people were meeting."

It didn't matter anymore. He wasn't thinking about that.

He was thinking that dancing wasn't like making a monument in bronze. With dance you did it once, perfectly or not, and then it was gone forever.

Whereas he was too clumsy for that, and so had to sweat and gnaw his mental cuticles.

When she got up to pour the tea, he tried his best. He didn't have a pen handy, so he had to sound it out in his head:

At nine, her mother watches from her wheelchair
As she dips and leaps and pirouettes.
This girl, once curled inside a body
now curling in on itself
has been commissioned, on a patch of floor
in Scarsdale
to move for both of them.

Or something like that. Eugene could see it now. The scene, if not the words. But he could feel them up there, queuing inside his head. He just had to wait and let them out. Then fuss with them until they hardened. Until they weren't going anywhere, anymore.

# *Protozoa*

FROM *New England Review*

ON A THURSDAY in May, Noa ditched her friends after school and jumped in a Lyft with Paddy. She wanted to pet his baby mustache in the back seat of the Kia. Instead she floated her arm out the window and bounced it to the hip-hop leaking from his earbuds. The air was warm and dense and sweat curled in the backs of her knees.

They rode along Venice Boulevard past shaggy stumps of sawed-off palm trees and sun-faded billboards hemmed in graffiti. Noa's friends Wren and Annaliese messaged her from the carpool lineup: *Why the little toad? He'll use you. Roast you.* They sent flame emojis.

Noa turned away from Paddy, just slightly, so he wouldn't see the messages. *Homework at my house,* she replied.

Wren and Annaliese were still preoccupied with complex cake recipes. They fastened back their sleek hair with headbands tricked out in enormous, furred pompoms. To Noa they seemed all parts light, which was good if you could meet them there, in the light, with the horses. Noa had come to feel like another species around them, a graceless mouth-breather. Their distaste for Paddy held no sway with her.

Someday they might understand how it was necessary to take a risk for a boy. Yes, she was afraid. That was the point.

Paddy bowled his backpack down the hall and free-fell onto the couch in Noa's living room. They played and replayed his latest post, a video poking fun at Callan from school. Paddy roasted people online under the name PaDWack. He had built a fan base after winning the school's slam poetry competition. As his rhymes got meaner his followers adored him more intensely.

"This is legit brilliant," Paddy said as he watched himself rap in the school bathroom with his porkpie hat pulled over his eyes:

*Maestro Callan with his hobo pants.*
*Taking a bath in the school trash cans.*
*Today in the lab he gets a nosebleed.*
*Keep off my keys, and stop picking at these* [pointing to his nose].

Callan was an easy target, a loner who used to slide out of his chair and finger his nostrils constantly when they were younger.

"Hobo pants, so true," Paddy said.

"Told you," Noa said. She'd fed him that line about Callan's jeans, which were tattered and torn off at the knee.

"You're wicked, Protozoa."

"Protozoa." She savored the word as she spoke.

"The cells?" Paddy said.

"I know what they are."

In a few weeks they would graduate from the eighth grade at Windsong, where they'd been together since kindergarten. Paddy was set to attend a magnet high school for the highly gifted and sometimes forgot he wasn't smarter than everyone else. Noa was going to the local public school in Venice where her mother said she would develop certain life skills.

Paddy rhymed some more: Noa Noa Protozoa, swervy like a boa. They drifted to her room. A faraway lawnmower churred and sun soaked the window above her bed. That morning she had hidden in the closet a model of Hogwarts castle, forty-six posters of boy bands, a bracelet loom. She had placed on the desk a freakish pencil drawing of her father with distorted features, her best one. Paddy, immersed in his phone, paid no attention to any of it.

Noa grabbed her giant plush crab and nailed him with it.

"Hey!" His hat fell to the floor and he quickly stuffed it back on his head. "You have to respect the lid." Cowlicks made his hair stand in odd clumps. He'd worn a hat to cover it for years, a knit beanie or a bucket hat or his most recent porkpie. At some point he'd become known as Paddington instead of Trevor, his real name.

As he pushed her onto the bed a laugh caught in her throat, her heart beating savagely. He dove next to her and cupped his lips over hers, teeth knocking on teeth. His had white plastic buttons of invisible braces on them. She thought of licking candy dots off long sheets of paper as she'd done on the Santa Monica Pier.

Later she would share details with her new closest friend, Aurora Waters, who had been places with boys already. *It's happening, Aurora,* she nearly blurted out.

Paddy hitched up her tank top, exposing her belly.

"Wait." She drew back.

"I mean. You invited me, Protozoa," he said.

"Fine." She tried to soften her body. His fingers trotted around the hem of her skirt and rolled her blue fishnet tights all the way to her toes. Then her breath was taken, as if she'd slipped into water too deep and dark to touch bottom. She pressed her nose against lip hair and groped the twiney muscles of his arms. His tongue slid along her face to her ear.

"Don't," she said when he rooted a thumb under her panties. It was like being jarred from a dream. Her bralette had been pushed up so she covered herself with the plush crab.

"That's booey," he complained and then collapsed facedown on the covers. Without a shirt he appeared much smaller. He had the fragile shoulders of a child.

"Stop looking at me," he said.

"I wasn't."

His stomach rumbled. "You have any of that truffle-up-agus your mama makes?" Without waiting for an answer he skidded down the hall to the kitchen.

A moment later Noa's arms and legs still hummed, as if her own daring produced an electrical charge. Things had gone almost exactly as she'd hoped or probably better. She took a blast of selfies to document: pouting, mouth slack, wide-eyed.

*I did it,* she messaged Aurora Waters. Fat-tongue emoji.

As Paddy rattled kitchen drawers down the hall, Noa thumbed through her phone. Her mother had just posted a photo of rabbit roulade plated with smashed root vegetables. The photo was poorly cropped, with her mother's freckled arm in the background. Noa commented under the photo #MR, short for Mother Rabbit. Her mother would reply much later with a winking emoji.

Noa's parents opened the restaurant Jenney together a few

months before, but her mother was the force behind it. She'd had the investors for dinner, charmed them with her food. Noa's father never would have gone to the effort, he said. Before they had the space, they'd catered office lunches out of a truck and her father seemed satisfied with that.

The restaurant was a dozen blocks from their house in Mar Vista. In the late afternoons Noa's father rode his bicycle home to check on her. Most often he stole some time to sun his broad back on the patio. He would pore over books with pages thin as tissue paper; he called them a "compendium of philosophies." Or, he would strike up a conversation with the neighbor Sharn over a fence that pitched heavily toward her yard. They would chat about her tomato plants and David Hockney and the eyesore McMansion going up across the street. Sharn was retired, a widow, and always seemed to have an ear for Noa's father.

"Shouldn't you be getting back?" Noa said once as the sun edged behind Sharn's roofline.

"Soonish," her father said as he clapped at a bug tickling his neck.

"You should go now," Noa sang as she walked down the hall. Take-out boxes littered the kitchen counter, emptied of rabbit sausage and fritters with chunks of pear. Paddy had flung open the French doors to the yard and wandered with a box in hand.

"This is bomb," he said, sucking dramatically on a fork dipped in yellow custard.

"Spoonbread," she said. People called it a drug. She slipped into her mother's clogs and joined him outside. The brick patio was edged in nasturtium with flat round leaves like lily pads. Her father's surfboards leaned against the tilting fence.

Paddy offered a nibble but Noa pushed it away.

"Should we take a picture together?" she said.

He shook his head and handed her the fork and box. Then he pulled out his phone and scrolled down a feed of photos. "Your mama's getting mad famous. You call her MR?"

Noa's face went hot. He had found her mother's post. "Mother Rabbit. Boring. Don't follow her or anything."

"But that's catchy."

Paddy's mother walked with a limp, thick ankles ending in

spreading flat shoes. She was no one interesting. Paddy liked to say that he was adopted, that his real parents were famous actors in other parts of the world. He looked enough like his mother that he couldn't be believed. For a while his lies caught up with him at school, but he saved himself with his PaDWack roasts.

"Rabbit," Paddy said as they walked inside. "Bunny. Huh."

"It's popular in Europe and the South." Noa tossed the empty box in the sink. She didn't mention that he'd eaten some.

They moved to the front door, noses in phones. He typed something and Noa's phone buzzed. He had messaged her: *300 likes for nosebleed von hobo pants.*

*If you roast me, better make me look good,* she replied. She remembered that he'd made up a rhyme for their music teacher Inez, a "siren with all guns firin'." After he posted it all the boys began to fawn over her. *Like Inez,* she added.

*No promises,* Paddy replied. *Whims.* He leaned into her as if he would kiss her goodbye but instead he flicked her breast.

*What the fuck, Paddington!* He disappeared into another car, leaving her staring after him until she saw spots.

When he was gone Noa burrowed into the jumble of relics on her closet floor. She balanced her laptop on flattened posters and the backs of doll bodies and sought out Aurora Waters. *Can you chat?*

Aurora was older, in high school on the other side of the city in Hollywood. She had boasted of her own encounters with boys, insisted that she'd felt a "magic ripple." They had met online after Noa set up a new account. She projected a mood using carefully selected images: a series of a healing bruise, a collapsed building in the aftermath of an earthquake, the peculiar drawing of her father.

*Dark heart?* Aurora had written her, introducing herself. Noa did feel at times exactly as Aurora said. Images that used to make her happy now made her wince: shaved ice doused in rainbow syrup and a hedgehog so small it slept in a teacup. She didn't want to adore those things again, but nothing yet had taken their place.

Aurora popped up on Noa's screen in the middle of a yawn. Her hair, which was dyed blue, was pinched into a nest on her head.

"I hooked up with Paddy," Noa said. "The one with the hat?"

"Yeah, I saw the message. The rhymer," Aurora said.

"It's fun but kind of like drowning."

"Did he shove his tongue in your mouth?"

Noa nodded. "I see why you call it magic."

"So you liked it." Aurora peered into the camera as if it would help her suss out the truth. Her skin was pale and even, heavily powdered.

"He took my tights off," Noa said.

"You didn't let him bone, though."

"No, no, no."

"Good, because then you give up any power you have. At all."

"Have you tasted plastic braces?"

"I didn't think you would do it," Aurora said.

A hoarse woman's voice hollered on Aurora's end, bags and keys settling on the counter. Aurora walked to her bedroom door, put her ear against it and slid the chain lock. In slim black overalls she could have been six feet tall. She'd written on the pockmarked walls, in Sharpie, words from one of her favorite trip-hop songs: *Ride the Night. Liberate your heart.*

The most exotic thing was that Aurora went out as she pleased any night of the week, hopped into a hired car and roamed the hills above the Sunset Strip and the bluffs in Pacific Palisades. Noa's favorite picture of Aurora was taken on those bluffs. With crazy eyes she pretended she was about to jump off the edge of an overlook, like the ocean was a trampoline she could bounce on.

Aurora sat in front of the camera again. "You don't seem sad today," she said, pulling a thumbtack out of a plastic breath-mints case. Her cuticles had been eaten away. "I have to hurry."

It was their secret ritual to watch each other cry. Aurora said that sharing tears was a high and a release. In Japan, she said, entire rooms full of grown men bawled together.

"Well, Paddy was in my bedroom just now," Noa said. "It's playing in my head like a movie."

"Yesterday you even said how fucked up the world is. Remember the starving dogs that no one loves?"

Noa nodded and sniffed her old dolls, molded plastic faces and synthetic hair.

"Or think about this," Aurora said. "What if it never rains again? It won't, I bet."

Aurora scratched at the inside of her arm with the thumbtack. She whimpered and her mouth twitched. The tics of emotion were familiar to Noa though they'd only known each other for two weeks.

Aurora stopped herself and cleared her throat. "If you can't be deep, it's not helpful," she said. "There's nothing I get from it."

Noa crumpled her face as if she could trick herself, but failed. Aurora cried steadily for three minutes and then snapped from it like a switch had been hit.

Late-afternoon fog nuzzled the house, casting Noa's room in darkness. From inside the closet, she heard the clicks of her father's bicycle spokes and the creak of the gate.

His flip-flops slapped against the kitchen floor. "Noa!"

She scurried down the hall.

"What's this mess?" He swatted a takeout box into the sink. A sweat stain bloomed over his heart on a threadbare T-shirt. The chef's jacket her mother had ordered for him was probably rumpled and stuffed into his backpack.

"Well, I ate already," Noa said. "So I'm not hungry."

"You ate everything? Not buying it."

"I had a homework group after school." She nudged a crumb along the floor. "They love the food."

He raked his whiskers. "Didn't we say no friends when you're alone?"

"I won't do it again. I'll FaceTime with you at the restaurant, I swear," Noa said.

"Nobody wants Roberta back," her father said. Roberta, the old babysitter, had taught him how to track Noa on his phone even though he claimed he wouldn't do it. Noa had persuaded her parents to let go of Roberta when they opened a restaurant so close to home.

"No one in eighth grade has a babysitter," Noa said. "Aren't *you* my supervisor now?"

"Aye. But this is a trial run." He narrowed his eyes at her then walked over to the French doors and rested his forehead against the glass. "Let's go surfing," he said. "Tomorrow, before school."

"I got pounded last time. And there's so much trash."

He looked at her. "If we see animals, that'll be worth it. Dolphins? Maybe a ray?" He tapped on the window.

Noa's father tried to coax her outside once in a while. On a recent afternoon he'd begged her to draw a portrait of him while sitting on towels in the yard. It was awkward to stare at her father, so she didn't try to get a realistic drawing. Instead she gave him broken and misshapen teeth and made his whiskers a long, braided beard.

"I like this," he'd said, leaning back on his hands. "You're off the phone, doing something in the actual world."

"The actual world?" she'd said as she exaggerated the hollows under his eyes. On paper he was a hillbilly tweaker.

"Yeah. You know." He leaned over and tore a leaf off the nasturtium and waved it in her face. Then he ate it. He might have understood that her world was entirely different, but he was romantic about what could be touched and tasted.

Paddy posted a new roast that evening during peak hours. In the video he chanted:

> *Noa Noa Protozoa.*
> *Bish hungry so get out your boa* [grabbing his crotch].
> *Form a line at the doa.*
> *But Harry Poe-tare not welcome anymoa.*

After his rap, he flashed his nipples. He'd taped over them two photos of protozoa, glassy and oval as seen through a microscope.

*Delete!!!* She messaged him. *I'm a hungry bish? You're the most hungry.*

*But it's about you. My muse,* he replied. Four emoji faces laughing so hard they were crying. *You asked for it, Proto.*

A ball of sickness formed, swelled against her ribs. She messaged Aurora: *P did it. Roasted me. So bad, right?*

Her phone pulsed with new people wanting to follow her. They'd jumped from Paddy's video to her accounts. Not strangers, really, because she had heard of them loosely. They were curious, of course. She added them all as followers.

*Want someone to call me hungry,* Aurora messaged an hour later. *You get all the attention.*

*Makes me look desperate,* Noa replied. Cracked-heart emoji.

*He likes you.*

*OK.*

*The titties though. So juvenile.*

By eleven the rhyme had more than four hundred views and Noa was being called *dirty ho*, being sent pictures of body parts that looked like cutaways from porn. Dick pics were normal but she'd never been flooded with so many. She was sure the people calling her names were jealous. Words were always thrown at girls looking to be wild. The smartest girls, the girls Noa admired most online, just ignored them as if they didn't matter.

*Protozoa.* Aurora messaged. *What do you think he'd call me?*

*A-snore-a. No. A-whore-a.*

*Ha. Cruel.*

"Noa," her mother called gently, poking her head into the room. Noa shoved her phone under the mattress. Her mother crept in and lowered herself onto the bed, swung a bare, dimpled leg over Noa's body.

Noa groaned. "I don't want to talk about food," she said.

Her mother sighed like she'd been wounded, but she didn't go away. Noa took her mother's hand and guided it to her own back. Her mother began to scratch.

"Tell me again," Noa said. "The first boy you liked. Wasn't he New Wave or Mod?"

"He rode a Vespa," her mother said. "Gunter. He had those thin suspenders."

Noa looked up at the ceiling. She tried to imagine her mother on the back of a scooter, bare-skinned knees darting through cars.

Her mother gathered Noa's hair and fanned it across her back. "Daddy's panicking. He wants you to stop wearing those stockings."

"The fishnets? What else did he say?"

"Well, they're provocative. It makes him uncomfortable, and he can't say that to you."

"Stop!"

"Listen," her mother said. "I told him that's not how you raise an empowered woman. I'm not having any part of it."

Noa pulled her mother's arm tight around her. "He's so lost."

"He doesn't know what a girl's like." Her mother pressed her cheek against Noa's back.

Noa sensed there was more to her father than that, acting like he had nothing to do in the afternoons. Tanning, chatting up Sharn. She stayed silent. It seemed dangerous to mention those things, as if that would turn them into real problems.

The next morning Noa walked through the elementary playground in long strides, the low angle of morning sun at her back.

Finger paintings dried on clotheslines. She bobbed under them, passed the soft rubber slopes and the climbing structure with a sail hoisted high like a ship. Either Windsong had shrunk overnight or she had grown into a giantess.

In the middle school building Paddy waited for her at her locker surrounded by his baller friends. Everyone could see that he liked her, the way he stood there waiting. She threw her shoulders back.

"Protozoa," he said, making his friends snicker. His fists were thrust deep in his pockets and he waggled them. "Under the bleachers at lunch?"

"If I have time," she said to be aloof.

All morning her insides lifted and turned as though she'd swallowed hundreds of moths. *Hooking up at school,* she messaged Aurora from the bathroom under the stairwell. It was the only bathroom on campus with total privacy, a locking door.

Aurora FaceTimed her right away. "Why?" She was hiding in a stall at her own school, whispering. "Don't be so public with it."

"I thought you said this was good."

"You're getting played." Aurora gnawed on her fingers.

There was a knock at the door and Noa hung up. She was done listening anyway.

In the hallway between classes, people walking behind Noa broke into a murmur of "Pro-to-zo-a." Boys snapped the waistbands on their Dri-FIT shorts. The attention made her flush but she didn't mind it. No other couple had started with any kind of sensation.

At lunch Paddy was not in the gym as planned. Noa roamed the school, checking the computer lab and the music studio. She saw Wren and Annaliese in the room where a nursery had been set up for teachers' babies. They each held an infant on one hip. When they caught Noa looking in at them the pity that came across their faces made her seethe. She'd deleted their messages that morning: *Toad called you a slut. Told you.* What if Paddy roasted them next, she thought. They could be joined twins, sharing one brain.

On the yard the *Rent*-heads had taken over the climbing structure. They swayed and sang "Aquarius," warming up for that night's performance of the musical *Hair* in the school theater.

Noa covered her ears and circled back to the gym, where Paddy's friends Asher and Finn sat on the floor. They maneuvered basketballs under bent knees and tipped potato chip dust into their mouths.

"He got called to the office," Finn said. "Had to go on leave. For a week."

"He left with his mommy," Asher said, and belched.

The thought made her shiver. "He was sent home for a nose-bleed rhyme?" Noa said. "People are too sensitive."

The boys looked at each other.

"You snitched," Finn said. "It was the Protozoa."

Noa's mouth dropped open. "I would never. I told him to do it."

"Snitch." Finn lobbed his basketball at her. She dodged it and ran across the campus to the school theater.

The dressing room was dark and swampy with costumes. Noa dropped into a heap of tie-dyed shirts. *I said nothing!* She messaged Paddy. *Want spoonbread? I'll send some. Postmates.*

Fatal, black hole of no reply.

She saw that the PaDWack account and all of his rhymes had been erased.

*He's gone,* she messaged Aurora. *Fuck my life.* Smoking gun emoji. She folded her knees to her chest. *Can you?* Crying-face emoji, blue-face emoji. She took a raggedy breath.

"Are you going to cry?" a voice said. She shrieked. It was Callan, nestled in a corner.

"Don't sneak up on me like that," she said.

"This is my perch," he said, bugging his eyes.

"His phone was taken," she said. "Paddy's. I feel bad now."

"Poor baby," Callan whined, batting a ballet shoe across the room. "When he's back I'm going to tackle him and blow snot all over his hat."

Noa cringed. "You saw the roast."

"I tried not to," he said. "'Cause I think the internet's garbage. But my sister follows him."

His sister, who was Aurora's age, had sent Noa a follow request in the night.

"Then he burned you too, calling you amoeba or some crud," Callan said.

"I know, but. It's a little different when he teases me."

Callan laughed so hard he held his stomach.

*Just deal,* Aurora messaged.

"Maybe your sister knows my friend. She lives near you." Noa showed him a photo of Aurora: halter top, pale hollowed waist, and pants that pooled at her feet. "Works at Vintage Cache on Melrose?"

"That goon?" He grabbed her phone away. "She's around. If you want to see her, the actual person, I know the spot." He said Friday nights an army of kids invaded a construction site off Sunset. He would take Noa if she could get across town.

*You going out to the spot?* She messaged Aurora. *You have to!! We can chill.*

All of the online girls Noa admired most said that strong eyebrows were critical to the face. In the vanity mirror on top of her desk she brushed and gelled her brows. Soon she would meet Aurora Waters at a secret spot. She was closer than ever to the future she wanted to have.

She had FaceTimed her father, so he could see that she was alone at home. She'd convinced him not to bother with her, said she'd be attending the school's production of *Hair* that evening with Wren and Annaliese. He said that she was making a good choice and he was glad for it. His words felt right, even though she'd misled him. She *was* making a good choice. She borrowed from her parents' closet a vintage Dodgers jersey, Valenzuela, and wore it as a dress with the fishnets and gold ankle socks and her creepers with platform soles.

In her frenzy to put herself together, Noa stopped thinking so much about Paddy. She was surprised when, on her way out the door, she received a message from him.

*Look what I found,* he wrote. He attached a video of her mother, an instructional on how to butcher a rabbit. The video was one in a series produced by a farm collective her parents belonged to. Noa had completely forgotten about it.

In the video her mother cuddled a spotted rabbit to her chest, then held it out and stretched its legs. Next her mother stood over a slaughtered animal, guiding the viewer through the separating of its parts. Wide smile, arms glistening. She was completely absorbed.

*Bunny killa,* Paddy wrote.

*Just like pigs and cows and . . . ,* Noa started to type. She deleted it. Too much effort was required to explain her mother's thoughts about rabbit: the versatile flavor, the small impact on the earth.

In fact her mother looked demented in that video. It was shot during her mohawk phase. She'd since grown her hair in on the sides.

*She's a chef. What does your mom do?*

She would let him hang there. His mother couldn't compare with hers.


Callan waited for her on the corner of Sunset and Doheny in front of a liquor store. "The spot!" He pointed uphill and they began to climb. It was dusk and billboard lights began to flip on, washing color out of the sky.

A canteen swung from Callan's shoulder. "My grandpa's, from Nam," he said. When they were far enough above Sunset he offered her a chug. "Jack and coke."

She coughed and her eyes watered but she drank again.

He gave her a military salute.

"Don't be hyper," she said.

"I haven't been in three years."

They meandered past steep driveways that led to homes built into the craggy hillside, homes on stilts.

"Freedom!" Callan yelled, spinning with his arms skyward.

Noa copied him but got dizzy.

They came to a chain-link fence that had been pushed down between drooping eucalyptus. Callan boosted her over and upslope they clambered, through spindly trees that had dropped a carpet of needles. A girl's laughter carried down the hill. *Come on,* the laughter said. *Hurry.*

*A, are you at the spot?*

Noa's insides were churning when they arrived at a place where the hillside had been flattened and cleared. In the near-dark she made out kids pushing each other in shopping carts across the dusty lot. Others had climbed on the Porta-Potties and hung upside down from them taking selfies.

"When security comes you have to just—" Callan said, thrusting a fist toward the trees. He led her to the opposite end of the lot, where kids lolled on a tarp fastened over a mountain of gravel. Smoke ribboned upward from them.

"Bruddah!" a girl called out in a taunting voice. Callan's sister, who called herself EmZee online. He scaled the tarp and sat next to her.

"Where's Aurora?" Noa said. She pulled herself up next to Callan.

He took a black pen from EmZee and sucked, then expelled vapor with a practiced flourish. "Juul," he said. "You want?"

Noa shook her head but took a hefty swallow from his canteen. She shuddered. A swarm of city lights below seemed to move, like they'd let go of whatever held them to earth.

"She's the one in that rhyme," Callan said to EmZee, hanging a thumb at Noa. "I told you."

"Hey, I follow you now," EmZee said.

Noa nodded.

"Follow back."

"Yeah, OK." Noa found the girl on her phone and sent a follow request.

Callan pulled his T-shirt over his knees, over the torn-apart jeans, and rested his head on them. His cheekbone was sprayed with acne, his Converse gaped at the toes as if his feet were growing right in front of her.

"Come on, I want a ride in a shopping cart," Noa said.

"PaDWack?" EmZee said. "He slays me every day." She leafed through her phone. "Look, he posted again."

"Can't be," Noa said. "I've been checking."

"There's a new account," EmZee said. "Padman."

Noa leaned in to watch Paddy, who jeered at the camera:

*You know Protozoa.*
*She's hungry as fark.*
*She eats bunny rabbit.*
*She's just like a shark.*
*She eats hobo meat straight up in the dark.*

"Turn it off!" Noa said. She closed her eyes and pressed on the lids. "Trash talker."

EmZee latched on to Noa's hand to console her, but then she laughed. "Who eats bunnies? He's so full of shit."

Noa couldn't say anything, couldn't move. The drink in her belly riled, torching her throat and her nose. She was punched right through the middle, drained.

"You're the hobo, you know," EmZee said to Callan.

"Who cares," Callan said. "Horse's muff."

"None of that's true," Noa said.

She wondered how Paddy knew they were together, there at the spot. Someone had taken their picture or tagged her. She looked around. Nobody seemed to be watching her.

*Why do you hate me?* She messaged Paddy.

*No hate. So easy to mess with Proto.*

*You'll be kicked out.*

*I got free speech rights. My mama will sue.*

She messaged Aurora: *Where are you? P roasted me again.* Red-face emoji. Tornado emoji.

Rays of orange light rotated across the lot. "Shit. Rent-a-cops," Callan said. Noa skittered behind him to the trees where they'd come in. He took off ahead of her, nimble in the brush. She half-crawled downhill all the way to Sunset.

From the Lyft home, Noa tried to FaceTime Aurora Waters.

*Not picking up,* Aurora messaged.

*OK, love you,* Noa replied.

She waited a minute.

*Why not?* Noa messaged.

*Too much babyness.*

*No! I was at the spot. I got drunk as fuck, A.*

*I don't even go there.*

Noa checked all of Aurora's accounts. In the last few hours Aurora had found online a new favorite person, Rileyyy424, who was shown in a scruffy animal costume with matted fur and ears. Looked like she'd slept outside in it. Aurora had liked and commented on all of Rileyyy424's posts. There was nothing special about that girl.

The next minutes blurred together. Noa got to her bedroom without speaking to her father, who was laughing in the yard with Sharn. She hid away in the closet with her laptop and trained its camera on herself. She was already swallowing hard over the lump but quickly drew cat eyes with a soft and runny liner. Then she hit record.

She didn't need to wind doll hair around her finger to get started. Her eyes became wet easily. Tears traced the contours of her cheeks, dragging black makeup. She watched herself in the monitor, sobbing freely in her own company. She went on until she was completely emptied.

Then Noa played back the entire video. The first flash of pain in her face was the most impossible not to watch. She cut the video to a continuous three-second loop: tears forming, crawling, repeat. The video made the hair on her arms stand up.

She posted the loop on all her online accounts. *A, made a crying GIF. Check it out.*

She waited for something to happen.

Her father rapped at her bedroom door.

"Hold on!" she said. She would have to face him. She thought he was desperate, to seek the friendship of an old woman. Her Mother Rabbit had become too much for him, with ambitions too massive.

Seconds later one of the girls who followed Noa, one of her new friends, posted a video of herself crying with a bloated nose and a chin dripping with tears. Another crying video popped up, and another. A face with makeup-dotted zits, a tongue coated in white scum, lips stretching to bare teeth with metal braces, a set of knuckles with H-A-R-M drawn on them.

Her father rapped again. She must come out now, he said. She was in all kinds of trouble.

"Privacy! Please!"

Ten crying girls. Twenty. It was as though they'd all been waiting for Noa, full of feelings that no one else wanted to deal with. They were right behind her. So many that the echo of sobs was almost unbearable. Gathering momentum, they pushed outward like a tide.

NICOLE KRAUSS

# Seeing Ershadi

FROM *The New Yorker*

I'D BEEN IN the company for more than a year by then. It had been my dream to dance for the choreographer since I first saw his work, and for a decade all my desire had been focused on getting there. I'd sacrificed whatever was necessary during the years of rigorous training. When at last I auditioned and he invited me to join his company, I dropped everything and flew to Tel Aviv. We rehearsed from noon to five, and I devoted myself to the choreographer's process and vision without reserve, applied myself without reserve. Sometimes tears came spontaneously, from something that had rushed upward and burst. When I met people in bars and cafés, I spoke excitedly about the experience of working with the choreographer and told them that I felt I was constantly on the verge of discovery. Until one day I realized that I had become fanatical—that what I had taken for devotion had crossed the line into something else. And though my awareness of this was a dark blot on what had been, up to then, a pure joy, I didn't know what to do with it.

Exhausted after rehearsal, I'd either walk to the sea or go home to watch a film until it got late enough to go out and meet people. I couldn't go to the beach as often as I'd have liked, because the choreographer said that he wanted the skin all over our bodies to be as white as the skin on our asses. I'd developed tendinitis in my ankle, which made it necessary for me to ice it after dancing, and so I found myself watching a lot of films lying on my back with my foot up. I saw everything with Jean-Louis Trintignant, until he got so old that his imminent death began to be too depress-

ing, and then I switched to Louis Garrel, who is beautiful enough
to live forever. Sometimes, when my friend Romi wasn't working,
she came to watch with me. By the time I finished with Garrel it
was winter, and swimming was out of the question anyway, so I
spent two weeks inside with Ingmar Bergman. When the New Year
started, I resolved to give up Bergman and the weed I smoked every night, and, because the title was appealing and it was made far
from Sweden, I downloaded *Taste of Cherry*, by the Iranian director
Abbas Kiarostami.

The film opens with the actor Homayoun Ershadi's face. He
plays Mr. Badii, a middle-aged man driving slowly through the
streets of Tehran in search of someone, scanning crowds of men
clamoring to be hired for labor. Not finding what he's looking for,
he drives on, into the arid hills outside the city. When he sees a
man on the edge of the road, he slows the car and offers him a
ride; the man refuses, and when Badii continues to try to convince
him the man gets angry and stalks off, looking back darkly over
his shoulder. After more driving, five or seven minutes of it—an
eternity in a film—a young soldier appears, hitchhiking, and Badii
offers him a ride to his barracks. He begins to question the boy
about his life in the army and his family in Kurdistan, and the
more personal and direct the questions are the more awkward the
situation becomes for the soldier, who is soon squirming in his
seat. Some twenty minutes into the film, Badii finally comes out
with it: he's searching for someone to bury him. He's dug his own
grave into the side of one of those bone-dry hills, and tonight he
plans to take pills and lie down in it; all he needs is for someone
to come in the morning to check that he's really dead, and then to
cover him with twenty shovelfuls of earth.

The soldier opens the car door, leaps out, and flees into the
hills. What Mr. Badii is asking amounts to being an accomplice
to a crime, since suicide is forbidden in the Quran. The camera
gazes after the soldier as he grows smaller and smaller until he
disappears altogether into the landscape, then it returns to Ershadi's extraordinary face, a face that remains almost completely
expressionless throughout the film, and yet manages to convey a
gravity and a depth of feeling that could never come from acting—
that can come only from an intimate knowledge of what it is to be
pushed to the brink of hopelessness. Not once in the film are we
told anything about the life of Mr. Badii, or what might have led

him to decide to end it. Nor do we witness his despair. Everything we know about the depth contained within him we get from his face, which also tells us about the depth contained within the actor Homayoun Ershadi, about whose life we know even less. When I did a search, I discovered that Ershadi was an architect with no training or experience as an actor when Kiarostami saw him sitting in his car in traffic, lost in thought, and knocked on his window. And it was easy to understand just by looking at his face: how the world seemed to bend toward Ershadi as if it needed him more than he needed it.

His face did something to me. Or, rather, the film, with its compassion and its utterly jarring ending, which I won't give away, did something to me. But, then again, you could also say that, in some sense, the film was only his face: his face and those lonely hills.

Not long after that, it became warm again. When I opened the windows, the smell of cats came in, but also of sunshine, salt, and oranges. Along the wide streets, the ficus trees showed new green. I wanted to take something from this renewal, to be a small part of it, but the truth was that my body was increasingly run-down. My ankle was getting worse the more I danced on it, and I was going through a bottle of Advil a week. When it was time for the company to go on tour again, I didn't feel like going, even though it was to Japan, where I'd always wanted to travel. I wanted to stay and rest and feel the sun, I wanted to lie on the beach with Romi and smoke and talk about boys, but I packed my bag and rode with a couple of the other dancers to the airport.

We had three performances in Tokyo, followed by two free days, and a group of us decided to go to Kyoto. It was still winter in Japan. On the train from Tokyo, heavy tile roofs went by, houses with small windows. We found a *ryokan* to stay at, with a room done up with tatami mats and shoji panels, and walls the color and texture of sand. Everything struck me as incomprehensible; I constantly made mistakes. I wore the special bathroom slippers out of the bathroom and across the room. When I asked the woman who served us an elaborate dinner what happened if something was spilled on the tatami mat, she began to scream with laughter. If she could have fallen off her seat, she would have. But the room had no seats at all. Instead, she stuffed the wrapping for my hot towel into the gaping sleeve of her kimono, but very beautifully, so that one could forget the fact that she was disposing of garbage.

On our last morning in Japan, I got up early and went out with a map, on which I had marked the temples I wanted to visit. Everything was still stripped and bare. Not even the plum trees were in blossom yet, so there was nothing to bring out the hordes with their cameras, and I'd got used to being mostly alone in the temples and the gardens, and to a silence that was only deepened by the loud cawing of crows. So it was a surprise when, having passed through the monumental entrance gate of Nanzen-ji, I ran into a large group of Japanese women chatting happily in singsong fashion on the covered walkway that led to the abbot's residence. They were all outfitted in elegant silk kimonos, and everything about them, from the ornate inlaid combs in their hair to their gathered obi belts and their patterned drawstring purses, was of another age. The only exception was the dull-brown slippers on their feet, the same kind offered at the entrance of every temple in Kyoto, all of which were tiny and reminded me of the shoes that Peter Rabbit lost in the lettuce patch. I'd tried them myself the day before, shoving my feet into them and gripping with my toes while attempting to slide across the smooth wooden floors, but, after almost breaking my neck trying to climb stairs in them, I'd given up and taken to walking across the icy planks in my socks. This made it impossible to ever get warm, and, shivering in my sweater and coat, I wondered how the women didn't freeze wearing only silk, and whether assistance was needed to tie and wrap and secure all the necessary parts of their kimonos.

Without noticing, bit by bit I'd worked my way into the center of the group, so that when suddenly the women began to move in unison, as if in response to some secret signal, I was swept along, down the wide and dim open-air corridor, carried by the flow of silk and the hurried pitter-patter of tiny slippers. About twenty feet down the walkway, the group came to a halt and spat out from its amoeba-like body a woman dressed in normal street clothes, who now began to address the others. By standing on my tiptoes, I could just see over the women's heads to the four-hundred-year-old Zen garden that was one of the most famous in all of Japan. A Zen garden, with its raked gravel and precise minimum of rocks, bushes, and trees, is meant not to be entered but to be contemplated from the outside, and just beyond where the group had stopped was the empty portico designed for this. But when I tried to make my way out by tapping shoulders and asking to be excused, the group seemed only to tighten around me. Whomever I tapped would turn to me with a bewildered look, and take a few quick little steps to the left or the right so that I could pass, but immediately another woman in a kimono would flow in to fill the void, either out of an innate instinct to correct the group's balance or just to get closer to the tour guide. Enclosed on all sides, breathing in the dizzying stench of perfume, and listening to the guide's relentlessly incomprehensible explanations, I began to feel claustrophobic. But before I could try to elbow my way out more violently, the women suddenly started to move again, and by flattening myself against the wall of the abbot's residence I managed to stay put, forcing them to move around me. They crossed the wooden floor in a chorus of scuffling slippers.

It was then that I saw him making his way along the covered walkway in the opposite direction. He looked older, and his wavy hair had turned silver, making his dark eyebrows seem even more severe. Something else was different, too. In the film, it had been absolutely necessary to project an impression of his physical solidity, which Kiarostami had done by keeping the camera closely trained on his broad shoulders and strong torso as he drove through the hills outside Tehran. But even when Ershadi had got out of the car to gaze at the arid hills and the camera had hung back at a distance, he'd appeared physically formidable, and this had given him an authority that, combined with the depth of feeling in his eyes, had made me want to weep. But, as he continued down the covered walkway, Ershadi looked almost slender. He'd lost weight, but it was more than that: it seemed that the width of his shoulders had contracted. Now that I was seeing him from behind, I began to doubt that it was Ershadi. But just as disappointment began to pour into me like concrete, the man stopped and turned, as if someone had called to him. He stood very still, looking back at the Zen garden, where the stones were meant to symbolize tigers, leaping toward a place they would never reach. A soft light fell on his expressionless face. And there it was again: the brink of hopelessness. At that moment, I was filled with such an overwhelmingly tender feeling that I can only call it love.

Gracefully, Ershadi turned the corner. Unlike me, he had no trouble moving in those slippers.

I started to go after him, but one of the kimonoed women blocked my path. She was waving and gesturing at the group, which was now peering into one of the shadowy rooms of the abbot's house. I don't speak Japanese, I explained, trying to get around her, but she kept hopping in front of me, gibbering away and pointing with more and more insistence at the group, which had now begun to move down the hall toward the anterior garden —move with an almost imperceptible shuffle of their combined feet, as if, in fact, thousands of ants were carrying them along. I'm not with the tour, I said, making a little cross with my wrists, which I had seen the Japanese do when they wanted to signal that something was wrong, or not possible, or even forbidden. I was just on my way out, I said, and pointed toward the exit with the same insistence with which the woman in the kimono was pointing at the group.

She grabbed my elbow and was trying to pull me forcibly back in the other direction. Maybe I had upset the delicate balance of the whole, a balance determined by subtleties that I, in my foreignness, would never understand. Or perhaps I had committed an unpardonable act by leaving the group. Again I had a feeling of impenetrable ignorance, which for me will always be synonymous with traveling in Japan. Sorry, I said, but I really have to go now, and, with a tug more violent than I'd intended, I freed myself of her hand and jogged toward the exit. But when I turned the corner there was no sign of Ershadi. The reception area was vacant except for the Japanese women's shoes lined up on old wooden shelves. I ran outside and looked around, but the temple grounds were occupied only by large crows, which took clumsily to the sky as I ran past.

Love: I can only call it that, however different it was from every other instance of love that I had experienced. What I knew of love had always stemmed from desire, from the wish to be altered or thrown off course by some uncontrollable force. But in my love for Ershadi I nearly didn't exist beyond that great feeling. To call it compassion makes it sound like a form of divine love, and it wasn't that; it was terribly human. If anything, it was an animal love, the love of an animal that has been living in an incomprehensible world until one day it encounters another of its kind and realizes that it has been applying its comprehension in the wrong place all along.

It sounds far-fetched, but at that moment I had the feeling that I could save Ershadi. Still running, I passed under the monumental wooden gate and my footfalls echoed up in the rafters. A sense of fear began to seep in, fear that he planned to take his life just like the character he'd barely played, and that I had lost the brief chance I'd been given to intercede. When I reached the street it was deserted. I turned in the direction that led to the famous pathway alongside the narrow river and ran, my bag slapping against my thigh. What would I have said to him if I had caught up to him? What would I have asked him about devotion? What was it that I wanted to be when he turned and at last his gaze fell upon me? It didn't matter, because when I came around the bend the path was empty, the trees black and bare. Back at the *ryokan,* hunched on the tatami floor, I searched online, but there was no news about Homayoun Ershadi, nothing to suggest that he was traveling in Japan, or no longer alive.

My doubt only grew on the flight back to Tel Aviv. The plane glided above a great shelf of cloud, and the farther it got from Japan the less possible it seemed that the man had actually been Ershadi, until at last it seemed absurd, just as kimonos and Japanese toilets and etiquette and tea ceremonies, which had all possessed irrevocable genius in Kyoto, at a distance grew absurd.

The night after I got back to Tel Aviv, I met Romi at a bar. I told her about what had happened in Japan, but in a laughing way: laughing at myself for believing for even a moment that it was actually Ershadi I'd seen and run after. As I told the story, her large eyes became larger. With all the drama of the actress that she is, Romi lifted a hand to her heart and called the waiter to refill her glass, touching his shoulder in the instinctive way she has of drawing others into her world, under the spell of her intensity. Eyes locked with mine, she removed her cigarettes from her bag, lit one, and inhaled. She reached across the table and laid her hand over my hand. Then she tilted her chin and blew out the smoke, all without breaking her gaze.

I don't believe it, she said at last in a throaty whisper. The exact same thing happened to me.

I began to laugh again. Crazy things were always happening to Romi: her life was swept along by an endless series of coincidences and mystical signs. She was an actress but not a performer, the difference being that at heart she believed that nothing was real, that everything was a kind of game, but her belief in this was sincere, deep, and true, and her feeling for life was enormous. In other words, she didn't live to convince others of anything. The crazy things that happened to her happened because she opened herself to them and sought them out, because she was always trying something without being too invested in the outcome, only in the feeling it provoked and her ability to rise to it. In her films she was only ever herself, a self stretched this way or that by the circumstances of the script. In the year that we had been friends, I had never known her to lie.

Come on, I said, you're not serious. But as she was never less than completely serious, even while laughing, Romi, still gripping my hand across the table, launched into her own story about Ershadi.

She had seen *Taste of Cherry* five or six years ago, in London. Like me, she had been utterly moved by the film and by Ershadi's face. Disturbed, even. And yet, at the last moment, she had been released into joy. Yes, joy was what she had felt, walking home from the theater in the twilight to her father's apartment. He was dying of cancer and she had come to take care of him. Her parents had divorced when she was three, and during her childhood and her teenage years she and her father had grown distant, very nearly estranged. But after the army she had gone through a kind of depression and her father had come to see her in the hospital, and the more he'd sat with her at her bedside the more she'd forgiven him for the things she had held against him all those years. From then on, they had remained close. She had often gone to stay with him in London, and for a little while even attended acting school there and lived with him in his apartment in Belsize Park. A few years later, his cancer had been diagnosed and a long battle ensued that looked to have been won, until at some point it became clear, beyond a shadow of a doubt, that it had been lost. The doctors gave him three months to live.

Romi left everything in Tel Aviv, and moved back to her father's apartment, and during the months that his body began to shut down she stayed by his side, rarely leaving him. He had decided against having any more of the poisonous treatments that would have prolonged his life by only a matter of weeks or months. He wished to die with dignity and in peace, though no one ever really dies in peace, as the body's journey toward the extinction of life always requires violence. These large and small forms of violence were the stuff of their days, but always mingled with her father's humor. They took walks while he could still walk, and when he couldn't anymore they spent long hours watching detective series and nature documentaries. Seeing her father's transfixed expression in the glow of the TV, it struck Romi that he was no less deeply invested in these stories, the stories of unsolved murders, of spies, and of the struggle of a dung beetle trying to roll its ball of manure over a hill, now that his own story was quickly drawing to a close. Too weak to get out of bed to go to the bathroom at night, he would try anyway, and then Romi would hear him collapse on the floor and would go and cradle his head and pick him up, because by then he was no heavier than a child.

It was during this time, the time that her father could no longer make it even the short distance to the bathroom and the round-the-clock nurse had to throw him over her large Ukrainian shoulder, that, at the nurse's insistence, Romi pulled on her coat and left the house for a few hours to go to see a film. She didn't know anything about the film, but she was drawn to the title, which she had seen on the marquee on a trip to or from the hospital.

She took a seat toward the back of the nearly empty theater. There were only five or six people there, Romi said, but, unlike when the theater is full and everyone disappears around you as the screen comes alive, she felt acutely aware of the presence of the others, most of whom had also come alone. During the many wordless stretches of the film, stretches in which one hears car horns and the sound of bulldozers and the laughter of unseen children, and the long shots when the camera rests on Ershadi's face, Romi felt aware of herself watching, and the others also watching. At the moment when she understood that Mr. Badii was planning to take his life and that he was looking for someone to bury him in the morning, she began to cry. Soon after that, a woman stood up and walked out of the theater, and this made Romi feel a little bit better, since it created an unspoken bond among those who remained.

I said that I wouldn't give away the end, but now I see that there is no way around it, that I will have to, since it was Romi's belief that if the film had come to a normal end what happened to each of us later almost certainly would not have happened. That is, if, after presumably swallowing the pills and putting on a light jacket against the cold, Mr. Badii had just lain down in the ditch that he'd dug, and everything had grown dim as we watched his impassive face watch the full moon sail in and out from behind the smoky clouds, and then, as a clap of thunder sounded, when it had grown so dark that we could no longer see him at all until a flash of lightning illuminated the screen again and there he was, still lying there, staring out, still of this world, still waiting, as we are still waiting, only to be plunged into darkness again until the next bright flash, in which we'd discover that his eyes had at last drifted closed, and then the screen turned black for good, leaving only the sound of rain falling harder and harder, until finally it crescendoed and faded away—if the film had just ended there, as it seemed to have every intention of doing, then, Romi said, it might not have stayed with her.

But the film did not end there. Instead, the rhythmic chanting of marching soldiers drifts in, and slowly the screen comes to life again. This time, when the same hilly landscape comes into view, it's spring, everything is green, and the grainy, discolored footage is shot on video. The soldiers march in formation onto the winding road in the lower left corner of the screen. This new view is surprising enough, but a moment later a member of the film's crew appears, carrying a camera toward another man, who is setting up a tripod, and then Ershadi himself—Ershadi, whom we just saw fall asleep in his grave—casually walks into the frame, wearing light, summery clothes. He takes a cigarette from his front pocket, lights it between his lips, and without a word hands it to Kiarostami, who accepts it without pausing his conversation with the DP, and without so much as looking at Ershadi, who in that moment we understand is connected to him through a channel of pure intuition. The shot cuts to the soundman, a little farther down the hill, crouching down out of the wind in the high grass with his giant microphone.

Can you hear me? a disembodied voice asks.

Down below, the drill sergeant falters and ceases his shouting.

*Bâlé?* he says. Yes?

Tell your men to stay near the tree to rest, Kiarostami replies. The shoot is over.

The last line of the film is spoken a few moments later, as Louis Armstrong's mournful trumpet starts to wail, and the soldiers can be seen sitting and laughing and talking and gathering flowers by the tree where Mr. Badii lay down in the hope of eternal rest, though now the tree is covered with green leaves.

We're here for a sound take, Kiarostami says.

And then it is just that huge, beautiful, plaintive trumpet, without words. Romi sat through the trumpet and the credits, and, though tears were streaming down her face, she felt elated.

It was not until some time after she had laid her father in the ground, and shoveled the dirt into his grave herself, pushing away her uncle, who tried to pry the tool from her, that Romi recalled Ershadi. So many intense things had happened to her since she had walked home full of joy in the twilight that she hadn't had time to think about the film again. She had stayed on in London to take care of her father's things, and when there was nothing left to take care of, when everything had been finalized and squared away, she remained in the nearly empty apartment for months.

During the days, all of which passed in the same way, she lay around listlessly, unable to apply herself to anything. The only time she could feel any desire was during sex, and so she had started seeing Mark again, a man she had dated during the year she was at acting school. He was possessive, which was part of why their relationship had ended in the first place. And now that she had been with other men since they'd broken up, he was even more jealous and obsessive, and wouldn't stop pushing her to tell him what it had been like with them. But the sex they had was hard and good, and she found it bracing after the months of feeling as though she had no body, as though her father's failing body were the only body there was.

At night, after Mark came home from work, Romi would go to his place, and in the darkened bedroom he would scroll through pornography until he found what he was looking for, and then would fuck her as she lay on her stomach and they watched two or three men penetrating one woman on the massive screen of his TV, pushing their dicks into her pussy and her ass and her mouth, everyone breathing and moaning in surround sound. Just before he came, Mark would slap Romi hard on the ass, thrusting himself into her and calling her a whore, enacting some ancient pain that drove him to believe that the woman he loved would never remain true to him. One night after this performance Mark had fallen asleep with his arms around her, and Romi had lain awake, for, exhausted as she always was, she couldn't sleep. Finally, she shimmied out from under him and crawled around on the floor in search of her underwear. Having no desire to stay, and no desire to go, she'd sunk back down on the edge of Mark's bed and felt the remote control under her. She switched on the TV and surfed the channels, passed over the stories of mother elephants and bee colonies that she had watched with her father, over the cold cases and the late-night talk shows, until there, nearly filling the enormous screen, was Ershadi's face. For a second, it appeared larger than life in the otherwise dark room, and then it was lost again, because her thumb had continued its restless search before she realized what she was seeing. When she flipped back, she couldn't find him. There was nothing on about film, or Iran, or Kiarostami. She sat there, startled and bewildered in the dark, and then slowly a sense of longing came over her like a wave, and she started to laugh for the first time since her father had died, and she knew it was time to go home.

There was no choice but to believe Romi. Her story was so precise that she couldn't have made it up. Sometimes she exaggerated the details, but she did it believing the exaggerations, and this only made her more lovable, because it showed you what she could do with the raw material of the world. And yet, after I went home and the spell of her presence wore off, I lay on my bed feeling sad and empty and increasingly depressed, since not only was my encounter with Ershadi not unique but, worse, unlike Romi, I'd had no idea what it meant, or what I was supposed to do with it. I had failed to understand anything, or take anything from it, and had told the story as a joke, laughing at myself. Lying alone in the dark, I started to cry. Sick of the pain throbbing in my ankle, I swallowed a handful of Advil in the bathroom. The pills swilled in my stomach with the wine I'd drunk, and soon enough nausea overtook me, and then I was kneeling on the bathroom floor throwing up into the toilet.

The next morning, I woke to banging on the door. Romi had had a sense that something was wrong and had tried to call, but I hadn't picked up all night. Still woozy, I started to cry again. Seeing the state I was in, she went into high gear, boiling tea, laying me out on the couch, and cleaning up my face. She held my hand, her other palm resting on her own throat, as if my pain were her pain, and she felt everything and understood everything.

Two months later, I quit the company. I enrolled in graduate school at NYU, but stayed on in Tel Aviv through the summer, and flew back only days before the start of the semester. Romi had met Amir by then, an entrepreneur fifteen years older than her, with so much money that he spent most of his time looking for ways to give it away. He wooed Romi with the same singular drive he applied to everything he wanted. A few days before my flight, Romi threw a goodbye party for me at our favorite restaurant, and all the dancers came, and our friends, and most of the boys we'd slept with that year. Amir didn't come because he was busy, and the following day Romi left for Sardinia on his yacht. I packed up my things alone. I was sad to leave, and wondered if I'd made a mistake.

For a while, we stayed in close touch. Romi got married, moved to Amir's mansion on a cliff above the Mediterranean, and got pregnant. I studied for my degree, and fell in love, and then out of it a couple of years later. In the meantime, Romi had two children, and sometimes she sent me photos of those boys, whose faces were hers and seemed to borrow nothing from their father. But we were in touch less and less, and then whole years passed in which we didn't speak at all. One day, soon after my daughter was born, I was passing a cinema on Twelfth Street and I felt someone's gaze, and when I turned I saw Ershadi's eyes staring out at me from the poster for *Taste of Cherry*. I felt a shiver up my spine. The screening had already passed, but no one had taken down the poster. I took a photo of it and that night I sent it to Romi, reminding her of a plan we'd once hatched to go to Tehran—me with a fresh American passport without Israeli stamps, and her with the British one she had through her father—to sit in the cafés and walk the streets that were the setting of so many films we loved, to taste life there, and lie on the beaches of the Caspian Sea. We were going to find Ershadi, who we imagined would invite us into the sleek apartment he had designed himself and listen while we told him our stories, and then tell us his own while we drank black tea with a view of the snowcapped Elburz Mountains. In the letter, I admitted to her the reason that I'd cried the night she told me about her encounter with Ershadi. Sooner or later, I wrote, I would've had to admit that in the blaze of my ambition I'd failed to check myself. I would have had to face how miserable I was, and how confused my feelings about dancing had become. But the desire to seize something from Ershadi, to feel that reality had expanded for me as it had for her, that the other world had come through to touch me, had hastened my revelations.

I didn't hear back from Romi for weeks, and then finally her answer arrived. She apologized for taking so long. It was strange, she said. She hadn't thought of Ershadi for years until three months ago, when she'd decided to watch *Taste of Cherry* again. She'd recently left Amir, and on nights when she couldn't sleep in the new apartment, with its unfamiliar smells and noises from the street, she would stay up watching movies. What surprised her was how differently Ershadi's character struck her this time. While she'd remembered him as passive, nearly saintlike, now she saw that he was impatient and often surly with the men he approached, and manipulative in the way he tried to get them to agree to what he wanted, sizing up their vulnerabilities and saying whatever was necessary to convince them. His focus on his own misery, and his single-minded determination to carry out his plan, struck her as self-absorbed. What also surprised her, because she didn't remember it, were the words that appear for a moment on the black screen before the film begins: *In the name of God.* How could she have missed that the first time? she wondered. Of course she'd thought of me as she lay in the dark and watched—of that year when we were still so young and spoke endlessly of men. How much time we wasted, she wrote, believing that things came to us as gifts, through channels of wonder, in the form of signs, in the love of men, in the name of God, rather than seeing them for what they were: strengths that we dragged up from the nothingness of our own depths. She told me about a film that she wanted to write when she finally got the time, which followed the story of a dancer like me. And then she told me about her boys, who needed her for everything, it seemed, just as the men in her life had always needed her for everything. It was good, she wrote, that I had a daughter. And then, as if she had forgotten that she had already moved on to other things, as if we were still sitting across from each other, deep in one of our conversations without beginning, middle, or end, Romi wrote that the last thing that had surprised her was that when Ershadi is lying in the grave he's dug and his eyes finally drift closed and the screen goes black, it isn't really black at all. If you look closely, you can see the rain falling.

# *Pity and Shame*

FROM *Tin House*

Hard lot! encompass'd with a thousand dangers;
Weary, faint, trembling with a thousand terrors;
I'm called, if vanquish'd, to receive a sentence
Worse than Abiram's.
—W. Cowper, "Lines Written During a Period of Insanity"

AT FIRST MR. COWPER just lay there like a heap of bedclothes, laundry for the wash. His face was so blank it was like it was erased off a slate. Doc Mac said he was concussed and he'd probably get over it and probably survive, awful as his injuries looked. Mostly there was nothing to do for him but get him to drink water or beef broth when he'd take it, and use the bedpan.

It had been Pete's idea to take in a lodger, but then he'd complained all week about living in two rooms instead of four. Now that the man was there all the time and she had to be up nights to look after him, Pete was ugly about it, spite of the good pay Doc got her for nursing. He stayed out a lot. When he was home he'd come in and watch what she did like he was suspicious. One night she was giving the bedpan, he kept crowding her till she finally had to say, "I need some room, Petey." He pressed closer. Annoyed with him, she said, "Guess you've seen one of them before."

"Some bigger'n that," he said.

"Come on, honey, I'm on the job."

"Not much of a job."

"More than you got," she said.

After she said it she realized it had another meaning than the

one she'd meant, and felt her face get red. She didn't know how
Pete took it, but either way it was unkind.

"Yeah, what the hell, I'm going," he said. And he went.

"I could use a hand with this," Doc Mac said. "Where's Pete at?"

"I can do that," she said. He let her show him she could keep
the hold he needed while he adjusted the splint.

"Radius is back in line, we'll get that scaphoid tucked back
where it belongs," Doc said. "It'll take a while."

She liked how he said "we." He was a tough thin man like a
dried-out leather whip, but he always spoke pleasantly. She didn't
know what some of the words he used meant, but she could figure
it out, or if she asked, he'd answer. It was not an arrangement she
was used to, but she liked it.

"How did the night go?"

"He was awful restless. Hurting. He hollered some."

"Coming to, I hope. Feeling what happened to him."

"I wish I could do more for him."

"Get some breakfast for yourself. Sounds like you had a
long night."

"I don't mind," she said, not knowing why she said it, but it
was true.

"God intended you for a nurse, Mrs. Tonely."

She watched him washing and salving places where the rocks
had torn up Mr. Cowper like he'd been dragged by a runaway
horse.

"My name isn't Tonely," she said. "I'm Rae Brown."

He nodded, working away. "That don't change what I said about
God's intentions."

Embarrassed all round, she tried to explain. "Well, my aunt Bess
was sick for a long time after an operation, and I was looking after
her. And my stepdad had these carbuncles I had to learn to treat."

He nodded again. "Just what I said. —Look there. No infection.
So far . . . But you get time off to eat, you know."

"I will," she said.

He was a kind man. She wished she could tell him about last
night. It had disturbed her. Mr. Cowper had been quiet for a while,
so she fell asleep in the chair, and then she woke because somebody was calling out. The voice was strange, like it came from a

long ways off, out in the woods or in the hills, somewhere else. It was a name he was calling, Cleo, Cleo. His voice wasn't loud, but pleading, like he was saying, please come, please come, but not really hoping for it. A heartbroken voice in the darkness. The night was silent, getting on toward morning, everything finally quiet at the saloon. She was nearly asleep again when he called out once more in that soft desolate voice, "Cleo!" This time a rooster answered him from across town with a little bugle call broken off short. She got up from the chair and went over to the bed and put her hand on his sweaty hair, whispering, "It's all right, it'll be all right," wanting to comfort that sorrow that came from far away and maybe long ago while he lay here a stranger among strangers. Things were so hard. And no way to talk about them.

Pete hadn't earned anything since the Bronco Saloon let him go last March. She'd kept the money from her cleaning for Mr. Bingham and the church, and then the two weeks' advance rent from Mr. Cowper, in a Twinings tea tin. When she needed some cash for groceries she found it had all had gone with Pete. It wasn't a big surprise, but it was a hollow feeling. She told herself Mr. Bingham wouldn't put her out of the house so long as she could pay the rent or work it out, and now she had good pay for boarding Mr. Cowper and nursing him.

That night, though, a bad thought came to her as she drowsed in the old rump-sprung armchair near the bed. Where did Mr. Cowper keep his money?

She couldn't worry about it then, in the middle of the night. But she did. Next day as soon as she'd got him looked after she went into the other room of the two he'd sub-rented from her and Petey two weeks ago and looked around. She felt like a criminal, but she looked into his coat pockets, and at the pocketbook she found there, which had twelve dollars in it. She checked the little chest of drawers where he'd put his shirts and stuff. There was nothing else of his in the room but some books and papers on the worktable, and under the table the little humpback trunk that was all his luggage.

He'd locked it, but there was a trunk key lying out on the table with what had been in his pockets when he went up to the mine. She had to look.

Down at the bottom of the trunk she found a billfold with more than two hundred dollars in it in paper and three fifty-dollar gold pieces. Relieved, she shut it all up quick, shoved it back under the table, and wondered what to do with the key. She went out and hid it behind the paper-wasp nest in the outhouse. The wasps were long gone, but it didn't seem like a place Pete, if he came back, or anybody would go sticking their hand in. Let alone if they knew about the black widow. She only wished she didn't, but she'd seen it twice.

She'd said truly that she didn't mind doing this job. She had minded nursing Roy's boils because he was a hateful man, but caring for Aunt Bessie had been a job she loved. The only trouble had been that Bess was a heavy woman and when she first came home from the hospital, Rae at thirteen couldn't even help her to turn over. Rae was a lot stronger now than she'd been then, and Mr. Cowper wasn't a big man. Doc Mac showed her how to change the sheets. And there really wasn't much to do for him. She wasn't lonely or bored. She was grateful for the silence. The house had felt small and cramped when it was full of Pete's big body and deep voice, and his friends that sat around with their hats on, smoking cigars and always talking. Now the quiet spread out in it, and her soul spread out in the quiet.

Some blue jays were yelling cheerfully at each other outside. The window was full of the gold August light. She sat thinking about things.

She thought a good deal about opening Mr. Cowper's trunk. She'd hardly known him in the short time he'd been there; Pete had shown him the rooms. They'd all signed the agreement Mr. Bingham insisted on, and shaken hands. He had a pleasant manner, but good morning and good evening was about it. He had been gone all day at his work with the mine company, and had boarded at Mrs. Metcalf's. It felt bad to go through his things, with him there in the next room knowing nothing about it, and she knowing nothing about him. She had needed to be sure his money was there, but she kept remembering when she looked for it and the memory troubled her. It was very clear; she could see the tray of the little trunk with papers and letters in it and some socks and handkerchiefs. She had lifted out the tray. Under it were some winter clothes and a dress shirt and coat and shoes, and under them a photograph in a cardboard frame of a dignified lady in 1870s dress, a small unframed blurry photograph of a little girl who looked unhappy, and a couple of books. He'd set his work books out on his worktable. The two in the trunk were *Little Dorrit* by Charles Dickens, and *Poems* by William Cowper. His billfold was between the books. She was careful to replace the photographs on the cover of *Poems*.

That was a puzzle. His name was William Cowper. He said it Cooper, but he wrote it that way, like "cowboy." She wondered why. Had he written that book? It was none of her business. She had had no business looking at his books anyhow. The trunk was locked now and the key was in the outhouse with the black widow.

Well into the shaft, almost past the daylight, he'd heard the framing creak loudly and thought that would be how a sailing ship would creak in a storm. He remembered that. He had set down his lantern to make another note. Looking up, he saw the weak glimmer on the rough pine beams. And that was it. That was all.

It came and went.

So did the ceiling of a room, slices of daylight, voices, blue jays squawking, the smell of tarweed. They came across his being and were clear but incomprehensible, like the pain. What ceiling, what room, what voices, why. It didn't matter, it was all at a remove from him, none of it concerned him. A man he knew, MacIver, a girl's face he knew but not who she was. They came, they went. It was easy, careless, peaceful.

There was a black rectangle in front of him. Just black, just there. Light around it, so it was like a hole in the light. It didn't move. At the same time he saw it, a rhythm began to beat in his head like a hammer. It was made of words.

*I, fed with judgment*

The black rectangle was right in front of him but he couldn't tell how large it was, how close or far. There was a great pressure on him, paralyzing and sickening him, holding him so he couldn't move. He couldn't get away from the black rectangle. It was there in front of him. It was all there was. The words beat at him. He tried to cry out for help. There was nobody to help him.

*to receive a sentence*

*to re CEIVE a SEN tence*
*WORSE than a BI ram's*

Whether he opened his eyes or shut them there was the black space, the bright glare around it, and the words in the terrible rhythm.

The timbers creaked, he saw the glimmer on them overhead. He tried to cling to that because it was before the judgment, before the sentence, but they were gone, there was dirt in his mouth and the words beating, beating him down.

*I, fed with JUDG ment*
*in a FLESH ly TOMB*
*AM*

He came back. MacIver was talking to the girl. He didn't understand what they said. He couldn't. He was being thrown around on long, sickening waves. He was in a ship tossing, creaking, sinking out from under him. In a train swaying, swaying as it ran, running off the track, falling down into the canyon. He tried to call out for help. The wheels were beating out the rhythm he dreaded. Then MacIver's face. Then it was all gone again.

He came back. Somebody was holding him, an arm around his shoulders, a comforting presence, but he heard something whimpering like a hurt dog. It made him ashamed.

"Hey," she said, "you're here. Aren't you?" She was looking at him from close. He saw the gray-green irises of her eyes and the tiny springy hairs of her eyebrows. He understood her.

He tried to say yes or nod. Great pain closed in on him and he shut his eyes. But he had the understanding. It held him, held him here.

"What," he said to MacIver.

"Tell you about it later."

"What."

MacIver watched him. Judging. Finally he said, "Cave-in." The

way he said it made it sound unimportant. Cowper had to think
it out.

"Quake?"

MacIver shook his head once. "We have your notes. You wrote,
'Unsafe at 200 yards.' You'd gone on some past that."

"Damn fool," he wanted to say, meaning himself, but it was too
difficult because of his chest. Instead after a while he asked again,
"What."

MacIver kept watching him. He reached a judgment.

"Stove you in some, William. Compound in the right leg, three
ribs, maybe four, I'm not sure. Right wrist. Contusions and abra-
sions from here to Peru. Not to mention concussion. Satisfied?"

"Lucky."

"Call that luck?"

"Left-handed."

"God damn," MacIver said softly, like a man admiring an
ore vein.


Goldorado was just another mean little town, but one thing she
liked about it was the water, mountain springwater clear as air. The
house had a standpipe in the yard and water piped to a faucet
in the kitchen sink. Mornings, after emptying the chamber pots
in the outhouse, she could rinse them clean right there at the
standpipe. The plentyness of water made housework easy and
bathing luxurious. She could clean up and cool down whenever
she felt like it, and do the same for her patient. These hot days
there wasn't much cross draft in his room even when she opened
the front door, and having to lie in bed with his leg and arm all
splinted and bandaged, hardly able to move, he got sweaty and
miserable. Doc Mac gave her a bottle of rubbing alcohol to use
where it was important not to get the dressings wet, and she took
to sponging him off a couple of times a day. Anything cool was
pleasant in the July afternoons, and there was nothing disagreeable about the job itself.

Treating Roy's carbuncles had been disgusting, the sores, and
the hair that grew all over his shoulders and back like a mangy old
buffalo robe, and Roy always either moaning or cussing dirt at her
for hurting him. She hadn't seen a lot of men and it was interesting to learn Mr. Cowper's body and compare it to the few others
she'd seen. He didn't have a potbelly like Roy. Pete had a lot of

wiry gold hair all over him and was milky white where he wasn't tanned. Where it wasn't all bashed and bruised, Mr. Cowper's skin was an even pale brown, like baked bread instead of dough. He was neat, somehow, like an animal. Doing for him had never been hard as soon as she learned what needed doing.

Having to learn it had come unexpectedly. But when had she ever been able to expect anything?

They'd brought him down from the old mine on a stretcher straight into the house and laid him on the bed that had been her and Pete's bed. A whole crowd came in after them, the little house was jam full of people, men women and children all jabbering with excitement about the accident. A couple of dogs got in with the crowd, putting Tiger into a panic fury, so she had to shut him into the kitchen and then into the cubby room, because people kept coming into the kitchen for something that was needed, water or a bowl, or just to stand and chatter about the cave-in. Most of the people had never spoken to Rae since she came there and didn't speak to her now. Then all of a sudden they were gone. Doc Mac had cleared them out.

She knew him from when she'd had to go to him soon after they got to Goldorado, when she was bleeding, losing the baby. He had been kind then, and he always spoke to her in the street.

He stood in the hall when he'd got the door shut on the crowd, and said, "Will you come in here, Miz Tonely?" looking very serious. She followed him into the bedroom. She took a quick look at the man on the bed, not much of him to be seen for bandages. She was glad of that. People had kept saying how he was all torn up and his bones crushed, and she didn't want to see it.

"I need to know if you can help me. He may not make it. I'll do what I can for him, but I need help at it. I need a nurse. I haven't found one yet. He's completely helpless. Have you cared for anybody sick?"

"Some," she said, scared by his hard, fast way of talking.

"I'll try to get a trained nurse up here from Stockton or Sacramento. I'll tell you exactly what to do. I'll get you nurse's wages from his company." What he said came at her so fast she couldn't keep up with it and didn't answer. "There's no place to put him but here," the doctor said with so much trouble in his voice that she said, "I can try."

His face cleared up. He looked at her keenly. She remembered that direct gaze from when she had gone to him with the bleeding. "All right!" he said. "Now let me show you what you'll be doing." He didn't waste any time.

But in the middle of telling her about what she'd be expected to do he stopped as if he'd run out of steam.

"You're a married woman," he said.

She said nothing.

"If you were a girl. But you've seen a man."

After a minute she said, "Yes."

She might have been angry or embarrassed except that he was embarrassed, scowling and fidgeting, and she almost wanted to laugh.

"He will be as helpless as a baby. With the same needs." His voice had gone hard again.

She nodded. "That's all right," she said.

She appreciated Doc Mac for thinking she might be too delicate minded to be able to look at a naked man and tend to his privacies, and the bedpan and all, but she wasn't. And this man was so broken, so beaten, he had been treated so rough that for a while you couldn't see him for his injuries.

She'd never minded having empty time, time by herself. She'd been worrying more than she knew about Pete and money and what next. She could admit to herself now that it was a relief as well as a grief that she'd lost the baby. And Pete.

She didn't have any tears when he went like that, not a word. But she was sad that the good time they'd had ended that way. She'd gotten to feeling scornful of him for always being disappointed and discontented and giving up on things, and she was sorry about that now. He couldn't help the way he was. But anyhow, gone was gone, and she could look ahead again.

It was all right being on her own. Enough money was coming in that she could really save some, enough to take her out of Goldorado. She didn't know where she'd go, her last letter to Aunt Bess had come back stamped NO LONGER AT THIS ADDRESS. But she'd worry about that when the time came.

When there was nothing to do for him and the house was as clean as she cared to bother making it, she would sit in the armchair in his room sometimes with Tiger asleep in her lap and do nothing at all. She'd been worried in this town, and lonely. Now she wasn't. She sat and thought.

She thought again about bodies. She didn't like the word *body*. It was the same word for a living person and a corpse. Her own body, or Pete's, which she knew every inch and mole and hair of, or the unconscious damaged body on the bed, were all alive, were what life was. A live body was absolutely different from a dead one, as different as a person from a photograph. The life was the mystery.

And then, holding and handling the hurt helpless man all the time, she was as close to him as she had ever been to Pete, but in a different way. There was no shame in it. There was no love in it. It was need, and pity.

It didn't sound like much, but when you came to the edge between life and death where he was, and she with him, she saw how strong pity was, how deep it went. She'd loved making love with Petey, back when they ran off together, the wanting and fulfilling. It had made everything else unimportant. But the ache of tenderness she felt for her patient did just the opposite, it made things more important. What she and Pete had had was like a bonfire that went up in a blaze. This was like a lamp that let you see what was there.

It was a while before the doctor would tell him how he'd been found. He couldn't hide his night horrors from Rae Brown, and she told MacIver about them. Maybe he thought they'd be worse if Cowper knew what had happened to him. Cowper was certain that they couldn't be any worse and maybe might be better. So MacIver finally told him.

Ross, the local company manager, had appointed to meet him up at the old Venturado Mine around noon that day to check out what he'd found.

Knowing that, he remembered the climb up to the mine in the morning sunlight, a steep haul through scrub oak and wild lilac that were growing back across the red, rocky scar of the old access road. It was less than a mile from town but felt like wilderness, full of birdsongs and strong scents, young sunlight slanting bright through the pines and tangles of mountain mahogany. The sun was already hot on his shoulders when he saw the mine entrance, a black rectangle in all that brightness.

He had no memory of going in. Nothing. All he had was the creaking in the shaft, the lantern light on the roof beam.

Ross had got there a couple of hours after he did and went into the adit to call him. Going farther in, he saw and smelled the air full of sour dust, and saw Cowper's lantern burning on the floor of the drift just in front of a chest-high tumble of rock and timber. "I thought it was a wall somebody built there," he said. He was looking at it trying to understand what it was when he realized that something blue he saw sticking out from under it was Cowper's shirt sleeve. He was facedown. Ross determined he was breathing. He hauled a couple of the bigger rocks off him but couldn't move the beam across his legs, and hurried back down to town for help.

"He was still wheezing when he located me at Metcalf's treating the old man's piles," MacIver said. "Never seen Ross out of breath and no hat before. Don't expect to again. He's asked about you. But he don't come round to see you."

"I owe him my life, I guess."

"Heaviest debt there is," said the doctor. "Just hope he forgives it."

Cowper brooded for a while. "Who's Abiram?"

"A-byerum? Darn if I know."

"In the Bible, I think."

"Oh well then," MacIver said, "damned if I know, and damned if I don't."

"Miz Brown?"

"In here," she called from the kitchen.

"You got a Bible?"

She came to the doorway of the room wiping her hands down her apron. "Oh, no, Mr. Cowper, I don't, I'm sorry." She really was sorry, wanting to amend her fault. She was like that, like a child. "Maybe Mr. Robineau would have a spare one? I'll go by the church and ask him when I go out."

"Thank you," Cowper said.

"But don't bring old Robineau back with you," said MacIver. "If this house is going to get filled with righteousness, I'm out of it."

MacIver made him laugh. When he laughed his chest hurt so sharp the tears came into his eyes.

They had known each other two years ago in Ventura, when Cowper was first with the company. They met at a poker game and liked each other. MacIver had a practice there, but he also had a habit. Cowper had been in a low, lonesome place in his life.

He was at a bar most nights. He was always glad to meet up with MacIver. The doctor had a keen wit, never lost his temper, was good company. He was such a gentlemanly drunk it took Cowper a while to realize that he was killing himself.

The company took Cowper on full time and sent him to inspect the Oro Grandy Mine, and he lost track of MacIver.

His first afternoon in Goldorado, he was not feeling encouraged about his stay there. Ross, the company's local boss, was a buttoned-up, all-business man. The kid they'd found for him to rent rooms from was unfriendly. The town had popped up on the strength of a couple of shallow-lode mines and was giving out along with them; the four mines he had been sent to inspect were almost certainly played out or barren holes in the ground. A lot of downtown windows were boarded up, bleak even in the blaze of midsummer. A hound dog lay dead asleep in the middle of Main Street. It looked like a few weeks could be a long time there.

The doctor came out of the bank building, saw him, and said, "William Cowper," half-questioning, as if not quite certain he had the name or the man right. When Cowper greeted him he looked relieved. He also looked like he'd been through the mangle. Otherwise he was much as he had been, and they picked up easily and pleasantly where they'd left off. Heading off the inevitable invitation to have one at the Bronco or the Nugget, MacIver made it clear that he wasn't drinking. "Where do you get a real dinner here?" Cowper asked him instead. They went off to the hotel and dined early, but in style, with a white tablecloth, oysters, and chicken-fried steak. They drank each other's health in seltzer water.

She had gone back to sleeping in her bed in the little back room off the kitchen. The walls were thin, and she left the doors open so she could keep an ear out. When he first started having the horrors and screamed out and thrashed trying to get up, she'd been scared of him, afraid she couldn't keep him from hurting himself or hurting her. But he still couldn't get up, and didn't have much strength even in a panic. Once when she was trying to calm him down he flailed out his arm and struck her on the face. It hurt, and she had a bruise next morning. She thought she might have to explain it. Like her mother when Roy hit her, it was just an accident, I was a little tipsy, we both were, he didn't mean any harm. But Mr. Cowper really hadn't meant any harm. It wasn't her he was trying to fight off or get away from. When she could get him to quiet down he was so worn out and confused he didn't know what he'd been doing or who he was talking to. Sometimes he was in tears like a child, crying, "I'm sorry, I'm sorry!" His tears meant he was out of the nightmare, coming back to himself. She liked to watch that relief happening, the mind coming back into his eyes, the quietness into his face. He always thanked her.

She didn't know anything about him of course, but she thought he was a lonely man. He didn't complain about the pain he was in, he joked and toughed that out the way a man expected himself to. But there was a grief in him that showed in his face. It went away when he talked with anybody, but it always came back, it was his look when he was by himself. Desolate.

She knew that word, like so many others, from Aunt Bess. "Oh my sakes, this is a desolate place!" Aunt Bess had cried out once, her first look at one of the dusty little East Colorado towns Roy kept moving them to. She had been so upset Rae hadn't asked her what the word meant then, but later on she had, and Aunt Bess said, "It means alone. Sad. Forsaken." And she'd said some of a poem that started, "Desolate, oh desolate!"

It was a lonesome word. *Forsaken* was even lonesomer. She valued words like that and the people who said them, Aunt Bess, old Mr. Koons, some of the schoolteachers she'd had, the boarding-house lady in Holt. She had treasured her McGuffey Readers with stories and poems in them. They got left behind in one of the moves to a new town. After that she knew she had to keep what she learned in her head. Even if she didn't say them, knowing words for things she felt and knowing there were people who said them used to help some when she was feeling desolate and forsaken, in those places, in those days.

She hadn't had friends her own age, and envied those who did. She'd used to think the girls just didn't like her, but now she could see that her stepfather and his friends had put them on the out-side right away in every town he'd moved them to. Just after they'd come to Grand Junction, Aunt Bessie had had to go back to Kansas to nurse Grandmother Brown, who was dying. She wanted to take Rae with her and Rae wanted to go, but Roy wouldn't have it. Soon after Aunt Bessie left, Roy started bringing his new friend Mr. Van

Allen over several nights a week. Rae's mother entertained Mr. Van Allen and the rent got paid.

Girls Rae had begun to know at school stopped speaking to her. It didn't seem to her it was her fault what her mother did. In fact she didn't think it was really her mother's fault. After Daddy died, when Rae was eleven, Mother had done nothing but cry, and before the year was out she married Roy Daid, as if he was the answer to anything. Mother wasn't strong, like Aunt Bessie was. Not everybody was strong. But people wouldn't speak to them now, and the neighbor woman said out loud to somebody in the street, "I'm not used to living next door to a slut."

Rae was so angry at everybody by then she wouldn't let anybody even try to speak to her. There was nobody. Nobody till Pete Tonely showed up with some of Roy's business friends. He was so different. Younger, and really handsome. He didn't hound her and paw her like Roy's friends tried to, but she knew he noticed her a lot. The day after she turned eighteen and found that Sears Roebuck had turned her off from her warehouse job there, Pete had come over. He said something nice to her, and she started crying. She made herself stop crying right away, and they sat out on the back steps talking for a long time. He said, "Rae, I came over to tell you. I'm pulling up stakes. Going to Denver. Tonight." She just sat there, dumb. He took her hand and said, "Listen. I want to take you out of this. If you want to come. I thought about going on to Frisco." She met him down at the train station that night.

The first year had had a lot of excitement in it, and joy. She didn't forget that. But poor Pete was always finding wonderful new friends and new prospects and then they didn't pan out. He got fired, or he quit. As time went on, it seemed like nothing satisfied him anymore. He was never hard on her, but the joy was all gone out of it. A few months after they got anywhere, he was talking about pulling up stakes. When they were in Chico, he'd met some man from a mining town who told him what a great job bartending was, and good money in the tips. And so she'd ended up in Goldorado. Still on the outside.

Mr. Cowper's boss came one afternoon. She made sure Mr. Cowper had his shirt on and was sitting up, and then left Mr. Ross with him. She went to the kitchen to start dinner. She couldn't help but hear what they said. She didn't much like Mr. Ross, a pink-faced man with cold eyes. He was a gentleman but it wasn't the same kind of gentleman as Doc Mac and Mr. Cowper.

She heard him tell Mr. Cowper that the company was going to keep on paying him while he was laid up. He said, "They think very highly of you down in Sacramento, Cowper," and you could tell that he tried to say it nicely, although it was a strain on him to do so and it came out sounding superior. That warmed her to Mr. Ross.

He chilled her down right away. As she showed him out he said, "No doubt you know, Mrs. Tonely, that your husband has several creditors here who would appreciate knowing when he might return."

Nobody in their senses would have made Pete a real loan. If he'd borrowed money privately that was none of Mr. Ross's business. Unless it was Ross he owed. But Ross wouldn't have lent Pete money any more than the bank would. He had spoken out of pure meanness.

She let her eyes cross his pink face without looking at it, the way he always did to her, and said, "My name's Rae Brown, Mr. Ross. I don't have a husband."

That shocked him maybe more than she meant it to. His pink cheeks went dark red and his jaw shook up and down. He turned away and strutted off like a turkey gobbler.

Well, she certainly was parading her shame. First to Doc Mac, then Ross. Might as well announce, "I was living in sin!" with a megaphone like they had at the rodeo.

She went in and passed Mr. Cowper's door without speaking to him to see if he needed anything. In the kitchen she stood there for a while and felt her face burn red hot. Going around announcing her name, as if being Rae Brown was something to be proud of. It didn't make any difference if she wasn't ashamed. Other people were. They were ashamed for her, of her, that she lived among them. They blushed for her. Their shame was on her, a weight, a load she couldn't get out from under.

"All right, let 'er buck."

MacIver handled the book like it might go off if he wasn't careful. He got his finger on the page and line he wanted, grimaced, and began to read in a jerky mumble.

And Moses sent to call Dathan and Abiram, the sons of Eliab: which said, We will not come up:

Is it a small thing that thou hast brought us up out of a land that floweth with milk and honey, to kill us in the wilderness, except thou make thyself altogether a prince over us?

Moreover thou hast not brought us into a land that floweth with milk and honey, or given us inheritance of fields and vineyards: wilt thou put out the eyes of these men? we will not come up.

"This making any sense to you?"

"Well, it might if you didn't read it like you were spitting gravel."

"I am not a reading man, William," the doctor said with dignity. "Given time, I have made sense of a medical text. But what's all this stuff? Which, and thou, and putting out eyes?"

"I don't know. If I could look at that book I might could figure it out. But it's not a one-handed book."

"Never heard it mentioned as such," MacIver said. "Hey, Rae?"

"She's hanging out the wash."

MacIver went to call out from the back door. "Rae! You ever done any Bible reading?"

Cowper heard her cheerful voice call back, "I used to read it to my auntie sometimes."

"Will you come make sense of this stuff to the divinity student in here?"

MacIver came back and she followed him. The smell of sunlight on newly washed sheets came in with her and she was laughing. "You two are reading the *Bible*?"

"Not real successfully," Cowper said. "Maybe you could help us out."

She took the thick, heavy, black-bound, red-edged book the minister had lent them. She held it with affectionate respect. "I haven't seen this for a long time. It's just like the one my aunt had."

"Don't lose the place! We had enough trouble finding it! See, there? It's called Numbers 15. Now just start there, and look out for the whiches."

She sat down in the straight chair, studied the page for a minute, and began to read. She read slowly, hesitating over a word now and then—*wroth, tabernacle*—but easily and with understanding. There was a music in it. A couple of times she glanced up to see if they wanted her to go on.

And Dathan and Abiram came out, and stood in the door of their tents, and their wives, and their sons, and their little children.

And Moses said, Hereby ye shall know that the Lord hath sent me to do all these works; for I have not done them of mine own mind.

If these men die the common death of all men, or if they be visited after the visitation of all men; then the Lord hath not sent me.

But if the Lord make a new thing, and the earth open her mouth, and swallow them up, with all that appertain unto them, and they go down quick into the pit; then ye shall understand that these men have provoked the Lord.

And it came to pass, as he had made an end of speaking all these words, that the ground clave asunder that was under them:

And the earth opened her mouth, and swallowed them up, and their houses, and all the men that appertained unto Korah, and all their goods.

They, and all that appertained to them, went down alive into the pit, and the earth closed upon them: and they perished from among the congregation.

And all Israel that were round about them fled at the cry of them: for they said, Lest the earth swallow us up also.

She looked at Cowper, and stopped.

After a minute MacIver said, "Whatever this Dathan and Abiram did, their wives and sons and little children didn't, did they? That's awful stuff."

Cowper was having some trouble breathing. The doctor had his eye on him as he went on. "You read like an angel, Miss Rae. You come of a religious family?"

"Oh my sakes no. Aunt Bessie and I read her Bible because she liked to be read to when she was sick and there wasn't anything else in the house. Then a neighbor heard she wanted something to read and brought over a whole box full of cowboy adventure stories."

"Made a change from Moses and Korah and them, anyhow." He got up and came over to Cowper. "Got trouble, William?"

Cowper nodded.

"I'll go finish the wash," Rae said, and slipped out, leaving the Bible on the side table. A black rectangle. Cowper shut his eyes and tried to breathe.

He went down into the pit, the earth swallowed him. But he was buried above ground.

*

Lying there in the long afternoons with nothing but time on his hands he felt what time was. It was his element, like air. It was a gift. His breath had begun to come easily again, the gift restored. He watched the slow unceasing changes of the light on the walls and ceiling and in the sky out his window. He watched July becoming August. The hours washed over him soft as the mild air.

Angus MacIver came in one morning, told him he'd been lying around like a hog in a wallow long enough, and began teaching him exercises to keep his muscles from wasting and get some strength in the good leg and arm. He did them faithfully, but doing anything at all both exhausted him and made him impatient to be doing more. It made the possibility of getting up off the damn bed, walking, walking back into the world, imaginable. But imagining it now, when it wasn't possible, threatened his gift of ease, made him restless. Doing nothing, he could let peace flow back into him.

And often now the peace lasted through the night. He would wake at what had been his worst hour, just before the turn of night toward day, black dark, the town and the hills dead silent, and watch the stars in his window grow paler and fewer and the chairs and bureau and doorway taking on substance, a long untroubled wakening.

He knew he counted on the doctor visiting most days, sitting down and talking a while, but he hadn't known how much until MacIver went off on one of his rounds, out to people on ranches up in the hills and at the big sawmill down the creek where, as he said, the hands kept practicing their sawing on themselves.

MacIver didn't keep a horse, renting a mare and a buckboard from Hugh at the livery stable for his rounds, or a riding horse for an emergency when the patient couldn't get into town. Rae said that he was liked and respected in Goldorado, but Cowper had wondered if his practice there was enough to live on. He was open about things like money that some men wouldn't talk about, so Cowper asked him. MacIver told him that two years ago a friend had given him a half interest in a going lumber business over in the redwood country. "Staked me for life," he said. "I'm in the clover. So long as people keep building houses."

"Man doesn't get many friends like that," Cowper said, thinking of Mr. Bendischer.

MacIver nodded, but his face closed down. Some part of Angus MacIver had a fence around it that was posted KEEP OUT. No barbed wire, but the sign was clear from a distance. It just wasn't clear to Cowper what was inside it.

Talking about himself to get away from whatever had shut MacIver down, he had said, "I got staked like that. When I was a kid." He stopped. He didn't want to tell the story.

But MacIver wanted to hear it. "Ran away from home?"

"My parents died. In a train wreck." He stopped again, but couldn't leave it there. He had to make his recitation. "On a switchback. My father worked for the Tomboy Mine up there. Near Ouray. The track had buckled since the last inspection. On a downgrade. Engine went off the rails down into the canyon and took the first car with it. They were in it. Me and my sister had gone back to the last car. The observation platform."

"How old were you?"

"Cleo was fourteen. I was eleven."

MacIver waited.

"Well, our next of kin was my mother's uncle. He took me and my sister with him to Pueblo. Then he fixed it up somehow with the bank and skipped out with everything Father left us." He heard his voice dull and level, like a rote recitation in school. "There was an old lawyer there in Pueblo, he'd have liked to get our uncle to justice. He tried. Couldn't do it. But he took an interest in my sister and me. Cleo wanted to work and keep me in school, and he helped her do that. He saved us. Robert Bendischer. I honor his name. He put me through the mining school in Golden. Mrs. Bendischer never liked us."

"How about your sister?"

"Cleo died of diphtheria. Two years after our parents."

After a while MacIver said, "God moves in a mysterious way." He had asked his questions gently, but spoke now with savage bleakness.

When he left that day he put his arm around Cowper's shoulders. In his helplessness the doctor had handled him all the time, deft and gentle. This was different, awkward, a sudden half embrace that hurt. MacIver left without a word, scowling.

He had been away five days now. It seemed like nothing happened and nothing changed. He did his exercises, but they didn't

get easier, and except for the scabs healing over he didn't feel he
was getting any better. His leg and wrist were still in heavy bandages, immobile, hot in the long hot afternoons and evenings. His
side still hurt and his breath came short when he moved. Even the
bruises didn't seem to fade much. He still needed Rae to help him
do anything at all.

She was good at thinking of what he might need and asking him
about it or just doing it. He knew that and appreciated it. But he
was so sick of still having to ask, can you do this, will you do that,
that he didn't always treat her the way he ought to. She was patient
with his crankiness up to a point. Then she went silent, and when
she'd done what was needed she'd leave him silently, going to another room or outside. But always in hearing.

When she had to leave the house, she told him, and made sure
there was somebody within earshot, usually the ten-year-old from
the only other house on South Fifth Street, a shy boy who wouldn't
meet your eyes. Tim always brought with him a game board that
had a star design with indentations for marbles. He sat for hours
moving the marbles into patterns. It should by rights have driven
Cowper mad to watch the poor kid, but in fact he found that silent
absorption soothing. And he wanted soothing. He was losing the
sweet, idle flow of uncounted time. Often now he felt irritable,
babyish, stupidly emotional, finding himself often in a fit of anger, or a panic, or halfway to tears. He lay there listening to the
endless chorus of grasshoppers out on the dry, hot, gold hillsides,
sweating, comfortless, desperately pushing despair away. Then Rae
would come in and smile. She didn't hold grudges any more than
the cat. He was glad to see her, glad she was there. He didn't know
how to say so, but she seemed to be glad to see him and be there,
so it wasn't necessary.

There was still nothing much to do but think. He found he had
a good supply of things to think about. What went on outside the
house in this town he scarcely knew, and it didn't concern him, so
he thought mostly about the past and about what was there right
now, like Rae.

Whoever the handsome sullen kid was who'd been there with
her, he'd evidently walked out, but she didn't seem like her heart
was broken. She wasn't much more than twenty and had the stunning health and grace and glow of her age, but she didn't have

the self-consciousness girls had, that always tied him up in knots. She wasn't hard, but in a way she was sophisticated. Maybe more than he was. He felt that sometimes, although he must be ten years older than she was. Or it was that she was a woman. Like Cleo, she knew what had to be done and went on and did it. A lot of what she had to do for him was embarrassing to him, shameful. It would have been unbearable if she'd felt the same way about it. She didn't. She took necessity for granted. She was grown up.

Cleo. A steady kindness. A buoyancy. A spring rising.

Thinking of her brought them all together into his mind, his sister and father and mother. Their good nature, their good cheer. It was like a firelit room. His memory of it was a window that showed it to him warm and bright. But there was no door, no way back in. They were alive there. He was the ghost, whimpering outside in the dark.

He hadn't left that room by choice, but men did. Probably he would have. A man went off alone to prove he wasn't soft. Didn't let himself depend on anybody. Didn't let down with anybody, didn't trust them, because that gave them the advantage over him. Cowper had lived in a man's world since before he was one himself. It was all the world that was left to him. The job cut out for him was a man's job: to fight the battle of life, to compete, succeed, win. Mr. Bendischer had talked about that with him, and had given him the weapons and the armor he needed for the battlefield. And so far he'd done all right.

But what a barren life it was. Always farther from the firelit room.

He liked his work. He was satisfied by knowing what he was doing and doing it well. But to most of the people who ran things, the men who kept the battle of life going, that wasn't enough, wasn't what it was all about.

Men dug tunnels after gold, he thought, but they didn't build them right. If they'd take pity on each other and themselves, they'd build right. At least shore up their ratholes with timber you could count on.

His thoughts went winding around that way, following each other's tails, and the afternoon would pass while he let them lead his mind back to paths it used to walk long ago and places it hadn't been before. He must have been needing some time to think, to take stock, because coming out of one of those long reveries he felt peaceful again, and it didn't seem so bad to be stuck helpless and useless in a bed in a hot little room in a half-dead little town in Amador County, California.

Then in the night he woke facedown with dirt in his mouth and eyes, blind, paralyzed, trying to get his breath with no breath, and the beat pounding in his ears. Buried above ground.

He struggled awake, struggled to calm himself. Holding his mind away from the beat of the terrible words, he sat up and watched daylight slowly transform the sky.

He knew he'd be afraid to go to sleep that night. He thought about it all morning. When he slept there was no way to keep it from happening. He'd learned something about keeping off the horrors, but he had to be awake to do it.

Reciting poetry he'd learned by heart in school and singing songs in his head, it didn't matter what, "Red River Valley" or "Praise God, from Whom," could keep him from slipping into the awful rhythm. If he could get "The boy stood on the burning deck" going, even that could keep Abiram away. He wished they'd made him memorize more in school. He lay hunting for bits of poetry and tunes that had been stuck deep in his mind like little gold veins in granite since before he could remember. "The cow's in the meadow, the sheep's in the corn . . ."

He'd ask Angus to find him something to read. He'd manage holding a book and turning the pages somehow. What the hell, he was an engineer, couldn't he figure out something that would hold a book where he needed it?

"Are there any books in the house, Rae?"

"Just yours," she said. "You want some more to drink?"

She refilled his glass from the pitcher on the bureau and set it on the crate they'd rigged up as a table, which he could reach with his left hand. The bed was close to the wall so that now he could sit up he could see more than sky out the window. His view was an old plum tree in the side yard and a triangle of Sierra foothill forested with white oak, scrub oak, madrone, and a couple of Jeffrey pines. To get to the crate-table Rae had to go between the bedside and the wall. The windowsill stuck out so she had to squeeze past it a little, turning sideways, away from him. Watching her hips and buttocks negotiate that passage in and then back out was an unfailing pleasure.

"I guess you gave that Bible back."

"Did you want to hear some more?"

"I liked hearing you read it."

"I like reading. I read a lot to my aunt when she was sick. I can borrow it back from Mr. Robineau."

"Maybe something that isn't the Bible," he said.

"There's some books in your other room."

He thought about it. "Materials stress resistance calculation tables are on the dry side."

She said, not turned toward him as she said it, "There's some other books in your trunk."

His trunk, what he'd put in it packing it in San Francisco. Another world. "What are they?" he asked more of himself than her.

"A poetry book and a book by Charles Dickens."

"Ace in the hole!" He was delighted. "Fetch 'em in here, Rae!" Of course he'd brought the Dickens—he'd bought it in the city to bring here, thinking there might be some long evenings. And he'd traveled with Cowper's *Poems* so long he'd forgotten about it.

Rae turned around. He saw with surprise that she had gone red, which with her was no modest-maidenly-pink business. She turned burning red, fire red, face, ears, throat, whatever could be seen of her. Then, more slowly, she turned white and stayed that way for some time. He'd seen her go through this once before, but not so extremely as now. It was distressing, and he felt sorry for her and sorry about causing the distress. But he had no idea what he'd said to cause it. Had he told her to fetch the books like an order?

"Mr. Cowper, I had to unlock your trunk and look in it. A while ago. I had to."

"That's all right with me, Rae." His first thought was that there was nothing of any value in the trunk, then he remembered he'd stuck some bills and coins in under the other stuff. Trying to ease her disproportionate embarrassment, he said, "If you ever get short of cash money, there's some in the bottom, did you find that?"

She burst into tears. The tears ran down her pale face. The sobbing shook her hard. She cried like a child, openly. It had come on her so suddenly she couldn't hide it and didn't try. She just stood there weeping. He tried to reach out to her but of course couldn't get anywhere near her. All he could say was her name, don't cry, it's all right.

She got the sobbing under control and with one of his handkerchiefs from the top bureau drawer wiped her eyes and nose. Doing that allowed her to turn away from him for a while. When she turned back she was still pale, and she'd missed some of the snot on her left cheek. He had never felt pity so sharp, so urgent, pity like a knife stab. It made him reach out to her again, sitting up and turning as much in the bed as he was able to. She saw his gesture, but did not put out her hand to his, though she came a little closer to the bed and tried to smile.

"I was afraid Pete might have taken your money. It's all right, it's there. He didn't. I hid the key. I wasn't sure if Pete might come back." She frowned and her mouth drew back in a grimace repressing another rush of tears.

"Well you did just right," he said, talking to her as if she were a child, letting his useless right arm drop back to his side, feeling his own tears ache in his throat and behind his eyes. "You did just right, Rae. Thanks."

Something relaxed between them then. An inner movement, very deep down, definitive, almost imperceptible.

She poured a little water from the white tin pitcher into the washbasin on the bureau and splashed her face and used his handkerchief with better success. She took the basin out to the front door to toss the water onto the scraggly rosebush by the steps. She came back into the room and said resolutely, "See, when he left, he took my money. So I was afraid maybe he'd—I'm sorry, Mr. Cowper."

Nothing came to him to say to her but, "That's all right." Then, "Look, Rae. We could drop the Mr., maybe. My name's William."

She stood looking at him. Head cocked, but serious. Judging. "I guess I can do that," she said. She did not smile. "Thank you."

When Doc Mac came in, she was sitting close to the lamp so she could go on reading *Little Dorrit* aloud. William was sitting up in bed. The old cat was asleep on the bed by his legs. "Well this is a pleasant domestic scene," Doc said with a grin, looking in from the dark of the hallway at them in the glow of yellowish light.

"Hey Angus," William said, and she could hear how glad he was to see him. "It's been a while."

"Bunch of fools out there in the sticks. Everything wrong with 'em from scurvy to bunions to a ten-month pregnancy. They need looking after."

"Did you get any dinner, Doc? We've got some pork and beans left I could quick heat up, and corn bread—"

"Thanks, Rae, they fed me at the Mannhofers'. Klara's a good cook, I generally try to get there around a mealtime. How's your sixth costa vera doing, William?"

"It'll do. You missed a shindy, Saturday night."

"Heard something about it. The Edersons again, right? I keep hoping someday some of that lot will manage to murder at least a few of each other."

"Carl Ederson went to shoot his brother Peer but he hit his cousin's horse. Or he was trying to shoot the horse and hit Peer. Which is it, Rae?"

He made her laugh. "Nobody really knows what happened," she said. "Just that Erland's horse got shot, and then Carl left town. And old Mr. Ederson says he's going to shoot Carl soon as he sees him. And old Mrs. Ederson threw his gun into the creek." They were all laughing. Coming past her to sit down in the straight chair, Doc touched her shoulder, a little light brush of the hand, the way he did sometimes. It was close in the small room. She and Doc were near the lamp, batting off or slapping at tiny mosquitoes. William was sitting up against the pillows, and his strong profile partly in the yellow light and part in deep shadow looked like an old photograph or a stone carving.

"I came in on a reading," Doc said. "More of the Scriptures? You trying to figure out what Abiram actually did to bring God down on him and his wife and the babies?"

"No," William said. "Don't reckon I ever will. We're reading the Gospel by Dickens."

"*Pickwick Papers*? I saw a play made out of that in KC once."

"This is *Little Dorrit*. More on the serious side."

"Well give me a shot of it. I am tired, to tell you the truth. Sitting here getting read to by a beautiful woman sounds like just what the doctor ordered." She tried to beg off, but he meant it. "Go on from where you were." Rae picked up the book and found her place.

"He's asleep."

"I know. Just go on reading."

"He's going to fall off the chair."

Doc started, half stood up, shook his head, sat down, and woke up. "Well, God damn, I went to sleep!" he said, and then, "Rae, I'm sorry. I am truly sorry."

She thought he was apologizing for going to sleep. She had got so used to Roy and the men he knew and then Pete and the men he knew cursing all the time, language a lot worse than "damn," which she hadn't even noticed. When she understood, she was embarrassed and touched, and said at random, "You didn't know what you were saying. I don't mind. You must be worn out. I was getting tired reading, anyhow."

"Foul-mouthed old cuss," William said. "Can't have you around the ladies. Go home and go to bed. We're all pie-eyed. It must be past midnight."

"It is," Doc said, looking at his silver watch. "Thank you for the fine entertainment." He yawned enormously. "Good night!"

He lurched out, waving the back of his hand at them vaguely.

"Never thought it had got so late," William said.

"I love that man," Rae said. "He's just good."

She felt dreamy, half there, half in the story she had been reading to them. She got Mr. Cowper—she still called him that in her head when "Mr. Cowper" made things easier than "William" did— seen to for the night, blew out the lamp, and bade him good night.

It seemed pitch dark for a moment, but the starlight and an old moon just clearing the mountains made a gray light in the house, enough for him to find his chamber pot if he had to, and for her to get to bed, still in the half dream of the story.

It tickled her that Doc had called her a beautiful woman. She knew that from him it meant nothing except his kindness. But for some reason she was glad he'd said it in front of William.

As she undressed the story came back around her. It had been hard going at first when they were all in Marseille, which she had to remember to pronounce "Marsay," and the prison there, and the quarantine. She could see the places, but what was going on didn't begin to make much sense until the third chapter, called "Home," when Arthur Clennam was with his mother in the old house. And then when the story got to Mr. Dorrit and Amy and her sister in the Marshalsea Prison. She had gone right on tonight to the chapter called "The Lock" because she didn't want to stop, even though she knew it was late. Arthur Clennam followed Amy to the prison and met Amy's father, and then she had to stop reading because Doc was tilting over in his chair like a tree about to fall. That room and her bedroom were all mixed up in her head with Mr. Dorrit, and his brother Frederick, and Amy bringing her dinner for her

father to eat. Jail cells and old dark places with heavy doors locked
on the fragile human souls inside them. And the sweet night air
pouring down the mountains through the house. She began going
to sleep before she'd gotten all the way into bed.

It was a Sunday morning. He knew because things had been very
loud at the Nugget last night and didn't quiet down till late, after the cricket trilling died away. Anyhow it felt like Sunday. And
presently they began hymn-singing away down Main Street in Mr.
Robineau's church. He'd been such a short time in Goldorado
before the tunnel fell in on him that he didn't have much picture
of the town. He remembered or imagined a little clapboard chapel with a kind of halfhearted try at a steeple. The congregation
sounded pretty thin on the ground from the way they wailed out
a hymn he didn't know, or maybe he couldn't tell what it was because half of them were out of tune and all of them singing it like
a dirge. Why did people drag out hymns like that? A good hymn
deserved a good tempo. They went caterwauling on and on, it always sounded like the last verse at last, but it never was. Sitting up
straight, breathing easy, and feeling good in the bright morning
light already warming the air, he sang to show how it should be
done—not loud, but moving right along with the beat. He sang
his own hymn.

> God moves in a mysterious way.
> His wonders to perform;
> He plants His footsteps in the sea
> And rides upon the storm.

Rae was in the doorway, bright-eyed, half laughing. Cowper
waved his left hand like a choirmaster and sang on.

> Deep in unfathomable mines
> Of never failing skill,
> He treasures up His bright designs
> And works His sov'reign will.

He stopped and looked at her. "Cowper's Hymn," he said.
"Go on!"
"That's the part I like. It's in the book, if you want to read it."
He reached for the smaller book that she had fetched from his
trunk along with *Little Dorrit*. She had put them both on his crate-

table, and the smaller one had stayed there. He held it out to her. She was shy about taking it from him, so he opened it to the title page. Before that was the flyleaf, with the inscription on it in spidery legal writing, *To my dear young friend and namesake of the Poet, William Cowper, on the occasion of his matriculation. May you find Honor and Contentment in your chosen profession. September 1889. R. E. Bendischer.* He knew it without reading it. He showed Rae the title page, and then turned to the hymn. It took a while, one-handed, but he knew the page. He knew all the pages.

"He called it 'Light Shining out of Darkness,' but mostly it gets called 'Cowper's Hymn.'"

She took the book from him at last.

"I never heard you sing," she said.

"I didn't feel much like it lately."

"I guess not." She was still shy, not looking at the book, or at him. He never could figure out her shynesses, her embarrassments. They were mysteries. The more he knew Rae, the more her mysteries. Endless. Unfathomable.

"I like that word," she said. She was blushing some, but went ahead. She was looking down at the open book now. "It's a grand word. *Unfathomable.*"

After a while Cowper said, "It is."

MANUEL MUÑOZ

# *Anyone Can Do It*

FROM *ZYZZYVA*

HER IMMEDIATE CONCERN was money. It was a Friday when the men didn't come home from the fields and, true, sometimes the men wouldn't return until late, the headlights of the neighborhood work truck turning the corner, the men drunk and laughing from the bed of the pickup. And, true, other women might have thought first about the green immigration vans prowling the fields and the orchards all around the valley, ready to take away the men they might not see again for days if good luck held, or even longer if they found no luck at all.

When the street fell silent at dusk, the screen doors of the dark houses opened one by one and the shadows of the women came to sit out on the concrete steps. Delfina was one of them, but her worry was a different sort. She didn't know these women yet and these women didn't know her: she and her husband and her little boy had been in the neighborhood for only a month, renting a two-room house at the end of the street, with a narrow screened-in back porch, a tight bathroom with no insulation, and a mildewed kitchen. There was only a dirt yard for the boy to play in and they had to drive into the town center to use the pay phone to call back to Texas, where Delfina was from. They had been here just long enough for Delfina's husband to be welcomed along to the field-work, the pay split among all the neighborhood men, the work truck chugging away from the street before the sun even rose.

When Delfina saw the first shadow rise in defeat, she thought of the private turmoil these other women felt in the absence of their men, and she knew that her own house held none of that. Just days before the end of June, with the rent due soon, she thought that all the other women on the front steps might believe that nothing could be any different until the men returned, that nothing could change until they arrived back from wherever they had been taken. She was alert to her own worry, to be sure, but she felt a resolve that seemed absent in the women putting out last cigarettes and retreating behind the screen doors. She watched as the street went dark past sundown and the neighborhood children were sent inside to bed. The longer she held her place on her front steps, the stronger she felt.

From the far end of the street, one of the women emerged from a porch and Delfina saw her moving along toward her house, guided by a few dim porchlights and the wan blur of television sets glowing through the windows. When the woman, tall and slender, arrived at her front yard, Delfina could make out the long sleeves of a husband's work shirt and wisps of hair falling from her neighbor's bun. Buenas tardes, the woman said.

Buenas tardes, Delfina answered and, rather than invite her forward, she rose from the steps and met her at the edge of the yard.

Sometimes they don't come back right away, the neighbor said in Spanish. But don't worry. They'll be back soon. All of them. If they take them together, they come back together.

The woman extended her hand. Me llamo Lis, she said.

Delfina, she answered, and as Lis emerged fully out of the street shadow, Delfina saw a face about the same age as hers.

Your house was empty for about three months, said Lis, before you arrived. That's a long time for a house around here, even for our neighborhood. Everything costs so much these days.

It does, Delfina agreed.

Was it expensive in Texas? Lis asked. Is that why you moved?

Delfina looked at her placidly, betraying nothing. She had not told this woman that she was from Texas, and she began to wonder what her husband might have said to the other men in the work truck, or in the parking lot of the little corner store near Gold Street, where the owner said nothing about the men's loitering as long as they kept buying beer after a day in the fields.

Your car, Lis said, pointing to the Ford Galaxie parked on the dirt yard. I noticed the Texas license plates when you first came.

We drove it from Texas, Delfina answered.

You're lucky your husband didn't take that car to the fields. They impound them, you know, and it's tough to get them back.

The woman reminded Delfina of her sister back in Texas, who had always tried to talk her into things she didn't want to do. It was her sister who had told her that moving to California was a bad idea, and who had repeated terrible stories about the people who lived there, though she had never been there herself. Her sister had given all the possible reasons why she should stay except for the true one, that she had not wanted to be left alone with their mother.

My husband says they stop you if you don't have California plates, Delfina said. So I try not to drive the car unless I have to.

On the long drive from Texas, she had learned that strangers only approached when they needed something. She could refuse Lis money if she asked, but it would be hard to deny her a ride into town if she needed it.

Even in the dark, she could tell that Lis was coming up with an answer to that. She had turned her head to look at the Galaxie, her face back in shadow under the streetlight.

Gas is expensive, Lis said, drawn out and final, as if she had realized that whatever she had wanted to request was no longer worth asking about. But she kept her sight on the car and said nothing more, which only convinced Delfina that she would, in time, come out with it.

We got our work truck very cheap before the gas lines started and we didn't realize how much it would take to keep it filled up. Did you have to stand in line for gas in Texas?

We did, said Delfina. It was like that everywhere, I heard.

Not everywhere, said Lis. They tell me that Mexico is OK again, but family will always tell you whatever they need to get you home.

Where are you from?

Guanajuato. And you?

From Texas, said Delfina. Where we drove from, she added, as if to remind her.

Lis's face had fallen back into shadow, making it hard to see if she was pressing her lips into a vague smile about the fact that Delfina's husband had been rounded up with the rest of them. The old man who used to live in your house a long time ago was from Texas, from the Matamoros side, she said. He lived here so long he

said this street used to be the real edge of town and that it backed
up to a grape vineyard.

Is that right?

He passed away a while back but he was too old to work by then.
He always said he wished he could go back to Mexico because he
was all alone. Pobrecito. Sometimes I think he had the right idea.
It's a terrible thing to be alone.

If she knew this woman better, if this woman knew her better,
Delfina thought, she would tell her that this was only half true,
that it was hard to make a go of it alone, but that it could be just as
hard to live in a house without kindness.

But then you two came. With your niño. How old is he?

He is four.

So little, said Lis. How sweet. My girl is a little older. Ten.

I think I've seen her before, said Delfina, though she didn't remember.

Children never understand the circumstances, said Lis.

No, they don't, said Delfina. I don't think they should ever
learn that.

It's part of life, said Lis. Ni modo. You know, that old man, I
think he would've liked what we were doing with the work truck.
All of us going together, as many people as we could load in the
back. He always said people were better neighbors in Mexico.

The Texas side?

Claro, said Lis, half-smiling. Listen, our rent is due on the first,
she said. Yours, too, no?

Delfina didn't want to say yes, not even in the dark, but only
"no" would mean this wasn't true.

Lis looked over at the Galaxie. I learned something the last time
this happened, that I had to keep working instead of waiting. It's
not good to run low on money.

Delfina could hear her voice press in the same way her sister's
used to, her sister who talked and talked, who thought that the
more you talked, the more convincing you sounded. Her husband
had said that anyone who asked too hard about anything really
wanted something else.

What would you say about taking the car out to the peach orchards and splitting what we get? I'd pay for half the gas.

Oh, I don't know . . . , Delfina began.

My girl is old enough to care for your niño, if you trust her, Lis

offered. It could be just us, she said, if you don't want to bring
along anyone else in the neighborhood.

I don't know . . . , Delfina hesitated, though she knew she could
not say that more than twice and she steeled herself to say no.

I know the farmer, said Lis. We could go out to the orchards
and pick up a few rows before he gives all that work away.

I'll have to think about it, said Delfina. My husband doesn't like
me driving the car. She remembered what her neighbor had said
about impoundment and she tried that: If they take the car . . .

You're from Texas, said Lis, but she pressed no further. Her face
was clear and open, but the way she said these words stung, as if
being from one side or the other meant anything about how easy
or hard things could be. It was none of any stranger's business, but
Delfina's husband had never allowed her to work and she knew
what women like Lis thought about women like her.

I don't know the first thing about working in the fields anyway,
Delfina said. She tried to say it in a way that meant it was the truth
and not at all a reply to what Lis had said about Texas.

It's easy but hard at the same time, said Lis. Anyone can do it.
It's just that no one really wants to.

I'll have to think about it, said Delfina.

I understand, Lis answered and backed a step out to the street,
her arms folded in a way that Delfina recognized from her sister,
the way she had stood on the Texas porch in defeat and resigna-
tion. Que pases buenas noches, Lis said and began walking away
before Delfina had a chance to reply in kind. When she did, she
felt her voice carry along the street, as if everyone else on the block
had overheard this refusal, and she went back into the house with
an unexpected sense of shame.

Very early the next morning, after a restless night, Delfina woke
her little boy from the pallet of blankets on the living room floor.
We're going into town, she told him, when Kiki resisted her with
grogginess as she struggled to get him dressed. She was about to
lead him to the car when she pictured herself driving past Lis's
house, how that would look to a woman she had just refused,
and her pride took over. She grasped Kiki's hand in her own with
such ferocity that he knew that she meant business and he walked
quickly beside her down the street and around the corner, past
the little white church empty on a Saturday morning and toward
town. The boy kept pace with her somehow and, to her surprise,

he made no more protests, and twenty minutes later, when they reached the TG&Y, she deposited Kiki in the toy aisle without saying a word and marched to the pay phone at the back of the store to call her mother in Texas.

He left you, her mother's voice said over the line. Nothing keeps a good father from his family.

They took other men in the neighborhood, too, Delfina said. He wasn't alone.

How many times did he go out to work here in Texas and he came home just fine? I told you that you shouldn't have gone. Your sister was absolutely right . . .

Delfina pulled the phone away from her ear and the vague hectoring of her mother barely rippled out along the bolts of fabric and the sewing notions hanging on the back wall of the store. Delfina gripped the remaining dimes in her hands, slick and damp in her palm, and clicked one of them into the phone, the sound cutting out for a moment as the coin went through.

How's the niño? Is he dreaming about his father yet? That's how you'll know if he's coming back or not.

Did you hear that? she interrupted her mother, dropping another coin. I don't have much time left.

Why are you calling? For money? Of course, you're calling for money. If he's a good father, he'll find a way to send some if he can't get back.

If you were a good mother, Delfina began, but it came as hardly even a whisper, and she lacked the real courage to talk back this way, to summon the memory of her white-haired father who had died years ago and taken with him, it seemed, any criticism of his late-night ways. Her voice was lost anyway as her mother yelled out to trade the phone over to Delfina's sister, and in the moment when the exchange left them all suspended in static, Delfina hung up the receiver. She had not even given them the address for the Western Union office and she would have to apologize, she knew, when the worst of the financial troubles would be upon her. But for the moment, she relished how she had left her older sister calling into the phone, staring back incredulous at her mother.

Come along, she said to Kiki when she went to collect him from the toy aisle, where he had quietly scattered the pieces of a board game without the notice of the clerk. He started to cry out in protest, now that he was in the cool and quiet of the five-and-dime and she was pulling him away from the bins of marbles and plastic army men. Delfina imagined the footsteps of the clerk coming to check on the commotion and, in her hurry to shove the board game back onto the shelf, she let slip the pay phone dimes, Kiki frozen in surprise by their clatter before he stooped to pick them up.

Come along, she said again, letting him have the dimes. Ice cream, she whispered in encouragement, and led on by this suggestion, he followed her out of the store. Kiki fell meek and quiet once again, as if he knew not to jeopardize his sudden fortune. It was only right to reward him with the promised treat, and she led him down the street to the drugstore with its ice cream stand visible from the large front window. It was only ten in the morning and the young woman at the main register had to come around to serve them two single scoops, but Delfina didn't even take the money from Kiki's hands to pay for it. She had a single folded dollar bill in her pocket and she handed it to the clerk, foolish, she thought, to be spending so frivolously. But her boy didn't need to know those troubles. His Saturday was coming along like any other, his father sometimes not home at sundown and always gone at sunrise. There was no reason to get him wondering about things he wasn't yet wondering about.

Delfina led him to the little park across the street from the town bank. He gripped his cone tightly and his other hand held the fist of dimes. She motioned him to pocket the change for safekeeping. Put it away, she said, sitting on one of the benches. But her little boy kept them in his grip and so she patted his pocket more firmly to encourage him and that's when she felt it, a hard little object that she knew instantly was something he had stolen from the toy aisle.

Let me see, she said, or I will take away your coins. Kiki struggled against her, smearing some of the ice cream on his pants, which finally distressed him into actual tears. Ya, ya, Delfina said, calming him, and fished what was in his pocket, a little green car, metal and surprisingly heavy. Her little boy was inconsolable and the Saturday shoppers along the sidewalk stopped to look in their direction. Sssh, she told him, there, there, and took the time to show him the car in the palm of her hand before she slipped it back into his pocket. Ya, ya, she said one more time, and leaned back on the bench, the Saturday morning going by.

Later, when they rounded the corner back into the neighborhood, she saw Lis out in her dirt yard. She was tending to a small bed of wild sunflowers, weeding around them with a hoe, her back turned to the street. The closer they got to Lis's yard, the harder the scuffling of Kiki's shoes became and Lis turned around to the noise.

Buenos dias, Delfina greeted her. She wanted to keep walking but Lis made her way toward her and she knew she would have to stop and listen, much like the time in Arizona on the trip out here, when she had accidently locked eyes with a man at a gas station, and he had walked over to rap on the window of the Galaxie and beg for some change.

Good thing we didn't go to the orchards after all, said Lis. I would've felt terrible if your car had stalled out there.

No . . . , Delfina began. I . . . The more she stumbled, the less it made sense to make up any story at all. There was no reason to be anything but honest.

The car is fine, she said. I just wanted him to walk a bit. We got ice cream.

For breakfast, Lis said, looking down at Kiki and smiling. What a Saturday! The morning's sweat matted her hair down on her forehead and she wore no gloves, her fingers a bit raw from the metal handle of the hoe, but she was cheerful with Kiki, recognizing his exhaustion. Her daughter, Delfina realized, was not out helping her, but inside the cool of the house, and she took this as a sign of the same propensity for sacrifice that she believed herself to hold.

I've thought about it, Delfina said, though she really hadn't. I think it's a good idea.

I'm glad, said Lis.

I wish I had said so last night. We could've put in a day's work. But I'm happy to go tomorrow.

Tomorrow's Sunday, said Lis, and when Delfina put her hand up to her mouth as if she'd forgotten, as if she might change her mind, Lis moved even closer to her, looking down at Kiki. But work never waits, she said.

El día de Dios, said Delfina. I didn't even think of it.

People work, said Lis. Don't worry about it.

We can wait until Monday. That way the children can be at school.

Like I told you, my daughter is old enough to watch him, if you trust her. I leave her alone sometimes. Or we can bring them out with us and stay longer.

Delfina could make out the shadow of a child watching from behind the screen door and, catching her glance past her shoulder, Lis turned to look. She called her forth and her daughter stepped out, a girl very tall for ten years old. This is our neighbor, Lis explained, and we'll need you to watch her little boy tomorrow. Will you do that?

The girl nodded and she stuck out her hand to Delfina in awkward politeness.

What's your name? Delfina asked.

Irma, the girl said, very quietly, her voice deferential. She had very small eyes that she squinted as if in embarrassment and Delfina wondered if she needed glasses but was too afraid to say.

We can trust you, can't we, said Lis, to take care of the little boy? If I leave you some food, you can feed him, can't you?

Oh, I can leave them something . . .

Don't worry, said Lis. I can leave something easy to fix and you can bring out something for us in the orchard. I have a little ice chest to keep everything out of the sun.

After Delfina nodded her head in agreement, Lis made as if to go back to her yard work. At dawn, then, Lis said. I'll bring everything we need.

For the rest of the day, Delfina was restless, anxious that every noise on the street might signal the return of the men. To have them come back would mean the lull of normalcy, of what had been and would continue to be, just when she was on the brink of doing something truly on her own. But the street stayed quiet. The afternoon heat swallowed the houses and by evening, some of the shadows resumed their evening watch, sitting stiffly but without much hope or expectation. They turned back in before night had fully come and Delfina went to bed early, too.

At dawn, she roused Kiki from the blankets strewn on the living room floor and poured him some cereal. He blinked against the harshness of the kitchen light at such an early hour, surprised at his mother wearing one of his father's long-sleeve work shirts, and even more surprised by the knock at the door. Lis stood there, her daughter behind her. Buenos dias, Delfina said and waved the girl Irma inside. She poured her a bowl of cereal, too, and Irma sat quietly at the table without having to be told to do so.

Thank you for taking care of him, Delfina said. We'll be back in the middle of the afternoon. She knew she didn't have to say more than that, trusted that Lis had spoken with the same motherly sense of warning that she used. Still, it was only now, on the brink of leaving them alone for the day, that she wished she had asked Kiki if he had been dreaming about his father, if he might have communicated something about what was true for him while he slept.

Lis showed her the gloves and the work knives and then the two costales to hold the fruit, a sturdy one of thick canvas with a hearty shoulder strap and a smaller one of nylon mesh. Her other hand balanced a water jug and a small ice chest, where Delfina put in a bundle of foil-wrapped bean tacos that would keep through the heat of the day.

In the car, Lis pointed her south of town and toward the orchards and Delfina drove along. They kept going south, the orchards endless, cars parked over on the side of the road and pickers approaching foremen, work already getting started even though the dawn's light hadn't yet seeped into the trees.

Up there, Lis said, where a few cars had already lined up and several workers had gathered around a man sitting on the open tailgate of his work truck. Wait here, she said.

Before Delfina could ask why, Lis had exited, approaching the man with a handshake. He seemed to recognize her and then looked back at Delfina in the car. Lis finished what she needed to say and the man took one more look at Delfina and then pointed down the rows.

Lis motioned her to get out of the car.

He says he'll give us two rows for now and we do what we can. If we're fast, he'll give us more. And he's letting us use a ladder free of charge.

That's kind of him . . .

They charge sometimes, Lis said. She took one end of a heavy-looking wooden ladder, the tripod hinge rusty and the rungs worn smooth in the middle. So fifty-fifty?

Half and half, Delfina agreed.

I can pick the tops and you can do the bottoms, if you're afraid of heights. Or you can walk the costales back to the crates for weighing. Give them your name if you want to, but make sure the foreman tells you exactly how much we brought in.

They worked quickly, the morning still cool. Delfina parted the leaves where the peaches sat golden among the boughs and the work felt easy at first. The fruit came down with scarcely more than a tug and when she yanked hard enough to rustle the branches, Lis spoke her advice from the ladder above: Just the redder ones and not too hard. Feel them, she said. If they're too hard, leave them. Someone else will come back around in a few days and they'll be riper then.

They did a few rounds like this, Delfina taking the costales back to the road to have them weighed. Sometimes Lis was ready with the smaller nylon sack and sometimes Delfina had to wait for other pickers to have their fruit accounted for. The morning moved on, a brighter white light coming into the orchard as they got closer to noon. As they picked the trees near clean, they moved deeper and deeper into the orchard and the walk back to the crates took longer, Lis almost lost to her among the leaves.

They had not quite finished the row when the sun finally peaked directly overhead and their end of the orchard sank into quiet. Delfina let out a sigh upon her return.

I should've brought the ice chest while I was there.

I can get it, said Lis. You've walked enough. She came down with the half-empty nylon costal and pulled a few more peaches from the bottom boughs as Delfina rested. She started walking toward the road, then turned around. The keys, she said, and held out her hand.

Delfina watched her go. Lis walked quickly with the nylon costal dangling over her shoulder. Maybe the weight of Lis's work was all in her arms from stretching and pulling, and not heavy and burning in the thighs like hers. Delfina sat in the higher bank of the orchard row, catching her breath, massaging her upper legs and resting. It was a Sunday, she remembered, and Lis had been right after all. People did work on this day, even if it felt as tranquil and lonely as Sundays always did, here among the trees with the leaves growing more and more still, the orchard quiet and then quieter. Sundays were always so peaceful, Delfina thought, no matter where you were, so serene she imagined the birds themselves had gone dumb. El día de Dios, she thought, and remembered Sundays when her white-haired father had not yet slept out the drunkenness of the previous night. Her own husband had sometimes broken the sacredness of a Sunday silence and she was oddly thankful for the calm of this orchard moment that had been brought on only by his absence. Delfina looked down the row to soak in that blessed quiet and the longer she looked, the emptier and emptier it became. The empty row where, she realized, Lis had disappeared like a faraway star.

She started back toward the road. The walk was long and she couldn't hear a sound, not of the other workers, not other cars rumbling past the orchards, just the endless trees and her feet against the heavy dirt of the fields. The day's weariness slowed her and made the trees impossible to count, but she walked on, resolute, the gray of the road coming into view. She emerged onto the shoulder of the road and saw the foreman and the foreman's truck and a few other cars, but the Galaxie was gone.

Excuse me, she said, approaching the foreman, who seemed surprised to see her, though he had seen her all morning, noting down the weight of the peaches she had brought in, saying the numbers twice, tallied under the last name Arellano.

You're still here, the foreman said, very kindly, as if the fact was a surprise to him too, and his face grew into a scowl like the faces of the white men Delfina had encountered in Texas, the ones who always seemed surprised that she spoke English. But where their faces had been steely and uncaring, his softened with concern, as if he recognized that he had made a serious mistake.

I thought you were gone, he said.

We were supposed to split . . . She held a hand to her head and looked up the road, one way and then the other, as if the car were on its way back, Lis having gone only to the small country store to fetch colder drinks.

Arellano, the foreman said, tapping his ledger. Arellano is the first name on the list, he said. I paid it out about a half hour ago.

That was my car, Delfina said, as if that would be enough for him to know what to do next. But the foreman only stared back at her. It was my husband's car, she said, because that was how she saw it now, what her husband would say about its loss if he ever made it back.

She told me that you two were sisters, the foreman said. If he only knew, Delfina thought, her real sister back in Texas. The mere mention made her turn back toward the orchard and walk into the row. She could sense the foreman walking to the row's opening to see where she was going, and when she reached the ladder, she folded it down and heaved it best as she could, its legs cutting a little trough behind her as she dragged it back to the road.

You didn't have to do that, the foreman said.

You did right by letting us use it, Delfina said. It's only fair. Other pickers had approached the foreman's truck and he attended to them, though he kept looking over at Delfina now and then, his face sunken in concern. None of the workers looked at her and she let go of the idea of asking any of them for a ride back into town. She sat in the dirt under the shade of a peach tree and watched while the foreman flipped out small wads of cash as the workers began to quit for the afternoon. When the last of them shook hands with the foreman and began to leave, she rose to help him load all of the wooden ladders back on to the truck.

He accepted her help and opened the door of the truck cab, motioning for her to get in. They drove slow back into town, the ladders clattering with every stop and start, the weight of them shifting and settling. Neither of them said a word, but before the orchards gave way back to the houses, the foreman cleared his throat and spoke: I think it's the first time I ever had two women come out alone like that, but I was raised to think that anybody can do anything and you don't ask questions just because something isn't normal. Even just a little bit of work is better than none at all and I kept thinking about the story she told me, that you two were sisters and that your husbands had gotten thrown over the border. You can tell a lot by a wife who wants to work as hard as her husband, you know what I mean? I wasn't sure you could finish two rows just the both of you, but you kept coming and coming with those sacks and that's how I knew you had kids to feed.

At the four-way intersection, just before the last mile into town, the foreman fished into his pocket and pulled out a bill. Take it, he said. He handed it to her, a twenty, and almost pushed it into Delfina's hands as he started the turn, needing to keep the steering wheel steady. The bill fluttered in her fingers from the breeze of the open passenger window, but the truck wasn't going to pick up much more speed. She wouldn't lose it.

Thank you, she said.

It's not your fault, he said. And I'm not defending her for what she did. But I believe any story that anybody tells me. You can't be to blame if you got faith in people.

You're right, she agreed. And though she didn't have to say it, she followed it with the words of blind acceptance before she could stop herself. I understand, she said, and it was not worth explaining that she really didn't.

Where should I take you? asked the foreman.

She didn't hesitate. There's a little store right near Gold Street, just across the tracks, she said. If you could stop, just so I can get something for my boy.

Of course, he said, though there could have been no other possible way to respond, since Delfina's request came with a small hiccup of tears, which she quickly swallowed away as the truck pulled into the store's small lot. Other workers had stopped there, too, and men from other neighborhoods lingered out front with their open cases of beer and skinny bags of sunflower seeds, staring at her as she wiped at her face with her dirty sleeves. She brought a package of bologna and a loaf of bread to the register and fished out three bottles of cola from the case at the front counter. The clerk broke the twenty into a bundle of ones, and she held them with the temporary solace of pretending there would be money enough for the days ahead and that money was going to be the least of her worries anyway.

She directed the foreman just a couple more blocks and when they turned the corner, the neighborhood held a Sunday quiet that made her think first of an empty church, but she had not been to a service in years. No, it was a quiet like the porch of the house in Texas when she and her husband had driven away, leaving her sister and her mother, a stillness that she was sure held only so long before one of them had started crying, followed by the other. A calm like that could only be broken by the bereft and that was how she understood that neither of them would ever forgive her. But that didn't matter now. The hotter days of July were coming, Delfina knew, and the work of picking all the fruit would last from sunup to sundown. Something would work out, she told herself, clear and resolute against the emptiness of her neighborhood, Lis's house stark in its vacancy. There, she said, pointing to her house, and she wasn't surprised to see Kiki sitting there on the front steps all alone.

There he is, waiting for his mama, the foreman said, as he pulled up, and Kiki looked back at them, with neither curiosity nor glee.

She handed the foreman the third cola bottle.

You know, he said, it'll work out in the end. Sisters always end up doing the right thing. She'll be back, you'll see.

What story had he figured out for himself, Delfina wondered, after she hadn't bothered to correct him about Lis not being her sister, and she decided that this also mattered little in the end, how he would explain this to his wife back home. She would not explain this to her husband when he came back. All her husband would care about was what happened to the Galaxie and that would be enough of a story. She might even tell her husband about the luck of the twenty-dollar bill but she would hold private the detail of the ring on the foreman's finger. She would hold in her mind what it felt like to be treated with a faithful kindness.

Thank you, she said, and descended from the truck cab, nodding her head goodbye.

On the steps, Kiki eyed the tall bottles of cola in her hand. But first there was the heavy field dust to pound away from her shoes and the tiredness she could suddenly feel in her bones. Delfina kicked her shoes off and sat on the front steps. She lodged one of the bottles under the water spigot to pop the cap, a trick she had seen her husband do. She handed that bottle to Kiki and he took it with both hands, full of thirst or greed for the sweetness, she couldn't tell. She took some of the bread loaf and the bologna for herself and offered him a bite, knowing he wouldn't eat one of his own. He was hungry and this was how she knew that Irma was gone, too. She was a girl who did what she was told and Delfina didn't blame her. Kiki crowded close to her knees, even in the heat of the afternoon, and so she popped the cap of the second bottle to take a sip herself and asked her little boy of no words to tell where he thought the older girl had gone, and where he dreamed his father was. Dígame, she said, asking him to tell her a whole story, but Kiki had already taken the little metal car from his pocket and he was showing her, starting from the crook of his arm, how a car had driven away slowly, slowly, and on out past the edge of his little hand and out of their lives forever.

# *The Plan*

FROM *LitMag*

HE WANTED TO HAVE more culture. This was what he always thought when he found himself at Lincoln Center. He remembered coming here on a school trip once, about ten years ago, when the complex was still partly under construction. There'd been some kind of tour and a concert-lecture for kids from different schools in the city. It had gone on and on, of no interest to him. He had never been back. He'd never even thought of going back. But earlier that summer of '76, on one of his long city walks, he happened to arrive at the plaza.

It was evening but the sun was still very bright. From a distance he could see rainbows dancing in the fountain spray. He had started to walk closer for a better view, though, of course, as soon as he did that the rainbows vanished. Since then he had returned several times, more than once around the same hour. But he never saw the rainbows again.

Tonight he'd been walking for almost two hours. He sat down to rest on the lip of the fountain, refreshed by the spray that dampened the back of his shirt and his neck. He had an image of his mother, spritzing shirts from an atomized plastic bottle as she ironed them. Unless he was mistaken, this was the first time he'd thought of his mother in a long while.

He sat smoking a cigarette, cooling off and looking around him. It was near curtain time, and the plaza streamed with people going to the various theaters. Most of the men were in suits and ties. The women wore dresses that bared their shoulders, high heels,

and evening makeup. The warm air was infused with the mingled
smells of their perfume and hair spray.

It would not have occurred to him to see if he could get a ticket
to any of the performances. Not just because he was out of his element, but because, from what he could tell, everyone seemed to
be with somebody else. A person by himself would stick out—like
a person eating alone in a fancy restaurant. If you were rich you
could get away with that kind of thing, you'd only be seen as eccentric, maybe. But he thought an ordinary person, especially a man,
would be looked on with suspicion.

So he wouldn't have thought of going to a performance alone,
and he didn't know anyone he would ask to go with him. He had
no idea if he'd enjoy a concert here any more than he'd enjoyed
the one he'd been to as a kid. But, starting with the first time his
rambles had led him to Lincoln Center, the idea had taken shape:
he would like to know more about music and art.

As a kid, he'd been a big reader. Later, for some reason he lost
the habit. Now he thought he would like to read more, not just
newspapers and magazines, but big, interesting books—books that
a lot of other people were also reading.

*Get more culture.* He put that on the list. The list of things to
do *after.* For now, though, too much thinking about anything not
connected with his plan was a distraction, and too much distraction would not do. That was how these walks had gotten started.
He had discovered how, when you had something important to
work out, long walks could be helpful. He couldn't think well at
home, not even when he was alone. And when Harley was there
he couldn't think at all. Harley's effect on his thinking was like the
effect on their TV when their neighbor was in his garage using
one of his power tools. It would not take living much longer with
Harley to turn his brain into mush.

Where they lived people didn't walk. He was sure he'd never
seen anyone in his neighborhood out walking unless it was with a
dog. Again, a lone man would have stuck out. He would have felt
too conspicuous strolling through the streets. The town had a park
but it was small, and since lately it had become the turf of drug
addicts it was often cruised by the cops. In the city, on the other
hand, you could walk forever, invisible, unhassled. It was a mystery
to him how all the bustle only made it easier for him to think.

Two young women sat down next to him. They began talking,

raising their voices above the splash of the fountain. They had been shopping. They were pleased silly with themselves and the swimsuits and sandals they'd snagged for next to nothing thanks to the big end-of-summer sales. He had no desire to listen to their babble, but they could not be ignored. Both had high-pitched, almost squealing voices, and one had the bad habit of saying everything twice.

He flicked his cigarette butt into the fountain and stood up.

"Why'd that guy give us a dirty look?" said one of the women.

"I don't know," said the other. "I don't know."

This would not do. It had been automatic—he wasn't at all aware of having given those two any special look—and it would not do. Not knowing exactly how he was behaving and how he was being perceived could be fatal. *(Yes, I remember him vividly: he looked at me like he wanted to strangle me.)*

Most crimes were never solved, and heading the list of reasons was the failure of people to notice things. Everyone knew that. Like most people planning a crime, he was counting on it. He had no intention of getting caught, and yet he often found himself picturing a TV reporter standing in front of his house: *Neighbors of the twenty-three-year-old alleged killer were stunned to learn . . .*

It might be bad luck to keep imagining the scene of your own arrest, but the point that needed hammering was that everyone should be shocked. *(Roden Jones? He was the last guy we'd have suspected!)*

Walking down Broadway, he watched the colored lights glow brighter and more lurid as the sky grew darker. As always, when he reached Times Square his pace slowed and his heartbeat accelerated. He had to maneuver around the crowds that collected to gawk at the street acts. One was a shirtless skeleton singing falsetto. *Night in the CITY looks PRETTY to me.* It amazed him that anyone would reward a person who sang like a cat getting fucked. And he hated Joni Mitchell. Joni Mitchell was a candidate. But the open guitar case at the man's feet was filled with bills, even a couple of twenties.

Most of the other panhandlers out tonight weren't bothering to offer entertainment—unless you counted the Hare Krishnas chanting.

Knots of cops stood around, looking sullen and bored. Or maybe just pretending to be bored. A man with a tattered Bible

preached Christ's coming. ("And maybe when He come He get
you a new Bible, huh, bro?" jeered a passerby.) A girl sat on a
subway grate, hugging her knees, a paper Orange Julius cup at
her bare toes. Fifteen, sixteen years old, pretty, but filthy. A born-
too-late hippie. She was nodding with closed eyes when he first
saw her. But just as he passed she jerked her head up and looked
straight at him.

The contrast between the pure blue pools of her eyes and her
smut-streaked face was startling. But the look she gave him—a
look of unmistakable horror and sadness, as though she knew exactly what he was planning—made him flush and sharply turn his
face away.

He'd meant to catch the next train home, but instead he
stopped in the Emerald Pub near the station. It was a place he
knew well, though he always ignored the other regulars and behaved as if he'd never seen the bartender before.

The encounter with the street girl had rattled him. But he
was not superstitious—she was obviously just some deranged kid,
maybe high, maybe even hallucinating—and after two scotches he
was himself again.

By the time he got home Harley would probably have gone to
bed. If not, she'd give him a hard time. If she'd been hitting the
scotch herself, she might throw or break something. But it was all
a sham. She didn't really care where he'd been—not in her heart,
anyway.

On the train back to Long Island he found himself sitting
across from a woman slumped in her seat, nodding. She was about
his age, attractive despite a few pimples. She was wearing a tight
denim skirt short enough to create a mouse hole at the top of her
bare thighs. He and several other men sitting nearby glued their
eyes to the spot like cats, collectively willing her to relax deeper.

Suddenly she pulled herself upright. She glared at Roden and
made a big show of placing the handbag she'd been holding at
her side onto her lap. He ignored her, but inside he was sniggering. Wearing a skirt that all but exposed your crotch when you sat
down, being outraged when men took notice—that was women.
Earlier that day, he'd witnessed another one—in a dress that,
folded twice, would've fit like a hanky into his pocket—tear into
an old bum for whistling at her.

The girl opened her bag and dug out a stick of gum. She tore off the wrapper, dropped it to the floor, and crammed the gum into her mouth. Soon she was happily chewing and snapping. She was some kind of champion, apparently. It didn't seem possible anyone could snap gum that loud.

When he got up to move to another seat she shot him a smug look, as if she'd scored a triumph over him.

She is a candidate, he thought. What a joy it would've been to go back and make her choke on that gum, to squeeze her neck until the pimples burst.

When the train reached his stop he did not go straight home but drove instead to a nearby street, where at least half the houses stood deserted. The last house on the right was reddish-pink in daylight, the walls peeling badly, as if the house had sunburn. But at night it might have been any color.

In a front window throbbed a lime-green neon sign: READINGS BY LOLA.

He was let in by a man wearing Ho Chi Minh sandals and a soiled undershirt who shuffled wordlessly back to his beer and the TV show he'd been watching in the dark.

The lights in the room at the back of the house were on, and though the TV was so loud that it might as well have been in there with her, the woman had been sleeping. She rubbed her eyes and uttered a low, disgruntled sound when the door opened. She was wearing a red bra and a black nylon half slip.

When she saw who it was she made an effort to smile, saying, "Hey, Jake"—the name he'd given her—and rolled onto her stomach. She slid the slip up over her hips, exposing blue-mottled thighs and a massive doughy rump. On one cheek, a mark the shape and color of a plum, as if a giant had pressed his thumb there.

As though from a tower he plunged into that familiar paradoxical state in which his senses were both blunted and incredibly heightened. He no longer asked himself why, no matter who the woman—girlfriend or stranger, whore or lawful wedded wife—he had never had sex without shame.

If it was going to look like a robbery, it would be better if it wasn't at home. For one thing, break-ins were infrequent in their neighborhood, and besides, there was an alarm.

Two years ago, when they were on their honeymoon, their hotel room had been robbed. This was in Aruba, and that particular

night they were out at a club. In spite of warnings from hotel management, they had neglected to lock their patio door. It was no
big loss—just a few pieces of Harley's costume jewelry. Other than
that, they'd been delighted with Aruba and with that particular
little two-story hotel, where every room had either a balcony or
a patio facing the sea. Harley had been talking about going back
ever since.

He remembered how easy it had been for the thief to enter.
And he thought how often it happened that a thief caught in the
act ended up committing murder—usually out of panic, but surely
in some cases because, at the sight of a helpless victim, the thief's
blood jumped, and the beast that might otherwise have slept
roared to life.

Strange, that he couldn't remember the precise moment when
he'd decided to subtract Harley. Sometimes it seemed as if the
idea had always existed, ever since they'd known each other, as it
seemed he had always hated her, though of course he knew this
was false.

He'd been barely out of his teens when he proposed to her. His
mother's death that year had left him alone. His father had died
a few days before Roden's fifteenth birthday—killed one day on
his way to work when his Pontiac hit a giant pothole and threw
itself into an oncoming car. After the settlement, his mother had
bought a house near the ocean and, with the help of a string of
boyfriends, proceeded to go through the rest of the money at such
a pace that there might have been nothing left if she hadn't succumbed to a bad case of lupus.

Roden's uncle Gene was afraid that inheriting a large sum of
money would squelch what little motivation Roden appeared to
have. It was true that he'd come of age with no particular goals,
but he believed this would have happened anyway. It was how he
was made. He'd always been a bad student, and in spite of an IQ
score he was told was above average he'd never had any interest in
going to college.

He was still in school when his mother's health first started to
fail. He'd stayed with her till the end, not thinking much about
the future, and after she was gone he wasn't sure what to do with
himself. He believed he'd think of something—he was still young,
after all. Look how the money had come to him. His uncle warned
him that a dollar didn't go as far as it used to, and Roden shouldn't

forget that most of his life was still ahead of him. But Roden believed that if everyone would just leave him alone, let him think in peace, he'd discover what to do. And for the moment he was glad he didn't have to work at some shit job like so many other people. The very idea made him sick. He was sure he'd become a thief or some kind of con man, or a drug dealer, like his old school pal Lanny, before he'd ever have let that happen. Those who chose the path of crime earned more respect from him than all the working stiffs.

Not that he was afraid to get his hands dirty. Gene, who worked as a contractor, put him on a crew from time to time, and he liked the achy, wasted feeling he had at the end of a day of manual labor, the hard-earned cash Gene stuffed into his shirt pocket. But that didn't mean he wanted to make a career of it.

That sizzling August day when he met Harley for the first time (at Jones Beach, posed on a towel like a pinup in a leopard-skin bikini), she was a key-punch operator working in an office in the Chrysler Building. But once they were engaged she quit. She was two years older than Roden, who was surprised to learn that she was in no hurry to get pregnant. He'd always thought a woman couldn't wait to have kids. Though she was never a loving mother herself—though she heaped sarcasm on her son and beat him with an extension cord—his mother had always assured him this was a universal truth.

But it meant nothing to him, either, that Harley wanted to put off motherhood. His cousin and best man, Ryan, warned him that, wedding accomplished, everything would change. This was another universal truth.

"Suddenly, she's got you where she wants, she thinks she's the boss of you, and everything you do is wrong. And once the first kid arrives, she's got no more time for you. And then the weight comes on, and there's something about this weight that seems to cause headaches or cramps most nights of the week. Next thing you know, high heels and makeup, not to mention screwing, are for special occasions. A blow job, like your birthday and Christmas, comes but once a year, and soon you're like, whoa, did I marry my girl or her fucking mother?"

Sometime between their first and second anniversaries, Harley stopped talking about putting off having kids. She stopped talking about having kids at all. She couldn't be accused of letting herself go, though. If anything, she was sleeker and better dressed than ever.

He had never committed a serious crime, but he had a criminal's instincts, including the one that said it was the small stuff you had to worry about. The smallest detail was the one that would bust you, like the sneeze that busts the last hijacker at the end of *The Taking of Pelham One Two Three*.

He goes over the plan again and again, step by step, even writing it all down (though careful afterward to tear the paper into tiny strips and throw them away).

They would be in their hotel room, getting ready to go out. She would be eager to go out. She loved nightclubs—clubs, fancy restaurants: these were the kinds of places where Harley shone. Above all, she loved to go dancing.

He would wait till she was in the bathroom. He would wait by the bathroom door, and when she came out he'd pounce. Even for a woman she was weak, couldn't open a jar without a rubber husband, or a bag of chips without using her teeth. Add to that the element of surprise, and it'd be a cinch to wrestle her down and gag and bind her. As an extra precaution he'd put a pillowcase over her head. Turn on the TV.

While she lay there, *figuring it out*, he'd toss the room. Then he'd leave and go down to the hotel bar, where he'd order a beer and take it to one of the tables in the courtyard. Remember to bring a newspaper or magazine. He'd sit by the pool and drink some of the beer, savoring it. Savoring her fear.

After a few minutes he'd get up, leaving the unfinished beer and the paper or magazine on the table. Just needed to use the men's room or buy cigarettes or make a phone call. He'd go back to the room and strangle her, using the telephone cord. Ten seconds or so and she'd be unconscious (he'd done his research, at the library—*in* the library, rather than checking out any possibly incriminating evidence). *With the application of continuous pressure, death will occur in four or five minutes.*

It had to be quick. No matter how exciting it might be to go slow, resist temptation. Oh, but of course he'd remove the pillowcase: he wanted to see her face. And she must see him. Must watch him do it.

Tear off gag and bonds, stuff into pockets to be discarded later, race back to courtyard. He'd sit down at his table and calmly take up his reading again, take up his beer, and when the beer was all gone he'd go back inside to the bar.

Looking at his watch, he'd ask the bartender if he could use the phone to make an in-house call. He'd dial his room number, let it ring several times before hanging up. Thank the bartender for the use of the phone. Decline if asked whether he'd like another beer. Wait around another minute or so, hands in pockets (gestures were very important) as if expecting someone momentarily to arrive. Finally, check watch again, shake head, furrow brow, leave bar.

Back in the room, he'd take a few seconds to make sure all was in order before calling the police.

Long before this moment, he would have rehearsed in front of a mirror the facial expressions and gestures that would show shock and grief without seeming hammy.

It was not what they called an airtight alibi. If anyone happened to notice how long he'd been gone from the courtyard, it could be established that, in theory, at least, he'd had enough time to do the killing. If asked where he'd gone, he planned to say to the john. But suppose, on his way to or from his room, he passed somebody? This was a risk he must be prepared for. He must make absolutely sure that the person did not get a good look at him.

But even if his alibi wasn't perfect—even if the police suspected him (which, of course, they would)—as long as they had no hard evidence he was safe. Besides, an airtight alibi was a necessity only when there was a glaring motive, and in his case there was none. No history—not even hearsay—of domestic abuse. He had never beaten Harley, and because he detested petty squabbling he rarely even argued with her. He was a master of the silent treatment, and his way when a fight began escalating was to put on his coat and leave. Growing up, he'd watched his father do the same and learned how divinely it worked against his mother.

There'd be no one to say they'd heard fighting coming from the hotel room. In fact, no one had ever witnessed them fighting anywhere. The marriage might have been a flop, but appearances meant everything to Harley. She was too proud to let others know the truth. Instead, she liked to gloat, to make others envious, especially her girlfriends. "He treats me like a queen," she'd lie. And he never denied it. Sometimes he thought maybe she was even fooling herself. "He's my little puppy dog, aren't you, doll?" And he'd play along, making silly little yapping or whimpering noises.

No one had ever heard him say a word against his wife, or that he wished he were single again. He had his pride, too, and it would not let him whine. It would have killed him to be seen as one of those crushed and bitter husbands like Ryan. Better that the world believe any lie about you than that you were not your own man.

There was no sheet on him. As a kid, he'd committed plenty of vandalism and petty theft, but he'd never been caught, let alone arrested. There was no Other Woman. Harley had no money of her own and no life insurance policy. Tourists everywhere attracted robbers, everyone knew that, and though the murder of a tourist was a rare thing in the Caribbean, crime in general had been creeping up.

And, of course, this would not be the first break-in at The Nook in Blue Heaven.

That the balcony door wasn't locked would not cause suspicion: guests were advised to lock their doors only when they were away from the room.

He goes over it, again and again. He works it out, scene by scene. Sitting in the darkness of himself, he watches it play and replay, like a movie. He assures himself that, for a prime suspect, a perfect alibi would only increase suspicion. He reminds himself that to believe that you are capable of a perfect crime is delusional. You took your chances as with everything else in life. And as with everything else in life, fortune favored the brave.

He tells the travel agent to make all the necessary arrangements for the last week of January. Harley is ecstatic. Nothing she liked more than the prospect of flaunting a winter tan.

It was a change so subtle that, for a while, he thought it was only because he was watching her so carefully. Yet he could have sworn she was more subdued than usual, as if she was under the weather, or under some kind of special pressure, and there were times he believed she was watching him as carefully as he watched her.

But why? Was she worried that he was thinking of leaving her? Maybe. But hadn't he been the one to suggest a second honeymoon in Aruba? She couldn't possibly have guessed his plan. If she had even an inkling, would she dare stick around?

But what if some sixth sense was trying to warn her. He'd never known her to be afraid of him. In fact, he'd always had a grudging respect for her in this regard: she might have been physically weak, but compared with most women Harley was fearless.

The last week of January was still months away—a long time to cope with the anxiety that was now eating at him. Night after night he closed his eyes only to see that strange hippie-girl's blue ones widen in horror. He slept badly, then spent his days in a fog. Which would not do. He must keep a clear head.

Harley was sympathetic, offering him some of the Seconal her doctor had prescribed for the insomnia that sometimes plagued her when she was getting her period.

An old news story came back to him—from somewhere in England, if he remembered correctly—about a former army major who couldn't get along with his wife. One day, after one of their many fights, he read an apology she'd written him—*Darling, I'm sorry. No one is to blame but myself. Please forgive me*—and saw a made-to-order suicide note. He arranged it to look as though she'd hanged herself. And he'd have gotten away with it, too, except that he confessed to a friend and ended up swinging from a rope himself.

It amazed Roden that someone strong enough to kill another person would not have the willpower to keep a secret. But he knew that it happened all the time.

Drugging Harley with some of her sleeping pills and tying a plastic bag over her head: of course he'd considered it. But he didn't have any convenient little note, did he.

Summer was gone, but while the weather was still warm he continued to haunt the city. With the new season the streets were more crowded, people moved faster, with more purpose and energy.

Having studied the posters, he now had a better idea of what went on at Lincoln Center. He still thought about wanting to have more culture in his life. But he didn't have to sit through a whole opera or ballet to know he would hate it.

Once school started, he found himself drawn north to the neighborhood around Columbia University. At first he felt self-conscious in places that were obvious student hangouts. Then one day a waitress asked him if he had his ID—there was a student discount, she explained—and he realized that he'd been silly to think he stood out. In a T-shirt and jeans and the denim or army jacket he usually wore, he could easily pass for a student.

On campus one afternoon, obeying an impulse, he trailed some students into a building and found himself outside a lecture hall where a class was just starting. The room was about two-thirds full. Ducking his head, he went to sit in an aisle seat in the last row. He glanced sideways at the teacher, who faced the class from behind a small wooden table with a glass of water sitting on it, like a man waiting to be served dinner. Roden was astonished that a professor would show up to work like this man: tieless, with a big stain on the front of his sweater vest, chin stubble, and a mop of uncombed hair.

Roden slumped in his seat, wondering what he'd say if the teacher asked what he was doing there. But why did he feel so fucking nervous? His heart was pounding, for Christ's sake. Self-loathing rose like mercury in his gut. He could barely listen to what the teacher was saying.

But even after he'd calmed down, he had trouble following. The name Marx kept coming up. The name was pretty much all Roden knew about Marx. He figured he'd have understood more if he'd been to the previous classes.

Soon he stopped listening. If he'd been less self-conscious, he'd probably have dozed off, as he noted two other guys in the room had done already. The teacher must have seen them, too, but to Roden's surprise he ignored them. He remembered the Catholic schools he'd gone to, where no kid ever would've gotten away with that, and it struck him that college life must be pretty breezy.

There was one student who kept interrupting the teacher by raising his hand as if he had a question. It never was a question, though, but always just his own thoughts—usually at some length—about what the teacher was saying. The teacher appeared to have no problem with this, but Roden thought the kid was showing off. Even more annoying was the fact that he wore his long hair in two pigtails, with a headband. When he looked in the mirror he probably saw a Comanche brave. What he should have seen was a girl. A very homely girl.

Later, he came across a course catalogue in a student lounge and learned that the course he'd been trespassing on was called Introduction to Marx. The surprise was that it was listed as a philosophy course. He'd always thought Marx was a politician, not some kind of philosopher.

At first he thought he'd misheard when the homely girl called the teacher Professor Marx. But in fact it was just one of those funny coincidences—and not really such a big coincidence, either, he thought, remembering that there'd been a Lenore Marx in his high school. A real cunt, as he recalled. Lenore Marx had been a candidate.

Toward the end of October he and Harley went to a wedding. The bride was his cousin, Gene's youngest daughter, Shay. At the reception, which was held at a restaurant in Montauk, Roden and Harley were dancing. Harley preferred fast music, because, unlike most husbands, hers danced well, and with him for a partner she could put on a show. But this was a slow song.

She had a habit when slow dancing of rubbing her forehead back and forth against his chin. The coconut scent of a new cream rinse she'd started using filled his nostrils, reminding him of suntan lotion. Reminding him of the beach. Of Aruba.

"Do you remember the first time we ever danced together?" she said.

"Yes," he lied. He wondered if she'd felt his heart jump. But what the fuck was she talking about? What had made her ask him that now?

Just then the song ended, and they pulled apart. His heart jumped again when he saw her expression. It wasn't like Harley to be sentimental—that was another way she was different from other women. Yet here she was, out of the blue, looking misty-eyed, talking mush.

To cover his discomposure he said, "I'm out of smokes. I'll meet you back at the table." There was a cigarette machine in the lobby. He took a few minutes longer than necessary, but he was still agitated when he returned to the banquet room.

Instead of going back to their table, Harley was now sitting at another table, next to her friend Angie. The two had their heads together, but when Roden approached they sprang apart as if a bee had flown between them.

It could have been anything, he told himself later. Any kind of girl talk. Women often huddled like that, looking all urgent as if they were discussing matters of state when in fact they were just gossiping, or, even more likely, tearing apart one of their friends. Besides, he didn't like Angie and she knew it, and she tended to go quiet around him.

Several times in recent days he'd been on the point of asking

Harley if something was wrong, but he was leery about where the question might take them. Until they got to Aruba, he thought, the less said between them, the better. But all his admirable patience was wearing thin, and January had started to feel very far away.

He was afraid of losing focus. He wanted it to be ever clear before him: his purpose, his decision, the reason Harley had to die.

Though he still didn't know what he was going to do with his life, he often felt on the verge of an important discovery. At the same time, he felt that Harley was in the way. Her very existence was holding him back, preventing him from being who he was meant to be.

He knew he would never marry again. Marriage was all wrong for him—he should have learned from his parents, who'd only made each other miserable. The truth was, he couldn't bear to live with the mistake he'd made, the humiliation of it.

And there was something else, something that had started long before he'd ever met Harley. By high school, it had already become a habit. He'd pick out a certain person because of something about her, maybe the way she talked, or the way she dressed or wore her makeup or her hair—some particular thing that got to him. She might have a sarcastic streak, like some of his teachers. Or she might be stuck up (Lenore Marx), or maybe just obnoxiously loudmouthed or conceited or dumb. And he'd feel a flood of venom and think, *She is a candidate.*

It was always by strangulation. And it wasn't that he never had murderous feelings toward any male—he did, often—but, for the full-blown fantasy, the candidate had to be female.

In his head he had strangled the assistant principal, several teachers and fellow students, and dozens, if not hundreds, of strangers. And one particular snub-nosed cheerleader many times.

His sickness—he did not shrink from calling it that—was something he waited to outgrow, like his habit of lifting purses, or his other juvenile delinquencies. But though once he'd reached manhood he wouldn't have dreamed of slashing the tires of a stranger's car, of murder he did dream. Of murder he dreamed more and more.

This candidate. That candidate.

But there were times when it wasn't just this or that particular female. It was everyone. People he knew, people he didn't know.

People. *They were all candidates.* And whenever he let his thoughts run free in that direction, the wildness of his own imagination shook him to the core.

Then, during the last year of his mother's life, his thoughts of murder waned. Though she'd had a full-time home nurse, her dying gutted Roden, leaving him hollowed out like a jack-o'-lantern, and when she died his grief was far worse than when he'd lost his father. It was the strongest emotion he'd ever known.

And then he met Harley.

Was blinded by the luster of her silver-blond hair—

Her lean tanned legs—

Her sumptuous breasts—

Her mouth with its taste like vanilla.

No sooner were they man and wife than the sickness returned. But there was this difference now. He was no longer appalled. He was not a child anymore, the fear of God had long left him. He hadn't believed in God since he was ten years old.

Time passed, and the two feelings grew equally, like twin demons developing inside him: the desire to be wifeless, the desire to kill.

He thought of it as a correction. Striking through his marriage, his mistake. Burying his humiliation.

Clear and simple. Or at least it had been clear and simple—before. But then things for which he wasn't prepared started happening. He was tortured by the fear of a flaw in his plan, the fear that he lacked some essential piece of information. Or he was losing his nerve.

Driving away from the wedding reception, he asked Harley as casually as he could if everything was OK and he felt her go rigid at his side. A chill little laugh, followed by her clipped assurance that of course everything was OK, why wouldn't it be OK, followed by a yawn. Her tell: Harley always faked a yawn when she was lying. They were both silent for the rest of the way home.

That night, Harley took a double dose of Seconal before going to bed. Roden got up several times in the night. He paced the room, stopping to gaze down at her sprawled, inert body. *Dead to the world.* He pondered the expression, running it like a bit of ticker tape through his head until it was drained of sense.

Why does she have to die?

She has to die so that he can be free.

She has to die because he has to kill someone, and she is the obvious candidate.

He isn't going to waste a lot of time thinking about whether or not she deserves to die.

Kneeling by the bed, the way he'd been taught as a small boy to say his prayers, he went over the plan again, step by step.

*There'd be no time afterward to fuck her.* Not for the first time does this thought leap and bark at him. The idea has always excited him, but he knows it's too risky.

Dead to the world. She doesn't even flinch as he stands there loudly cursing her in the dark.

Were it not for the Valium and the nitrous oxide they'd given her, he might never have learned the truth. But when she came home after what was supposed to have been a breakfast date with Angie, Harley was weepy and babbling.

When Angie tried to hustle her upstairs—"She's just a little dizzy, she just needs to lie down"—Roden asked her to leave. Angie looked scared then, obviously reluctant to leave Harley alone with him. But he'd spoken in a way that made her go at once.

He followed Harley up to their room, where she crawled into bed and blurted out everything.

When he tried telling her that it was OK, he wasn't upset, he wasn't angry at her, it was as if she was deaf. It soon became clear that his feelings were not what she was concerned about. Nor was she crying because she'd had a change of heart about the baby.

She was afraid of going to Hell.

"Oh, Roddy, what if God won't forgive me?"

"What are you talking about? You don't believe in all that Catholic crap anymore, remember?"

It was true. They'd been married in a church because Harley wasn't going to be denied the lead role in a big church wedding. But neither of them had been to Mass in years.

There could be no doubt, though, that she was genuinely scared. A Catholic upbringing is something you never really leave behind.

He could not calm her fears. He was having enough trouble trying to stifle his own feelings, or at least not give them away.

He was thinking that now he wouldn't need a suicide note.

He was torn. Part of him said better stick with the Aruba plan, switching to a whole new plan was reckless. On the other hand, now that this unexpected chance had come, shouldn't he seize it?

Harley didn't discuss her feelings with him again, but he eaves-dropped on her phone calls with Angie.

What if the Catholic Church was right? In that case she had committed a mortal sin: premeditated, cold-blooded murder.

She was not herself. Don't take his word for it, ask her best friend. Harley was frightened, depressed, tormented. That guilt would drive her to swallow all her pills at once was tragic but un-derstandable.

He knew Harley well enough to know that her state of mind wouldn't last forever. He must act while she was still in the throes. On the other hand, he mustn't be too rash, or he might trip him-self up. But now that he knew he wasn't going to have to wait till January, some of his old patience had returned. He decided to give it a week.

*I wish I could explain to you in a way you'd understand. Believe me when I say I never meant to hurt you. But I've been living a lie for too long. We both have. This whole marriage has been a lie from the start. Now I've met someone else, someone who loves me more than you ever could. And I've gone away with him. I don't know what else to tell you, except to repeat that I didn't mean to hurt you. And that I feel sorry for you. You are so out of touch with your own feelings. You are so self-absorbed you don't see what's going on right under your nose! The abortion was a terrible thing for me. I didn't know if the baby was yours or his. Not that it matters now. But in the end I see that it was really a good thing because it got me to decide once and for all which man I truly wanted to be with.*

He didn't stop to think—the whirring, crashing activity of his mind could not be called thinking. He threw back some scotch, got in his car, and drove to the little sunburned shack near the train station.

"Hey, Jack, what's happening, man?"

"*Jake,*" he corrected.

He used his bare hands, choking her from behind, surprised at the force with which she reared, nearly throwing him. When he got his breath back he removed her bra, the same red bra she always wore.

The man was watching TV, as usual. The sound very loud, as usual. He turned his head at the last minute but it was too late.

This one was harder. The man had thick, rubbery rings of flesh around his neck. Roden was afraid the cheap bra would snap.

A black-and-white movie was playing. An old western. Roden could watch what he was doing superimposed on a scene of masked men on horseback bearing down on a stagecoach.

It was done. For an instant he felt sapped of all strength. He had to resist the urge to drop to the floor.

Driving away from the house, he marveled at how quick it had been. How quick and easy.

It was done. It could never be undone.

With the woman he'd felt the euphoric rush and release his fantasies had prepared him for. But it was killing another man that made him feel proud.

He'd never known what the man's name was, or exactly what his relationship was to the woman. The woman had called herself Marilyn, a name Roden had always liked.

He didn't think Marilyn deserved to die. But he didn't feel bad for her, either. She was a whore, and whores got murdered all the time. It was one of the things whores were for.

MARIA REVA

# Letter of Apology

FROM *Granta*

*Don't think.*
*If you think, don't speak.*
*If you think and speak, don't write.*
*If you think, speak and write, don't sign.*
*If you think, speak, write and sign, don't be surprised.*

NEWS OF KONSTANTYN ILLYCH BOYKO'S transgression came to us by way of an anonymous note deposited in a suggestion box at the Kozlov Cultural Club. According to the note, after giving a poetry reading, Konstantyn Illych disseminated a political joke as he loosened his tie backstage. Following Directive No. 97 to Eliminate Dissemination of Untruths Among Party Cadres and the KGB, my superior could not repeat the joke, but assured me it was grave enough to warrant our attention.

One can only argue with an intellectual like Konstantyn Illych if one speaks to him on his level. I was among the few in the Kozlov branch of the agency with a higher education, so the task of reeducating Konstantyn Illych fell to me.

Since Konstantyn Illych was a celebrated poet in Ukraine and the matter a sensitive one, I was to approach him in private rather than at his workplace, in case the joke had to be repeated. Public rebuke would only be used if a civil one-on-one failed. According to Konstantyn Illych's personal file (aged forty-five, married, employed by the Cultural Club), the poet spent his Sundays alone or with his wife at their dacha in Uhly, a miserable swampland thirty kilometers south of town.

Judgment of the quality of the swampland is my own and was not indicated in the file.

The following Sunday I drove to Uhly, or as close as I could get to Uhly; after the spring snowmelt, the dachas were submerged by a meter of turbid water and people were moving between and around the dachas in rowboats.

I had not secured a rowboat for the task as the need for one was not mentioned in Konstantyn Illych's file, nor in the orders I was given.

I parked at the flood line, where five rowboats were moored: two green, two blue, one white, none black. Our usual mode of transportation was black. I leaned on the warm hood of my car (black) and plucked clean a cattail as I deliberated what to do next. I decided on the innocuous white; anyway I did not want to frighten Konstantyn Illych and cause him to flee by appearing in a black one.

The dachas were poorly numbered and I had to ask for directions, which was not ideal. One man was half-deaf and, after nodding through my question, launched into an account of his cystectomy; another elderly man, who clearly understood what I was saying, rudely responded in Ukrainian; one woman, after inquiring what in hell I was doing in her brother's rowboat, tried to set her German shepherd on me (thankfully, the beast was afraid of water). I was about to head back to the car when an aluminum kayak slid out of the reeds beside me, carrying two knobble-kneed girls. They told me to turn right at the electric transformer and row to the third house after the one crushed by a poplar.

A few minutes later I floated across the fence of a small dacha, toward a shack sagging on stilts. On the windowsill stood a rusted trophy of a fencer in fighting stance, and from its rapier hung a rag and sponge. When no response came from an oared knock on the door, I rowed to the back of the shack. There sat Konstantyn Illych and, presumably, his wife, Milena Markivna, both of them cross-legged atop a wooden table, playing cards. The tabletop rose just above water level, giving the impression that the couple was stranded on a raft at sea. The poet's arms and shoulders were small, boyish, but his head was disproportionately large, blockish. I found it difficult to imagine the head strapped into a fencing mask, but that is beside the point.

"Konstantyn Illych?" I called out.

"Who's asking?" He kept his eyes on the fan of cards in his hands.

I rowed closer. The wood of my boat tapped the wood of the table. "I'm Mikhail Igorovich. Pleased to meet you."

Konstantyn Illych did not return my politesse, did not even take the toothpick out of his mouth to say, "You here for electric? We paid up last week."

His wife placed a four of spades on the table. Her thick dark hair hung over her face.

I told Konstantyn Illych who I was and that the agency had received reports of how he had publicly disseminated wrongful evaluations of the leaders of the Communist Party and the Soviet society at large, and that I was here to have a conversation with him. Konstantyn Illych set his cards facedown on the table and said in a level tone, "All right, let's have a conversation."

I had conducted dozens of these conversations before and always began from a friendly place, as if we were two regular people —pals, even—just chatting.

"Quite the flood," I said.

"Yes," said Konstantyn Illych, "the flood."

"I'll bet the children love it here."

"No children."

Usually there were children. I stretched my legs out in the rowboat, which upset its balance, jerked them back.

"No parents, grandparents, aunts, or uncles either," said Milena Markivna. Her upper lip curled a little—the beginning of a sneer, as if to say, *But you already knew that, didn't you?*

There had indeed been mention of a mass reprimand of Milena Markivna's relatives in the fifties, but amid all the other facts about all the other citizens of Kozlov—all their sordid family histories —the detail had slipped my mind. Still, the woman did not need to dampen the spirit of the conversation.

Konstantyn Illych broke the silence. "So what's the joke?"

"I haven't made a joke," I said.

"No, the joke I supposedly told about the Party."

Already he was incriminating himself. "The term I used was *wrongful evaluation*, but thank you for specifying the offense, Konstantyn Illych."

"You're welcome," he said, unexpectedly. "What was it?"

"I cannot repeat the joke." I admit I had searched Konstantyn Illych's file for it, but one of the typists had already redacted the words.

"You can't repeat the joke you're accusing me of telling?"

"Correct." Then, before I could stop myself: "Perhaps you could repeat the joke, and I'll confirm whether or not it's the one."

Konstantyn Illych narrowed his eyes.

"We aren't moving any closer to a solution, Konstantyn Illych."

"Tell me the problem first," he said.

A brown leaf, curled into the shape of a robed figurine, floated by Milena Markivna's foot. She pressed the leaf into the murky water with her thumb before turning to her husband. "Just say sorry and be done with it."

I thanked her for her intuition—an apology was precisely what was in order, in the form of a letter within thirty days. Milena Markivna advised me not to thank her since she hadn't done anything to help me, in fact she hated officers like me and it was because of officers like me that she had grown up alone in this world, but at least she had nothing to lose and could do anything she wanted to: she could spit in my face if she wanted to, which I did not recommend.

Konstantyn Illych was tapping his fingernails on the table. "I'm not putting anything in writing."

It is usually at this point in the conversation, when the written word comes up, that the perpetrator becomes most uncomfortable, begins to wriggle. Most people fail to grasp the simple logic of the situation: that once a transgression occurs and a case file opens, the case file triggers a response—in this case, a letter of apology. One document exposes the problem, the second resolves it. One cannot function without the other, just as a bolt cannot function without a nut and a nut cannot function without a bolt. And so I told Konstantyn Illych, "I'm afraid you don't have a choice."

He reached for the small rectangular bulge in his breast pocket. "Ever read my poetry?"

I expected him to retrieve a booklet of poems and to read from it. Dread came over me; I had never been one to understand verse. Thankfully he produced a packet of cigarettes instead.

"Come to my next reading," he said. "You'll see I'm as ideologically pure as a newborn. Then we'll talk about the letter."

*

Normally I'd have a letter of apology written and signed well under the thirty-day deadline and I took pride in my celerity. Even the most stubborn perpetrators succumbed under threat of loss of employment or arrest. The latter, however, was a last resort. The goal now was to reeducate without arrest because the Party was magnanimous and forgiving; moreover prisons could no longer accommodate every citizen who uttered a joke.

In Konstantyn Illych's case, next came gentle intimidation. If Konstantyn Illych stood in line for sausage, I stood five spots behind him. If Konstantyn Illych took a rest on a park bench, I sat three benches over. He pretended not to see me, but I knew he did: he walked too fast, tripping on uneven pavement; bills and coins slipped from his fingers regularly. His head jerked right and left to make sure he never found himself alone on the street. He needn't have worried—always the odd pedestrian around—and anyway I did not intend to physically harm or abduct Konstantyn Illych, though that would have been simpler for both of us. My older colleagues often lamented the simpler times.

Four days passed without a word exchanged between us.

On the fifth day I went to see Konstantyn Illych give his poetry reading at the Kozlov Cultural Club. I took a seat in the front row of the lecture hall, so close to the stage I could see the poet's toes agitate inside his leather shoes. In the dim light I was able to transcribe some of his poetry:

> Helical gears, cluster gears, rack gears,
> bevel and miter gears, worm gears, spur gears,
> ratchet and pawl gears, internal spur gears,
> grind my body
> meat grinder
> grinds
> gr gr grrr
> ah ah ah
> aah aah aah
> ah haaaaaahh

And also:

> The bear
> bares his flesh
> skinless, bears the burden
> of the air woooooooooooooooosh

And also:

Dewy forget-me-not
not me forgets.
Stomp.

I cannot guarantee I transcribed the onomatopoeic bits with accuracy; Konstantyn Illych's reading gave no indication of the number of *a*'s and *o*'s, etc.

At the end of the reading the poet placed his pages at his feet, unbuttoned his faded blue blazer, addressed the audience: "Time for a little trivia. I'll recite a poem and one of you will guess who wrote it. Get it right and everyone here will admire you, get it wrong and you'll be eternally shamed." A few people laughed.

Throughout the challenge poets such as Tsvetaeva, Inber, Mayakovsky, Shevchenko (this one I knew), and Tushnova were identified. The audience expressed their enjoyment by whooping and clapping between names.

Konstantyn Illych waited for the lecture hall to quiet down before he leaned into the microphone. "Who, whom?"

This apparently was also a poem; the crowd erupted in fervid applause. I made a mental note to alert my superiors that local culture was going down the chute.

Konstantyn Illych scanned the audience until his eyes locked with mine. "The gentleman in the front row, in the black peacoat," he said. "Who wrote that poem?"

Once more the hall fell silent.

I turned right and left, hoping to find another man wearing a black peacoat in my vicinity, when I saw Konstantyn Illych's wife sitting behind me. She crossed her arms, her great bulging eyes on me, beckoning me to answer. One of her hands, nestled in the crook of her arm, resembled a pale spider waiting to pounce.

Konstantyn Illych's voice boomed above me. "The greatest poet of all time, Comrade, and you do not know? I'll give you three seconds. Three . . ."

I froze in my seat. The man to my right, whose nose looked like it had been smashed many times, nudged me in the ribs.

"Two . . ."

The man whispered, "Grandfather Lenin!" which I found absolutely in poor taste.

"One!" Konstantyn Illych bellowed. "Who was it, esteemed audience?"

The words rose up from the crowd in a column. "Grandfather Lenin!"

Konstantyn Illych looked down at me from the stage, tsked into the microphone. Each tsk felt sharp, hot, a lash on my skin.

It was around this time I began to suspect that, while I had been following Konstantyn Illych, his wife had been following me. I forced myself to recollect all I could of the preceding week. Milena Markivna never figured in the center of the memories—the bull's-eye had always, of course, been Konstantyn Illych—but I did find her in the cloudy periphery, sometimes even in the vacuous space between memories. If I stood five spots behind Konstantyn Illych in line for sausage, the hooded figure four spots behind me possessed Milena's small, narrow-shouldered frame; if I sat three benches from Konstantyn Illych, the woman two benches over had the same pale ankle peeking out from under the skirt. I began to see the task of retrieving the letter of apology in a new light.

What I suspected: It was not about the letter, rather the lengths I would go to retrieve it.

What I suspected: I was being vetted for a position of great honor.

What I knew: "Who, whom?" had been a simple test, and I had failed it.

What I knew: My mother had been subjected to the same tests as a young woman, and had succeeded.

When I was a child, my mother was invited to join the Honor Guard. According to my father, she had always been a model student, the fiercest marcher in the Pioneers, the loudest voice in the parades. She was the champion archer of Ukraine and had even been awarded a red ribbon by the Kozlov Botanist Club for her Cactaceae collection. One evening, an officer came to our door and served my mother a letter summoning her to the Chief Officer's quarters. Within six months she was sent to Moscow for special training, as only special training would suffice for the Guard that stands at the mausoleum of Lenin. Since our family was not a recognized unit—my parents hadn't married because my paternal grandparents (now deceased) didn't like my mother—my father and I could not join her in Moscow. I was too young to remember much about this period, but do have two recollections: one, I could not reconcile the immense honor of the invitation with the grief that plagued the family; two, my father assumed care of my mother's cactus collection and every evening, when he thought I was asleep on the sofa bed beside him, wrapped his fingers around the spines of the plants and winced and grit his teeth but kept them there until his whole body eased into a queer smile. For many months his hands were scabbed and swollen. Within a year my father was gone also; he had at last been able to join my mother in Moscow and my grandparents told me that one day I too would join them.

When Milena Markivna entered my life, I felt I had finally been noticed. The vetting process for the Honor Guard was still possible. My reassignment to Moscow to see my mother and father was still possible. I believed it was possible to make gains with hard work.

From that point on I followed Milena Markivna's husband with greater vigilance and Milena Markivna followed me with greater vigilance. If Konstantyn Illych riffled through his pockets for a missing kopek for a jar of milk, Milena Markivna's voice behind me would say, "Surely you have an extra kopek for the man," and surely enough, I would. If I dropped a sunflower-seed shell on the floor while pacing the corridor outside the couple's apartment, behind the peephole of Suite 76 Milena Markivna's voice would say, "It's in the corner behind you," and surely enough, it was. She was a master observer, better than me.

(It should not go unsaid that, beyond mention of the reprimand of Milena Markivna's family, her file contained little information. This may have been because she was born in the province surrounding Kozlov and not in the city itself, but I suspected it was a matter of rank: if Milena Markivna were indeed my superior, tasked with the observation of my conduct and aptitude for ceremonial duty, I would not have access to her full history. Information is compartmentalized to mitigate leaks, much like compartments are sealed off in ships to prevent sinking.)

Konstantyn Illych, in turn, grew accustomed to my omnipresence, even seemed to warm to it. After a bulk shipment to the Gastronom, I watched him haul home a thirty-kilogram sack of sugar. By the time he reached his building, the sack had developed a small tear, which meant he could not haul the sack up to the ninth floor without losing a fair share of granules. The elevator was out of the question due to the rolling blackouts and so I offered to pinch the tear as he carried the load over his shoulder, and he did not decline. Many minutes later we stood in front of Suite 76, Konstantyn Illych breathless from the effort. Since I was there I might as well come in, he said, to help with the sack. He unlocked the steel outer door and the red upholstered inner door, then locked the doors behind us. The apartment was very small, surely smaller than the sanitary standard of nine square meters allotted per person. After we maneuvered the sack to the glassed-in balcony, I scanned the suite for a trace of Milena Markivna— a blouse thrown over a chair, the scent of an open jar of hand cream, perhaps—but saw only books upon books, bursting from shelves and boxes lining the already narrow corridor, books propping up the lame leg of an armchair, books stacked as a table for a lamp under which more books were read, books even in the bathroom, all of them poetry or on poetry, all presumably Konstantyn Illych's. A corner of the main room had been spared for a glass buffet of fencing trophies and foils, and on the top of it stood a row of dusty family portraits. I tried to find Milena Markivna in the photographs but these, too, were Konstantyn Illych's—the large head made him recognizable at any age. I wondered if she lived there, if she was even his wife.

Milena Markivna entered the apartment a few minutes after us, with a soft scratch of keys in the locks. She appraised me as I imagined she might appraise a rug her husband had fished out of a dumpster. Would the piece be useful, or would it collect dust and get in the way? Her expression suggested the latter, but her husband was leading me into the kitchen, the point of no return. Once a guest steps into the kitchen, to have them leave without being fed and beveraged is of course unconscionable.

Milena Markivna leaned her hip against the counter, watching Konstantyn Illych mete out home brew into three cloudy shot glasses. "Lena, fetch the sprats, will you?"

Milena Markivna said she needed the stool, which I immediately vacated. She stepped on the stool to retrieve a can from the back of the uppermost cupboard and set the can down on the table, with some force, and looked at me, also with some force, as if daring me to do something about the unopened sprats. I produced the eight-layer pocketknife I always kept on my person. In an elaborate display of resourcefulness, I flicked through the screwdriver, ruler, fish scaler and hook disgorger, scissors, pharmaceutical spatula, magnifying lens, hoof cleaner, shackle opener and wood saw, before reaching the can opener. Its metal claw sank into the tin with so little resistance, I could have been cutting margarine. Milena Markivna must have noticed the surprise on my face, asked if I knew about the exploding cans.

I conceded I did not.

"It's something I heard," she said, "something about the tin, how they don't make it like they used to. People are getting shrapnel wounds." After a moment she gave a dry mirthless laugh and so I laughed as well.

Before Konstantyn Illych passed around the shots, I laid a sprat on my tongue and chewed it slowly to let the bitter oil coat the inside of my mouth and throat to minimize the effects of alcohol.

Milena Markivna also chewed a sprat before the first shot, which I did not fail to notice.

Three rounds later, Konstantyn Illych spoke of the tenets of Futurist philosophy and was about to show how he employed them in his poetry when I asked about the letter of apology, due in fifteen days.

"Mikhail Igorovich," he said. "Misha. Can I call you Misha?"

"You may." The home brew was softening my judgment and there was only one sprat left.

"Fuck the letter, Misha. What is this, grade school?"

I told him about the possible repercussions, about his getting fired or arrested. "You're lucky," I said. "In earlier times, a political joke meant ten years."

Konstantyn Illych set his empty shot glass upside down on his pinkie like a thimble, twirled it in languid circles. "Once upon a time," he began.

I wanted to shake the letter out of him.

"I got the flu," he continued. "Ever get the flu?"

"Sure."

"The flu turned into pneumonia and I ended up in the hospital. Not only did I get my own room, but by the end of the week the room was filled, and I mean floor-to-ceiling filled, with flowers and cards and jars of food from people I didn't even know, people from all around the country."

Milena Markivna placed the last sprat between her lips and sucked it in until the tip of the tail disappeared into her mouth.

Konstantyn Illych leaned in. "Imagine, Misha, what would happen if you tried to get me fired."

Milena Markivna smacked her lips. "Shall I grab another can? Maybe this time we'll get lucky."

Another week passed without success. My superior remarked that I was usually quicker at obtaining a letter, and was I not dealing with someone who specialized in the written word, who could whip up a heartfelt apology in no time? I tried what I could with the poet. I considered bribing him, but the mere thought felt unnatural, against the grain, against the direction a bribe usually slid. I began to neglect other tasks at work, but believed my persistence with Konstantyn Illych would be rewarded. I admit I thought of Milena Markivna as well, and often. She followed me into my dreams. Throughout my life, she would tell me, I was being watched over. She would award me with a certificate signaling my entry into the Honor Guard, would place on my head a special canvas cap with a golden star on its front. I cannot say if this is true to the initiation ceremony but it was how I imagined it had happened with my mother. I would wake at night to find myself alone in my dark room but was never afraid. I knew I was being watched over.

The day before the deadline I stood at the back of the town cinema, watching Konstantyn Illych watch *Hedgehog in the Fog*. I cannot recall when I began to watch the animated film myself. I had already seen it a number of times and always found it unsettling, in the way heights are unsettling. En route to see his friend for tea, Hedgehog gets lost in the fog that descends on the forest. It isn't the fog or the forest that troubles me, as it troubles Hedgehog, it is this: Hedgehog sees a white horse and wonders if it would drown if it fell asleep in the fog. I've never understood the question. I suppose what Hedgehog means is: if the white horse stops moving, we would no longer see it in the white fog. But if we no longer see it, what is its state? Drowned or not? Dead or alive? The question is whether Hedgehog would prefer to keep the fog or have it lift to discover what is behind its thick veil. I would keep the fog. For instance, I cannot know the whereabouts of my parents because they are part of me and therefore part of my personal file and naturally no one can see their own file, just like no one can see the back of their own head. My mother is standing proud among the Honor Guard. My mother is standing elsewhere. She is sitting. She is lying down. She is cleaning an aquarium while riding an elevator. Uncertainty contains an infinite number of certainties. My mother is in all these states at once, and nothing stops me from choosing one. Many people claim they like certainty, but I do not believe this is true—it is uncertainty that gives freedom of mind. And so, while I longed to be reassigned to Moscow, the thought of it shook me to the bones with terror.

When the film ended, I felt a cold breath on the back of my neck. Milena Markivna's voice came as a whisper: "Meet me at the dacha at midnight. I'll get you the letter."

It was a weekday, a Wednesday, the dachas empty of people. The swamps were still flooded but this time a sleek black rowboat waited for me. It barely made a seam in the water as I rowed. Northward, the overcast sky glowed from the city. My teeth chattered from the cold or excitement or fear; it is difficult to keep still when one knows one's life is about to change. Already I could feel, like a comforting hand on my shoulder, the double gold aiguillette worn by the Guard. The tall chrome boots tight around my calves.

I tried to retrace the route I had taken the first time I visited the dacha, but found myself in the middle of a thicket of cattails. The glow of the sky switched off. Normally electricity is cut not at night but in the evening when people use it most and thus the most can be economized—this is the thought I would have had had I not been engulfed in panic. Darkness closed in on me. I circled on the spot. The cattails hissed against the edge of the boat. Willow branches snared my arms and face. A sulfurous stench stirred up from the boggy water. Milena Markivna had given me the simplest of tasks and I was about to fail her.

A horizontal slit of light appeared in the distance, faint and quivering. I lurched the boat toward it. Soon I recognized the silhouette of the shack on stilts; the light emanating from under its door. I scrambled up the stairs, knocked. The lock clicked and I waited for the door to open, and when it did not, I opened it myself.

A figure in a white uniform and mask stood before me, pointing a gleaming rapier at my chest. The figure looked like a human-sized replica of the fencing trophies I had seen inside the glass display at Suite 76.

"Close the door." The voice behind the mask was calm, level, and belonged to Milena Markivna.

I tried to keep calm as well, but my hand shook when it reached the handle. I closed the door without turning away from her, kept my eyes on the rapier. The ornate, patinated silver of its hilt suggested the weapon had been unearthed from another century.

"Down on the floor. On your knees."

I had not imagined our meeting to be like this but did as I was told. I inquired about the utility of having my ankles bound by rope and Milena Markivna said it was to prevent me from running away before she was done. I assured her I wouldn't think to run from such an important occasion and she, in turn, assured me she would skewer my heart onto one of my floating ribs if I tried. Before she stuffed a rag inside my mouth I told her I had been waiting for this moment since I was a child and she said she had been waiting for it since she was a child as well. I told her I was ready.

She said, "I'm ready too."

I do not know how much time passed with me kneeling, head bowed, as Milena Markivna stood over me.

I tried to utter a word of encouragement, mention the canvas cap with the golden star on its front, but of course couldn't speak through the rag in my mouth. All I could do was breathe in the sour, pickled smell of the fabric.

At last she knelt down in front of me, one hand on the hilt of the rapier, its tip still poised at my chest. With the other hand she took off her mask. Hair clung to her forehead, moist with sweat. I searched her face for approval or disappointment but it was closed to me, as if she were wearing a mask under the one she had just removed. I wondered how this would all look if a stranger barged through the door: she almost mad and I almost murdered.

Milena Markivna stabbed the rapier into the floor, which made me cry out, and said there really was no hurry in what she was going to do. She brought over a candle that had been burning on the table and dipped my fingers into the liquid wax, one by one, as she named her relatives who had been executed, one by one, thirty years ago. The burning was sharp at first—I dared not make another sound—but soon felt like ice. Milena seemed calmer then. She took the rag out of my mouth, unlaced her boots, set her feet on them and gave me a series of instructions. As I enveloped her warm toes in my mouth, she reminded me how she hated me. I removed my lips from the mound of her ankle long enough to tell her that we were not so different, she and I; that I too had grown up alone even though that would change soon. As she brought a second candle over and began to tip it over my scalp, she asked how it would change. Barely able to speak now, I told her that it would change when she inducted me into the Honor Guard and I would go to Moscow and see my family again. She laughed as if I had told a joke. The smell that greeted me was of singed pig flesh, sickening when I realized it was my own hair. My head pulsed with pain; tears blurred my vision. Milena Markivna set the candle down and asked how I knew where my family was. I said it was what I had been told. As she slid her fingers along the blade of the rapier, she said the neighbors had told her that her family had gone to a better place too, but never specified where or why they never wrote. The darkness of the night filtered in through the cracks of the shack and into my mind and I began thinking things I did not like to think about—my mother and father and where they might be. Milena Markivna wrapped her hand around the hilt of the rapier again and told me to take off my coat and shirt and lie facedown on the floor.

As I did so, one thought knocked against another, like dominoes:

There was a possibility I was not, at present, being recruited.

If not, there was no Honor Guard waiting for me.

If not, my parents' rank did not matter.

If not, my parents did not have rank.

If not, my mother was not in the Guard.

If not, they were not in Moscow.

The blade dragged from my tailbone up the thin skin of my spine, searing my mind clean. I screamed into my mouth so that no one would hear. When the blade reached between my shoulders it became warm, and from its point a sweet numbness spread through my arms. I thought of my father with his bleeding hands, understood that queer smile. My head spun and the walls began to undulate. My voice came hoarsely. "How do you know what happened to your family?"

After a moment she said, "They disappeared. That's how I know."

"They could be anywhere."

"Do you believe that?"

"Yes." My body shook against the damp floorboards. "No."

It was when I welcomed the blade that it lifted from my skin. I felt a tug between my ankles, then a loosening. She had cut the rope.

"You can go."

"You're not done."

"No," she said, but pushed my shirt and coat toward me with her foot. I lay limp, spent. Through the window I could see the glow of the city flicker back on. I remembered why I had come to the dacha, but could not rouse myself to bring up the letter. I found I did not care about it much myself. I would be the one who would have to issue an apology to my superior the next day, give an explanation for failing to complete my task. I would write it. My superior would read it. I would be dismissed. What next? I would go to the market for a jar of milk, search my pockets for the correct change. If I weren't to have it, a voice behind me might ask if someone has a kopek for the man. Surely enough, someone will.

Before leaving I asked Milena Markivna, "What was the joke your husband told?"

"Oh." She said, "██████████████████████████? ████████ ██████████████████████████."

"All this trouble for that?"

It was the first time I saw her smile. "I know. It's not even that funny."

# Black Corfu

FROM *Zoetrope: All-Story*

## Žrnovo, *1620*

THE DOCTOR SLEEPS NAKED, which is not widespread practice
on the island of Korčula, not even in summer. As if to atone for
his bared skin, his wife sleeps in cake-like tiers of bedclothes. Only
she is privy to the doctor's secret shamelessness; in public company, he is the model of propriety. Once upon a time, she found
this and his other bedroom vagaries irresistibly appealing. Tonight
he startles awake from his nightmare to find her surfacing from
yards and yards of white linen. She rises like a woman clawing out
of snow.

*I have never lost a patient.*

He studies the tiny, halved heart of his wife's earlobe. Their
room pulses with the moon. He can almost hear the purr of the
rumor, yawning awake within her, stretching and extending itself.
Does she believe it? Is she beginning to believe it? The naked doctor shudders. He imagines a man who resembles him exactly. That
man is moving inside his wife.

What tool can he use, to extract their rumor from her body?

The doctor's costume is hanging on a hook. It is not nearly
so frightening as the hooded uniform donned by physicians during the Great Plague of 1529, the beaky invention of Charles
de l'Orme. He wears a simple black smock, black waxed-leather
gloves, and his face, when he operates, is bare.

"It is not true," he says in a clear, sober voice.

His wife's face is planked white and blue with moonlight. The one eye that he can see in profile is streaming water. She is like a stony bust granted a single attitude by her sculptor. Silently, the doctor begs her: *Look my way.*

*Crack.*

"You must promise me that you will put it out of your mind." His voice is still his own. "You betray me by imagining me as that man."

His wife parts her dark hair with the flats of her palms. Does this again and again, like a woman bathing under the river falls. Outside, the moon shines on with its eerie impartiality, illuminating this room, illuminating also the surrounding woods, where the doctor knows a dozen men are fanning out, hunting for his patient.

"Please. Please. I performed my duty perfectly. I could never make such a mistake."

"I am not even thinking about you. I am listening for the girls."

She says this without turning from the door. Now the doctor hears what must have awoken her. Not his nightmare but their middle daughter's sobbing. Ashamed, he reaches for his robe. "Let me go to her."

The girl sits tall in the bed, with white, round eyes that seemed to pull in opposite directions, like panicked oxen. Her sleeping sisters bracket her, their faces slack and spit-dewed. The doctor has long suspected that his middle child is his most intelligent.

"Papa, will they punish you? Will you go to prison?"

"Who told you such a thing?"

In fact, the punishment will be far worse than that, if it comes.

"Nobody," his daughter says sadly. "But I listen to what they tell one another."

So the rumor has penetrated the walls of his home, the mind of his child. He grows so upset that he forgets to console her, flees her side. In two hours, the dawn bells will begin to ring. Bodies will congregate at the harbor. What if the miasma of the rumor is already changing? Becoming even more poisonous, contagious—

*I will have to keep the girls indoors from now on, to prevent their further contamination.*

What will happen to him, if he cannot stop the rumor from spreading, transforming? He might be sent to the Venetian garrison. He might be strung up in the dark Aleppo pines before anything so official as a trial. Yet unofficially, of course, his punishment is well underway. A second death would be only a formality.

He had once dreamed of being the sort of doctor who helps children walk again; instead, he found himself hobbling them. Children of all ages were carried to him on stretchers, with blue lips and seamed eyelids. A twisted plot, without a single author to blame. As a younger man, he'd ventilated the pain through laughter. Sometimes the circumstances of his life struck him as so unbearably absurd that he'd soar up to a blind height, laughing and laughing until his red eyes shut and spittle flecked his chin. ("Open your eyes," his wife would beg. "My love, you are frightening us—") But it has been many years now since such an episode. Only behind the roped bedroom drapery does the doctor indulge such wildness today.

His wife is very proud of the doctor's accomplishments. Because he loves her, he never shares the black joke. Not once does he voice an objection to the injustice of his fate, or rail against what the island has made of his ambition. Aboveground, the *chirurgo* practices medicine in his warm salon—performing salubrious bloodlettings, facilitating lactation for the pretty young noblewomen. Whereas this doctor must descend into the Neolithic caves, under the cold applause of stars.

His formal title is the Posthumous Surgeon of Korčula, yet all the bereaved know him by name. Centuries after his passing, he will be reverenced on Black Corfu as something more and less than a man. He operates on the dead—the only bodies an occupant of his caste is permitted to touch. Before his good reputation was gutted by his accusers, the doctor had a perfect record: during his twenty-three-year tenure on the island, not a single *vukodlak* had been sighted. Everyone slept more peacefully for his skill— the living and the dead. Whose relief was manifest in the verdant silence of the woods, in the solemn stillness of the cemetery air. Inside that pooling quiet he could hear, unwhispered, *Thank you, Doctor. Bless you, Doctor.*

These islands off the coast of Dalmatia, with their fertile dusks and their thin soils, breed a special kind of monster. A corpse that continues to walk after its death. Animated by wind from some other world, spasming emptily on, mute and blue and alone. *Vukodlak, ukodlak,* and *vuk*—appellations to distance a grieving family from a terrible and familiar face in the moonlit forest, now bloated and drained of light.

Korčula is entirely covered by woodland, rising out of the mirror-bright Adriatic like a hand gloved in green velvet. It seems to belong to a long-expired age, lush and prehistoric. Trees peer blindly down at the sea, black Dalmatian pines and soaring cypresses laddering their thousand ruddy arms over the azure water, and over the low macchia, that snarling undergrowth that breaks into sudden shouts of yellow and violet like the singsong joy of the mad. Korčula is the home of shipbuilders and explorers, the fabled birthplace of Marco Polo. That the dead also wander its pitched slopes should surprise no one; when the Greeks established a colony here in the sixth century BC, they named the island for its sepulchral hue. Korkula Melaina. Corcyra Nigra. Black Corfu.

The doctor was born during the longest period of Venetian rule over Korčula, two centuries before the republic would fall to Napoleon. He was the child of a child of a kidnapped child, a cook who escaped from the galley kitchen of a Portuguese ship and oared with seven others through driving winds to reach Black Corfu's shoreline. They lived as freedmen at the base of the cliffs, in the poorest quarter of the stone-walled city, in dwellings evincing the fragile tenacity of the red and blue barnacles spiraling out of the rocks. They paid rent to the hereditary counts.

As the doctor's mother recounted this lineage in whispers, her tone taught him more than her words about the precarity of their position. And yet, despite their color and station, she grew old loving the sight of her face in the mirror. She pushed through the market stalls in a perfume of oblivion, ignoring the catcalling sailors, the curled lips of the upper-class women, whose chins reminded her son of the hard nipples on lemons. Their derisive stares seemed to pass painlessly through her, like blades slicing at water. She resented no one. And he, trailing her elbow, quietly learned to subsume his rage; by the age of seven, he knew well the taste of fury as it sank into the body, that nasal salt of swallowed things. *I am smarter than my mother,* this child decided.

Not until he was a father himself did the doctor understand that her docility had been a strategy. Always she had been protecting him. He'd missed the teeth inside his mother's smile, and only now could he fathom the resolve required to raise dark-skinned

children under the flag of an unequal truce. From his crabhole
he watched the gold and scarlet clouds cluster over the hills. To
survive here required one to sip the air; the wide sky belonged to
the nobles.

Still, sometimes he emerged at first light, as fishing boats
slipped the grasp of the harbor for the expanse of the open sea,
and allowed himself to feel otherwise. Wasn't it possible that a
posthumous surgeon might one day be promoted from his abyss
to the upper world? Ambroise Paré, a barber's apprentice, became
physician to the kings of France, securing his ascent by eschewing
the common practice of scalding battlefield wounds with boiling
oil, instead dressing them with rosewater and turpentine. Perhaps
the doctor would be granted a similar opportunity to impress the
Venetian Council of Ten. To restore the sick to health would have
been his preference, but to keep the dead in their coffins was a
service certainly no less valuable to the republic.

The new student continually looks back to the shrinking harbor,
where the ship that delivered him to Black Corfu that morning is
now small as a toy. At the wide cave mouth, his legs jerk to a stop,
twin animals balking in tandem.

"Few people on the Continent know the real dangers the dead
pose," the doctor says, his voice growing ever more sonorous as
they descend a dim tunnel. Candles lean out of natural sconces in
the rock, dozens of red hands along the mossy walls, waving them
on. "Yet a body is at its most defenseless at this time, soon after
expiration, orphaned in its coffin."

"In Lastovo," the boy mutters, "we all know the dangers now.
Nobody can escape the knowledge."

On his home island, there has been an outbreak of *vukodlaci*.
The first in three generations. The boy describes a scene out of the
doctor's insomniac fears. Mass exhumations, emergency surgeries
performed in the open. Gravediggers undoing their handiwork,
spading up dirt. ("They toil under the moon, looking like large
rabbits on tethers," he says, with plainspoken horror.) Torches lip-
ping orange syllables over the toppled stones. The only posthumous surgeon in Lastovo is nearing seventy and half-blind; in any
case, no single surgeon can attend to so many patients at once.
And so this boy has been sent here to learn a new trade.

A quarter mile deeper into the caves, the new student intro-
duces himself: his name is Jure da Mosto, and he belongs to one
of the most tightly closed aristocracies in all of Europe. Thirteen
families have controlled Lastovo for centuries—patricians who
are identical, in their threatening languor, to those pale raptors
wheeling over the trees, their idle talons tearing at the seafaring
clouds.

"A face like yours must irritate your parents, eh?" the doctor
offers mildly.

Despite the Italian ancestry the boy claims, his complexion will
always raise suspicions. Who can account for the colors wreath-
ing out of the buried past, and where and when they might resur-
face? Jure da Mosto looks no older than sixteen, and already with
the stink of some precocious failure on him. The doctor thinks: *It
would be a joy to be wrong about even one of them.*

They've sent him another reject, perhaps. A dropout from the
Ragusa hospital. The family disappointment. Councilmen, too, often assume that any half-wit can hack away at the dead. Nobody
but the posthumous surgeons themselves, a subterranean guild,
understands what is required—the magic necessary to the practice, in addition to the science, and something ill-expressed in language: an instinct for the right depth when making the first cut.
This cannot not be taught.

"What do you mean—a face like mine?"

"So . . . overcast. So dark with worry."

The doctor has very little patience for the boy's fear. Even less
for his self-pity.

"Once upon a time, I also dreamed of being another sort of
man—"

The ashen student startles awake. "Many of us would have preferred a different fortune."

The doctor has worked his entire life to attain this rank. And
yet the pinnacle of his achievement is considered, by this boy's
people, a valley of shadow.

They reach the cave's largest hall, which has served since the
medieval period as a medical theater. A rock awning sprawls over
their heads, a bright wishbone chandelier of white calcite suspended from its apex. Bodies are delivered here by runners paid
by the families, who take pains to avoid encounters with the doc-

tor. On the operating table, a patient quietly waits, a pearl comb glinting in her red hair.

All bodies rotting under the moon run the risk of becoming *vuko-dlaci*. How does a posthumous surgeon protect the dead from this fate? By severing the hamstrings.

Few think of the humble hamstring as the umbilicus that tethers a corpse to our spinning world. But cut that cord, and no body can be roused to walk the earth. Hamstrung cattle are crippled for life, the doctor reminds Jure. On the other side of dawn, their patients are securely moored in their coffins, guarded against every temptation to rise up.

Vocabulary is key, when communicating the risks posed by the *vukodlaci;* all posthumous surgeons take great care with their articulations. The bereaved must understand that should they cross paths with a *vukodlak,* this shell is not their beloved. Only the flesh has been reanimated; the soul, it is presumed, is safe with God. "An evil wind is blowing Cila's body around" is a chilling pronouncement to the surviving family, but far less damaging than the deranging hope bred by "Cila walks again."

As for what the doctor tells his own children of his work? "Clipping a bird's wings" is his preferred euphemism. He is determined not to frighten them.

His daughters touch one another's shoulder blades, giggling, feeling for secret pinions.

But the girls are too smart for this; they know their father does something shameful, something ugly, doesn't he? Otherwise, why must he leave at night, in his black robe, for the distant caves?

"The hamstring extends between the hip and the knee joints."

For the third time, the doctor explains the surgery to Jure da Mosto.

"First, we locate the tendons at the back of the knee . . ."

Jure wants to know: Do the eyes of a cadaver never flutter open? Has there never once been—?

"Never," says the doctor.

The bug-eyed boy wipes a gloved hand across his mouth, leaving a shiny spider line. His lips curl, as if he is repulsed by his own interest.

"And in all cases, the surgery is a—a success?"

"I understand that these are dark days in Lastovo. You have my every sympathy. But you should know that here on Black Corfu, no such error has ever occurred."

The doctor claps his hands, as if dismissing a horde of demons from the room.

The surgery on the young woman takes a quarter hour, and is wholly unremarkable. She is the only daughter of one of the hereditary counts. From this man, the doctor will collect triple his ordinary fee. "The surgeries I perform on the wealthy pay for those on the poor," he explains to young Jure, who is staring at the countess's colorless mouth. Each lip looks like a tiny, folded moth. *She is about your age, isn't she?* the doctor thinks, wondering how many bodies the boy has seen in his short lifetime.

Terrible things do happen to the people in the hills, but such cases are viewed as tragedies, aberrations of nature. This unfortunate countess died of a sickness known locally as "throat rattle" —an illness that has claimed dozens of lives in the doctor's quarter, where the death of children is commonplace.

Midway through the surgery, the student wanders away from the table, drawn to a gemstone sparkle in the corner—the doctor's lectern, a naturally occurring pillar that supports a priceless book, a gift from the former rector of Zagreb's Jesuit college: a copy of the anatomical sketches of Vesalius. Jure thumbs through the book with a pouty expression, as if he has already anticipated every flowering organ.

"This is the brain, then?" He yawns.

"Watch what I am doing," the doctor snaps.

The boy's face goes purple in the torchlight, which the doctor takes as a hopeful sign. Perhaps young Jure knows enough to feel ashamed of himself.

She has rare red hair, bright as a garnet, a comet that resurfaces in her genetic line every eight generations. The doctor had never spoken to or touched her in life, but had seen her scarlet tresses moving through the market stalls and known: the Nikoničić scion. *At last,* he thinks sadly, making the final cut, *her body will sleep without rousing, while her soul flies to the Lord.*

As the night wears on, they operate on an old sailor, now at anchor. The doctor draws the boy's fingers down the hairy thigh to the sunken divot of the kneecap. Together their hands fly across a wintry isthmus of skin, tracing the muscles they will handicap. Is the boy attending to the lesson?

The boy stiffens. "Oh, God," he says, jerking back with a shudder. "There has been some mistake. I do not belong down here with you. Please, I want to go home."

"Home" being synonymous, for this lucky young man, with the sunlit world above.

*Blessed are the living*, thinks the doctor, his scalpel poised.

Animals, too, can become *vukodlaci*. Almost certainly, some of the birds circling Korčula are bloodless, caught in their old orbits. Many passing sailors have reported sightings of the great, mixed flocks of living and dead gulls. The latter are easily identifiable, looping over the bay with a fixed-wing soar, their cerulean feathers shining continuously, even on gray afternoons. They sing, and their song is unmistakable, weirding out over the sea.

As a boy, the doctor dedicated himself to tending injured animals. He freed foxes from traps and cauterized their wounds, bandaged swallows with broken blood feathers. He begged his father for stories of doctors who cured their patients of lameness, madness, blindness, gout. The miracles of saints, he understood, were original events, contingent on the action of the Holy Ghost, whereas surgery was a human achievement—it could be practiced, perfected, repeated. His father had allowed the boy's belief that he could become the city physician, leaving his mother to extinguish this hope.

"Have you ever seen a doctor who looks like us, my son?"

There were two doctors on the island: The first was the city physician, a wealthy old Croat who, it was whispered, had been unable to cure his own sterility. The second was the Jesuit. His skin poured forth a yellow light, and his age was unguessable; he seemed to be simultaneously flush with health and minutes shy of death. He refused to treat those who had not first made confession.

"Where do the doctors live?"

"With us, on Black Corfu."

"No. Be more precise, my son. Think like they do. What answer would a doctor give?"

The doctor's mother often spoke to her son as if she were trying to gently jostle fruit from a tree without puncturing its skin. She believed in his extraordinary intelligence and did not wish to deform its natural progression.

"They live above the rocks."

"Yes."

Where the hereditary counts of Korčula also resided, those pale rulers with belled chests and short femurs who paced their marbled balconies and reported to the Council of Ten. Together, his mother explained, these families—Kanavelić, Izmaeli, Gabrijelić, Nikoničić —determined everything that happened on the island. And no count would permit somebody who looked like her son to treat his relations.

Heartbroken, the boy approached the Jesuit to plead his case. Should he be prohibited from his life's vocation, owing simply to an accident of birth?

"I am a precocious young man," he said, repeating the compliment he'd overheard a tutor giving his thin-nosed student in the parish hall moments earlier. "You can teach me anything, and I will master it." He was a week shy of thirteen.

The Jesuit clapped a heavy hand on the boy's shoulder. Unbeknownst to most, he had been filling an open post, covertly severing the hamstrings of the island's deceased. And a year later, after an exacting apprenticeship, the young doctor found himself performing the same surgeries under the ground.

From the doctor's first entry in his log:

*13 February 1597. Absolute rest, starvation, sedation, bloodletting. These are remedies for living bodies. What I do is a sanctioned desecration.*

And from his initial impression of his student:

*3 January 1620. What a petulant boy they have sent me. Mere fear of the outbreak infects him, and he counts himself foremost among its victims. How terrible, to have one's mind occupied by the suffering of others.*

When he was a petulant novitiate himself, the doctor would heap effervescent salts into the boiling cauldron of his mind— black grief, red rage, crystals quarried from his deepest wounds —until his eyes were wet and raw.

At last, he split the strictures of his mentor's patience. With a sharp cane-rap to the boy's shin, the Jesuit boomed, "Enough! You think it is *beneath you* to attend the dead? Let me avail you of a truth, which you have proven too dense to realize: We treat the living. We treat the fears of the living."

The following night, the boy from Lastovo appears in the theater looking dire. Yellow torchlight puddles around his boots. He squirms miserably.

"You are two hours late."

Already the doctor has cut the hamstrings of two patients.

"I was afraid to leave my room. Something was howling and howling. Circling right outside my window!"

The bright-eyed *čagalj*, explains the doctor. Jackals. "Late in winter, when there is no food for the *čagalj*, we hear them howl until dawn."

"But sir, we have barely passed the solstice."

The doctor presumes the boy is describing a vivid dream, haunted by the terrors of Lastovo.

"Yes, I suppose that's true. Perhaps the hunger has overcome them prematurely."

"I know what I heard. It was no animal."

He wears a look of such open hatred that the doctor can only laugh.

"Do you find this work beneath you? Tell me, will you regret our time together when you return to a home overrun with *vukodlaci*?"

Jure says nothing, and his gaze falls to the cave floor.

At this, the doctor softens a little, recalling how far the young patrician has traveled from his home. "If the howling comes again," he counsels his student, "walk outside and confront the source. I trust it will flee at the first sound of your footsteps."

It's a terrible night. *Even his reflexes are lazy,* the doctor thinks irritably. The boy yawns and leaves his mouth hanging open. He sneezes like a cannon, his arms limp at his sides. He seems to forget, for long stretches, to blink. How can a person stare and stare and still take in nothing? Only from his patients can the doctor tolerate such vacant inattention.

"Repeat what I just said."

"This block is to assist the . . . extension of the thigh?"

"Incorrect."

After the last surgery, the doctor dismisses the sulky Jure, then sits on the table and watches a black and orange spider ascend the craggy wall. It moves like a fugitive hand. At the seam where the wall becomes ceiling, it deftly flips itself and continues to the other side.

"I have risen as far as this world will permit me," the doctor tells his subterranean audience of none. "To rise farther, must I also invert myself entirely?"

Cave fauna had impressed a lesson on the young doctor. He observed the fat, blue worms wiggling through centimeter clefts. The tiny bats hooking by the hundreds into the limestone. They held on wherever they could, dark gasps in the glittering fissures. The lesson was this: Fit yourself to your circumstances. Wrap your wings tightly, and settle into your niche. Go smooth, stay flat. Do your breathing in the shadows. Grow wider, or wilder, and your home could become your tomb.

However, the doctor sometimes wonders if his pragmatism has undermined his ambition. He watches the worms move almost imperceptibly through the cracks. If only there were other rooms, other worlds than this one.

The following morning, the doctor and his daughters walk through the freezing *bura,* encountering a funeral procession for the son of a count. A wailing train of mourners moves down the street, women with golden eyeshadow and charcoal lips, men in round black hats and scarlet vests, music springing from the gaudy mouths of trumpets.

"Papa," his eldest child asks, "why do so many people come to cry for him? When little brother died, we told no one."

Pneumonia is a frequent visitor to their windswept quarter. When informed that her infant brother had stilled, the seven-year-old girl had wept adult tears, comprehending immediately, with a heartbreaking precocity, that there was nothing against which to struggle.

Half a vertical kilometer separates the counts' floating quarries from the hovels of the barnacle people. Their rooms he cannot enter, not even with the lockpick of his imagination. It amazes the doctor, that the distance between their realities can be measured to the meter. They are neighbors, and yet their breath barely overlaps.

At dusk, they come to the doctor's house. Four men from the hills, trailed by the city investigator. Flanking the parade is young Jure.

With his back to the doctor, the boy addresses the *chirurgo* in Venetian.

"What are you doing here?" the doctor asks. Everyone ignores him. He knows only a smattering of the language. Each word he catches is a cold, discrete surprise, raindrops falling from a high ceiling and exploding into meaning: *girl, red, mistake.*

The doctor hears his own name several times, spoken in a tone that frightens him.

So Jure has found a fellow nobleman, the snowy Croat—the "real" doctor—with whom to lodge some complaint. What is it?

The *chirurgo*, his trapeze-thin brows knotted in astonishment, translates: "Your patient Nediljka Nikoničić, daughter of Peter, has been sighted in the woods behind the western cemetery."

"Impossible."

"This boy says the procedure was done improperly."

*Improperly.* The boy does not look up to receive the doctor's glare.

"She is a *vukodlak* now, walking the woods."

"As I said, impossible." Perhaps the famished young visitor has hallucinated a girl in the woods. Or confused the early howling of jackals. As waves of contempt sheet off his skin, the doctor asks what proof the boy can offer. He keeps his voice low and controlled, aware of the open door. Behind him, a child's voice rises: "Papa?"

"No one, the boy says, could mistake the color of her hair."

The *chirurgo* smacks his dry lips.

"A blood-red color, known to all of us."

"The committee has opened an inquiry."

Hunters are already mounted, searching the woods.

Without turning, the doctor can feel his wife's warmth at his back. His three daughters hide under the awning of her shadow, listening. His throat closes with panic. *What if they believe this?*

Now Jure tugs at the investigator's sleeve, whispering something behind the closed shades of their shared dialect. One hand lifts and falls, pantomiming slashing. Locked out of their deliberation, the doctor is nevertheless certain that the boy is lying.

"This boy does not even know where the hamstring is located. Interrogate him, and you shall quickly exhaust his knowledge—he has none. Ask him what he believes I did improperly."

A translation comes promptly: "He remembers seeing your hand slip."

Jure has retreated behind a human wall of his elevated caste. His lips spread into a pinched, jammy smile, one eye rolling off into space. He does not look like a malicious genius. He looks like the child he is, and embarrassed by his fright. It runs in circles around his pallid face, like a horse he cannot bridle. Why has he invented this story? The doctor imagines the point of his scalpel driving toward the boy's open blue iris, expertly peeling back layer after layer of falsehood until he reveals the true memory of the surgery.

"On the basis of one troubled boy's testimony, you have summoned hunters?"

"Other sightings," the *chirurgo* says, "are being reported."

The doctor shudders at the tense shift. Many people in the hills, it seems, have been waiting for this chance to give form to their fears, to accuse the Moorish doctor of malpractice.

The *chirurgo* abstracts the developing allegations—gargling his words, as if their common tongue has become distasteful to him —before reverting to Venetian.

"Papa!" the doctor's youngest cries again, as his wife finally herds the girls away. He swallows the globe in his throat.

"Who claims to have seen her?" he asks softly.

And so the doctor learns the names of his enemies.

That night, his wife presents to the doctor with no symptoms of the rumor's progress inside her save one: her wounded, streaming eyes. He sweeps her black hair from her scalp to examine them, thinking, *The eyes are so easily bruised.* He is afraid that the trauma is done, that her love for him is leaking away.

"Hundreds upon hundreds of deaths," he mutters. "Thousands of successes. Years of my life spent under their earth. Which counts for nothing, it seems."

"If you made a mistake," his wife tells him gently, "it means simply that you are fully human." She touches the top of his cheekbone, as if feeling for the lever of a secret door. "Only admit it to them, so we might begin to make amends."

The doctor is speechless. In an act of spontaneous reformation, his wife immolates her image of him as a perfect man, resurrects him, and forgives him.

*But that's not me! That's an imposter—flawed, ugly, clumsy, deluded.*

He recoils from her reprieve, disgusted, even as her eyes pool with love, and he wonders if it is animal or alien—her ability to pardon him for this thing he has not done. Once more her affect is luminous and calm, the way a lake recovers its composure after a hailstorm. Blue to the bottom again, the stitches dissolved. *You are a better surgeon than I am,* he thinks, horrified. *It is a ghastly scene to behold: my death.*

There is suddenly, he feels, no one left to defend—that man has been swallowed up into this forgiveness.

"No. No. I did nothing to deserve this, this—"

This love badly frightens him. He does not want it. If she could believe that he'd failed his patient, and lied to everyone about it—

He watches his hands shoving her away.

"If only you believe me, in all the world, I will live," he promises her.

His wife looks up at him with injured surprise; never before has he touched her roughly.

"I myself have made a thousand errors."

"But if you do not believe me," he says ominously. "If you have become like them—"

Her small mouth drops open as she reaches for him. She has the face of someone at the top of a fall, her arms wheeling in space. She grabs for his shoulders, sobbing; the sound seems to echo from somewhere else. Her small hands press into his chest.

Shadows dart down the hall. The children.

"No woman wanders the woods." He's drawn her close, his lips fluttering over her ear. "But if you do not believe me, if you have lost faith in me, then you are no longer my family."

As her arms sink to her sides, he turns and leaves for the caves, climbing the briary path, although of course no patients await him; he has been suspended from performing surgeries pending the counts' investigation. At the cave mouth, the doctor pauses. It occurs to him that they might be waiting for him deep below. An ambush. The hunters converging on their true quarry.

Two nights pass. The doctor is unjailed. His wife and daughters do not leave the house. No hunter has captured or even glimpsed the *vukodlak;* at the same time, her presence drapes over the island like a fog. The wailing women in the harbor chapel see nothing else, kneeling in the candlelight with oil-slick eyes like seals.

Another doctor is now caroming around Korčula: Leering and

fiendish and floppy-handed. Apocalyptically incompetent. The doctor's twin, ruining his good name. *Open your eyes. Give me a chance to fight him, the Other Man. The usurper who has replaced me in your memory.*

Those few who do meet the doctor's gaze still fail to recognize him. Their paranoia trawls over his skin, and a monster springs into their nets. His timbre shakes, and they presume his guilt.

Moving behind the market stalls, he eavesdrops on once-familiar voices, now corrupted and rusty with fear:

". . . because she was *interfered* with . . ."

". . . the soil disrupted . . ."

". . . and blood in her mouth!"

He haunts the homes of his friends: Nicolas and Matthias Grbin, John and Jerome Radovanović. "Look at me," he begs. "Could I do these things?" Warmed by some ember of tenderness, they unshade their eyes, which flare with a wild and mounting horror.

Three more nights without fresh news. The hunters chase a redtailed squirrel. Many reputations are now at stake: the hunters grumble that perhaps the boy misled them, while the *chirurgo* defends the investigation to the Council of Ten. So when the doctor learns that the searchers have dug up the grave of Nediljka Nikoničić, over the family's protestations, and discovered an empty coffin, he can be certain only that Jure da Mosto is not conspiring alone.

"Her body is missing," he tells his wife.

"So I've heard."

Astonishingly, she takes his hand.

On the night before his deposition is to be taken, the rumor infects the doctor himself, feasting on his doubts. Parasitically it grows— stronger, brighter, more vehemently alive. How to combat it?

"My hand did not slip," he practices in the mirror. "Never once, in a thousand surgeries, has my hand slipped."

The doctor tries to conjure his wife's face, the faces of his daughters; he needs a shield. Instead, he sees red hair, ablaze in the moonlight and advancing through the forest, descending toward the town.

"Why do you credit this boy's account?" he shouts at his anguished reflection. "An interloper who arrived mere days ago?"

But it's too late. The *vukodlak*'s face has lodged inside him, throbbing and pillary white. In his mind's eye, he watches himself lurching over the operating table, a character in their tale.

Now it is not his patient who torments him, her bare feet stepping crunchingly over the pine cones. It is the Other Man.

For the Other Man is everywhere, leaping from mind to mind, eclipsing him as darkness covers the sun. He finds it impossible to forgive his wife for forgiving him. If she is capable of loving such a creature, what can he ever have meant to her? He cannot accept the dreadful love pouring his way. It will erase him entirely.

He sees his hand, rising and striking her. Her neck, snapping back. He projects these visions into the minds of his friends, imagining them imagining him. That he does nothing of the sort does not, in the end, matter. The doctor thinks: *I am whatever they wish to make of me.*

"I can be trusted with any patient."

The tribunal has been assembled since dawn. When the bell tolls again, the doctor stares from face to face to face, for the eternity of those ten deafening gongs. All of these men are well known to him. He has operated on many of their fathers, brothers, mothers, and sons. His voice is hoarse but measured.

"As evidence, I remind the court that I have performed this procedure on one of my own children."

His composure breaks; at the worst possible moment, his memory betrays him, sucking him into the past. He sees himself walking through the pinewoods of Žrnovo, his only son in his arms—stillborn, the dear boy would never take a single step. "What risk could he possibly pose?" his wife had pleaded. "Leave him be, my love. Please." But the doctor had insisted. The infant's face was his own face—a tiny, blue cameo. The bud of his nose was a cartilaginous copy of his grandfather's; the lips a larval clone of his lips, which he bent to kiss goodbye. In the freezing, white theater, a part of the doctor lives in permanent exile, floating over his breathless son in the blank air.

"I can be trusted—"

He winces to hear the reverb in his voice, as tears breach their banks and flow freely. He has lost already.

"On 3 January, year of our Lord 1620, the hand of our posthumous surgeon slipped while performing his paralyzing surgery. It is possible that this slip was, in fact, deliberate."

After they state the charges against him, he is returned home. Still, no *vukodlak* has been discovered in the woods; and nevertheless, the case will be sent on to the Council of Ten—already the ship bearing the investigator's files is leaving the harbor. Months will pass before a verdict.

In later centuries, new etiologies will evolve. Miasma theory will yield to germ theory, superstition to science. Yet every novel treatment breeds an equally novel genetic resilience, as only the hardiest survivors spawn. And so the cure teaches the disease how to evade it.

The day after the tribunal adjourns, the investigator appears at the doctor's door.

"The boy remembers more and more of that night."

"Does he?"

"Something else came back to him."

Seagulls scream above the harbor. All over the island, in the minds of his neighbors, the red-haired *vukodlak* is waking.

"Tell me, what has returned to young Jure now? What illusory memory?"

As it turns out, the doctor has badly underestimated his puerile foe, whose gift for creative invention belies his bland, seed-hull face. Upon introduction to this latest and darkest variant of himself, the doctor walks stiff-legged to the docks and retches the contents of his stomach into Korčula Bay. Small, red fish rise to nibble at the bilious cloud, and the doctor is consoled by this alone: the voracious appetite of nature, and its utter indifference to his wretched reflection, floating on the water.

That evening, returning to his family, the doctor discovers that his quarantine has failed. His wife sits by the window, watching a pale-green sliver of sea; when she finally speaks, it's her calm that shakes him.

"They say that you were in love with her."

"No."

"That you did something . . . to her body. That you—"

"And you are seduced by such vile falsehoods?"

"Oh, my love."

"I see that even the most hideous crimes are not foreign to your imagination."

Because she has already witnessed such evil, hasn't she? She has been entertaining him, the Other Man, all afternoon.

She sleeps at the outer edge of their bed, her back to the doctor, like a caterpillar clinging to its leaf. And yet her palm is flung behind her, for him to take if he so desires—her arm bent backward, reaching for him. He stares at it in horror.

The doctor spends the next three nights knocking on doors, an uninvited guest. He pleads his case to whoever answers, incapable of rest until his reputation is restored. He begins in their own impoverished precinct, crabbing his way across the sea-slick docks.

"You behave like a guilty man," his wife admonishes. "You make their case for them. Can you not see that?"

He gazes at her blearily, his mien that of the *vukodlak* itself, driven to circle the nocturnal streets.

"The rumor has polluted every mind on the island. If I cannot defeat it, I see no possibility of redemption for us. I would have to change our names, burn off my skin."

His daughters adopt their mother's pitch, blocking the doorframe with their slight bodies. "Stay here, Papa! Please do not leave us!"

The doctor blinks at the four of them, as if surprised to find intruders in his home. His thumb covers his lower lip, forming a little crucifix to dam a loosening cry.

He is genuflecting in a light dusting of snow, midway along the stair cut into the limestone cliffside that spirals up to the ivory compound of Peter Nikoničić. Leagues below, the dark sea rolls into the coastline, detonating soundlessly on and on. The doctor has never before climbed to such an elevation; vertigo momentarily convulses him, and he scrapes at the rock face for some ballast, before regathering his senses and pressing on.

Reaching the summit, he pauses to admire the unity of the architecture: the main house with its colonnade of white stone quarried from Vrnik, its luminous domed roof like an exhumed moon. *The windows of these fortressed palaces leave the rich surprisingly vulner- able,* the doctor thinks. *Any spectral eyes can follow the starlight into their private rooms.* Edging closer, he exploits this privilege of the already dead.

A dozen plates are set along a long, black table, interspersed with bouquets of nettles. The table itself is an elegant ungu- late, an Italianate species of furniture, with legs that end in oak hooves. Perhaps it, too, has been hobbled, so that it can- not gallop off with the crystal candlesticks, the golden decant- ers. The Other Man, the doctor guesses, dines here often. Peter Nikoničić, no doubt, invites the ghastly twin into his thoughts a hundred times a day.

Roasted meats appear on silver platters. Dried berries heaped like red plunder, and boiled vegetables deliquescing into soup. And there, stealing impertinently into the middle seat, flanked by half a dozen healthy children, is the doctor's assassin, Jure da Mosto. In this house, where his family would be relieved he'd found a berth, he looks younger than his sixteen years. With his long bangs combed over his eyebrows, and his thin torso swal- lowed by a scarlet vest, he is eleven, ten, too puddled and small to support the doctor's hatred. It is suddenly all too easy to under- stand why the boy from Lastovo would move the countess's body.

*We are in the same predicament, then,* the doctor considers. *You do not want to be a liar, any more than I want to be a monster.*

Bones stack up beside the drained chalices, as the noblemen and their rapacious progeny consume the dishes with remarkable speed. His former student laughs, one hand clapped to the hole of his mouth; the scene is muted by the roaring wind buffeting the doctor, yet his mind supplies the sound. It is nothing so light as laughter, this noise he hears, or imagines he hears, pouring out of young Jure.

The doctor had intended to stand before the meal's end and stride into their midst; but as the table is cleared by three servants, he merely watches, hypnotized by the ebb and flow of life and shadow inside the great hall, unaware of the snowflakes collect- ing on his stooping back. One by one, Jure da Mosto and every Nikoničić scion and servant disappears. Soon the room has emp- tied of people, and yet the doctor remains, bowing outside the window, addressing himself to the count's empty chairs: *I am an innocent man. As the Posthumous Surgeon of Korčula, my record of service is faultless—*

One can become numb to numbness, a tertiary disavowal of the body, and this is precisely what occurs to the doctor, kneeling in snow. He might be kneeling there still, had two hands not clapped onto his shoulders, wrenching him to his feet.

"You do not belong here."

Craning around, the doctor collides with the Other Man, reflected in the gray, frightened eyes of the count pinning him to the stone wall. At once, the vertigo returns, and he collapses into the man's embrace. A bright quarter moon floats over the harbor, winding light around their bodies in lean stripes. The doctor fights through an endless moment. Elevating his gaze to meet the count's, he beholds himself dissolving into his double.

"Peter Nikoničić." His voice, when it comes, is barely intelligible. "Peter Peter Peter Peter *Nikoničić!* Estimable sir, your lordship, Peter *Nikoničić.*"

His tongue, that trained slug, as yet incompletely thawed, lurches to form the words.

"Forgive my intrusion, but I have come to, to, to—"

The doctor is not a drunk, but it occurs to him that he might become one, in the count's future testimony of this encounter.

"I do not belong here. That is true." A whirl of disordered feeling threatens to pitch him over the ledge. "You people let me fly to the roof of a cave and no farther. You have blocked my ascent to the true sky. You call me the Moor, Peter Nikoničić, although my family has lived on Black Corfu for as long as your family."

Giggles escape him, seeming to originate not from his mouth but from the crinkling corners of his red eyes, and evaporating into the night. He gapes up, for a moment confusing the rising hysteria with the falling snow.

"Oh, you people should have hobbled me long ago! You must have guessed that I would one day climb your hills. But I imagined a different kind of advancement, Peter Nikoničić—a promotion!"

The joke of his life seizes him once more, and he vibrates with silent mirth. "Ah, look," he murmurs. "We have an audience."

Blue light floods through one of the upstairs windows; this would be Jure, the doctor is somehow certain. Jure in his guest room, looking down on them. Looking down is the boy's sole talent, isn't it? Quite a feat, for an inbred adolescent.

With great effort, the doctor regains himself, grasping the count's wrists.

"That boy in your house is a liar. To protect himself, he has hidden the body somewhere. But the surgery was routine, and your daughter is no *vukodlak*." He leans in until their clammy foreheads touch. "Peter Nikoničić, I never harmed her. You must believe me."

Loosening his grip on the doctor, the count steps back. Both men are breathing heavily. He lowers his lantern. Now only a slice of him is visible, caught in the light: his wide, flaring nostrils, his quivering mustache. Still, it is enough to reveal the grief of Peter Nikoničić. The doctor is prepared for rage. He is prepared for blows. He is unprepared for the horsey bellows of the big man's sorrow in the dark. He quiets, recognizing the rhythm of his own despair, for which he's found no cure.

"She is gone." Peter Nikoničić's face has passed into blackness. "And now you must go, too."

On his return descent, retracing his steps through the forest, the doctor notices two sets of prints in the drifts.

"Who is following me?" he cries.

Something is moving in the thicketed darkness, agitating the branches. An almost human whimpering, unbearably familiar.

"Nediljka?" he whispers.

His middle daughter steps from the shadows.

"Papa!" Her voice flutters in the frigid air.

*How lost must I be,* he wonders, *to have no awareness of this little girl at my heels?*

"I am very cold, Papa."

She slips into his arms, and it's an agony to feel her slight frame trembling, to have no further protection to offer. He walks as fast as she can manage, and when the snow deepens he carries her. They move through a ravine of solid moonlight. In this lunar meadowland, they are not alone. His daughter sights the creature first, and screams.

The thing rears on its hind legs, its coppery hair matted to its heaving sides. The doctor's mind, grasping for a name for the humanoid storm cloud, can find only *monster*. It is his daughter who roars back, "Bear!"

For an instant, the doctor experiences a surge of elation, thinking: *I can explain everything to them and repair my reputation.* But of course that's not true. The boy's story has moved into the tower of fact, of history. It will not be evicted.

From her perch on his shoulders, his daughter is eye level with the bear, whose snout falls open. He sees black teeth. A levitating, slate tongue. Great, shaggy arms thick as oak boughs, and whetted claws that rend the very air. A deafening sound erupts from the chasm beyond its flashing jaws, shaking the island to its bedrock; and inside that sound, a miracle happens. The three animals surrender to some spell of mutual hypnosis. Life beholds itself, a radiance ricocheting off three mirrors, multiplying; and from their conjoined attention, a fourth mind surfaces, vast enough to encompass them all—an anonymous, ephemeral intelligence. Before its collapse, each creature glimpses itself through the eyes of another. The girl sees herself small as a blossom atop the shoulders of her father, who is, after all, only a man; the doctor recognizes himself in the bear's awareness, a nameless silhouette in the landscape, cleansed of every accusation; as for the bear, the nature of her realization floats outside the net of human language. Dropping to her paws, she disappears into the pines.

The doctor is left with only a fleck of the knowledge that engulfed them a moment ago: there is another country in which he exists, running parallel to this one.

Just before sunrise, they reach another clearing, now a plain of fresh snow. Birds throb into the sky, startled from their feeding. Their cries are like thunder flattened by a rolling pin, silvery and faraway. Even skimming the earth, they echo remotely.

"Why do they sound like that, Papa—both here and not here?"

"They are dead and alive," he replies.

His daughter's skin has a blue cast, and her eyes are half-lidded. Her slender hands swim inside his gloves, her shivering body in his robe. The cold has invaded her.

Before them, along the apron of the harbor, warming floes split and sink into the sea. Ships loom like alien beasts, their gunwales transformed by icicles into slick gums with violet fangs. *They will lose a thousand teeth before noon*, thinks the doctor. His daughter stirs, nuzzling her face into his hair.

In the doctor's home, the freeze is only beginning. With a shriek to silence the morning gulls, his wife falls upon him.

"Where have you been? How could you take her out into this weather?"

She wrenches their daughter from his grasp, enveloping the child in her warmth.

"She followed me," he says weakly. He touches the girl's cheek. "Tell your mother what you saw."

She blinks at him and coughs.

"Tell her," he urges.

"Nothing."

"Get out," says his wife. She looks at him as if he were a stranger.

The doctor sighs, feeling an almost hallucinatory unburdening. "You did love me."

That night, the doctor sleeps on a pallet in one of the sailors' brothels, where even the seven-foot proprietor is afraid to place a hand on him. He wakes at dawn and wanders the herringbone maze of the walled city, watching impassively as his neighbors wince away from him.

The close of day is a violent spectacle on the island of Korčula. The sun falls from the sky as if shot, collapsing into the horizon as light ribbons away from the moored ships. He sits on toothy rocks, in the spray of unending waves. The wind has chased everyone else inside. Once the moon has risen fully, he stands and turns toward the forest, toward the Other Man. Twin crescents of a lunar powder mar the seat of his trousers. The ordinarily meticulous doctor has not visited the barber in a fortnight. Scalpel in hand, he starts up the hill.

"I can be trusted with any patient."

He speaks aloud to the watchful rabbit. Her pink nostrils swell and fall, and he feels a rush of love for her, for her immunity to the swirling lies of man.

As he descends to the theater to prepare for a final surgery, the rabbit remains on her beetle-bored log, peering after him, down the throat of the cave to where the shadows jump.

From the doctor's final, undated entry in his log:

*I am coming to see this plan as the only means by which I might exonerate myself of the charges brought against me and vanquish my ubiquitous, invisible adversary. With a steady hand, I will sever my hamstrings. I will complete this procedure perfectly, and so mark my first and last operation on a living body. After hobbling myself, I will cut my throat, thus proving to my faithless family and fellow citizens that neither nerves nor emotion could ever compromise my dexterity, or vitiate my efforts on behalf of our dead.*

The complete exculpation and defense runs to nearly forty pages.

It whistles out of the cave—not stumbling, not lurching, but running nimbly down the hillside, between the pines. On steady legs, it stalls beside two yellow-mossed boulders. Thoughtfully, it pops a finger into its mouth—as cold and as dry as this clear winter's night, devoid of even a drop of fluid. Undergrowth lisps up and around in the salty breeze, dark vines pocked with turbulent blossoms. It bends a knee and genuflects, staring up at the towering canopy. Arid incisions split the backs of its thighs. It caresses these wonderingly, bewitched by the supple angle of its leg unbending. Has the surgery been a failure, then? For here it stands.

"Perhaps," the doctor's *vukodlak* admits softly to the thousand whispering trees of Black Corfu, "I have made a mistake."

SAÏD SAYRAFIEZADEH

# *Audition*

FROM *The New Yorker*

THE FIRST TIME I smoked crack cocaine was the spring I worked construction for my father on his new subdivision in Moonlight Heights. My original plan had been to go to college, specifically for the arts, specifically for acting, where I'd envisioned strolling shoeless around campus with a notepad, jotting down details about the people I observed so that I would later be able to replicate the human condition onscreen with nuance and veracity. Instead, I was unmatriculated and nineteen, working six days a week, making eight dollars an hour, no more or less than what the other general laborers were being paid, and which is what passed, at least for my self-made father, as fairness. Occasionally, I would be cast in a community-theater production of Neil Simon or *The Mystery of Edwin Drood*, popular but uncomplicated fare, which we would rehearse for a month before performing in front of an audience of fifteen. "You have to pay your dues," the older actors would tell me, sensing, I suppose, my disappointment and impatience. "How long is that going to take?" I'd ask them, as if they spoke from high atop the pinnacle of show business. In lieu of an answer, they offered a tautology. "It takes as long as it takes," they'd say.

It was spring, it was rainy, it was the early nineties, meaning that *Seinfeld* was all the rage, and so was Michael Jordan, and so was crack cocaine, the latter of which, at this point, I had no firsthand knowledge. As for Jerry Seinfeld and Michael Jordan, I knew them well. Each evening, having spent my day carrying sixty-pound drywall across damp pavement and up bannisterless staircases in one of the state-of-the-art family residences being prewired for the internet—whatever that was—in a cul-de-sac eventually to be named Placid Village Circle, I would drive to my apartment and watch one or the other, Seinfeld or Jordan, since one or the other always happened to be on. They were famous, they were artists, they were exalted. I watched them and dreamed of my own fame and art and exalt. The more I dreamed, the more vivid the dream seemed to be, until it was no longer some faint dot situated on an improbable time line but, rather, my *destiny*. And all I needed to turn this destiny into reality was to make it out of my midsized city—not worth specifying—and move to LA, where, of course, an actor needed to be if he was to have any chance at that thing called success. But, from my perspective of a thousand miles, LA appeared immense, incensed, inscrutable, impenetrable, and every time I thought I had enough resolve to uproot myself and rent a U-Haul I would quickly retreat into the soft, downy repetitiveness of my hometown, with its low stakes, high livability, and steady paycheck from my father.

The general laborers came and went that spring, working for a few weeks and then quitting without notice, eight dollars apparently not being enough to compensate even the most unskilled. No matter. For every man who quit, there were five more waiting in line to take his place, eight dollars apparently being enough to fill any vacancy. I was responsible for showing the new recruits around on their first day, which took about twenty minutes and got me out of carrying drywall. Here's the Porta-Potty. Here's the foreman's office. Here's the paper to sign. They wanted to know what the job was like. They wanted to know if there were health benefits. They spoke quietly and conspiratorially, as if what they asked might be perceived as treasonous. They wanted to know if they might have the opportunity to learn some plumbing or carpentry. "You'll have to talk to the boss about that," I'd tell them, but the answer was no. What they should have been asking me was if there was a union.

No one knew that I was the boss's son. About once a week my dad would show up in his powder-blue Mercedes and walk around inspecting the progress, displeased and concerned, finding everything urgent and subpar, showing neither love nor special dispensation toward me, nor did I show any toward him. This seemed to come easily to the two of us. I was just another workingman in wet overalls and he was just another big shot in a three-piece suit and a safety vest. The roles we played were generic, superficial, and true. Later, he'd tell me, "I'm doing this for you, not for me." What "this" was was not entirely clear. "One day all of this will be yours," he'd say. "This" was three subdivisions and a ten-story office building downtown. "This" was the powder-blue Mercedes. According to my father, he wanted me to learn the meaning of hard work up close and personal so that I would know what life was really like, but also because he wanted me to experience what he had gone through growing up on the outskirts of town with six siblings, odd jobs, and no help from the government. In short, I was living a version of his life, albeit in reverse.

From time to time, I would be paired up with a guy named Duncan Dioguardi, who was my age but looked ten years older, and who liked to order me around—put this here, put that there. He enjoyed the power, while I enjoyed the cold comfort of knowing that I could burst his bubble by telling him who my dad was, but a good actor never breaks character. Clearly, I was a novice and not very good at hard work, as Duncan and my father had already surmised. I got winded fast. I got apathetic fast. I cut corners when I could. I waited for opportunities to go to the Porta-Potty. I waited for opportunities to smoke cigarettes. The cigarettes got me winded faster. "You need to get into shape," Duncan would tell me. "Why don't you use your next paycheck to buy yourself a ThighMaster?" This was a joke for him. He would walk around in short-sleeved shirts, impervious to the chill, a tattoo of a snake coiling around his bicep and crawling up toward his neck, en route to devour his face, a dramatic and striking image if ever there was one, doubly so against his pale skin, slick with drizzle. In the meantime, I slouched beneath drywall, imagining LA in the spring, waiting for lunchtime, quite proficient at not being the boss's son, and all the while reassuring myself that one day in the future I would be performing some version of this role with nuance and veracity, out of shape or not. *What did you draw from to create the character?* the critics would ask me. *Why, from real life,* I would say.

When lunchtime arrived, I'd sit around with the other general laborers, thirty of us on upturned crates in an unfinished living room with a spring breeze blowing through the glassless windows, eating roast-beef sandwiches and talking about money problems, home problems, work problems. My problems were not their problems, but I wished they were. Their problems were immediate, distinct, and resolvable; mine were long-term, existential, and impossible. When I spoke, I tried to approximate the speech patterns of my coworkers—the softened consonants and the dropped articles—lest I reveal myself for the outsider that I was. No hard *k*'s, *x*'s, or *f*s. The irony was that my father's specified plan of self-improvement for me dovetailed with my own: experience real life up close and personal.

The other general laborers knew one another from high school or the neighborhood or the previous work site, which had paid ten dollars an hour. They hoped that the subdivision wouldn't be finished until fall, maybe even winter. They didn't mind working forever. They were still counting on a chance to learn a trade—but half of them would be gone in two weeks. As for me, I'd grown up in Timpani Hills, where none of these men would have had any reason to visit unless they'd come to do some roofing. I'd gone to the best schools and had the cushiest upbringing, including a pool in the backyard and weekend acting classes, where my dad would watch me perform on parents' night, misty and proud in the front row, his boorishness temporarily abated, supportive of his son's passion and talent until he realized that his son was intending to pursue acting as something more than a hobby. Now all that history was inconsequential, pulsed inside the blender of collective toil. No one would have been able to tell me apart from any of the other general laborers I sat with on my lunch break, smoking cigarettes amid exposed crossbeams. Just as no one would have been able to tell that I was the boss's son. To the latecomer entering the theater, I was indistinguishable from the whole.

Just as no one would have been able to tell that I didn't really want to give Duncan Dioguardi a lift to his house after work, but his car had broken down—yet one more item to be added to the list of immediate problems. What I wanted to say was *Why don't you ride home on a ThighMaster?* But what I actually said was "Sure, jump in!" I could hear the sprightliness in my voice, all false. It was Saturday. It was four o'clock. The foreman was letting us off early because the drywall hadn't been delivered on time. The new recruits wondered if they would still be paid for a full day. Theirs was an argument that made sense only on paper. "Go enjoy the weather," the foreman said, as if he were bestowing the good weather upon us. Indeed, the sun was high and there was no rain. When the breeze blew, it blew with promise. I should have been savoring the first official nice day of spring; instead, I was driving an hour out of my way down Route 15. The traffic was slow-going. We stopped and started. We stopped again. Duncan Dioguardi apologized for the traffic. Inside the car he was surprisingly thoughtful and courteous. He had his seat belt on and his hands were folded in his lap. "Setting is everything," my dear old acting teacher had once told me, and then we had done exercises to illustrate this concept: forest, beach, prison cell.

"I don't mind traffic," I told Duncan. I was being courteous, too. I softened my consonants. I dropped my articles. Through the windshield, our midsized city crawled past at a midsized pace. Midsized highways with midsized cars. Midsized citizens with their midsized lives.

We talked about work and then we talked about ourselves. Away from the subdivision, it was clear that we had little in common. He told me that he'd been doing manual labor since he was fifteen, beginning with cleaning bricks at a demolition site on the north side of the city. I was taking weekend acting classes at fifteen. "A nickel a brick," Duncan told me. "You do the math." I wasn't sure what math there was to do. Duncan was the one who should have been taking acting classes, not me, receiving instruction on how to transform his supply of hard-earned material into that thing called art. He'd already lived twice the life that I'd lived, while having none of my advantages. He was what my father had been before my father hit it big. But Duncan Dioguardi was most likely never going to hit it big. His trajectory seemed already established. If I wasn't careful, *my* trajectory would soon be established. The tattoo of the snake heading up to Duncan's face was not an affect but as apt a metaphor as any of what the past had been like for him, and what the future held. He needed no affect. *I* was the one who needed an affect. "Don't ever get a tattoo," my acting teacher had told me. "A performer must always remain a blank slate." So here I was, playing the role of general laborer, with flawless skin and stuck in traffic.

It was four thirty. If I was lucky, I'd be home by six. Maybe I would take a nap, assuage my fatigue and apathy, wake up fresh and do something productive, like read a script and enlighten myself. Sometimes I would lie in the bathtub and read aloud from my stack of current and classic screenplays, playing every single character, men, women, and children. Even the stage directions were a character: *Fade in. Int. bathtub—night. Fade out.* Everything was deserving of voice. Meanwhile, Duncan Dioguardi and I lit cigarettes, one after the other, inhaling first- and secondhand smoke. We fiddled with the radio. Tupac came on. Tupac was all the rage. We nodded our heads to Tupac. Apropos of Tupac, I told Duncan about how I was planning to move to LA. I said it casually, as if this plan were already in the works rather than a doubtful dot on an undrawn time line, and I was unexpectedly filled with a brief but heartening sense that, merely by my vocalizing that something would happen, something would actually happen—as per pop psychology. Duncan told me that he had lived in LA, between starting high school and dropping out of high school. What else had Duncan done by the age of nineteen? Where else had Duncan lived? He was so far ahead of me in the category of life that I would have been unable to catch up even if I began living *now.* "What was LA like?" I asked him. I could hear my counterfeit casualness being usurped by genuine yearning. "It was magical," Duncan said. He got quiet. He contributed no follow-up details. He stared out the windshield. "See this traffic?" he said. I saw this traffic. "This isn't LA traffic," he said. I pictured LA traffic on a Saturday at four thirty, sun high, never rain, bumper-to-bumper, all of it magical.

Suddenly, I was telling Duncan Dioguardi about my innermost desires, speaking confessionally, spilling my guts, spelling out exactly how I was going to become an actor, how I was going to rent a U-Haul, not give the boss any notice, fuck the boss, drive a thousand miles in a day, arrive in LA, find an agent, find a place to live, start auditioning for film and television, maybe even *Seinfeld.* "Keep an eye out for me on *Seinfeld,*" I said. If you say it, it will happen. Somewhere along the way, I had stopped dropping articles and softening consonants, because it was too difficult a ruse to maintain while also trying to be authentic. I told Duncan about having performed in *The Mystery of Edwin Drood,* twice, at the rec center, one fall and the following fall. I'd had only a small part but I'd got some laughs. I didn't tell him that there'd been fifteen people in the audience. Perhaps he'd heard of the production? There had been a four-star review in the *Tribune.* No, he hadn't heard of it.

"You can do better than that bullshit," he said.

*

It was five o'clock. We were moving fast now. The traffic was gone.
So were my cigarettes. We were inspiring each other with our uplifting stories of promise and potential. Duncan was telling me
about his own plans for the future, which mainly involved having
realized that he'd wasted the previous year, and the year before
that. He was determined to make up for it. He knew precisely
what needed to be done. He spoke generally. In response, I spoke
generally, too, providing platitudes where applicable. "You can do
whatever you set your mind to," I said. "It's mind over matter,"
he said. "That's right!" I said. "That's right!" he said. We were in
agreement, and yet I had the peculiar feeling that we were referring to different things.

He was telling me where to turn. Turn here. Turn there. Left.
Right. Right. I was entering territory with which I was unfamiliar,
because I'd grown up cushy. We drove beneath an overpass that
led into a down-and-out neighborhood of weather-beaten, two-
story, redbrick homes, a hundred of them in a row, every one
identical, just as the houses in my father's subdivision were identical, but at the other end of the economic spectrum. This was a
neighborhood of odd jobs and no help, where people shopped
for dinner at the convenience store. "I trust them as far as I can
throw them," Duncan said, referring to I know not what. This was
outsized struggle in a midsized city. Turn. Turn. Turn. The Spice
Girls came on. The Spice Girls were all the rage. Apropos of the
Spice Girls, Duncan was asking me if I wanted to party tonight.
He was asking as if the thought had just occurred to him. It was
Saturday, after all. It was five thirty. It would be a shame to let
these windfall spring hours go to waste. It would be a shame to
go home as I always did, lie in the bathtub, have another night of
living life through the soggy pages of screenplays, getting closer
to twenty years old, my time line unraveling like a ball of yarn.
I somehow knew that the word *party* in this context meant one
thing: getting high. What I really wanted was to stop at a convenience store and get more cigarettes. "Don't waste your money,"
Duncan said. He could buy me more cigarettes, no problem.
He pointed to one of the identical buildings. If I gave him ten
dollars he could get me a carton of cigarettes at half price. If I
chipped in thirty dollars he could get the two of us cigarettes
*plus*. "Do you want cigarettes *plus*?" Duncan asked. "Do you want

to party?" He was speaking now entirely in the language of euphemisms, and I was fluent.

"Yes," I said. "I want to party."

It was six o'clock and we were in the basement of Duncan Dioguardi's house. Or, more to the point, we were in the basement of his *mother's* house, where he was staying until his security deposit cleared. "Banks," he said, generally. His mother wasn't home, but she kept a nice house, much nicer on the inside than it appeared on the outside, with hardwood floors and crown molding, and I thought about how these were the kinds of detail that would have eluded a person who had merely driven through the neighborhood without bothering to stop, like the passenger on a cruise ship who thinks he knows the island from the port. Duncan's basement was more bedroom than basement, with Mom's touches, sheets tucked in, cozy and comfortable, except for a boiler in the corner that was making clicking sounds. Stacked up in a pile were some carpentry manuals for beginners, yellow books with hammers on the covers. "I dabble with those sometimes," he said. Then he added, "But they won't give a guy like me a chance." I wasn't sure if "whatever you set your mind to" would apply in this instance.

On his dresser was a Magnavox TV, twenty-five-inch, with a built-in VCR, presumably left on all day, tuned to ESPN, where the announcers were oohing and aahing over, who else, Michael Jordan, who was doing, what else, winning. He glided down the court. He floated through the air. He elbowed his defender in the chest. Everything he did had style, even his mistakes. He was the perfect blend of beauty and power, of grace and aggression. No one would have dared tell Michael Jordan, "It takes as long as it takes."

My carton of cigarettes was in my lap, cradled lovingly, half price, as promised, already torn open by me, cigarette smoke going straight up into my face, and in Duncan's palm was the adventure I had come here for, two small white cubes—yellowish, really, crumbs, really—bought at full price. "This is what you get for twenty dollars apiece," he said. "You do the math." Had I been the latecomer to this play, I would have thought that these two small cubes had been chipped off the edge of some drywall, so insignificant did they look. If Duncan had accidentally dropped them on the floor, they would have been lost forever in the grain of the hardwood. But Duncan, handling them with such care and attention, as if he were a doctor operating over a nightstand, demonstrating speed and precision, using one of Mom's table knives to gently break the two white chips into even smaller white chips, would never let them drop on the floor. This was the stuff of theater, basement theater, the six-o'clock show, and I had a front-row seat to the action, from which I was able to watch what happens when the actor does not have the right props with him, because this actor is "not a pro, and not intending on becoming a pro." What Duncan was, though, was ingenious, withdrawing a roll of aluminum foil from beneath his bed, no doubt procured from Mom's cupboard, and a box of Chore Boy, also from beneath his bed, with little Chore Boy wearing a backward baseball cap, a big grin on his face, because life is nothing if not delightful, especially when one is cleaning. He could have been a character from a fairy tale, Chore Boy, innocent and archetypal, his stumpy arm beckoning the consumer toward some enchanted land. Soon, a perfect aluminum foil pipe emerged from Duncan Dioguardi, glinting silver in the Magnavox light, reminding me of the way some family restaurants will wrap your leftovers in aluminum foil in the shape of a swan. But into this particular swan's mouth disappeared a piece of the Chore Boy, followed by one small chip off the drywall, and then Duncan Dioguardi ran his lighter back and forth, orange flame on silver neck, and from the swan's tail he sucked ever so gently, cheeks pulling, pulling, until, like magic, he tilted his head back and out of his mouth emerged a perfect puff of white smoke.

He considered for a moment, eyes closed, then eyes opened, gauging, I suppose, the ratio of crack cocaine to baking powder, and then he offered an appraisal. "Not bad," he said. He looked at me. Was it my turn now?

No, not yet my turn. First we must watch Michael Jordan, because the aluminum foil pipe needed time to cool down, a necessary and dramatic interlude, the basement boiler ticking off the minutes. It was almost the end of the basketball game, and beads of sweat dripped elegantly down Jordan's shaved head as he huddled with coaches and teammates, half-listening to advice that had long ago ceased applying to him. He showed no signs of trepidation or anxiety about the fate of the game. He already *knew* the fate of the game. As for the advice that Duncan Dioguardi was now offering me, I listened carefully. This is how you hold the pipe. This is how you inhale the smoke. "This isn't a cigarette," he said.

"You don't suck it into your lungs." He was patient, the way a good coach should be. Then he clicked the lighter and I was pulling as he had pulled, not too hard, not too soft, just right. I had expected the foil on my lips to taste like something, but it tasted like nothing. I had expected the smoke to smell like something, but it smelled like nothing. I had expected the high to alter me in some profound and mystifying way, but the effect was underwhelming and anticlimactic. Mostly, I felt clear-eyed and levelheaded, disappointingly so. "Not bad," I said anyway. The only thing that was unexpected was the sudden sense of fondness that I had for Duncan Dioguardi, good coach that he was, and, dare I say, good friend. Sure, I barely knew him; sure, we had had different upbringings; but we had shared something on that ride down Route 15, and we were sharing something now, within his home, which he had welcomed me into, and in this way, yes, I could consider him a friend. The passenger who had remained only in the port, browsing the trinket shops, delighting in duty-free, would never have known this subtle but essential detail. Just as he would never have known that there was indeed a distinct smell hovering in the room, of the Chore Boy being cooked alive, not dissimilar to the odor when the plumbers had come through the subdivision, soldering the water lines, the new recruits watching them with envy and admiration.

That spring, my dear old acting teacher came to my rescue by way of a phone call, out of the blue, asking if I might be available to audition for a play that he was directing at the Apple Tree Theatre. "So wonderful to hear your voice again," he said. He said that he had always remembered me fondly from those Sunday classes years earlier—Intro to Acting I, followed by Intro to Acting II—where he would instruct a dozen teenagers in the world of make-believe. We played games, we played inanimate objects, we played adults. "There are rules even for make-believe," he would tell us. Everything he said had the ring of truth and revelation. He had the empathy and kindness of the elderly. If there had been an Intro III and IV, I would have taken those, too, all the way up to C. I was always forlorn when my dad arrived to pick me up in his powder-blue Mercedes, the engine kept running. On a few occasions, my teacher had taken him aside and told him that his son had a future in theater. "That's good to know," my father had said, but the future he was envisioning was real estate.

Now my teacher was calling to say that he had never forgotten me, that I had made a strong impression on him, even at the age of fifteen, and that he thought I would be perfect for the role he had in mind. The way he spoke made it sound as if he had already come to a decision, and reading for the role was only a technicality. Still, I knew enough to know that nothing was ever guaranteed, that auditioning was only one step toward being cast, that a play was only one step toward a movie, and a movie was only one step toward fame. But that my teacher had sought me out after all these years was a sign that I was truly talented, that the hope I had been harboring was not false, and that I was living a life where the unexpected could indeed occur.

When I showed up for the audition a week later, I was disheartened to see that it was far from a foregone conclusion. I was one of twenty young men who had apparently all been students of my acting teacher, and all of whom he had apparently remembered fondly. We were perfect replicas of one another, dressed in khakis, hair blow-dried, walking around doing the same vocal warm-ups that we had been taught: *B-B-B-B, T-T-T-T*—no softened consonants here. In our hands we held headshots of our giant faces, lit to make us appear older, wiser, and better-looking than we actually were, and on the back were our résumés, numbering ten or fewer credentials, twice for *The Mystery of Edwin Drood.* In thirty years, the list of credentials would be longer and our headshots would be younger.

Things were running behind. The auditions were supposed to have started at ten o'clock, first come, first served, but it was noon and they'd made it only through twelve hopefuls. I was No. 19 on the list. I was anxious. I was hungry. I was taking time off from work. "A dentist's appointment," I'd told the foreman. "Do that on your own time," he'd said. Instead of eating food, I smoked cigarettes, standing in the doorway, six feet from a sign that said NO SMOKING, exhaling out into the spring air, alongside my fellow actors who looked like me. We bantered, we joked, we lit one another's cigarettes, we pretended we were not consumed with insecurity and competitiveness. To help pass the time we talked about classical and postmodern theater. If I had gone to college, I might have known what I was talking about. The walls around us were adorned with posters of plays past, announcing four-week runs to nowhere. Every so often the big brown door of the theater, with its single round pane of glass, something like a porthole, would swing open, offloading the previous aspirant, a carbon copy of myself, whose face conveyed, in equal parts, relief, defeat, and premature delusions of being cast.

When it was finally my turn, I was surprised to see that my acting teacher, whom I had remembered at best as middle-aged, and at most as old, was probably only in his early thirties. He had seemed tall back then, too, but now he was short and I was tall. He was standing in the middle of a row of seats, with stacks of scripts beside him, and when I handed him my headshot he looked at me without the faintest recognition, but then when it suddenly became clear to him who I was and how much I'd changed in the intervening years he stepped forward and embraced me. I felt his empathy and kindness draped around my shoulders, expressed without reservation, and if the embrace had continued much longer I might have cried. He wanted to know how I'd been, and what I'd been doing, but since the auditions were running behind there was no time to catch up.

What was being decided here and now was whether I would be cast in a central role as a character who would be onstage for all three acts but had zero lines. I could not tell if this was a step backward or forward for my career. If I had to pick one, I would have picked backward. According to my teacher, it was forward. "He holds the play together," he said. To this end, he needed to see how I "moved through space," since moving through space would be the only thing I would be doing. So I took my place onstage, apprehensive beneath a single blinding spotlight, and waited for his direction, which was, simply, "Show me the color red."

This was not something I had been anticipating. I had been anticipating, for example, being asked to mime pouring a glass of water, something I remember being quite good at. Without warning, we had entered the realm of symbolism and abstraction. We had entered game playing and fun. But all I could think of was the tremendous predicament of being asked to embody a *concept*. Was a color even a concept? If I had been fifteen still, I would have done what he asked, happily, without thinking twice. I would have done every color. *Here's fuchsia! Here's cadmium yellow!* There would have been joy in exploration. Now my brain felt calcified and literal, the effects of aging. I could think only of making a semibold choice, like lying on my back and moving interpretatively. But lying on my back would obscure me from my teacher's vision. "If the audience can't see you," he would sometimes say, "then who are you doing this for?" I lay down anyway, the hard stage pressing against me, dust getting all over my khakis. The foreman would say to me later, "You got dirty from going to the dentist?" For lack of any other idea, I channeled the character of the foreman, and then I channeled the drywall, which was not a character, and I thought about smoking a cigarette, because in my world of make-believe the color red smokes cigarettes, which was what I did, lying on my back, eyes closed, moving conceptually, this way and that, blowing smoke into the yellow spotlight of blindness, and when I stood up and dusted myself off I had, most wondrously, been given the role.

The second time I smoked crack cocaine was the spring I worked construction for my father on his new subdivision in Moonlight Heights. By this point, the electricians had finished prewiring for the internet, whatever that was, the floors had been poured, the windows had been installed, and the general laborers had come and gone, eight dollars an hour not being enough. I would show the new recruits around, bathroom, foreman, paper to sign, and then I would go carry drywall in the sunshine. I was aware that I had been waiting for Duncan Dioguardi to invite me to party again, but no invitation had been forthcoming, and to broach it myself seemed as though it would traverse an essential but unstated boundary.

This time it was a Thursday evening, after our shift, around six o'clock. Duncan's car had broken down again. "Sure," I said, "jump in." I could hear the sprightliness in my voice, now authentic. The traffic was just as bad as ever and we crawled forward with our windows rolled down, the spring breeze blowing in, the cigarette smoke blowing out, dusk all around us. "I'm sorry about the traffic," Duncan said, as he had said before. "I don't mind," I said. We talked about the subdivision for a while, and then we were quiet, mulling over I know not what, and then I broke the silence with the fantastic news that I'd been cast in a play, and that the way I saw things it was only a matter of time before I would be renting the U-Haul and making my move.

Duncan was happy for me. He shook my hand. He slapped me on the back. "Whatever you set your mind to," he said. I told him that I'd get him a free ticket for opening night. He told me, "I'll be able to tell people I knew you *when.*" I was not used to such expansiveness. I could feel myself blushing. "Not many lines," I told him. Obviously, the truth was that there were *no* lines. But I thought it was important to at least try to keep things in some perspective. Humility first, fame second.

"Lines don't matter," Duncan said. Success was what mattered, and success called for celebration.

"Aw," I said, "I sure appreciate that." But it was a work night, after all.

No, it wasn't. It wasn't even seven o'clock. It would be a shame to let such good news go to waste. "Let's celebrate," Duncan Dioguardi said.

I knew that, in this context, *celebrate* was another word for *party*, which was, of course, itself another word.

The traffic was gone and I was driving fast. If I had had an ability to observe myself, I might have questioned why I needed to get where I was going in such a hurry. Under the overpass I went, fifteen miles above the speed limit. Turn, turn, turn. Duncan Dioguardi didn't need to tell me where to turn. He wanted to know if I had forty dollars to chip in. For forty dollars I'd have to stop at the ATM. The ATM was in the convenience store, where people were shopping for dinner. At the ATM, I noted with satisfaction that my savings were considerable—eight dollars an hour adds up.

His mother was home when we got there. "Meet my friend," Duncan Dioguardi said. The word *friend* was not a euphemism. His mother was sitting in the living room watching *Seinfeld.* She said, "You're welcome here anytime." She was being warm. She was being hospitable. She was laughing at what was happening on TV, and a few moments later Duncan and I were in the basement, also laughing at what was happening on TV. Jerry was saying something logical, and George was frustrated, and Elaine was rolling her eyes, and here came Kramer bursting through the front door. When Duncan opened his hand, I imagined for a moment that, instead of the insignificant chips off the drywall, he was holding a palmful of giant chunks, the size of golf balls, one pound each.

"You do the math," Duncan said.

Beneath his bed was the Chore Boy, but its symbolism had gone the way of the euphemism. Now when we smoked, we used, of all things, a broken car antenna, which, according to Duncan, he had found lying on the sidewalk. This was a neighborhood where car antennas lay on the sidewalk. The smoke came out of Duncan's mouth in the same white puff that lingered in the air of the basement theater. "Not bad," he said, again. And when it was my turn I also said, "Not bad," but I meant it this time. I was the passenger on the cruise ship who has become acquainted with the island. The same warm feeling of friendship for Duncan engulfed me, followed by an unexpected but welcome sense of optimism concerning my prospects—extraordinarily promising they were, weren't they, beginning with those three acts I was going to have onstage and heading toward a career. It was eight o'clock. Another episode of *Seinfeld* was just getting underway, the back-to-back shows courtesy of NBC, the interweaving story lines being established in that first minute: someone determined, someone displeased, the fatal flaw introduced, followed, thirty minutes later, by the abrupt resolution, and all of it funny, until all of it suddenly was *not* funny.

Suddenly I was in possession of that thing called clarity. I was watching the most vapid show in the history of television—it had always been vapid and we, the viewers, had always been duped. I could see straight through it now—solipsistic, narcissistic, false reality, easy tropes, barely amusing. The clarity that I *thought* I'd had moments earlier had not been clarity at all but, rather, its opposite, delusion, which was now being usurped by an all-encompassing awareness, horrible and heavy, through which I understood at once that I was not talented, had never been talented, that my life as a general laborer was proof of this lack of talent, and that being cast in a role with zero lines was not a step toward fame but a step into obscurity in a midsized city. Who but a fool agrees to move through space for three acts without saying a word?

The car antenna was coming back my way. It was nine o'clock. I had entered a strange dimension of time—it was progressing both slowly and quickly, as marked by the ticking of that basement boiler. Nine was early for night. It would be night for many more hours to come. I was nineteen. Nineteen was young. I would be young for many more years to come. What exactly had I been so troubled by a few minutes before? Light and airy clarity descended upon me. Ah, *this* was clarity, and the other, delusion. I had reversed things, silly, overstated them, compounded them, turned delight into cynicism. I was going to be onstage for three acts, moving through space, another credential to have on my résumé when

I arrived in LA. It was ten o'clock. Was ten o'clock early for night? Was night moving slowly or fast? Was Jerry funny or stupid? We were driving back to the ATM now. I knew I was traversing some essential but unstated boundary, but I traversed it anyway. I wondered if Duncan Dioguardi had ever had a broken-down car or if he had smoked the car, its antenna being the last piece remaining. I wondered if he'd smoked LA. I wondered if he'd one day smoke his Magnavox TV. This is the last time I'm doing this, I said to myself, even as I knew that saying so implied its inverse. At the ATM, I took out another forty dollars. I noted my balance. My savings account was still large. It was midnight. Midnight was still young.

# Natural Disasters

FROM *Ecotone*

WE WERE LIVING in Oklahoma ironically. Obviously it is not possible to live in a place ironically, but we were twenty-four and freshly married, so it was not obvious to us. It would not become obvious to me for a very long time; by then, by now, this clarity would be pointless, the thinly exhilarating *aha!* of a riddle solved at a cocktail party.

Three months before we relocated to the Sooner State, Steven had come home from work with the news that he'd been offered a promotion and a significant raise for a position in his company's Oklahoma City office. He shared this information tentatively. He was always tentative with me, always eager for my approval and watchful for the barbs of my scorn, and this was another thing that should have been obvious to me but wasn't. The company had 130 active oil wells in the state pumping out 120,000 barrels a day. Steven was a chemical engineer; he would monitor and, if necessary, modify the desalting process in the crude oil distillation unit at a refinery on the I-240 corridor. I don't mean to suggest that I understood any of this. I didn't, nor did I try to. I delighted in letting the particulars of Steven's work—all that *science,* all those *numbers* —sail over my head. I suppose I thought my mind too pure to be sullied by such things.

This would be Steven's first post away from corporate headquarters. We were living on First Avenue at the time, in a studio apartment the most notable features of which were its odor of mice decaying in the walls and its location across from the UN. The odor inculcated in us a sense of the small realities of our life, while

the UN, with its sweep of flags snapping in the wind, its kaftaned
and suited and dashikied diplomats eating hot dogs and shawarma
on the plaza before the glittering glass and marble of Niemeyer's
Secretariat building, reminded us of its spacious potentials.

In New York we were broke, but this was OK, even fun, because
we assumed that someday soon we would be comfortable, and
would look back on these days with a tender longing that was
not the same as actually wishing to relive something. Our faith in
this narrative made it possible to enjoy things that were not, in
themselves, enjoyable. I made a pot of chili con carne and fed us
for a week on six dollars. Steven discovered a bookstore near the
World Trade Center devoted exclusively to ornithology, where for
five dollars apiece the owner would let you sit all day in the air-
conditioning. Perhaps our faith in this narrative is what allowed
us to delight even in our frequent arguments, and to misappre-
hend them as markers of our marriage's durability rather than
its fragility.

It was the notion of spacious potentials that Steven's job offer
awakened in me. I remember the moment clearly. It was July of
1990, one of those callously hot New York nights when the urban
winds seem lifted from the surface of Venus. In the face of this,
our stalwart air conditioner may as well have been made of putty. I
was in the lightest thing I owned, a slip I'd bought to wear beneath
an unfortunate bridesmaid dress. Steven had just arrived home
from work, and was dressed uncomplainingly in a suit. We were
sitting on the corduroy couch in our tiny living area. ("You could
sit on the couch and touch the stove with your toes," I had told
our future children a hundred times in my head.) The origin of
the corduroy couch was a story we liked to tell. We had salvaged it
from the sidewalk on a drizzly summer day, and it took weeks for it
to dry out in our apartment. I can still smell it, like some colossal,
sodden basset hound returned from a hunt. The couch, the mice,
bodies underground on the 6, wine souring in an open bottle
on the coffee table . . . We lived a life of manageably unpleasant
odors. In my fantasies, our future was scentless as water.

As soon as Steven told me about the job offer, I saw us on a blanket in the prairie beneath a sky as solid and ardent as a conversion.
I saw an old Indian in a headdress of magnificent tail feathers,
his face canyoned with wrinkles, his eyes black and sad and weary.

(Years later I would visit a museum exhibit of the Indian portrait photography of Edward S. Curtis and realize that this mental image was not even mine; it was *Chief Three Horses, Dakota Territory, 1905*. But at the time, I confess, the image in my head seemed to me a thing I had conjured from some deep well of empathy within myself.) I saw a faceless woman in red cowboy boots and knew that she was me. The woman glanced at me through time and space with immense knowingness. *Yes,* I thought. We would go. Oklahoma would become part of the story of my life. As I sat beside Steven on the couch in the heat, with the pink night peering in at us through the window, I was also sitting on the edge of a small white bed, tucking in my children with a story about Mommy and Daddy's time in Oklahoma.

You see, I lived then guided by the unconscious notion that the story of my life as I was meant to live it was already written in a secret, locked-away text. At the end, I would finally be able to open it and read the story that had been written there all along—its arc, its twists and turns, its motifs and themes, its most evocative lines. For a moment before death, I would know what the world had intended for me and whether I had gotten it right or gone terribly astray.

In September, we loaded our first car with our scant possessions and said goodbye to the mice and the diplomats.

In Oklahoma, we moved into a house in a suburban development off I-40 called Amber Ridge. The neighboring development was Willow Canyon. There was neither a ridge nor a canyon as far as the eye could see, and we got a real kick out of this. We got a kick out of the house, too. It was brand-new, crisp as a toy yanked from the packaging, with an unseemly number of gables cramming the roofline and a potpourri of arched, circular, and Georgian windows on the facade—a jangling, architecturally screwy pastiche. The house was five times the size of the apartment we had left behind. It was a silly amount of space, more than two people could possibly fill. We had arrived in a place where space was completely unprecious, and this notion was as astonishing to me as if the same thing were to be true of time.

On our first night in the house, after Steven fell asleep, I wandered from room to room. Night in New York had trembled with residual light; here it was pure black, so that I could not even make out the walls, the edges of what was ours.

The next morning, one of Steven's new colleagues pulled up in a Ram pickup to give us "the grand tour." His name was Ward and he wore a bolo tie with a turquoise pendant. I stored this detail away. In the days and months that followed I collected many more like it: a church billboard that read, IF YOU THINK OKLAHOMA IS HOT . . . !; an octogenarian with a handlebar mustache and a bald eagle tattoo on his withered bicep; a gaggle of drunk, big-haired women stumbling out of a honkytonk. I tended my little collection with the vigor of an avid hobbyist, savoring the delicious irony of a place that conformed exactly to my hackneyed expectations. Another misapprehension: I believed that I could nail this place by triangulating among its details, that these typifying images converged upon a deeper truth.

As we sped west on 41, away from the suburban sprawl and out into the prairie, Ward told us that the region had no native trees. "Any tree you see was brought in one time or other," he said, waving generally at the landscape. To this day, I'm not sure if what he said is true, but the idea stuck with me. For the entirety of our brief time in the state, what few trees there were seemed to me to have a wavering, shimmering quality, as if they were projections you could slide your hand through. In lofty moments I think I saw my own presence there the same way. I loved Oklahoma because it had nothing to do with me. Ward, I learned later, was from Annapolis.

I said our house was cluttered with gables and Georgian windows, but when we moved in I didn't know what a gable or a Georgian window was. These were terms I learned through the part-time job I found six months after our move, working as a copywriter for a realtor named Bethany Parkhurst. Whether it took me so long to find work because I was depressed, or whether I was depressed because it took me so long to find work, I am no longer sure. I do know that in our first months in Oklahoma, despite my outward pleasure in our circumstances, I was depressed for the first time in my life, and maybe that is part of what I mean when I say that it is not possible to live in a place ironically. I was lonely in Oklahoma, the particular loneliness of an unemployed wife who knows no one but her husband for a thousand miles. Often I stayed in bed until noon. I ran errands in a sweatshirt with no bra underneath because why not? One afternoon I went to the supermarket planning on lamb chops for dinner, but they were out, and this seemed absolutely personal; I abandoned my cart, already loaded with cereal and juice and the cocktail nuts Steven liked, and rushed out of the store.

The next morning, I woke to find that I could not move my right index finger. I stared at it, willing it, but I could not bring myself to lift it. Then the phone rang and I got up to answer it and that was that. This kind of thing began happening regularly. I would be standing beside the car at the gas pump and suddenly I could not raise my left foot. At dinner with Steven's boss and his wife, it was my neck that separated from my control. These incidents ended only with some external interruption: a car honking for its turn at the pump; Steven's boss punching me playfully but *hard* on the shoulder and saying, "Right? Right?"

I spent a lot of time during this period driving through the prairie. I'd tell myself I needed to get out, that it would do me good to see some nature. The truth is that on these drives I stoked my growing terror of this place, of the on and on and on of it. Sometimes as I drove, the clouds above me would seem to coalesce around a brown center and then, suddenly, drop. Sometimes the thing I was driving past—a mailbox, a swimming pool—would suddenly be coated in black, glossy oil. I had developed a twinned obsession with tornadoes, on the one hand, and oil, on the other. They seemed to me to be part of a unified system, connected by some mystical-sinister energy. The tornadoes funneled destructive force down from the sky, the oil wells pulled it up from the ground, and I was living where these forces met, on the perilous surface of the earth.

In March, my best friend Kristin and her husband Rich, who were moving from New York to Los Angeles (where it was assumed Rich's screenwriting career would take off), stopped to visit on their journey across the country. I'd been counting down the days to their arrival, and when Kristin stepped out of the car I hugged her so tightly I frightened myself a little. We took them line dancing, and I watched with local smugness as they costumed themselves for this activity in western shirts and boots and jubilantly chucked the *g*'s from the ends of their gerunds. "Steven's company has wells all over the area. Ponca City, Enid, Waynoka, Fort Supply," I told them breathlessly, willing my utterance of these strange names to sound authoritative.

"Do you have a tornado shelter?" Kristin asked. We took them out back to see it. The house was so new the yard was still grassless, all loose yellow dirt.

"I see you're workin' on Dust Bowl: The Sequel," said Rich.

"You know us Okies," said Steven.

He pointed out the shelter, a reinforced steel door in the dirt.

"This would be just perfect for an abduction," said Kristin.

"Don't tell anyone, but we've got a little Polish babushka down there right now," I said.

"We take her out when we've got a yen for pierogi," said Steven.

It had been months since we'd had anyone for whom we could show off our verbal acuity. The next morning as I watched them drive away, next stop Santa Fe, I could hardly breathe.

That very day I picked up the local jobs newsletter at the grocery store and found the advertisement for a copywriter.

WRITER NEEDED TO BRING RESIDENTIAL PROPERTIES TO LIFE.
WORK FOR TOP-10 OKC REALTOR. PART-TIME, PAY NEGOTIABLE.

Within the hour I had mailed off a cover letter and résumé. Two days later I received a phone call from Bethany Parkhurst, the Top-10 OKC realtor who had posted the ad.

"The job is this," she said. "Every listing needs a description for the brochure. I hate writing and I'm not good at it. I've always done it myself but I want to stop. That's where you come in —I hope."

She asked about my experience and availability. I told her about my job in New York and tried to convey that I was very available without sounding too desperate; Bethany's voice was crisp and polished, and suddenly I wanted this job more than I had ever wanted anything in my life.

"Are you a good writer?" she asked.

"Yes," I said steadily. It was a relief to be asked a question about myself and to be so certain of the answer. I could dash things off quickly and I could make just about anything sound good. In college I got As on papers about books I'd barely skimmed. It was not that I was so smart; it was just that I was exactly what Bethany had asked for—a good writer. I could give the impression of meaning

and insight, of grand convergence, and if you weren't paying careful attention you might not notice that beneath the rhythms of
thought the argument was facile, even specious.

"I have a listing in Willow Canyon. Can you meet me there tomorrow at eleven?"

I told her I could. She proposed an hourly rate which I agreed
to. It wasn't until that evening, when I told Steven about the job
and he asked how it paid, that I realized I hadn't even listened to
the number.

Bethany Parkhurst was one of the most appealing people I have
ever known. I suspected this would be the case when I spoke to
her over the phone, and when I met her the next day in front of
a beige ranch in Willow Canyon, I knew immediately that it was
true. I couldn't stop staring at her. She was not beautiful, nor was
there anything unique or interesting about her appearance. Her
features exhibited a kind of generic perfection—hers was the face
an adolescent wishes for while examining the acne on her too-
wide forehead.

"You're on time," she said when I got out of my car. I would
later learn that she had been born and raised in Oklahoma City.
But she did not have the open drawl of most locals. She kept herself a little apart without seeming to keep herself apart. This was
one of her many talents.

"This house isn't much. The owners haven't put any money into
it at all. It really needs your special touch," she said as we walked
up the short driveway.

Warmth spread through me. *My special touch.* Bethany had asked
if I was a good writer, I had said yes, and that was that. The next
day I would send her the copy and ask if the style, length, and
structure were what she'd had in mind, and she would call and
tell me that it was perfect, and after that she would never mention
anything about the quality of the work I sent her ever again.

The owners weren't home. Bethany had a key and let us in.

"Oh no you don't," she said when we stepped inside. I looked
up, startled. Bethany was staring at a large painting on the living
room wall. It was one of those kitschy landscapes—a stone cottage
next to a babbling brook, a little wooden footbridge. "I told them
to take this down. It's part of my job to monitor taste. People have
to trust me."

Bethany walked me through the house, pointing out those features I should highlight (chair-rail molding in the dining room, a vaulted ceiling in the master bedroom) and those I should refrain from mentioning (linoleum flooring, a cracked concrete patio out back).

"What I've always done is, after I've seen everything I come back to the living room and just—" She breathed deeply in, out. "Reflect. Until I've sensed the house's essence."

She looked at me a bit sheepishly, and I was touched by this betrayal of earnestness. I imagined Bethany Parkhurst hunched over a desk late at night, typing and deleting—striving, as she had said in her ad, "to bring residential properties to life."

Together, we stood in the living room beneath the painting of the stone cottage. (Was this the home the owners of this shabby ranch wished for? Suddenly the trite painting seemed as personal as a wound.)

After a short while, Bethany turned to me. "OK," she said, and waved me to the door, as if the metaphysical process of sensing a house's essence always took precisely one and a half minutes.

I assumed that Bethany had spoken so bluntly about the painting because it was just the two of us, but I would come to learn that she had a single self, which did not adjust. Later that week, at a house in Colony Corners, I would hear her say the same thing she'd said to me—"It's part of my job to monitor taste. You have to trust me" —directly to the owner's face, this time about a homemade quilt, a retro item in shades of avocado and mustard draped over the back of a sofa. The woman bit her lip and silently moved the quilt to the closet. But before we left, she thanked Bethany. "I do trust you," she said, like a penitent seeking forgiveness from a priest; then she hugged Bethany.

"It's their home and people can be sensitive," Bethany said to me once we were outside. She said this in a voice absolutely empty of judgment. She'd spoken about monitoring taste in this same rinsed tone. There was nothing moral about taste to Bethany, no pride in having it nor shame in lacking it. It was simply necessary in the selling of residential property.

Soon I was visiting five or six properties a week. After the first few houses, Bethany did not accompany me. Sometimes, as at that first house, the owners were not at home, and I would be given instructions for getting in. The key was under the mat, or in the planter, or taped to the mallard whirligig. I would wander through the house taking notes: *walk-in closet, en suite master bath.* Exploring the houses alone felt wonderfully subversive. I especially loved to investigate the pantries. If I found items that suggested a sophisticated home cook—curry paste, anchovies, cornhusks—I would put in some extra effort with my writing. Often I found mountains of junk—jumbo tubs of cheese puffs, three different marshmallow cereals, a discovery that was like pressing my tongue to a battery, a sour thrill of pleasure at the poor choices of other people.

Frequently there were pets—terriers yapping from the garage, a marmalade cat slinking across the back of a sofa, gerbils spinning in the dark. Once, I stepped into a house where I'd been told no one would be home and a loud, clear voice said, "Go away, please!" I blurted an apology and was hurrying out the door when the voice said the same thing again with exactly the same intonation. "Go away, please!" It was a parrot, a splendid lime-green bird that lived in the kitchen in one of those old-fashioned domed cages. I recounted the story to Steven that night, and again to his coworkers and their wives at a dinner party that weekend. (It was all coworkers and wives; the extraction of resources, apparently, was the province of men.) I had become a person whose job came with that most valuable perk: good anecdotes.

Usually, though, someone was at home, and except for a single instance, that someone was a woman, which meant, almost automatically, a wife and mother. One house, I told Kristin on the phone, had so many shrieking, stampeding towheads that I found it impossible to ascertain how many children there actually were. In another, I entered the living room and a child of about four in spaceship pajamas looked up from his cartoons and said, very matter-of-factly, "We're moving to Texas because of Trashley."

Often the women were about my age, with a baby on a hip, a toddler hanging from a leg. "Can you imagine having *two kids?*" I would say to Steven at night, as if the idea were as lunatic as keeping wildebeests for pets. We would laugh together, delighting in our sense of ourselves as too urbane, too bright and scattered, to manage the exigencies of family life—exigencies about which we were intentionally very vague—at such a young age. (Though looking back, I wonder if Steven actually felt this way at all, or if he simply went along. I believed then that I understood him completely, but perhaps I had simply assumed he saw everything the same way I did.) The competence of these women, the hardened shapeliness of their lives, terrified me. Though none was quite as appealing as Bethany, many shared a certain ineffable quality with her—a diamond selfhood, hard and translucent. It turned out many of her clients attended the same church as she did, Radiant Assembly, an evangelical congregation that one of Steven's colleagues, a fellow transplant from the Northeast, referred to as "Rabid Insanity." I used to wonder whether it was the church's power shining through these women. Sometimes when I was touring a house and the woman was out of view, I would pretend that her house was my house and her children were my children. I had been born here and was among Radiant Assembly's faithful. I was friends with Bethany and fistfuls of women like her, like us. If I could get deep enough into that imagining, my self would sweep cleanly away and a feeling would fill me that was like being dipped in cool, sweet water.

My drives out to the prairie stopped. My work kept me busy in the suburban enclaves close to downtown, and I no longer felt the need to cultivate my own fear by traveling beyond these places. At unexpected moments, though, I would be overcome by an acute physical awareness of everything that was still out there. Once I was standing in an ersatz Arts and Crafts bungalow in Rivendell Corners, when suddenly I felt the vastness of the prairie and the sky tingling against my skin; I felt the oil beneath my feet, like swimming far out in the ocean and sensing all that black depth below you. Then I heard Bethany's voice in my mind— *You have to trust me* —and at once, I felt better.

Some of the things I saw resisted the transformation into anecdotes. Once, I found myself in the home of an elderly widow. I sensed the house had once been well kept, but it was badly neglected now, and the woman's daughter, who was also her live-in caregiver, apologized over and over for what she euphemistically called "the mess." The house needed everything—a new roof, new floors. The kitchen appliances were ancient. Mold speckled the wallpaper and the husks of flies collected on every windowsill. From a reclining chair in front of the television, the old woman muttered, "Tell her to write about the garden."

"She knows to write about the garden, Mom," the daughter said. She looked at me with an embarrassed smile that perplexed me until I went out into the yard and saw that there was no garden, just a mud patch where a garden must have been once.

"There's bluebells, foxglove, snapdragons," the old woman said when I came back inside, counting the flowers off on her fingers.

"She knows, Mom," the daughter said impatiently.

"Be sure to mention the hollyhocks. People like those. And the daylilies. Stargazers—"

The daughter closed her eyes.

I did not tell anyone this story or any of the others like it. They weren't meant for me. I witnessed them only as an accident of circumstance. *This is life. This is what it means to be human*, I would think to myself vaguely as I breathed in the humid air of other people's dramas. And I would feel pretty good about myself, both for bearing witness and for keeping their secrets.

The writing was a breeze. I developed an efficient process: I would draw up a list of evocative words and phrases that were more or less germane to the house at hand. Say: *curb appeal, mint condition, stately, pristine*. Or: *stunning, sought-after, the very best in country living, charmer*. Then I would string these words together with the pertinent information. *This pristine three-bedroom ranch oozes curb appeal, from its stately front lawn to its mint-condition brick facade*. Or, *For home-buyers looking for the very best in country living, this stunning charmer in sought-after Castlegate is a must-see*. The copy was like candy floss— voluminous clouds that dissolved to sweetness, to the idea of substance.

Months passed. At some point I realized that it had been a long time since a part of my body separated itself from my control.

One day Bethany called me about a house that was not located, as most of her properties were, in one of the developments that encircled Oklahoma City like a frill. This house was thirty miles away, out in the country. "Really annoying location," she said. She had a knack for stating opinion as fact.

I drove out to see the house the following afternoon. It was a cloudy, humid day, the air fuzzed with an electric tingling. I drove for miles down a two-lane highway that radiated northwest from the city. A few months earlier this drive would have terrified me, and I felt relieved, not because I could now speed past fields of switchgrass unafraid, but because it seemed to me that my resilience had been affirmed; I remember thinking that I was very good at handling a mental rough patch, and this pleased me the same way being good at anything pleased me.

I still remember the name of the street, Redtail Road. It was a narrow country road, straight as an arrow and shot dead into the abyss. The houses were spaced far apart. You could look down the whole length of the road and see them all at once, like dice cast on an enormous table. My destination turned out to be the last house. Just past the driveway the asphalt formed a tidy edge against an infinity of prairie.

For a minute before I got out of the car, I just sat and stared. This house was like none other I had visited for Bethany. It was *architecture,* a word whose variants I had deployed emptily countless times in my copy: *This three-bedroom home exhibits colonial architecture at its very finest. Gorgeous architectural touches abound in the formal dining room. Architecturally innovative yet effortlessly livable, this home embodies the elegance for which The Meadow Estates are prized.* The exterior was cedar and glass. The angles of the roofline fit together with the mysterious rightness of a poem. The roof was copper and, touched by the diffuse light of the overcast sky, it seemed to glow. Beside the house, a tall tree grew; it looked older than any other tree I had seen in the state, with a broad, generous crown of leaves. I blinked, half-expecting that when I opened my eyes the improbable house and tree would be gone.

I had just the last name of the seller—Follett. I rang the bell and a few seconds later the door opened. I blinked again. I was standing face-to-face with the most conventionally handsome man I had ever seen. I told you that except for a single instance, the people in the houses were women. This story, the one I've been getting to all along, is the story of that single instance.

"Mac," he said, holding out his hand. He was tall and leanly muscular and looked entirely sun made—skin darkened by it to the shade of a toasted cashew, hair lightened by it to gold filaments.

"Jen," I said, and shook his hand.

An image blazed into my head of him on a chestnut horse with a Marlboro between his lips. For a horrifying moment I was certain he had somehow seen it, too. In my head I was already on the phone with Kristin: "When I say handsome I mean beyond anything you could be imagining right now."

"I'll leave you to it," he said. "Let me know if you need anything." He walked down the hall and disappeared.

I stood in the foyer, flummoxed. Typically the owners wanted to show me around, at least a little. They wanted to be sure I noted the recessed lighting in the living room or that I knew the kitchen cabinets were solid maple. "The open floor plan is a fantastic kid-friendly feature," a woman once said to me. They had an idea of how they wanted their home portrayed and they wanted to be sure I got it right. I attributed Mac Follett's behavior to a certain male cluelessness—he didn't have the instinct to monitor and steer things the way a woman did, I thought.

I began to make my way through the house with my notebook. It was as beautiful inside as out: soaring post-and-beam ceilings, a fireplace with a stone hearth, tongue-and-groove pine floors. Outside it had begun to pour, and through a leaded glass window I watched the rain strafe the terrace.

I had noticed that Mac didn't wear a ring, and there was no evidence of a woman's presence in the house, at least not the kind I was used to seeing—no fashion magazines in the basket next to the couch, no lipsticks or lotions in the bathrooms.

"What do you think he's doing out there all alone?" Kristin would ask, and we would toss around theories.

"He used to live in the Rockies until he developed a debilitating fear of elevation."

"He was married, but his wife left him for a dirt farmer."

"It's a real sod story."

When I reached the master bedroom, he was sitting on the neatly made bed watching television. Golfers strolled across a velveteen green. I tried my best to do everything as usual. I jotted: *double exposure, built-ins.*

"So you go around looking in people's houses?" he asked, his eyes still on the golfers.

"Pretty much."

"Sounds interesting."

"Not all of the places are like this. Your house is amazing."

He smiled crookedly. I blushed. *Amazing*—another fatuous

word I used all the time in my copy. He must be used to women liquefying in his presence, I thought.

"It is, isn't it?" he said after a moment. The tone in which he said this was not at all boastful, but almost apologetic. I supposed that he was one of those rich people whose good fortune embarrassed him, the type who would refer to a family compound in Jackson Hole as "the cabin." Typically I found this sort of thing irritating, but in Mac Follett it struck me as oddly touching—such discomfort and unease in a man who surely received affirmation at every turn.

Lightning flashed, turning the sky briefly green. A sharp crack of thunder followed almost immediately. I flinched, and he smiled at this.

"Big one," he said. I wanted to say something witty, but I was all ooze. "You're not from here."

"How can you tell?"

Again lightning flashed and again I flinched.

"You'll get used to it," he said. The thunder came, this time a sound like a spray of gunfire. He cleared his throat. "Don't let me keep you." He returned his gaze to the golfers. I turned and left the room quickly, unsure if he was trying not to impose on my time or if he'd grown bored with me.

I surveyed the rest of the house. There were three other bedrooms, each sparsely furnished, the closets bare. A beautiful library with walls of knotty pine held only a few paperbacks. The pantry was stocked with things you might take on a camping trip: peanut butter, oats, jerky. I saw in these details an appealing asceticism, a minimalist self with no need for ornamentation. When I was finished, I stopped back at his bedroom. The rain had tapered. In the humid aftermath of the storm, the land that stretched beyond the windows appeared like soft fur.

"All set," I said, waving my notebook imbecilically.

"You saw the observatory?"

I looked at him quizzically.

"It's kind of hidden. Come. I'll show you."

He clicked the remote and the TV sucked in the golfers. I followed him down the hall. He stopped at a door I had assumed to be a closet and opened it to reveal a narrow spiral staircase.

"It's all one tree trunk," he said, sliding his hand along the banister. The wood was exquisite—intricately grained and polished to a whispery smoothness. I had the sense, then, that I was about to ascend into the house's "essence," that thing Bethany had spoken of with such unexpected earnestness.

He began to climb, and I followed after him. I could feel his movement drawing me upward, and I could hear Kristin: "He *took* you to his *observatory?*"

When I reached the top of the staircase he held out his hand for me. I took it, and he pulled me up into the gray light of the small room.

"It's something, isn't it?" he said, hands stuffed in his pockets.

I could only nod. There were no walls, only windows, and through them the prairie stretched in every direction. It would not be correct to say that it stretched to the horizon because I could not see any horizon line. At the edge of itself the prairie seemed simply to fade, land turning to dust turning to air.

"It's like floating," I said.

He smiled that crooked smile again.

"You can make out Norman if you squint," he said. "Over here."

Together we looked east, straining to make out the blurred gray rising. And because we were looking in the same direction when it happened, we both saw it: The clouds coalescing around a brown center. The center dropping from the sky to the ground.

In the years since that day I have lived many places: Florida with its hurricanes, California with its earthquakes, and, for the past decade, Maine with its blizzards that bury cars and houses in stunning, sinister white. If you stop to think about it, the idiosyncrasy of these forces is astonishing. A vortex of clouds kissing the earth. The solid ground splitting and rippling. You could never imagine such things, if you didn't already know they were possible. I have come to believe that life is different in each place, and I do not simply mean that in Florida you sandbag while in Maine you salt. What I mean is that a place and its disasters—its fathomless, inscrutable unknowns—are not separable. Oklahoma is its tornadoes, just as Maine, even on the mildest of spring days, is its snows, is a caved roof and a woman asleep in her bed, and then gone. The disaster is always there, because it takes up residence inside of you.

\*

Mac Follett didn't hesitate. He grabbed my arm and led me back down the staircase. Before the living room window I froze, transfixed. The funnel cloud was soft and brown. Against the plains it seemed to stay perfectly still, and I understood that this must mean it was moving toward us in a straight line.

"Come on," he said, tugging at my arm. "There's a shelter."

We hurried through the pelting rain, past the tree and across the terrace and the lawn, the tall grass whipping around my ankles. When we reached the shelter, he pulled open the heavy brown door and we climbed down into the earth. He closed the door behind us and I was plunged into darkness more total than any I have experienced before or since. I waved my hand in front of my face but saw nothing. For a moment the coherence of things seemed to break apart. I felt as if I were neither upside down nor right side up but tumbling through the darkness. Then suddenly it was light, and I was standing perfectly still with my feet on the packed earth floor. Mac had turned on a lantern that hung from a nail on the wall. I took in our surroundings: a few coolers stacked by the stairs, some cluttered shelves beyond the light of the lantern, two metal folding chairs in the center. The ordinariness of these things seemed wildly discordant with our situation, though I no longer remember if I found this comforting or unnerving. Honestly I think I was probably too panicked to feel much of anything. I sat. I hugged my knees to my chest and tried uselessly to slow my breathing.

Mac paced slowly back and forth, hands plunged in his pockets. He did not look at me. For a minute or two he seemed to go completely inside of himself, as if he had forgotten my presence altogether, and I thought that we must be in even graver danger than I'd realized. I was drenched, and though the rain had been warm—unsettlingly so, like bathwater—I shivered, and this movement seemed finally to pull him out of something.

He stopped pacing and looked at me. He unstuffed his hands from his pockets and squatted so that his eyes were level with mine.

"You're safe," he shouted over the noise of the storm. "I promise."

In that moment, in a storm shelter in Oklahoma, with my hair hanging around my face in wet strings and Mac Follett, round-shouldered in the lamplight, promising that I was safe, I had the exhilarating sense that for the first time I was living a page from the secret text of my life. It was obvious, suddenly, that the storm raging on the other side of the shelter door was here for me, to catalyze my life with its force. I was supposed to be here, and here I was, and the purpose behind my being here was effortlessly legible. I could see what would happen in this moment and the next and the next just as I had seen all of the houses along the length of Redtail Road at once. I would be unfaithful to Steven. Mac Follett would tuck a strand of wet hair behind my ear, testing my resistance, and I would offer none. When the storm passed I would emerge into the watery light of its aftermath with him, the cured scent of his body and the chlorine of semen on my skin. "Stay," he would say, and I would. For a day, then two. I would call Steven, and though there would be nothing I could say to explain, I would stay on the phone for hours, just talk, words strung together to create the impression of a gentle goodbye. Mac would not sell the house. We would remain there together, until my body was made of grass and dust.

I sat on the folding chair, waiting for him to tuck my hair behind my ear and set the story in motion. And as I waited, two things happened. First, the storm subsided, the roar giving way to soft, defeated wailings. Second, my eyes adjusted to the dim light, and things that had at first been hidden became visible. I could see, on one shelf, a jumble of fishing gear—rods and waders, a khaki vest pinned with lures. On another, a dusty golf bag stuffed with clubs and a tin bucket of white and yellow balls. And, on a shelf in the corner, still half-concealed in shadow, a big camouflage rucksack and a blue cap with a gold medallion.

"You were in the army?"

He looked away from me.

"My brother. In the Gulf."

"Oh," I said. I tried to convey with my expression an all-purpose weightiness. I knew nothing about the Gulf. I knew no one who had gone, no one whose life had brushed even lightly against this war or any other.

"This was his house. He built it himself. I'm just selling it. He died four months ago."

"I'm sorry," I said reflexively.

He winced.

I understood then that I had misapprehended everything that had happened since I arrived at the house, which wasn't his at all: the way he'd disappeared after letting me in; his unease when I told him how beautiful it was. And suddenly I felt very foolish, or maybe ashamed.

He walked over to the shelf and picked up the cap, passed it back and forth from hand to hand, then set it back down.

"I moved his things down here because I couldn't keep seeing them," he said.

I wanted to tell him he didn't need to explain, least of all to me, but I saw now that he did need to. The need glinted plainly in his eyes. It had been there all along, but I had missed it.

"It's OK," I said, though what was OK, or for whom, I couldn't tell you.

We stayed down there a few minutes more in silence. When the sound of the storm had faded away, he pushed open the brown door and we climbed out. The light was the watery way I had imagined. The house was untouched—whatever path the tornado had taken, I could see no trace of it.

Mac walked me to my car. "Thank you," he said. For days afterward, I would hear his voice thanking me, and I would feel sick with everything I was beginning to know about myself. I got in the car quickly, backed down the long driveway, and went straight home. Two days later, I sent the copy to Bethany Parkhurst. *On the market for the very first time, this exquisite post-and-beam home has been custom designed to take full advantage of its spectacular surroundings.*

In December, Steven's company transferred him again, and we left Oklahoma for Nevada. Two years after that, when they summoned him back to corporate headquarters, he went to New York alone. I continued west to California.

But first. Before we left the Sooner State, some months after that storm, I found myself in the dusty archives at City Hall. I couldn't help myself—I needed to know, though I was suspicious of this need, as I was by then suspicious of nearly all of my wishes and desires. It took me only an hour or so to find what I was looking for.

Terence Follett, 29, of Eakly, died January 16 from injuries sustained in a two-vehicle collision in Omega. An avid outdoorsman with a lifelong passion for astronomy, he enlisted in the army after graduating from West Central High. He was stationed in Landstuhl, Okinawa, and at Fort Irwin in California's Mojave Desert. He then returned to Eakly, where he bought twenty acres. Selling the mineral rights made it possible for Terry to build his dream house. During Desert Storm he re-enlisted and was deployed to Kuwait, where he assessed infrastructure damage in Al Wafrah. He had returned home in July. He is survived by his mother, Joanne Beams; his father and stepmother, Walter and Connie Follett; a brother, Maclean; and numerous aunts and uncles.

That's a good story, isn't it? Rich and diverse in its settings, with a real sense of arc and one hell of a plot twist—to return home from a war in a faraway land only to die in Omega, Oklahoma. Even that name, Omega, sounds like something from a story, almost too evocative, too on-the-nose, to be real.

I read an interesting article online last night. It said that earthquakes have come to Oklahoma. Scientists predict that this year seismic activity in the state will be six hundred times the historical average. Fracking is to blame. Wastewater injected into wells deep in the earth. After reading this I closed my computer, made myself a cup of coffee, and went out onto the heated porch to drink it. It's winter here. I stayed up much of the night, watching the snow fall onto the fields beyond my house, and wondering what it must be like to feel the earth tremble in a place meant for other disasters.

Maybe you think all of this is easy to interpret. A girl left the city and learned a thing or two. A silly young woman hoped to be ravished by a man who was not her husband. A marriage fell apart, and afterward a wife was wiser, though in some ways no better, than she had been before. Maybe it is only my personal stake in the matter that makes me want to believe it was not that simple. All I can say is that when I pulled up to the house on Redtail Road I thought life was one thing, and when I drove away I knew it was another. I knew, quite simply, that a life is not a story at all. It is the disasters we carry within us. It is *amazing,* it is *exquisite,* it is a *stunning charmer,* and it is noted in water and jotted in dust and the wind lifts it away.

## Our Day of Grace

FROM *Zoetrope: All-Story*

Camp near the TN River
Mon. November 21, 1864

Dear Lucy,

It commenced snowing at about dark here, & the wind is as cold as the world's charity & blowing at a terrible rate. Some of the letters I sent came back. It is very uncertain about letters nowadays, tho I suppose it will do no harm to write more, & I wanted you to know that I'm still right-side up, tho you ought to see me now if you want a hard-looking case. Whiskers have grown out all over & I am ashamed to scan a looking glass. C.W. calls me Chief of the Brigands & looks as rough as I do. I had Georgie cut my hair & he made such a hash of it that it will take 12 months to grow out right.

On the march north we lived 3 days on parched corn & then in the last week in the rain & mud just 2 biscuits a day to each man. When an officer rides by the boys all cry out, "Bread, bread, bread," & tonight there was a meat issue but it featured so many shanks & necks that our requisition officer said next they'll be throwing in the hoofs & horns. Still if nothing else the war has taught me to be less particular, & now when I see dirt in my victuals I just take it in.

In our last camp we made a hut by driving timbers into the ground in the fashion of a stockade but here we sleep in what we call gopher holes, after we've built fires in them to dry & harden the earth. We huddle together & shiver like Belshazzar did when he saw the vision on the wall. Everyone wants to get at the Yankees to pillage their blankets. There is still a great deal of sickness in the regiment with measles & dysentery accounting for most of the casualties. A good many get sick that never get well again. C.W. hasn't changed his shirt in 5 months & Georgie is a perfect tatter-demalion. He says that if his shirt rots any more he can make it a necklace. C.W. says in this army 1 hole in the seat of your britches means you're a Captain, 2 a Lieutenant, & if you're a private you don't need to unbuckle to relieve yourself. Georgie has tried fashioning moccasins from some scraped hides but says they stink & stretch out in the heel on the march & whip him nearly to death. Back when barefoot men were excused from fighting many threw away their shoes the night before a battle, but now they're compelled to perform as much duty as those well shod.

I'm happy to hear my Georgie stories charm Nellie in particular. Tell her he is so small some of the boys like to call for him to come out of his hat because they can see his legs. He walks like he's stepping over furrows & is always kicking his fellows' shins on the march. He regularly announces to one & all that if he can just get an eye on Lincoln with his musket he'll make a cathole through him. C.W. says that anyone who can make us smile so much is like loaf bread & fresh beef all the time, & that he is always hunting for something to raise his spirits given that he's forced to sojourn in those low haunts of Sorrow. He claims Georgie's tomfooleries & his wife's letters to be his only remedies. He reads me his wife's letters & I am always tired long before she closes.

We hear a great many things about reinforcements coming from west of the Mississippi, & also about the movement of Lee's army in VA. Ten thousand rumors are current & many believe them all.

Most of us are disheartened, even those who would not profess to it. C.W. calls Hood the Butcher & it is certain he is the most unpopular General in the army & some swear they will no longer fight under him. It's said that the Brigadier Generals & Colonels & company officers have all been called together to forestall an uprising & that everyone all around regrets that poor Joe Johnston is gone. Yesterday Hood rode past our column & when it came time to give 3 cheers our 3000 men did not make as much noise as you would hear at a schoolhouse on the election of a chalk-tray monitor. He blames all setbacks on poor morale resulting from his predecessor's continued retreats. He told us before our previous engagement that he would compare us to a mule team that had been allowed to balk at every hill: one portion would make

strenuous efforts to advance while another would refuse to move
& thus paralyze the whole. Many of us will not forget that in July
he lost 8000 killed & wounded in 2 days trying to do what Johnston said could not be done. But we like our Colonel, who in his
attentiveness to us puts me in mind of an old farmer gathering up
his stray cattle.

Lu! Do you miss your special friend? What a sight he now
makes! He is conventional but unmarried, young but unhealthy,
nostalgic but still isolate, war-weary but still the greenhorn, &
awake to absurdity but still humorless. He is in all ways lacking
polish, perspective, & resolve. He complains of others' shortcom-
ings but there is neither depth to his understanding nor breadth
to his compassion. Chariness & uncertainty are his trademarks, as
well as the desire for attachment without the willingness to make
a clean breast of it. He can only hope that the careless & thought-
less boy who left you 2 years ago will return, if Providence so pro-
vides, more judicious & more considerate, & perhaps at the least
he will have learnt how to associate with his fellow beings, however imperfectly, & that the world has not the narrow limits of his
own little heart. Send news of your father & Nellie. Send news of
your health, & thoughts. A rat just came right up to my candle
as confused as if he were home. & now I am very sleepy & must
close—

With great love,
Your William


Front Royal, VA
Mon. November 21st 1864

My dear CW,
I woke up very early this morning to find it had been sleeting in
the night. The early part of the day was so cold and disagreeable
we spent it around the fire eating nuts until it turned bright and
fair. Which was good news, I hope, for you in camp. The sunset
tonight was filled with crimson and gold.

I chastise myself for having but little system in this writing. It's as
if the first thing I conceive is the first I write down, up one side of
the sheet and down the other. I commenced this letter yesterday,
but laid it by unfinished at bedtime. After the boys retired I had
the light and fire all to myself. Before then we had a discussion as

to whose letters you read first. They said you choose mine and I said you choose theirs.

We had a bad Sabbath. I upset the churn and inundated the kitchen with sour cream. The boys were unhappy with the feeding boxes they made, so they just spread the fodder around in the hopes that on the frozen ground what the sheep left the cows would eat. I made jelly in the afternoon, but then my hands were all stained, so I couldn't sew. I paid a bridal call on Kattie Wetherell. She was full of chat and of the opinion that all the manly virtues are concentrated in her husband-to-be. Ah! Welladay: may she ever believe thus. She also reported that a drunken cavalry officer rode through town and dismounted from time to time to smash windows.

Thank you for what you sent. You ask how we are fixed for money. Well it goes about as fast as it comes. Even after all this time it is still an adjustment for me to be running a household. We women are told that our fragility is our strength and protection our right, but this War no longer allows us our frailty, or to assume the presence of guardians that are supposedly our due. I never thought things would go on as well as if you were here, but at least things have gone better than I anticipated.

You wish me to tell you about myself but there's not much to tell. I'm lately not able to stand going out into the cold, as it seems to take my breath and set me to coughing. But I feel well when in the house. No one has been sick of any consequence. Wellie is very careful of my health. He said tonight, "Mother, you had better go to bed. You can't stand it to work so."

Next week will be our anniversary. Nine years have passed on wings, it seems to me. I feel so widowed that I stay at home mostly. I am a wonder to myself when I think of all this time without you. Your mother talks of you with Asa and Wellie as if you were still about. Our nights together come back to me as sad as the sleet and as sweet as heaven. Last week when the house was quiet I dreamed I heard your footsteps, and you came to the bed and stood over me. And then I heard your name called, away in the distance and yet so plain. And then my body grew unruly and furious, however much I wished for sleep.

I cannot think of half I want to say but am thankful for what I can express. My mind is more harassed and unsettled without yours. Tell me if the cold has settled on your lungs, or if your cough is any worse. How much you are missed no one can tell but a wife who has had such a husband. You may not suppose I ever go to our warm bed without thinking of you. Wellie sends his regards to your messmates Georgie and William. Asa is determined to shoot a duck for Thanksgiving. I persuaded him to wear your coat and it looks much better than his.

Your loving wife,
Hattie

Camp near the TN River
Wed. November 23, 1864

Dear Lucy,
2 corporals returned with the brigade's mailbag but there was nothing for me. Rabbit today for dinner. He thought he had us outpaced but an emaciated Reb can give any sort of animal a lively run.

Your old friend Raselas Buck has gone. He asked his parents to write letters to our Captain telling tales of woeful conditions at home & when they had no effect he said he would write his own furlough. We all signed up together, 2 years & 2 months ago now, goaded on by the fire-eating element of editors & preachers & politicians. & C.W., who still tells one & all he despises the North for flouting the law requiring the return of fugitive slaves & for making a martyr of the likes of John Brown, who took an oath to murder Southern women & children. Do you remember I told you that when I dallied about volunteering C.W. sent me a petticoat in the mail? He was a one-man recruiting station. He asked Raselas if he intended to stay in his store & measure out his days weighing sowbelly, & in his presence I remember wondering if I wished to be that teacher who watched the seasons pass while laboring with middling success to drill some wisdom into wayward heads.

Maybe because we had no proper goodbye on my furlough I linger on our first parting back then, & the effects of our kisses on the platform. Remember our vexation with the brigade of other people's relatives & friends bidding them farewell & loading them down with parting gifts? Before you arrived we were addressed by a veteran of the Mexican Wars & a Miss Josephine Wilcox, accompanied by 3 maids of honor & a regimental color sergeant. She fancied herself quite the orator but C.W. said she went about it as smooth as you might come down a rocky hill in the dark. After we left it was so hot we broke holes in the boxcars' planking & stuck our heads out like chickens in a poultry wagon. At intermediate stations bolder swains took advantage of the slowdowns to leap off & steal kisses from the girls who graced the rights-of-way.

You mention your cousin's complaints in his letter about his training. I never told you but our officers & men started out in equal ignorance & blundered along through drill, drill, & more drill, & loading in ranks & preparing to fire, & in our first mock assault my messmate ran his bayonet through the back of the man in front of him. I remember one day some of the boys with their smoothbore muskets fired 200 shots at a flour barrel 150 yards away & registered only 13 hits. & yet we were fire-eaters all: on the march we yelled at everything we saw & heard. The cry might start at one end of the regiment & get taken up by brigade after brigade without anyone knowing or caring what it was about. & when we had a tent, C.W. & Georgie placarded it with a sign that read "Sons of Bitches Within."

See, Lu? I am trying to be the more candid correspondent you crave.

Tell your cousin we all wonder if we will stand the gaff or play the quaking coward, but with their first shot most become new men & give themselves over to the fight. He need only keep his courage through the preliminaries, whether he glimpses the surgeons preparing their kits or the litter-bearers stacking their stretchers, or that first flash of sunlight on an enemy rifle. & that he probably won't be so frightened that he can't obey all the orders, & that every fool mistake that can be made has already been made, from conscripts who forget to bite off the end of the paper before loading the charge, or fire so high they hit only those Yankees already in Paradise, to 2 of our recruits who pulled the trigger before withdrawing their ramrods, thereby sending their odd little missiles out over their fellows' heads.

Remind him that there will always be someone with whom to rally. At Peachtree Creek if it hadn't been for C.W. we would have all gone to hell in a pile. He led a group of us that returned fire prone in a bed of pennyroyal & came out looking like the latter end of original sin. Then he sat cross-legged & morose beneath a tree while we overran the Federals' position, & at a tipped wagon got some tin washpans & drew them full of molasses, which we scooped up with some good Yankee crackers.

But it's my turn at the picket so now I'll close with love—
William

Boone, NC
Tues. November 22

Dear William,

I received your letter of 7 November last evening and was so excited and happy I did not close my eyes until one. Awoke this morning to a hard rain and roads so awash that Nellie was weather-bound and unable to get to school. While circumambulating the chicken coop I lost my footing and rose from the mud covered from waist to hem, and Nellie enjoyed the spectacle so wickedly she needed to sit to regain her breath. Midafternoon when the skies cleared, Father seeing Nellie and me unusually mournful proposed a walk, and upon our return we found sitting on the porch a strange soldier who proved to be Cousin Mack. We had bread and a little fried meat and onions and beets for dinner, and we did enjoy it so. While I made up the bread Nellie read aloud from "Marmion," and Cousin Mack tarried with us until late: we played What's It Like, and he requested Nellie and I sing "There's Life in the Old Land Yet." Father thought he heard heavy cannonading in the distance and Cousin Mack reported that to the west the Yankees have supposedly been repulsed thirty miles. We had quite the discussion as to just how comprehensively the command "children, obey your parents" was to be heeded where matrimony was concerned, and it was all unprofitable, since at the close of the debate we each retained our original positions.

Mack promised to return tomorrow afternoon with a horse he found in the mountains and offered to carry any mail we wish to send on with him, so upon his leaving we drew up our table before the fire and commenced writing.

Friday is my birthday! 20 years old! How long I have lived on this sphere for all the good I have done. I am older than I am wise, and wiser than I am beneficent, and now a woman, decline the unwelcome thought as I might. What good has all my schooling done me? However much I wish to stay careless and free I am a woman not only according to the hunger of my heart but because I can now measure my deficiencies in every respect, from my awkwardness to my self-indulgence to these flashes of temper. Winter's harvest is nearly ended and I have planted few seeds of improvement in the meantime, so that the future will likely prove barren of the fruits of firm resolve or self-control. At least those we love, most of us, have been preserved and protected, but who knows what will come with another revolution of the year's wheel.

We sheltered two soldiers a few days ago, one intoxicated who came into the kitchen from out of the rain and commenced swearing and frightening everyone until Father settled him, and the other just a boy barely older than Nellie, who limped terribly and when we asked if he was wounded explained that he was crippled with rheumatism and that it had been a full year since he had slept under a roof.

William! Please report more of how you feel. You choose to bare enough of your heart to induce the belief that you have communicated all when in fact at times you have reserved so much as to have communicated nothing.

Remember when our tongues ran away with our fatigue and we talked as if for dear life until so late in the evening? When did I ever say so much, and in so short a time? You have always possessed an odd fascination for me, about which I give a poor accounting when cross-examined by Father or Nellie. They never tire of pointing out the number of opportunities you have flouted to expand your promise to me, but I still believe you have more depth of feeling than your acquaintances would suspect. And I am glad that in all we have been called to pass through at least you have been able to view the earnest desire of <u>my</u> heart. And I continue to trust that in a short time we will be permitted to enjoy each other's fascinations again.

And Cousin Mack is now waiting, and so here I cease—
Your faithful
Lu

Camp near the TN River
Sat. November 26, 1864

Dear Lucy,
Our Lieutenant died of fever. He leaves a wife & 4 children.

I was relieved from picket duty around 9 & have a little leisure & will improve it by writing to you. We had so much rain that for a mile & a half beside a marshland we were in it knee-deep, through country already flooded & rendered more inhospitable still by the downpour. I remember when we would take advantage of such rain to stay in the house courting all day, but here it turned to hail, & we had a freeze, a thaw, a rain, & another freeze. We all wish for a pair of boots. We keep a poor fire in a miserable little stove, & it is now so cold Georgie tells everyone the North has come down to shake hands with the South. Despite all this I have been afflicted with only a sore throat.

We may stay here 2 months or 2 days. If we further improve our sleeping-holes we will have to move as usual. Georgie & a few others begged provisions at farmhouse doors with anguished recitations, & today we each got 4 potatoes. Thoroughly cooked they were very good. Of the sick some were able to eat but were not much benefited. Otherwise we've had only hard bread & feed corn. For the hard bread we use a rifle butt & some water, after which we skim off the weevils, & for the feed corn an old coffee mill, which makes a workable mush but gives everyone the quickstep. Another forage returned a barrel of whiskey so villainous only the old soakers could stomach it. A cupful produced a beehive in the head & the boys all called it Nockum Stiff. It was a particular favorite of one of our corporals, shot through the hand & with such a terrible hole that when the dressings are changed he lets his friends peer through at objects in the distance.

During the night a man was taken with the tremens & performed some of the most horrid noises & gestures that any of us had ever witnessed. It took 5 men to hold him. Our newest messmate, a bog-trotter named Blayney, seems so pained by the joviality of others that few wish him welcome. Around the cook kettle he stands silent while the rest of us join the social round, & should the atmosphere get too congenial he takes his leave even before eating.

Georgie sends his regards to Nellie, & warns her to be careful of all soldiers. He claims he has not seen a girl in so long he would not know what to do with himself if he did, but reckons he'd learn before he let her out of his sight. He has a girl he's been writing but his method of courtship is so indirect & his advances so halting that the war will end before she becomes aware of his interest. He lives in fear that all the eligible women in his town will marry shirkers & civilians.

The Yankee lines are very close. On picket one shouted at me,

"Ain't you got any better clothes than those?" & I shouted back, "You think we put on our good clothes to go & kill the likes of you?" I think if the question were left to the contending armies we would restore the peace tomorrow & hang both Presidents' cabinets at our earliest convenience.

Before our last engagement the Federal artillery gave us their usual full force & good practice, & at our advance there was such heavy fire that boys were leaning forward as if pushing into a wind. We drew our heads down into our collars the way we would in a storm. The regiment before ours delivered its fire & then broke & ran. Men were flying in all directions from the field, & that scattered our regiment from hell to breakfast. Afterward the bodies lay around like loose railroad ties, the dead 3 & 4 deep, & after they froze to the ground the burial details had to resort to pickaxes. I have seen more depravity in the last month than in all my days previous. This war is a graveyard for virtues. Even our drummer boy could stare the devil out of countenance. C.W. bayoneted a boy who had killed our bugler after asking for quarter, & then dragged the boy's body onto the road so that the hospital wagons would make a jelly of his remains. He is very low & says that it requires the faith of a prophet to see any good resulting from so much mayhem, & that perhaps both nations must be destroyed when we consider how much corruption runs riot in high places, & that it may be that our country's day of grace is passed. But he also says that he will all the same see the thing play out or die in the attempt.

I regret having failed to be as unselfish to you as you have been to me, & I wish that while we were together I had made your happiness a more earnest study. I have considered of late how often promises of amendment are made & broken. I hold to hope that those favors forgotten & duties neglected will not rise up in judgment against me. I am grateful for the way during our goodbyes your kisses took each rebellious & ungenerous thought in my heart & hushed it to silence, & I pledge to improve my demonstrations of affection in return.

If Nellie would like to see where we are, tell her to map the Elk River up north of the Tennessee, toward Franklin. & now it is snowing, & I can hardly keep my eyes open, & so I will close —

With love,
William

*

Front Royal, VA
Fri. November 25th 1864

My dear CW,

I still have received no word from you since your letter of 20 October. How long is each day that brings no tidings.

Snow last night and freezing rain today. Not a soul on the roads. Even at noon it was windy. Did anyone ever see such cold?

Asa this morning coughed so hard he threw up his breakfast. I stewed some dried fruit and swept, and that used up much of the light. After dinner we walked over to see old Mrs. Hale, whom we found very blue but cheered before we left. She is always prophesying brighter times and telling us the news. She says Mary Hall is married and Mattie and Addie Burnham are better. I don't know how she lives but we brought her some flour, and the Newtons keep her in wood. I had my first coffee in 14 months, and she distilled it to such a strength that I was something like wild for the rest of the night. She compared our Republic to Hercules attacked in his crib, and I said all we sought was to go our way alone, and she reminded me that Dr. H in his sermon this last Sunday gave the most excellent discourse on "Vengeance is mine; I will repay, saith the Lord," and we agreed that we liked his views with regard to retaliation very much.

Your mother says she worries about my superintendence of our home, but I know you will not find fault with it. I have paid Mr. Sargent and am glad to have that bill straightened up anyway. Our mare has the stifles. I have decided that we will need the north lot for pasture this spring, and that the boys should not undertake to do too much and I would rather they do less and do it well. We have not yet dried any apples. They have been so busy through the days I have not had the heart to ask them to work nights. Asa is not interested in his studies and is taken up with the chores at home. As for Wellie, each dawn brings its changes and he finds what he can to interest him. I couldn't get him to write you, though it was so foul out and he had the time.

At his bedtime he and I had such a cry Asa asked how he was supposed to sleep. I now sit before my candle fretful and worn out. I feel less and less able to bear each difficulty that comes our way. I know it's wrong when we have so much to be thankful for, and I wish I could control this wayward disposition. I accommodate my low spirits like communion with a congenial friend. I wonder if I'm capable of a single hour of perfect contentment, one hour in which my soul is not yearning for something it cannot have. My specialty is despairing over disappointments that are entirely unavoidable. I have to remind myself to let trivial matters pass away, as I impart little cheer to my loved ones when I'm cast down. I suppose that is your gift. And I suppose that's why since you've been gone we have had so very few callers except relatives. When people resume their visits once you return I will know who they are coming to see.

I feel as though I could not sympathize with anyone tonight. And yet as I sit dry and sheltered in my house I think of he who has secured those comforts for me, and imagine him open to the elements and his enemies. O my poor lonely soldier boy, I would give a good lot to see you. I remind myself now and always that I have found the one who loves me, as I love him.

A house in town containing the bodies of smallpox victims was burned. Asa has still not gotten his duck. And while writing, my old disease (getting sleepy) is coming on, so I bid you good night and take my warm brick and go to bed alone—

Your loving wife,
Hattie

Boone, NC
Fri. November 25

Dear William,
No birthday greeting from you. Nellie baked a cake for me out of sorghum molasses and honey, and it was very nice too when done. I was awakened at five by her shouting, "Birthday gift!" into my ear after she had stolen into my room. For my birthday dinner Mr. Webb came, looking as usual satisfied with himself and the world in general, along with Miss Boyd and Doctor Turner. Her sister's baby is not well, and it worries us all a good deal. Around the table we each contributed a ghost story, and some of our party were more affected by the tales than they were willing to admit. Miss Boyd remarked when we were clearing in the kitchen that it is too bad you can't be here at home when we both wish you here so much. I retained custody of my expression and answered that there must be many who would be delighted to have you reappear, and she returned only a queer look in response. Afterward I felt so spiritless that even Doctor Turner's singing was no remedy. During

the rest of the visit Father and Nellie did the talking and I listened. Just as supper was over two soldiers came who wanted bread and milk, so it was late before we had the dining room cleaned up. Then, after we saw all our visitors off, they seemed to leave the house behind them very lonely.

Today I had a sore finger and could not sew. All morning was chill and disagreeable without, and I had a suspicion of the neuralgia. I hope a good night's rest tonight will restore my strength. I feel neither well enough to be up nor sick enough to be in bed. Nellie has recommended some gentle exercise in the open air, and says she also feels a good deal out of tune. Father claims all is well with me with the exception of a sore finger. My teeth ache.

Out of Nellie's earshot he asked if it could really be the case that both his daughters are having difficulties with beaux. He noted that when Alvin Blakemore visited last week to bring Nellie a few periodicals the young man had behaved very strangely, sitting with her only some 10 minutes and then suddenly rising and bowing himself out of the room. She has been fretting ever since that he was injured by some remark she made, and then last night during my birthday dinner he rode through the yard and did not call. What a cold, strange boy he is to be sure.

Three privates are currently sleeping soundly on our porch in their muddy blankets like a trio of resigned and happy pigs. They arrived midday and the poor souls are almost starved and soon we'll have nothing to give them. Nellie dressed the wounds of one and did so bravely, while I turned faint and sick while only holding the basin. The boy bade her to not let any Yankee officer carry her off, and she answered that she depended on boys like him to prevent such a possibility.

So I am not much of a nurse. Sometimes I feel poorly suited to any vocation but books. I am not as young as I once was, but I have no desire to go back and live my errors over. Should we reconsider the pledges we made during our goodbyes? Are there other pledges you made of which I remain unaware? I feel the way, after one has had a limb tightly bound and the ligature removed, he cannot for a long time accept his freedom from restraint.

Do "coming events cast their shadows before"? I wonder. Ever since I was a child I have worked as I work now to resist the millstone of my timidity. Write with whatever reassurance you can. It is lonely waiting for the last sands to drop from the glass.

Doctor Turner reports that all seems to be quiet with the Army of Northern Virginia. They've lacked the excitement of even the occasional skirmish. Lately there have been a large number of wagons coming from the west. It's said that deserters from both sides armed to the teeth have taken asylum in the hills, from whence they descend upon unprotected homes. I have commenced reading the life of Patrick Henry aloud to Father.

I hope this letter finds you in good health and good fortune—
Your expectant
Lucy

Camp near Columbia, TN
Mon. November 28, 1864

Dear Lucy,
We have relieved Forrest's cavalry, which was sent to scout for crossings along the Duck River. The Yankees have evacuated the town & burned the bridges, & the plan seems to be to attack them if not in Nashville then in Franklin.

Artillery caissons have moved up & dug in behind us. All night long the company has been agitated, as if mistrusting our own intentions. Bitter cold. Almost starved out. If anyone had told me before the war of what we could bear month after month I would have dismissed it as all talk. Georgie & C.W. are huddled around our fire, nodding & almost asleep, the ground too unforgiving for them to lie back on. Our chaplain was perfectly motionless for a day & a half before he died. Even after beating the feed corn between stones, chewing it leaves the gums too sore to touch. Our packhorses are so famished they're gnawing their bridle reins. 5 of our company deserted in the night, & some of the frozen dead have been stood up for sentries. A lot of fellows are drooping about trying to look sick.

Cheatham's & Stewart's corps have arrived as well. Our attacking forces are becoming so extensive as to resemble a migration. C.W. reported after foraging that we have filled every road leading north over the breadth of this entire area, with supply trains behind, & behind them the stragglers: the sick, the exhausted, the new recruits, the convalescents, & the shirkers. You can tell how many think they're up against it by the extent to which the roads are littered with discarded playing cards & dice. Most of the men would rather be a private in this regiment than a Captain in another, so the order to consolidate with other decimated units has been detested.

My hands are so numb I must stop & warm them before continuing. I write with a tinplate for a desk. Occasionally I have to study to comprehend my own words. I hope this note makes some sense since as I sit here there is commotion on every side. I hope you know how much you are missed. A chaplain from Cheatham's corps is headed to the rear loaded down with letters, & so I will run this to him—

Will

Front Royal, VA
Mon. November 28th 1864

Oh CW, CW, CW,

We can only hope that the God who shows us how little we know of what's good for us will help resign us to His will. It was very cloudy with snow falling this morning, and then it cleared off. I hate to imagine what trials this weather has brought upon you. I know worrying will not ease me, and I remind myself that letters get so easily miscarried and tell myself throughout the day that it will all come right by and by. I set my washing out by noon, while your mother was carding and spinning.

The Yankees are back. A wagon rolled up to our barn, and the accompanying soldiers loaded it with hay. Different regiments have been passing since early afternoon. A Captain approached our porch and announced his brigade would quarter in the meadow in front of the house, and then came the wagon trains with the horses and all the wheels cutting up the fields terribly. We hid the bacon in a packing box under Asa's bed and they crawled underneath and found it but left it there. The search was supervised by the Captain and a young, mortified boy whose only apparent task was to keep track of our expressions. Addie Burnham says they searched her house for guns and took from there one ham and an old rooster they pursued for a half hour straight. She thinks she came off pretty well all things considered. The Yankee Captain remarked to us that everywhere he goes he encounters people eating with their hands, and that he assumes the farther south he proceeds the less learning he will find. Father said after they left that the majority of the Federals have been recruited from the lowbred immigrant classes and induced to fight by sign language. He sees the breach between us and them as so wide that by the War's end the South can only be all Yankees or no Yankees at all. I saw in one detachment a mulatto in uniform, but I don't blame him near as much as his instigators.

Wellie fell from the toeboard of the wagon, and his knee is considerably swollen. I heard him tell Asa while they were in the barn turning the straw-cutter that he'll be glad when spring is here. I gave him some vinegar and salt for his cough, and he's taken to carrying a bag of pennyroyal leaves as a remedy against fleas.

Kattie Wetherell brought over a letter from her husband so he's not dead after all, and we're very glad. She gave me a mournful look when I told her I'd heard nothing from you.

Are we to be pitied? We had <u>those nine years</u> with each other. How many can claim that? I wish you could see our children and all the fruits of our labors. I need you to fill that place beside me in which only you fit. I write to you from my own ocean of consideration and love. Please send word even if it's only the shortest of notes—

Your privileged
Hattie

> Boone, NC
> Mon. November 28

Dear William,
There was some cannonading again in the night. I was up half a dozen times looking out the windows and finally dropped into a doze broken by Father coming in with a candle to fetch something for Nellie. I did not sleep until sunrise, and then was very early astir. Nellie has a sore foot.

This afternoon we all went to the mill to be weighed. I counted the same as the former occasion: 116 pounds. A cavalry company picketed in the depot lot and then rode away. Some stragglers came by for milk, and we gave them some. I went to my bed and lay down and heard the hail and was so tired I didn't know what to do so I didn't do anything. I read aloud to Father and made Nellie a tiara of winter jasmine and calendula so oversize that when she tried it on in the mirror she claimed to resemble a calf peering through a rosebush. Later I heard her stop playing the piano in the middle of her piece, and when I looked in she had lowered her head to the soundboard.

Yesterday we went to church for the first time in 11 weeks, and I was sad to think of the many changes that have taken place since. After the service Father invited Alvin Blakemore to lunch, which proved a calamity. Nellie, when she heard, announced that all luncheon parties were stupid and that this was no exception. We ate almost nothing so that there might be more for Father and Alvin, and the poor boy sat there like the Spartan whose fox was gnawing his vitals beneath his cloak. He was uncommunicative about the length of his furlough and seems to have an implacable conviction about his own inability to win affection, which Father and I discussed after he'd left, and it transpired that Nellie was listening in the hall, and in so doing realized the truth of the old adage that eavesdroppers never hear any good about themselves.

I feel I should end every letter with FOR GOD'S SAKE WRITE. Father reminds me that a peevish and fault-finding woman is utterly unfit for company in this or the next world, but I learned early in life to depend upon my own efforts, and I wish to renew my belief in what we possessed and our endless variety of ardent declarations. It may be that this national separation that wreaks its passion in slaughter is proof that what was once the best of all human governments was but an experiment and a failure, but I refuse to concede that your heart and mine are not as linked as they have ever been. I imagine all those left helpless and deprived and in need of a lover's care, and even in the face of what may be your eloquent silence I still desire only to smooth your pillow and tender your rest.

Father says he noticed a great commotion and lights at Doctor Turner's when he passed by, and we're afraid something has happened there. I tell myself I will receive your letter tomorrow, and with that I put out my light.

Your loving and furious
Lucy

Front Royal, VA
Wed. November 30th 1864

My silent CW,
It has been a cold morning after a heavy shower in the night. While still in bed I was gratified by a sensation of you and woke to your touch all along my arms. You were warning me that our hens were finding the strawberries as fast as they turned red. I heard the boys

already at their chores but felt too worn with care and anxiety to stir. I have to be mindful of scanning old scenes of our pleasures. That temptation for me is like rowing near a waterfall: if I get too near I will be swept over the edge.

Addie Burnham brought over a letter from her brother, who is now near you under Cheatham. She had just fetched it from town and Wellie's face when he spied it was terrible. We are never ready for bad news, though we know tragedy can lurk within any unopened envelope. After she read it Asa said it sounded like Hood was ready to give the Yankee Army of the Ohio a most complete dressing, and Wellie took himself to the barn. He has been saving a bottle of honey for your return, but when he checked it it had candied. I told him that I'm sure you don't feel hard toward him for not writing, and that maybe tonight we could put together a crate of food to send you.

I am so weak lately that a pail of water seems heavy and anything I do beyond the usual uses me up. I think I have never been more reconciled to my lot. But when I stand by the fire, or sit for our meals, or note Wellie's shoulders, I think of you. You created this version of me and now you are gone and I must manage my resentment and dismay. Asa never got his duck but promises he will once you're home. Billie is improved from hock to muzzle. Little Henry Rhodes, only just in the service, has been killed. His poor mother is almost crazy.

Your devoted
Hattie

Franklin & Columbia Turnpike
Wed. November 30, 1864

Lucy!
It's warmer today & we are all grateful for the sun. We moved up in the night, marching with a good road & a bright moon. The road was strewn with luxuries thrown away. I picked up a pocket inkstand & then discarded it myself a mile or so on. They say the water is healthy. It does not appear so.

I can't write much as it seems we are looking for a fight every minute. I am well with the exception of one ear, which has been deaf & roaring for some time. In the late afternoon yesterday, after listening to shelling since first light, we were sent forward on the double-quick to support Forrest's cavalry at a little town called

Spring Hill. We charged into the Yankees' fire, & many of the boys advancing looked bewildered, as if they wondered what they were expected to do. I loaded & shot until I had blisters as big as 10-cent pieces & my gun was so hot I could not touch the barrel. My cap box was shot off my belt & my rifle shot through the stock & split. The Federal sharpshooters throw a good ball & at long range too. The boy beside me had his brains scattered all over us. I have been like a foundered horse ever since.

Georgie has wept at every rest & interval. We kill scores of Federals but they seem to have no objections, for they know they will use us up in time & replace what we cannot. Meanwhile the practice here is to drag men along while they are of any use, & then once they are not to turn them out to die.

We have had our first view of the Federal entrenchments surrounding the village of Franklin. It is said that all Hood's subordinates including Forrest are arguing against a direct assault, & C.W. notes that we don't require a spyglass to realize the peril. The ground is level with no cover, & the breastworks astride the Nashville road are fearsome, & Yankee artillery positions to the NW & E will subject any attacking columns to enfilade fire. Their gunners have been double-charging their cannons with canister, & they will cover that ground like a fine-tooth comb. Georgie says a chicken could not live on that field once they open up on it, & C.W. answered that it was not so hard to get there as it looked but the trouble was to stay once arrived. Shielding half their line is also a thick hedge the branches of which have been sharpened into abatis. It's said that Hood hazarded $1000 on one card in a faro game & won. It's also said that with his lost leg & new fiancée he has much to prove.

Our boys are loading down the chaplains with watches & letters & photographs, but I still have a bit of time to write. Everywhere before us the Yankee regimental flags are dotting the slopes. Our forces are arrayed in all directions. When we step off, flurries of startled rabbits & quail will lead our advance. I thought when you finally saw me next you would see a boy who did not want to quarrel, & who wanted to work in concert with you to bring about good feeling. I thought until then of proposing we read together a Bible chapter each night so that we might share what we were thinking before retiring. But now I must close, as we are being ordered up to our positions. The air is hazy. Our bands are playing. I regret having provided you only stray glimpses into my interior, with its changeful exaltations & deprivations, & its clues as to the secrets of my heart already vanishing. I recognize it's all our task to argue not against Heaven's hand but to bear up & steer onward. & I see that Hope calculates its schemes for a long & durable life, & presses us forward to imaginary points of bliss, & grasps at impossibilities, & so ensnares us all.

# *Wrong Object*

FROM *Harper's*

*HE IS a nondescript man.*

I'd never used that adjective about a client. Not until this one. My seventeenth. He'd requested an evening time and came Tuesdays at six thirty. For months he didn't tell me what he did.

The first session I said what I often said to begin: How can I help you?

I still think of what I do as a helping profession. And I liked the way the phrase echoed down my years; in my first job I'd been a salesgirl at a department-store counter.

I want to work on my marriage, he said. I'm the problem.

His complaint was familiar. But I preferred a self-critical patient to a blamer.

It's me, he said. My wife is a thoroughly good person.

*Yawn,* I thought, but said, Tell me more.

I don't feel what I should for her.

What do you feel?

Gratitude, I suppose. And when I think of leaving, pity.

What do you wish you experienced?

He slumped in my old chair. (I'd just signed the lease; the furniture I'd ordered hadn't come yet.)

I don't feel enchantment . . . or the hope that we can make each other better. Married ten years, together thirteen. But I never had that.

That being enchantment.

He shrugged. All the things people say about being in love.

I never felt she was necessarily *the one,* he said.

The one, I repeated.

That we were destined for each other.

Do you have children?

Three. How about you, Doc? Do you think love is just a solitary fantasy system?

I believe in the existence of good fits, I said.

I took notes after each session. Most therapists allow ten or fifteen minutes between patients, but I scheduled mine a half hour apart. That first year, I had a notebook in a different color for each. His was brown, and the pages for our first six sessions were almost empty.

*Talks about wife, what a good person she is. Annoying.*

The blankness I felt regarding this patient—I'll call him K— may have been his most distinctive quality. My notes on other patients ran long. I found K boring. I didn't particularly like him. And I liked having patients I liked.

From Week 9: *His wife (C) has an internal compass, whereas he's not lying and grabbing and snatching because he's afraid of being caught.*

*How do you know?* I asked.

I noted that when he said "lyin' and grabbin' and snatchin'," he said it in caricatured Ebonics.

*K visibly not black,* I wrote.

If pressed, what could I have said? That K was slender and nearly bald. That he was in his forties. He dressed in the style of our Southern California community: good hard shoes but no jacket. Often he wore a gray, collared sweater, soft, close fitting. Probably cashmere. I wondered where he bought it. The shirts my husband chose faintly bothered me.

For the past eight years, K had been counsel for a transpacific company. I knew this because I'd googled; he still didn't talk about his work except once to tell me he'd have to cancel because he would be flying to Asia.

K devoted our sessions to his wife and the minor problems

of the rich. He'd bought a painting that was possibly a fake. He winced talking about his relationship with the dealer.

I suggested that K cultivate dreams by keeping a notebook on the bedside table, but he claimed not to dream.

He liked his wife to color her hair. Was that wrong of him? He asked me this and didn't notice my hand going rogue to my head, where wiry white strands curled out from the dark.

He decided to buy her a purse. He actually unfolded a picture to show me. See, it's made to look like a plastic shopping bag from Chinatown.

I loved that purse.

I told my supervisor about K at our monthly training session.

K had had a fight with his wife, who wanted the children to wash their own clothes. I'd said that everyone needs to learn how to do laundry. K had shrugged with a look of almost pleasurable guilt. I never did, he said.

What about in college?

Harvard has a laundry service, he said, flicking his wrist.

I hated him a little then. I'd not gone to Harvard. And I still did laundry. Too much of it. In that gesture of K's I saw what I feared a lot of people—my husband's family, maybe even my patrician supervisor—really thought of me: that I was less because I had been poor.

My supervisor was a very old, very tall man, a legend in the Los Angeles analytic community. He carried an aura of glamour, even then, in his eighties.

I told him about the purse.

I don't think you're less, he said. I admire you for having made your own way.

A lot of the time K bored me, I admitted.

My supervisor smiled, an expression of his never without a trace of pain. In the seventies, he said, a village priest asked the great Dr. Winnicott how to differentiate between a parishioner who could benefit from talking and someone who needed professional help. Winnicott said, if he is boring you, then he is sick and needs psychiatric treatment.

From the door, as I was leaving, I turned back to ask Dr. Bair, Where did you go to college?

The Farm, he answered. Then, seeing my confusion, he explained. Stanford; we used to call it the Farm. I don't know if they still do.

That same day, in the coffee shop near my office, I saw the purse. A young mother had hooked it over her stroller handle.

I immediately searched for it online. Seventeen hundred dollars.

Another spat with his wife. K wanted to visit Alaska. His descriptions of the wildlife were tender, reverential. He wanted to see the willow ptarmigan's feathered feet. Snowy owls. Loons. The endangered Steller's eider. In a decade, he said, so much will be gone.

C said she planned to stay put.

I suggested that that sounded cold.

He defended her then, as if I'd attacked, which I suppose I had. She has more important responsibilities, he said, than swanning around the world with me.

Let's talk about our relationship, I said.

*Our* relationship? K said.

Yes. We've spent a good deal of time discussing your feelings about your wife. Let's consider what's going on right now in this room and whether or not that's satisfying. This is a relationship we could end without damage.

Our rel*ation*ship, he said again. I hadn't really thought of us as having one. I'm all right with you, he mumbled.

Really? I said. Because I'm not sure I've been able to help you. Sometimes I feel we go over the same territory.

Well, that's probably my fault, he said. I haven't talked about everything. But I suppose that's what I'm here for.

And then he told me. At the time I had a pencil in my hand, and I wrote down the date: January 28, 2012.

I'm a pedophile, he said. The problem with my wife isn't . . . I've never been enchanted with anyone her age. Which is to say my age.

The light in my office made him look dangerously thin, pretzeled on the corduroy chair. (My furniture had finally arrived. K was the only one of my clients to notice.) I was aware of the narrowness of his shoulders in the gray, collared sweater, the niceness of his socks.

All the hair on my arms stood up. There are questions I want to ask, I interrupted, but I need you to be aware, first, that in the state of California I will be required to report you if . . .

Don't worry, he said. I've never touched a child. I never will. That's not why . . . he shrugged. Not a possibility. I have too much to lose. And, he paused, it'd be wrong. I get that. I have three kids.

As he talked in an even voice I felt, for the first time, that we were in something together.

OK, I said, sitting back. I had a hundred questions.

What age children? Girls or boys? When did this start? Were you abused?

That's what everybody'd probably think, right? But I don't think so. There were strange things, but . . .

He was not completely bald. He had a kind of hair I'd seen around LA the past few years. What time had left had been shaved to the length of a crew cut, but one absolutely distinguishable from the military forms of that style. All of a sudden his look entered the lexicon of handsome. *I'm getting old*, I thought.

It seemed not only that I could fall in love with this person (in the way therapists fall in love, with the poignancy of renunciation) but that whatever that motion was, like a rope being shaken, it had already begun.

We spent the next month hunting down a sexual predator in K's past. I saw the population outside my office differently during that time. People in my coffee shop appeared heroic; I began to believe that many carried damage and made it their purpose not to pass that damage on.

March 8 I quoted Auden in the brown notebook:

*I and the public know*
*What all schoolchildren learn*
*Those to whom evil is done*
*Do evil in return.*

*But not always,* I scribbled.

We exhumed an inappropriate babysitter, a chubby fourteen-year-old with a contralto laugh who liked to lie over his lap and make him spank her, and a difficult mother (the opposite of C).

But no real sexual evil. By the middle of the summer, we stopped trying.

If it's buried, it's buried deep, he said.

Why did you come to me when you did? I asked.

I called you because of a girl, he said. He hadn't in the least invited the situation. In fact, he avoided one-on-one time with his own daughters, he tended to take them places together, though he planned activities for himself with his son. I couldn't imagine that kind of carefulness with my children.

This girl, he said, followed him around at work for three weeks, as a project for school. And she fell for him, the eighth grader's crush so obvious it became a joke in the office. Even her father, the CFO, laughed about it. For K, this felt excruciating. Because there *was* a current between them, and she was showing it while he had to act as if it didn't exist.

She asked him for a three-day-a-week internship. He said no. She slows me down, he told her father. I spend all my time explaining the law. The CFO was offended because K had insufficiently gushed. Isabel, her name was. Everyone else in the office loves Izzy, the CFO pointedly said.

It was over now. He hadn't seen her or heard about her for eight months. He had never once asked her father what she was doing, or whether she'd trekked through Orange County for the Christmas bird count. She'd talked about that. She kept a notebook with her sightings of local birds. She'd told him about a population of wild red-crowned parrots that had been growing since the forties, when a flock escaped from a truck hurtling north from Mexico to a Bakersfield pet store. Now he read about birds whenever there was an article in the paper. He'd grown more attached to the family dog.

So you had your love story, I said.

I fell in love but in an impossible way.

That's what we call "wrong object." Our hope is to keep those feelings and direct them to someone else. (I said that, but I didn't know whether it was possible.)

Right object, he said. Well we all know who that would be. I sometimes think I love my dog more than my wife.

*

A generation ago, someone sat in a chair like mine and listened to a person talk about a different wrong object. In offices all over North America, psychiatrists attempted conversion therapies. My takeaway from those sad chapters of the history of psychology was that you could scare people and make them celibate, you could maybe stop them from doing what they had the urge to do, but it was nearly impossible to implant an alternate desire. The arc of gay liberation had a good ending, at least in California. But K's problem never could.

We'd already gone ten minutes over time and K was still talking when I told him we had to stop. He looked at me with gratitude as he stood. He seemed relieved. His secrecy was ending, but mine had just begun.

Now I knew there was a real child. I wished he hadn't told me her name.

Shrinks promise confidentiality, but everyone breaks that promise. I talked to my husband about patients, and not only to him. I'd once puzzled out a couple's case with my running partner. But I couldn't tell anyone about K; I didn't want to. I felt pretty sure no one would understand.

I spent a few hours on the internet. The case law was iffy. Child pornography was illegal and could have arguably been subject to mandatory reporting. I hoped he wasn't watching child porn.

I slid into bed next to my sleeping husband.

I may have been honor bound to tell my supervising analyst, but Dr. Bair was leaving for a nine-week writing retreat in Scotland, where he planned to devote himself to a memoir in verse about his first marriage, to a wife who died young.

Over the next weeks, K told me about his first object. We talked in it and around it, the way music reorganizes itself. We added a second session, Thursday mornings.

The summer he was thirteen K had fallen in love with a friend of his sister's, a girl named Anna Li. His family had rented a house in Malibu, and he followed the two girls everywhere. The ends of her hair touched her hips. She had stick legs, dark compared with his own freckled skin. He was a geek then, he told me, with acne. I thought I would grow out of that and be one of those guys who had a beautiful younger wife, he said. His mother, in fact, was a beautiful wife, sixteen years younger than his father. The three children slept on a porch cantilevered over sand, and heard the thunder of rippling waves all night long.

Anna Li's wrist had brushed against his, but that was all until the day before he left (his parents had decided to return home early), when the three waded into the ocean and his sister ran back to get a popsicle from the refrigerator. He watched her trudging up the sand and thought her bum was too big. Anna tied her hair up in a knot by touch alone, her elbows out to the sides of her ears. He was standing but just barely, with ridged sand under his feet; the waves lifted him up and down; it was like jumping without gravity. Their bodies found each other and he felt her legs waving underwater, like sea fronds, then her knees touching both sides of him. She placed her hands on his shoulders, which were rising up and down, too. She kissed him, and the inside of her mouth tasted of melon, the musky flavor he hadn't liked but now did. The smell of sea, the knob of her ankle on his back, her hands light on his shoulders, bobbing up and down with the surf. They laughed, looking at each other because they fit. Then, suddenly, a huge wave came and unlatched them, hurled them tumbling in foam, and when they emerged nine feet apart her face was covered with her netted hair, the rubber band lost to the sea.

His mother, in a yellow blouse, stood waving from the deck; his sister was returning, her splayed feet sinking in the sand with each step. The sun puckered the surface of the ocean. Their eyes shone; their hair plastered against their skin. He left for New York with his family the next day and never saw her again.

She runs a cosmetics company now, he said.

But the age of the girls he loved did not march up the staircase with him. He'd desired a thirteen-year-old when he was thirteen, when he was in high school, then when he was in his twenties and thirties. The penchant never changed. He'd married at thirty-six.

I asked if he'd thought of telling C then. He hadn't. I mean how would you bring it up? By the way, I'm not really all that attracted to you?

I thought that he could tell her now, but what if she ran out of the house with the children and hired a divorce lawyer?

*

I read about a Canadian psychiatrist who'd closed down his practice and sent former patients, on whom he'd attempted conversion therapy, letters of apology with refund checks. Eventually the
doctor went bankrupt.

My supervisor summoned me for one last meeting before he left
for Scotland. He had a fire going in his office fireplace. I'd never
known it worked. Gas, he said when I stared. He always offered
me coffee during our sessions, and I accepted, though it was late
afternoon. He wore a flannel shirt under his suit jacket and hiking
boots, already dressed for his retreat. He efficiently ran through
each of my patients. He asked me about K only once.

What about the purse?

I told him the truth: I'd forgotten it.

He's not boring you anymore?

No, I said.

I wished him well on his book, hoping I would see him again. At
his age, I couldn't be sure.

And then it was just K and me.

What does it mean to be a nonacting "minor-attracted person"?
I asked, which is what he'd started to call himself.

For some people, I suppose, it would mean they can't have sex.
Not real sex.

But that's not you, I said. You're not celibate.

Not exactly.

With that qualifier, it seemed I'd bitten a tip of cardboard.

If a guy in a bar says, My wife and I have great sex, and his
buddy says, Meh, ours is so-so, what does that even tell you? Maybe
the one's so-so would have been the other's nirvana.

I asked about his fantasies.

It's pretty much always the same, he said. We're in water. She's
skinny, teasing. She coaxes me. I have to be pulled into the game.
No face usually. But a girl. That body.

Do you think of this fantasy to become aroused with your wife?

My running partner once told me she had to imagine being raped
to come and the ickiness bothered her so much that orgasms
didn't seem worth the trouble. She'd read about arousal recon-
ditioning in a women's magazine. In the sixties, psychologists had

patients masturbate to a favorite fantasy and then replace that with something more acceptable just seconds before climax, when it was too late to stop. Gradually, they pulled the switch back, until finally, the idea went, the patient wouldn't need the fantasy at all. But arousal-reconditioning therapy failed—at least, it failed to make gay people straight.

My running partner said she couldn't completely obliterate the need for violence, but now she only required a minute or two. I'd also read about satiation training, which was kind of the opposite. Patients masturbated to their favorite fantasies over and over again until they wore them out.

I'll try number one, K said, now that we're picking from discredited therapies. How many times a week do I have to do this?

Two or three, I said.

She's gonna wonder what's gotten into me.

He had been having sex with his wife all along, but not a lot. Still, he said, not appreciably less than their friends. Unlike with those couples, though, K was the one who demurred. Sometimes during dinners out, the men made jokes about missing the sex-rich time before marriage, looking at their wives with blame. This humiliated his wife.

But after two weeks of the regime and K's apparently newfound appetite, they laughed together about their previous imbalance.

At the end of five weeks, C called a moratorium.

This is a little too much for me, she told him. Instead, she signed them up for a Ligurian cooking class. The chef would come to them.

How had it worked?

I don't know, he said. Without the fantasy, her naked face was like an old friend.

K had an unusually large mouth. His lips pressed together in an exaggerated tight smile, which he held a moment then let down. Oh, that's a grimace, I realized. Sometimes I understood what a word meant from reading but had never met it in life.

I asked again whether he could tell her. I thought it was worth the risk. But he didn't want to.

You've never asked me about porn, he said.

I raised a hand, meaning *Stop*.

He waved me off. I always knew it was out there, he said. Last night, I finally watched one on my computer. The thing felt homemade. There was a girl, eleven or twelve. She looked poor. More young than pretty. It was supposed to be her first time. You could see she was scared. He was much bigger and rough. The guy was hurting her, and you could see he wanted to. He was getting off on her fear. I closed my computer to stop it.

My fantasy, he said, it was never that at all.

He returned to his first concern: his marriage.

OK, so I don't have the sparkle, he said, or whatever that is. But my question is still the same. Do I love her enough? The problem is choice. If you turn away from your instincts, you're left with rationality, essentially with shopping. There is something repellent about deciding to pick a person that way. This one's a wonderful cook. That one looks great dressed up. The other one's fluent in three languages but disorganized.

Isn't that more or less what we all do? I said.

Really?

Well, few of us marry paraplegics.

You married a paraplegic? He asked.

No. I did the usual thing.


Maybe we're done, K said.

The one thing we haven't tried is telling your wife.

He shook his head. This is enough for me. Why should she have to learn that she had her children with a monster? She could have married plenty of other guys.

I'd written statistics on a three-by-five index card. But what could I say: You are not alone?

After that the life went out of our sessions. He canceled frequently for trips, more family trips, I noted, fewer business. He no longer seemed miserable. By the summer, he'd stopped coming altogether. That might have been the happy end of our story.

Dr. Bair eventually returned from Scotland, where he'd broken a leg, walking on a rocky crag. The footsteps, he said, helped his prosody. He'd had to spend the last six weeks of his retreat in a Swiss rehabilitation facility. This time no fire burned in the marble fireplace of his office. He offered coffee as usual, but I declined, in deference to the plastic boot on his leg. I summarized my cases, skipping lightly over K's termination.

I'm still not getting a clear sense of your work with him, he said. I always thought something would emerge from all that boredom.

Maybe now that it was over, I could tell him more. I wanted to talk about K. None of my current patients engaged me as much.

I looked at Dr. Bair's long face, pale and weaker from his trip, and remembered him saying, *I don't think you're less.* I decided to trust him. I started to describe our work, what we'd accomplished, what we'd left unfinished.

But his gaze focused. His eyebrows rose. I'm surprised at you, he said.

He never touched a minor. He came to get help.

According to his own report. Did he engage in pornography?

I could have lied. Well, only once, I finally said. I tried to remember my statistics. There are something like four million child-porn websites. And he hated it. He didn't do anything, I said, too loud. He came to me to learn how to live with these feelings. If something happened to him for seeking help that would be a really bad thing.

I saw I'd made a mistake. I wanted to ask him to promise he wouldn't report K, but instead I flattered him, asking how his work on the memoir had gone, whether he'd been able to finish.

He shook his head and told me that he'd made some progress, but not as much as he'd hoped.

A few weeks later, on a Tuesday evening, there was a knock on my office door. A woman introduced herself as Catherine.

Someone had reported her husband, she told me. There had been an investigation. He hadn't done anything, she said, and so of course he'd been cleared.

I thought of explaining that it wasn't me who'd reported him, but it was anyway, I supposed, my fault.

K had obviously told her almost everything. What I'd hoped for had come true; she stood here his ally, her black hair pulled back in a ponytail. They were no doubt closer from their mutual rage. She was stately, truly beautiful with large Grecian features. She was not carrying the purse that looked like a plastic shopping bag but dressed with classical good taste: a knit suit, modest heels at the end of long slim calves. He'd never once told me that C was beautiful, her proportions probably wasted on him. I'm sure he hadn't thought of me in those terms at all.

I'm sorry, I said. I didn't want this to happen.
He feels terribly betrayed, she said. We both do.

I left my office, taping a note on the door to cancel my later session, and I meandered on residential streets, walking in and out
of pockets of sound, leaf blowers, illegal but still used everywhere
here, and occasionally a choir of birds under an inexplicably hospitable tree. I'd started noticing birds. Without meaning to, K had
given me the inclination. It may have been all K still had from the
girl. I thought about Dr. Bair. I was just a beginner and he was an
eminence. But our relationship wasn't what I'd believed.

At least Isabel, the girl, had been spared. No doubt by now
she'd forgotten her crush. Perhaps she'd begun dating, in the way
of our high schoolers, via texts and Instagram. I wondered if she'd
kept her love of birds.

# They Told Us Not to Say This

FROM *Harper's*

THE FEW WHITE BOYS in our town could ball. Breakaway lay-ups, nothing-but-the-bottom-of-the-net free throws, buzzer-beater fadeaways. They slept with basketballs in their beds and told us about their dreams. We tried not to stare at the diamond studs in their ears as they talked about winning imaginary games in over-time or seeing blurry scoreboards. *It don't matter if I can see the score anyway, I finna play my hardest regardless,* Brent Zalesky said once, squinting his eyes in the sunlight. Brent Zalesky lived in the Crest. He didn't flinch at the sound of gunshots, he received detentions weekly, and he ganked tapes and CDs from Wherehouse with the clunky security devices still attached. Brent Zalesky knew how to get them off, armed only with pliers and a Bic lighter. This was 1996, and he never got caught. He took music requests and we'd find surprises in our lockers at school. We loved him for this. We loved his buzzed blond hair, his stainless-steel chain necklace, his jawline, his position. Brent Zalesky played point guard. All the boys on the team respected him. They called him Z.

When the boys got their basketball photos from Lifetouch, we collected them like baseball cards and kept them in hole-punched plastic sleeves in our day planners. Each year, Z's wallet-size bas-ketball pic slid into the front of our collections. Freshman year, he simply signed his name on the back: *Peace, Brent.* Junior year, he wrote more words on the one he gave Marorie Balancio: *Sup Rorie, I think you're hella fine. Peace, Brent.*

Back then there were two movie theaters in town and he took her to the one that didn't smell like Black & Milds and piss. Marorie said he drove up with a cigarette tucked behind his right ear, but he didn't light it until after he dropped her off at home. She saw the small spark hanging outside his car window because he had waited until she unlocked the front door. Marorie couldn't help but look back and wave before she walked inside. Earlier, during the movie, Brent Zalesky had fed her popcorn. She said it was like he knew exactly how much she needed and when she needed more in her mouth. We could only imagine what it felt like, to have his fingers so close to our open lips.

Our parents said no boyfriends until we were thirty. They didn't talk to our brothers like this because they wanted to bend down and kiss all their *titis* every day. Sons got brand-new Honda Preludes on their sixteenth birthdays. Our moms took wannabe directors to Circuit City and bought camcorders that ended up in corners collecting dust. Wannabe rock stars got Fender Stratocasters and we felt like those street performers in the city who stand on overturned milk crates and hope for quarters in an open guitar case. Still, we sang a cappella by our lockers on breaks. We wanted to be En Vogue, Xscape, TLC, SWV. Anytime Brent Zalesky walked by we got so weak in the knees we could hardly speak, you know? We wondered if we'd still know him when we turned eighteen, all of us desperate for him in our cotillions. Rosyl Manalo's mom said throwing a cotillion would be a waste of money, but she also bought a big-ass Louis Vuitton hobo and filed a police report like it was a missing person when it got stolen from her shopping cart at the Canned Food Grocery Outlet. *I had never seen her cry so hard before,* Rosyl told us, *not even when she thought someone kidnapped me at Service Merchandise.*

We weren't worth much, not as much as sons. Sons never fucked up. Sons never had to pay rent. Marorie's brother got a girl preggo when he was eighteen and they mooched off her parents for years. *His babies are good luck,* her mother said, excited about becoming a *lola.* But vacuuming at night was bad luck, cutting nails at night was bad luck, buying someone shoes was bad luck. *If you give shoes as a gift, that person will walk out of your life forever.* Moles, the color red, aquariums—all good luck. *If something bad is going to happen to you in the house, the goldfish will absorb it.*

We're not sure why we listened to women who pinched our noses in the kitchen when we were kids because we'd be so *maganda* if only our noses weren't so flat and our skin wasn't so dark. *The complexion of the poor people who work in the province.* We envied Lianni Benitez because her mother was dead. Still, it was ingrained in us all, to listen to our elders without question, to read their minds, to fetch things they pointed at with their chins. We barely knew our *lolas* and *lolos*, but every time we saw them, no matter how old we were, we reflexively reached out for the backs of their wrinkled hands to touch to our foreheads in greeting. *Bless, bless*, they would say. For all we know they could have been assholes when they were younger, but it didn't matter. They had white hair now. We had to obey them, no questions asked. Jason Lagundi showed up in a limo to take Rosyl to prom, and then her mother grounded her. She wouldn't have done that if it had been a white boy from Blackhawk, the kind who'd grow up to rock Brooks Brothers or Nantucket Reds from Murray's Toggery Shop, the kind who never liked working or practice because he never had to, didn't you know he was the kind who deserved everything? The kind who'd marry you only if you looked good on paper, the kind who apologized for sweating while he "made love" to you, the kind who wouldn't still eat you out after getting his lip busted in a fight because, well, he'd never thrown a punch in his life. These boys lived across the Benicia–Martinez Bridge and then some, far enough away to look better, even though they sagged their pants and wore backward caps. They thought they could wear Vallejo, you know, like it was a high school phase. They'd wear it and take it off when it was time to grow up.

*When you grow up, you should be a doctor. Did you know your lolo was a doctor in the Philippines?*

*When you grow up, you should be a lawyer. You can make a lot of money and buy a big house. Did you know I had a big house in Quezon City?*

It was always about the house. Lianni Benitez lived in an apartment, and they talked about it like it was a shame. Anyone with a four-bedroom in Glen Cove was automatically a good person. They shook their heads when we told them where Brent Zalesky lived.

*He's not going to go anywhere*, our mothers said.

Our *lolas* echoed them with *What, you think he's going to grow up to be a professional player, like on the TV?*

We didn't have an answer for that. What we knew was that Brent Zalesky played like it mattered. Real game or scrimmage, there was no difference. What we knew was that Brent Zalesky wasn't afraid to fight for his team, for our school, for us. What we knew was that he liked reading about all kinds of professional athletes for inspiration. He would talk to us about real-life things in the hallway. *Did you know Wayne Gretzky used to eat dinner with his skates on when he was a kid? Did you know Roberto Clemente used to stay late after practice and do one-hop throws into an overturned trash can at home plate over and over again, because it was the hardest throw to make from his position?* To Brent Zalesky, there was never a point where great athletes stopped working at being great. No buzzers, no finish lines. They couldn't rely on luck. They were always playing the game, working harder, trying to be better.

We tried to relay this to our parents. To them, it didn't matter that Brent Zalesky threw his heart out on the court for his teammates, night after night during the season. They couldn't admire how he made fast decisions, how he'd casually throw up fingers to call a play as he dribbled past the half-court line, how teammates leaned closer to him during a time-out, how he lifted off the floor in the paint and floated in midair. It didn't matter that he weaved and shot and fought for wins in a good-for-nothing gym in front of people like us.

In the middle of junior year, Brent Zalesky started dating Marorie. We covered for her and never told her parents where she really was. After dinner one night, he pulled her into his bedroom by curling one finger around a belt loop on her jeans. There was more desire in that move than anything I've ever felt in my whole life, she still insists.

He had one chick poster in his room, just one mixed in with his favorite athletes. Marorie was expecting to see a blonde (her mother had a pedestal for a coworker named Virginia. *My blond friend Virginia . . . Virginia and I did lunch today, did you know that she's white?*) but Jocelyn's hair was dark, like ours, only highlighted in ways we weren't allowed to think about. Some of us straight-up had mustaches, but our mothers never said anything, as if the longer we stayed furry, the longer they could keep the leashes on. *Don't wear lipstick,* our mothers said, *lipstick will make your lips turn brown and you don't want them to be brown.* This brown girl on the poster? She didn't have a mustache.

*Who's Jocelyn Enriquez,* Marorie asked.

*You don't know who this is?*

Marorie shook her head. She half expected him to talk about how Jocelyn Enriquez looked because that was the routine. When we wore flannel shirts from Choice, our mothers said we looked like farmers. When we stood up straight, they didn't like that we looked taller than them. We were too skinny, too fat, our hair was too long, our hair was too short. *Gain ten more pounds.* They'd force-feed us bowls of mashed potatoes and butter and sigh when the scales never changed. *Cut your hair.* None of us were just right. And when we did crave *arroz caldo* from Goldilocks, our parents took us to Red Lobster or Olive Garden instead. Marorie was still looking at Jocelyn Enriquez when Brent Zalesky pulled a pair of headphones from underneath a pillow. He carefully placed them over Marorie's ears, picked her up, and put her on the bed. These were the days of Walkmans, blank cassette tapes and running to the radio to push record. These were the days of working for what you wanted. No quick downloads, no Insta-anything.

We asked her if they hooked up that night.

*No,* she said, *we just listened to Jocelyn Enriquez music. He was surprised I didn't know who she was.*

That same spring, we started to find Jocelyn Enriquez tapes and CDs in our lockers at school. We knew they were from him. Then Candice Quijano discovered that Jocelyn graduated from Pinole Valley High School, just ten miles away from us, and we got hella excited when we learned Jocelyn was a member of the San Francisco Girls Chorus and had a recording contract by the time she was sixteen. Roberto Clemente was from Puerto Rico. Wayne Gretzky, Canada. And here was Jocelyn, who grew up so close to home. We listened to her voice in our bedrooms at night and turned the volume up a little when we heard a track in Tagalog.

Our parents were ashamed of the language even though they spoke it. We used to joke that they didn't teach us as kids because they didn't want us to grow up to have accents like theirs. *I don't have an accent, English was the medium of instruction in the Philippines.* But when we listened to that Jocelyn Enriquez song in Tagalog, it sounded beautiful. At the end of the chorus were the words *mahal kita.* We recognized this because of Brent Zalesky. He had written those two words at the bottom of a note in Marorie's day planner.

*What does that mean?* we asked her.

*It means I love you,* she said.

When we were in our beds that night, we thought about how strange it was, how we never heard our mothers and fathers say those words to us before, *mahal kita*.

When Marorie tried out for varsity, we joined her even though our parents said it was dangerous. They didn't want us doing anything outside of the house. We didn't think we would be any safer staying inside and listening to our mothers criticize us.

*You're going to get hurt,* they warned us.

*We want to get hurt,* we said.

Brent Zalesky came to all of our home games. We played for him. At the free-throw line, we slid our palms on the bottoms of our sneakers before taking the basketball from the ref. Our palms got dirty quick, but it made the ball feel secure in our hands. We bent at the knees and learned how to hunger for that sound, those flicks at the bottom of the net. In practice after school we did suicides until we felt like puking. We did them in our driveways at night too.

Somehow, in practice, we started to talk like the boys. When someone would miss a pass we'd say, *Where were you at, playa?* When someone shot an air ball, we'd put a fist to our mouths and boo like boys. It wasn't long before we started to spit into our palms as we lined up to slap hands against opposing teams postgame. *Good game, good game, good game,* we'd all say. Sometimes we couldn't hold in the laughs until the line was done.

We blasted music in the gym during warm-ups before home games. Coach let us turn up the music so loud that we could feel the beat on the floor, could feel it in our bodies, our hearts. Who cared that the Bulls dominated back then and that the Dubs were shit. On the court, we felt proud. During games, we took hits and threw elbows like champs. Who cared about girls from Napa who put their fingers in our faces and timed their pregame team chant with ours so you couldn't hear our voices? Who cared that we would grow up to have all kinds of girls interrupt us, correct us, cut us, talk over us, throw shrimp cocktail at us? Could we blame them? We were brown like their nannies, brown like the big-eyed dirty kids in those Save the Children commercials, brown like hotel housekeepers, brown like nurses who wiped asses, and brown like those Miss Universe runners-up who said things like, *You know what, sir, in my twenty-two years of existence, I can say that there is nothing major major I mean problem that I've done in my life . . . because I'm very confident with my family, with the love that they are giving to me. So thank you so much that I'm onstage. Thank you, thank you so much!*

Fuck.

We were brown like their daddies' secretaries, brown like the women their daddies beat off to and sometimes left the family for, brown like *me love you long time*, brown like I need to apologize for offending you, brown like *may I take your plate*, brown like *you think I need your charity*, and brown like *how can I help you, sir?* Back then, we helped ourselves. We dove out of bounds. We broke bones. We didn't care about sweat-slicked ponytails. Didn't care about the skinned knees or bruises or scars, didn't bother with bandages in the mornings before school. We got hard. All the marks on our faces and bodies said, *So what, I'm still here.*

# Omakase

FROM *The New Yorker*

THE COUPLE DECIDED that tonight they would go out for sushi. Two years ago, they'd met online. Three months ago, they'd moved in together. Previously, she'd lived in Boston, but now she lived in New York with him.

The woman was a research analyst at a bank downtown. The man was a ceramic-pottery instructor at a studio uptown. Both were in their late thirties, and neither of them wanted kids. Both enjoyed Asian cuisine, specifically sushi, specifically omakase. It was the element of surprise that they liked. And it suited them in different ways. She got nervous looking at a list of options and would second-guess herself. He enjoyed going with the flow. What is the best choice? she'd ask him when flipping through menus with many pages and many words, and he'd reply, The best choice is whatever you feel like eating at the moment.

Before they got there, the man had described the restaurant as a "hole-in-the-wall." He had found it on a list of top sushi places in central Harlem. Not that there were many. So, instead of top sushi places, it may just have been a list of all sushi places. Be prepared, he said. Nothing is actually a hole-in-the-wall, she replied. Yet the restaurant was as the man had described: a tiny room with a sushi bar and a cash register. Behind the bar stood an old sushi chef. Behind the cash register sat a young waitress. The woman estimated that the hole could seat no more than six adults and a child. Good thing sushi pieces were small. Upon entering, she gave the man a look. The look said, *Is this going to be OK?* Usually, for sushi, they went downtown to places that were brightly lit, crowded, and did not smell so strongly of fish. But tonight downtown trains were experiencing delays because someone had jumped onto the tracks at Port Authority and been hit.

That was something the woman had to get used to about New York. In Boston, the subway didn't get you anywhere, but the stations were generally clean and quiet and no one bothered you on the actual train. Also, there were rarely delays due to people jumping in front of trains. Probably because the trains came so infrequently that there were quicker ways to die. In New York, the subway generally got you where you needed to go, but you had to endure a lot. For example, by the end of her first month the woman had already seen someone pee in the corner of a car. She had been solicited for money numerous times. And, if she didn't have money, the same person would ask her for food or a pencil or a tissue to wipe his nose. On a trip into Brooklyn on the L, she had almost been kicked in the face by a pole-dancing kid. She'd refused to give that kid any money.

You worry too much, the man said whenever she brought up the fact that she still didn't feel quite at home in New York. And not only did she not feel at home; she felt that she was constantly in danger.

You exaggerate, the man replied.

At the restaurant, he gave the woman a look of his own. This look said two things: one, *you worry too much*, and, two, *this is fun —I'm having fun, now you have fun*.

The woman *was* having fun, but she also didn't want to get food poisoning.

As if having read her mind, the man said, If you do get sick, you can blame me.

Eventually, the waitress noticed that the couple had arrived. She had been picking polish off her nails. She looked up but didn't get up and instead waved them to the bar. Sit anywhere you like, she said sleepily. Then she disappeared behind a black curtain embroidered with the Chinese character for the sun.

When they first started dating, they'd agreed that if there weren't any glaring red flags, and there weren't, they would try to live together, and they did. To make things fair, each tried to find a job in the other's city. Not surprisingly, the demand for financial analysts in New York was much higher than the demand for pottery instructors in Boston.

*Huzzah,* he texted the day the movers arrived at her old apartment. She texted back a smiley face, then, later, pictures of her empty living room, bedroom, bathroom, and the pile of furniture and things she was donating so that, once they were living together, they would not have, for example, two dining room sets, twenty pots and pans, seven paring knives, and so on.

She was one of those people—the kind to create an Excel spreadsheet of everything she owned and send it to him, so that he could then highlight what he also owned and specify quantity and type, since it might make sense to have seven paring knives if they were of different thicknesses and lengths and could pare different things.

He was one of these people—the kind to look at an Excel spreadsheet and squint.

Before the big move, she had done some research on the best time to drive into the city in a large moving truck. She did not want to take up too much space. It would pain her if the moving truck was responsible for a blocked intersection and a mess of cars honking nonstop. The internet said that New Yorkers were tough and could probably handle anything. But the internet also said, *To avoid the angriest of New Yorkers during rush hour, try 5 a.m.* When she arrived at 5 a.m., he was waiting for her in the lobby of his building, with a coffee, an extra sweatshirt, and a very enthusiastic kiss. After the kiss, he handed her a set of keys. There were four in total: one for the building, one for the trash room, one for the mailbox, one for their apartment door. Because all the keys looked the same, he said that it might take her a month to figure out which was which, but it took her only a day. She was happy that he was happy. She would frequently wonder, but never ask, if he had looked for a job as diligently as she had.

I'll just have water, the man said, when the waitress gave them each a cup of hot tea. It was eight degrees outside, and the waitress explained that the tea, made from barley, was intentionally paired with the Pacific oyster, which was the first course of the omakase. The waitress looked no older than eighteen. She was Asian, with a diamond nose stud and a purple lip ring. When talking to her, the woman could only stare at the ring and bite her own lip. The woman was also Asian (Chinese), and seeing another Asian with facial piercings reminded her of all the things she had not been able to get away with as a kid. Her immigrant parents had wanted the best for her, so imagine coming home to them with a lip ring. First, her parents would have made her take the ring out, then they would have slapped her, then they would have reminded her that a lip ring made her look like a hoodlum and in this country not everyone would give someone with an Asian face the benefit of the doubt. If she looked like a hoodlum, then she would have trouble getting into college. If she couldn't get into college, then she couldn't get a job. If she couldn't get a job, then she couldn't enter society. If she couldn't enter society, then she might as well go to jail. Ultimately, a lip ring could only land her in jail—what other purpose did it serve? She was not joining the circus. She was not part of an indigenous African tribe. She was not Marilyn Manson. (Her father, for some strange reason, knew who Marilyn Manson was and listened to him and liked him.) Then, in jail, she could make friends with other people wearing lip rings and form a gang. Is that what you want as a career? her parents would have asked. To form a lip-ring gang in jail? And she would have answered no.

Tea it is, the man said. He smiled at the pretty waitress. She *was* pretty. The purple lip ring matched the purple streak in her hair, which matched the purple nail polish. Nevertheless, the man complimented the waitress's unremarkable black uniform. The waitress returned the favor by complimenting the man's circular eyeglass frames.

Oh, these silly things, the man said, lifting his glasses off his nose for a second.

They're not silly, the waitress said matter-of-factly. They're cool. My boyfriend couldn't pull those off. He doesn't have the head shape for it.

If the man lost interest, he didn't show it. If anything, knowing that the pretty waitress had a boyfriend only made the flirtation more fun.

Kids now are so different, the woman thought. She hadn't had a boyfriend until college. She wasn't this bold until after grad school. But the waitress might not have immigrant parents. Perhaps her parents were born here, which would mean different expectations, or parenting so opposed to the way they had been brought up by their own strict immigrant parents that there were basically no expectations. Another possibility: the waitress might have been adopted. In which case all bets were off. Kids now were not only different but lucky, the woman thought. She wanted to say to the waitress, You have no idea how hard some of us worked so that you could dye your hair purple and pierce your lip.

The man nudged the woman, who was sitting next to him like a statue.

You're staring, he said. The waitress had noticed, too, and huffed off.

The mugs that the tea came in were handleless. The tea was so hot that neither of them could pick up the handleless mug comfortably. They could only blow at the steam, hoping that the tea would cool, and comment to each other on how hot it was. Until now, the sushi chef had not said a word to the couple. But it seemed to irritate him as he prepared the Pacific oyster (which turned out to be delicious) to see them not drink the tea.

This is the Japanese way, he finally said. He reached over the bar for the woman's mug. He then held the mug delicately at the very top with two fingertips and a thumb. The other hand was placed under the mug like a saucer. This is the Japanese way, he said again. He handed the mug back to the woman. The couple tried to mimic the chef, but perhaps their skin was thinner than his; holding the mug the Japanese way didn't hurt any less than sticking their hands into boiling water. The man put his mug down. The woman, however, did not want to offend the chef and held her mug until she felt her hands go numb.

Now that the man knew the chef could speak English, he tried to talk to him.

What kind of mug is this? he asked. It looks handmade. The glaze is magnificent. Then the man turned to the woman and pointed out how the green-blue glaze of their mugs seemed to differ. The layering, he said, was subtly thicker and darker in this part of her mug than in his.

Hmm, the woman said. To her, a mug was a mug.

It's a *yunomi*, isn't it? he said to the chef. Taller than it is wide, handleless. Yes, handleless, with a trimmed foot. Used in traditional tea ceremonies.

The chef looked suspiciously at the man. Maybe he was wondering if the man was fucking with him, as people sometimes did when they encountered a different culture and, in an effort to tease, came off as incredibly earnest, only to draw information out of the person they were teasing until the person looked foolish.

He's a potter, the woman said.

The man quickly turned to her as if to say, *Why did you just do that? We were having so much fun.* Then he began to laugh, leaning back and almost falling off the barstool. I'm sorry, he said to the chef. I didn't mean to put you on the spot. The mug is beautiful, and you should be proud to have something like this in your kitchen. I would be.

The chef said thank you and served them their first piece of fish on similarly green-blue ceramic plates that the man promised not to scrutinize.

Enjoy, the chef said, and gave them a steady thumbs-up.

The man responded with his own thumbs-up.

The woman liked how easily the man handled everything. He never took anything too seriously. He was a natural extrovert. By now, the woman knew that, although he worked alone in his studio, he not only enjoyed the company of others but needed it. When out, he talked to anyone and everyone. Sometimes it was jokey talk, the kind he was having with the sushi chef. Sometimes it was playful banter, the kind he had with the pretty waitress. The flirting didn't bother the woman. Instead, it made her feel good that the man was desired. While he was not handsome, he had a friendly face and rosy cheeks. The word *wholesome* came to mind. He was someone who could have just stepped out of a Norman Rockwell painting.

Their first official date had been on Skype. It had consisted of each of them drinking a bottle of wine and watching the same movie on their respective laptops. He suggested *House of Flying Daggers,* and she said that she was OK with watching something else. Maybe something that wasn't so overtly Chinese and, no offense to the talented Zhang Yimou, so old-school.

What do you mean, "old-school"? he had asked.

I mean Tang dynasty, she had said.

She was fine with watching something more mainstream, set in modern day, with story lines about non-Asians. She didn't need the man to make her feel comfortable, if that was, in fact, what he was trying to do.

But it's a critically acclaimed movie, he'd replied.

So they ended up watching *House of Flying Daggers*. The entire movie was in Chinese, with English subtitles. As they got progressively tipsier, the man asked the woman if the subtitles were all correct. I guess, the woman said, even though she understood only half of what was said and was reading the English herself. The man knew much more about Wuxia than she did. He also knew much more about the Tang dynasty, especially the pottery. During that dynasty, the Chinese had perfected color glazes. Most famously, they had perfected the tricolored glaze, which is a combination of green, yellow, and white. He even said the Chinese word for it, *sancai*, and she was a little shocked. No, she was a lot shocked. You would know the glaze if you saw it, he said once the movie was over and the wine had been drunk. The next day, he sent her a picture of a Tang-dynasty camel with *sancai* glaze. It was the same camel that had sat next to her mother's fireplace for the past twenty-five years.

The woman asked some of her friends. Most of them were Asian, but she had a few non-Asian friends as well. A red flag? She did not want to continue with this man if he was interested in her only because she was Chinese. She had heard of these men, especially the kind you met on the internet. She had heard of "yellow fever." She didn't like that it was called yellow fever. To name a kind of attraction after a disease carried by mosquitoes that killed one out of four people severely infected said something about the attraction. Her closest friends told her that she was doing what she did best, overthinking and picking out flaws where there weren't any, hence the reason she was still single at thirty-six. As a potter, the man would obviously know about the history of pottery. And he probably just liked *House of Flying Daggers* as a movie. One of her non-Asian friends said, He's a guy and probably just thinks martial arts are cool. One of her Asian friends said, He probably just wants to impress you.

We'll see, she replied.

For their next Skype date, he suggested a romantic comedy set in England. The following week, an American action film. The next week, a Russian spy drama. After watching, they chatted first about the movie and then about other things. He told her that he had been in a few serious relationships, the most recent of which ended a year ago. What was she like? the woman asked, but really just wanted to know if she was Chinese. The man said that she was nice, though a little neurotic. But what was she like? the woman asked again, and the man said, What do you mean? She was Jewish and tall. He didn't suggest watching a Chinese movie again. When they visited each other, they ate not at Chinese places but at French, Italian, and Japanese restaurants. She was excited that he was turning out to be a regular guy. He met most of her friends, who afterward found a way to tell her how lucky she was to have met someone like him: single, American—an artist, no less— and her age. By "American," some of her Asian friends also meant "white," the implication being that she was somehow climbing the social ladder. She hadn't thought any of these things before, but now she did. Or maybe she had thought all of these things before and was just now admitting to them. Eventually, the woman felt comfortable enough to ask the man why he had picked *House of Flying Daggers* for their first date. The answer he gave was even less profound than what her friends had said. It was a random choice, he explained. That day, the movie had popped up on his browser as something that he might be interested in watching. It was critically acclaimed, he said again.

So it was settled. The big question of why he was dating her was out of the way. Her Chineseness was not a factor. They were merely one out of a billion or so Asian girl–white guy couples walking around on this earth.

The sushi chef worked quickly with his hands, and the woman couldn't help but be mesmerized. From a giant wooden tub of warm rice he scooped out two tiny balls. He molded the balls into elongated dollops. Then he pressed a slice of fish on top of the rice using two fingers, the index and middle, turning the nigiri in the palm of his hand as if displaying a shiny toy car. As a final touch, he dipped a delicate brush into a bowl of black sauce and lightly painted the top of the car. For certain pieces, he wrapped a thin strip of nori around the nigiri. For others, he left the fish slices on a small grill to char. The woman was impressed. This chef looked as though he belonged at the Four Seasons or the Mandarin Oriental. Between courses, he wiped down his cooking station and conversed with them. He spoke softly, which meant that the couple had to listen carefully and not chew too loudly. The man told the chef that they lived only a few blocks away. The chef lived in Queens but was originally from Tokyo. The man said that he had seen the chef working here before. The chef said that that was impossible. The man insisted that he had. He said that he walked by this restaurant every day on the way back from his studio, and though he had never come in, he peeked inside every now and then and saw a chef—you, he said—working diligently behind the bar.

The chef chuckled and said, That's impossible.

Why do you say impossible? the man asked.

Because this is my first day working here.

Oh, the man said, but, refusing to admit that he had been wrong, pushed on. He asked if the restaurant was a family-run business. He might not have seen the chef, as in *you*, but he might have seen a brother or a friend. And surely the chef must have come in for an interview. Perhaps when he peeked in that day the chef was actually there, learning the ropes from the previous chef, who might have been the brother or the friend. At this point, the woman put a hand on the man's thigh.

The chef chuckled again, longer and louder than before. He looked at the woman, and she felt herself unable to meet his gaze. It was not a family-run business, he clarified. He did not know the previous chef. He had been hired yesterday and had interviewed by phone.

The man finally let the topic slide, and the woman was relieved. If he'd continued, she would have had to say something. She would have had to explain to the man (in a roundabout way) that he sounded insensitive, assuming that the chef he'd seen in the window was this chef and then assuming that the chefs could have been brothers. The roundabout way would have to involve a joke—something like *Oh-don't-think-all-of-us-look-the-same*—and the man would have laughed and the woman would have laughed and the chef would have chuckled. It would have to be said as a joke, because the woman knew that the man hadn't meant to seem insensitive; he had just wanted to be right. Also, the woman didn't want to make a big deal out of nothing. She didn't want to be one of those women who noted every teeny tiny thing and racialized it. And wasn't it something that she and her closest Asian friends joked about, too—that, if you considered how people are typically described, by the color of their hair and their eyes, it did sound as though they all looked the same?

But joking about this with her friends was different from joking with the man.

For a moment, the woman felt a kinship with the chef, but the moment passed.

After the couple had finished their tea, the waitress came back and started them on a bottle of unfiltered sake. She still seemed miffed from earlier. She spoke only to the man, explaining that the nigori had herbal notes and hints of chrysanthemum. The woman tossed back her sake and couldn't taste either. The man hovered his nose over his cup for a long minute and said that he could smell subtle hints of something.

Alcohol? the woman said.

Something else.

Chrysanthemum?

Something else.

The woman wanted to add that perhaps what the man was smelling was bullshit, because the waitress was clearly making everything up. How the woman knew was that she had read the back of the bottle, which said the sake had a fruity nose with hints of citrus.

*What's wrong with me?* the woman thought. She was getting riled up over nothing. This was nothing. The man leaned over and rubbed a finger under her chin. She felt better, but not entirely right. The chef smiled at them while slicing two thin pieces of snapper.

When enough time had passed, the man began chatting with the chef again. He was curious, he said. The sushi was delicious, and he was wondering where the chef had worked before. He must have had years of experience. It showed. Speaking on behalf of both of them, the man continued, he hadn't had omakase like this in years and they went to some of the best places in the city.

Like where? the chef asked.

The man listed the places, and the chef nodded in approval and the man beamed. The woman felt a need to interject. Many of these omakase places had been her suggestion. To be honest, when they first started dating the man knew what omakase was but had never tried it. He said the opportunity had never come up, and the woman wondered if this was code for *I didn't know how to go about it, I didn't want to look like an idiot if I went in and ordered wrong*. So, for one of their early in-person dates she had taken him to a place in Boston. She knew the chef, who was Chinese. Many Chinese chefs turned to Japanese food, as it was significantly classier and more lucrative. She spoke with the Chinese chef in Chinese about the Japanese omakase, an experience that she would not have known how to describe to her parents, who had been taught to loathe the Japanese, or her grandparents, who had lived through the Sino-Japanese War and did loathe the Japanese. Thankfully, that history was not part of the woman's identity. She had grown up in the States. She felt no animosity toward Japanese people, culture, or food. Anyway, the point was that, when she'd visited the man in New York, she had looked up the places he had just listed. She had taught the man that, in Japanese, *omakase* means "I leave it up to you." There was one more thing. She had paid. Not always but most of the time, especially at the more expensive places. And it made sense for her to pay. She earned more, and trying omakase together had become one of their things. She liked that they had things.

There was also that place in Boston, the woman interjected. Remember? The one I took you to. The first time you had omakase. While she was saying this, the woman wondered if she was being too defensive, but she said it anyway.

Of course, the man said without glancing at her. So where did you work again? he asked the chef.

A restaurant downtown, he said. He then gave the name, but it was not one that either the man or the woman recognized.

You might not know it, he said. It was a very exclusive place. Very fancy. We didn't open every day. We opened only by reservation. And to make a reservation you had to call a specific number that wasn't listed, that was only passed by word of mouth. When you called, you asked to speak with the manager. The manager had to know you, or else he would say you'd called the wrong number and hang up.

You're kidding, the man said. Then he looked at the woman and asked if she'd heard that.

She had heard it. The chef wasn't whispering. The man leaned over the bar, so that his upper body was now above the trays of nori and the bowl of sauce. He was leaning on his elbows, like a little boy waiting for a treat from his mother in the kitchen. Adorable, the woman noted, and momentarily felt fine again.

So I'm guessing you got tired of that, the man said. Dealing with all those rich folks.

No.

It was probably the stress. I bet a place like that made you work terrible hours. All those private parties. People who have nothing better to do with their money.

No.

And not being able to make whatever you wanted. What the customer wants the customer gets. A place that exclusive, you probably got some strange requests.

Yes, but that's not the reason I was fired.

Fired?

The man looked even more interested. Did you hear that? he said to the woman. To him, if a high-class chef had been fired that meant that the chef had a rogue streak, which was something the man tended to respect. Also, he was getting drunk. The sake bottle was empty, and the waitress had brought another.

Fired for what? the man asked. He offered the chef a cup of sake, but the chef declined.

The woman turned her own cup in her hands and stared at the wall behind the chef, which had a painting of a giant wave about to crush three tiny boats. The woman liked the fact that she and the man worked in completely different fields. It meant that there was very little competition between them, and what they had in common was something genuine. The man had no interest in money, and that fascinated her. He seemed a free spirit, but how was he still alive today if he didn't care about money? She, on the other hand, was much more concerned about money and where it came from. She liked her job, but she liked it most because it was stable and salaried. Although she could not say those things to the man, who sometimes said to his friends, Bankers, when she made practical remarks about how they were going to split the check. After he said that, he did one of those comical eye rolls to show everyone that he was kidding. It was funny. She laughed along. But later, when she asked him why he did that, he would put a hand on her head and say that she was overthinking it. He was only teasing her because he was so proud of her. She did something he couldn't in a million years do. Numbers, graphs—just hearing

her on the phone made his head spin, but the work was clearly
important and necessary. And you're able to do this because, well,
let's face it, you're smarter than me. The man had said that. When
he said it, the woman felt a happy balloon rise from her stomach
to her mouth.

Fired for what?

The chef didn't answer. Instead, he washed his hands, which
were now covered in red slime, and picked up a blowtorch to sear
the skin of a nearby salmon.

A year into dating, she had taken the man to meet her parents.
They lived in a cookie-cutter suburb in Springfield, Massachusetts.
Her father worked for a company that designed prosthetic limbs.
Her mother was a housewife. Back in China, they'd had different
jobs. Her father had been a computer-science professor and her
mother had been a salesclerk, but their success in those former
roles had hinged on being loquacious and witty in their native
language, none of which translated into English. Every now and
then, her father went out for academic jobs and would make it as
far as the interview stage, at which point he had to teach a class.
He would dress as sharply as he could. He would prepare careful
notes. Then, during class, the only question he was asked, usually
by a clownish kid in the back row, was whether he could please
repeat something. Her mother took a job at JCPenney but eventually quit. In China, an efficient salesclerk followed customers from
place to place like a shadow, but no one wanted her mother to do
that at JCPenney. In fact, her mother was frequently reported for
looking like a thief. Nevertheless, her parents were now comfortable in their two-thousand-square-foot house, which had a plastic
mailbox and resembled everyone else's. Perhaps her parents liked
the sameness of suburban houses because, from the outside, you
couldn't tell that a Chinese family lived inside. Not that her parents were ashamed of being Chinese, and they had taught their
daughter not to be ashamed, either. You are just as good as anyone else, they'd told her, even before she realized that this was a
thought she was supposed to have.

The woman did not know how her parents would react. She
had brought home other boyfriends, and the reception had been
lukewarm. The man was the first boyfriend she had brought home
in a long time. Unfortunately, that made the question of race even

harder to answer, as he was also the first white boyfriend she had brought home. So, were her parents being welcoming out of relief that their daughter wouldn't become a spinster or out of surprise that she, as her friends pointed out, had got lucky? As with every complex question in life, it was probably a mixture of both. But was it a fifty-fifty mix or a twenty-eighty one, and, if the latter, which was the eighty and which was the twenty?

Throughout the weekend, the woman felt feverish. Her brain was in overdrive. She watched the man help her mother bring in groceries and then help her father shovel the driveway. She was in disbelief when her father went out and came back with a bottle of whiskey. She didn't know that he drank whiskey. She then had to recalculate the fifty-fifty ratio to take into account the whiskey. For each meal, her mother set out a pair of chopsticks and also cutlery. When the man chose the chopsticks, her parents smiled at him as if he were a clever monkey who had put the square peg into the square hole.

That he could use chopsticks correctly elicited another smile, even a clap. Then they complimented him on everything, from the color of his hair down to the color of his shoes.

The woman was glad that her parents were being nice, as it dispelled the cliché of difficult Asian parents. Previously she had explained to the man that her parents had a tendency to be cold, but the coldness was more a reflex from years of being underdogs than their natural state. When her parents turned out not to be cold at all, the woman was glad, but then she wondered why they hadn't been more difficult. Why hadn't her father been more like a typical American dad and greeted the man at their cookie-cutter door with a cookie-cutter threat?

By the end of the weekend, her mother had pulled her aside to say that she should consider moving to New York. The man had thrown the idea out there, and the woman didn't know how to respond.

I'm not sure yet, she told her mother. But we're going to look for jobs in both places.

Her mother nodded and said, Good. Then she reminded the woman that a man like that wouldn't wait around forever.

For their last piece of omakase, the chef presented them with the classic tamago egg on sushi rice. The egg was fluffy and sweet. How was that? the chef asked. He asked this question after every course, with his shoulders slumped forward, and their response—that it was the best tamago egg on sushi rice they'd ever had—pushed his shoulders back like a strong wind.

The Japanese way, the woman thought. Or perhaps the Asian way. Or perhaps the human way.

Dessert was two scoops of mocha ice cream. For the remainder of the meal, the man kept asking the chef why he'd been fired. Another bottle of sake had arrived.

It's nothing interesting, the chef said.

I doubt that, the man said. Come on. We're all friends here.

Though neither he nor the woman knew the chef's name, and vice versa. During the meal, no one else had come into the restaurant. People had stopped by the window and looked at the menu but had moved on.

Management, the chef finally said. He was done making sushi and had begun to clean the counter. He would clean the counter and wash his rag. Then he would clean the counter again.

His purpose wasn't to clean anymore, the woman decided. It was to look as if he had something to do while he told the story.

What happened? she asked. At this point, she might as well know.

I was fired three weeks ago, the chef said. The manager had booked a party of fifty for a day that I was supposed to have off. Then he called me in. I initially said no, but the party was for one of our regulars. I said I couldn't serve a party of fifty on my own and he would need to call in backup. He said OK, and an hour later I showed up. But there was no backup, just me. The manager was Chinese, and said that he had called other chefs but no one had come.

The chef stopped cleaning for a moment to wash his rag. I'm not an idiot, he continued. I knew that was a lie. So I only made sushi for two people. I refused to make sushi for the other forty-eight, and eventually the entire party left.

Bold, the man said.

The woman didn't say anything. There was a piece of egg stuck between her molars and she was trying to get it out with her tongue. When she couldn't, she used a finger. She stuck her finger into the back of her mouth. Then she wiped the piece of egg—no longer yellow and fluffy but white and foamy—on her napkin.

I'm Chinese, the woman said reflexively, the way her parents might have.

The chef went back to cleaning his counter. The man cleared his throat. He said, not specifically to the woman or the chef but to an invisible audience, That's not what the chef meant.

I know, the woman said. She was looking at the man. I know that's not what he meant. I just wanted to put it out there. I don't mean anything by it, either.

The man rolled his eyes and a spike of anger went through the woman. Or maybe two spikes. She imagined taking two toothpicks and sticking them through the man's pretty eyes to stop them from rolling. Then she imagined making herself a very dry martini with a skewer of olives.

Sorry, the chef said. He was now rearranging the boxes of sesame seeds and bonito flakes. He was smiling but not making eye contact. In a moment, he would start humming and the woman would not be able to tell if he was sorry for what he'd said or sorry that she was Chinese. A mix of both? She wanted to ask which one it was, or how much of each, but then she would sound insane. She didn't want to sound insane, yet she also didn't want to be a quiet little flower. So there she was, saying nothing but oscillating between these two extremes. In truth, what could she say? The chef was over sixty years old. And the Chinese, or so she'd heard, were the cheapest of the cheap.

The man never called her sweetheart. Sweetheart, he said, I think you've had enough to drink. Then he turned to the chef. Time to go, methinks.

The chef spoke only to the waitress after that. He called her over to help the couple settle the bill. The woman put her credit card down while the man pretended not to notice. She tipped her usual 20 percent.

What was that? the man said once they were outside. It had got colder. It would take them fifteen minutes to walk home.

I'm not mad at him, the woman said.

And you shouldn't be. He was just telling a story.

Again, I'm not mad at him.

The man understood. They walked in silence for a while before he said, Look, I wasn't the one who told the story and you have to learn not to take everything so personally. You take everything so personally.

Do I?

Also, you have to be a little more self-aware.

Aware of what?

The man sighed.

Aware of what?

The man said, Never mind. Then he put a hand on her head and told her to stop overthinking it.

*Contributors' Notes*

*Other Distinguished Stories of 2018*

*American and Canadian Magazines
Publishing Short Stories*

# Contributors' Notes

NANA KWAME ADJEI-BRENYAH is from Spring Valley, New York. He graduated from SUNY Albany and went on to receive his MFA from Syracuse University. He was the 2016–17 Olive B. O'Connor fellow in fiction at Colgate University. His work has appeared or is forthcoming in numerous publications, including *Guernica*, *Esquire*, *The Paris Review*, *Compose: A Journal of Simply Good Writing*, *Printer's Row*, *Gravel*, and others. *Friday Black* is his first book.

· In writing *The Era* I found a new way to arrive at a story. I discovered that sometimes just a voice could be the spark. I had what would become Ben's voice rattling in my brain for a while. It was a postapocalyptic-sad-boy chorus that was strange and funny and alive to me. An idea of a world emerged from this voice, a world that was brutal in the name of "honesty," a world that had learned to forsake kindness as a virtue. And once these general ideas were in place, I let the voice take me where it would.

Born in Northern California in 1988, KATHLEEN ALCOTT is the author of the novels *America Was Hard to Find*, *Infinite Home*, and *The Dangers of Proximal Alphabets*. Her work has appeared in the *Guardian*, the *New York Times Magazine*, *Zoetrope: All-Story*, *Tin House*, and *ZYZZYVA*; her short story "Reputation Management" was short-listed for the 2017 Sunday Times Short Story Award. A fellow of the MacDowell Colony, she has taught fiction and literature at Columbia University and Bennington College.

· Having lost my parents by my early twenties, I often considered how I might maintain a relationship with each—which stories of theirs might take on different meaning as my life changed, which objects left behind might alter in emotional valence. But at the center of these thoughts was a certain dynamic: myself as protean, my parents' lives as fixed where they left them—never, as the story begins, providing any new information.

As my parents' lives grew further away, I found that they were not the statuary I expected, and that certain truths I had took to be calcified were not; I learned, for instance, that a turquoise ring of my mother's, something she'd worn my entire life and whose sentimental value I believed to be significant, was actually a gift from a college boyfriend she nurtured no fond feeling for—she just couldn't, reported a mutual acquaintance of theirs to me, ever get it off. My experience of my father, after his death in my adolescence, was not dissimilar; once I was twenty, a well-meaning friend of his typed up some old correspondence of theirs, revising a narrative I'd built of his adventurous, politically driven early years as an itinerant journalist into something else: a portrait of a very troubled, potentially bipolar young man who seemed motivated mostly by the blankness of any new place.

I must have felt afraid of some other fact that lurked for me, regarding either of them, particularly in the wake of a very painful separation that left me, at the end of my twenties, without much of a plan for my future; it is always when I fear what's ahead that I begin to doubt and revisit what, or who, is behind. I spent the year after the relationship ended in a string of houses that did not belong to me, renting sublets in increasingly remote parts of the country, and wrote "Natural Light" during my stay in the last, in a ramshackle farmhouse in Maine, writing all morning and swimming all afternoon.

WENDELL BERRY is native to the community of Port Royal, Kentucky, to which both sides of his family have belonged for more than two hundred years. Since 1965, he and Tanya Amy Berry have lived on and from a marginal farm in the Kentucky River valley. He has written fiction, poetry, and essays. For most of his life he has maintained an interest in issues of land use, and he has tried to promote the good care and good health of the land and the people.

• I have always known more stories, and have told more, than I could write. Now and again, because of increasing age and experience or the accumulation of work, I have more or less suddenly become capable of writing so as to be read by strangers a story that, until then, had been only spoken and heard in my own neighborhood. Behind this now-written story is a lived one that, for a while, could be passed about among people who knew the setting and, so to speak, the original cast. Writing such a story calls for the characters and the situation to be newly imagined, in order to give it the plausibility previously supplied by local tellers and hearers. This can be accomplished by moving the lived story into a fictional community already prepared, as has been done here.

JAMEL BRINKLEY is from the Bronx and Brooklyn, New York. He is the author of *A Lucky Man: Stories*, a finalist for the National Book Award in

Fiction, the Story Prize, the John Leonard Prize, and the PEN/Robert W. Bingham Prize, and winner of the Ernest J. Gaines Award for Literary Excellence. His work has appeared in *Ploughshares, A Public Space, Gulf Coast, LitMag, Glimmer Train, American Short Fiction,* and *Tin House,* and other publications. A graduate of the Iowa Writers' Workshop, he was also a Carol Houck Smith Fiction Fellow at the Wisconsin Institute for Creative Writing. He is currently a Wallace Stegner Fellow in Fiction at Stanford University.

  • If my files are accurate, the opening line of the very first draft of this story was this: "The first time I heard 'Brooklyn Zoo' by Ol' Dirty Bastard, I was at a house party in Flatbush with my friend, a guy who called himself Claudius Van Clyde." For a while, "Brooklyn Zoo" was my working title, and I wanted to draw upon the energy, aggression, and arrogance that characterize that song in order to counter the passivity, inwardness, and timidity of the narrators I often find myself using in first-person stories. But then, in order to counter all that male intensity and assuredness, the story demanded that Ben and his friend be out of their depth, in terms of their age and maturity, and in terms of their understanding of their environment, of the women they pursue, and of their problematic, exoticizing desires.

  It is a cliché in fiction to have a scene in which a dog barks mysteriously in the distance, but what happens when a barking dog actually shows up? When it occurs here and the young women respond, Claudius, who has acted as the catalyst for much of the story, decides he's had enough, but then Ben, driven by his lust and his preoccupation with his father, takes the baton. I was excited to see what would occur after that, and while I was surprised by the specifics of what ensued, it made total sense to me to discover that neither of the two guys were ever really in control of what was happening.

DEBORAH EISENBERG's most recent collection of stories is *Your Duck Is My Duck.* She lives in New York City, teaches at Columbia University's School of the Arts, and has received many awards, including a MacArthur Fellowship.

  • I'd say that none of the stories I've written are what you'd call characteristic of my stories, but this one is possibly the least characteristic, as well as the most recently written. It began—uncharacteristically—with the title, which popped into my head one day. I thought, Somebody should write something called "The Third Tower," and after a time during which nobody seemed to do that, I thought, Oh, well, I guess I will.

  I really didn't know what snagged me on that title, but it was always in my mind as I worked, and eventually, after many trials, I finished the story. So then there I was, with a story set in a sort of near future or a parallel present, about a girl—a young laborer—whose imagination, curiosity, vitality, and quality of experience are being purposefully reduced.

Maybe it's asking a lot of the reader to explore the dynamic space between those two elements, but that's how it worked for me; the character and her plight arose from the title. The title obviously implies a relationship between an image of two towers—almost inevitably in this era the image of the two annihilated World Trade Center Towers—and a third tower. That third tower might suggest, for example, the Freedom Tower, a triumphalist tourist magnet erected ostensibly as a monument to those murdered on September 11, 2001, or the first of horrifyingly proliferating skyscrapers (this tower, that tower) signifying, above all, money, or just an abstract tower representing surveillance or domination.

So it turned out that what had interested me about that phrase, *the third tower*, were matters concerning the systemic opportunism of power and money: catastrophe as a rationale for increasing economic inequities, as a rationale for invasions and resource appropriations and wars and oppression that benefit only the powerful; catastrophe utilized as an instrument to make a population compliant or inadvertently complicit —incapable of significant dissent or incapable even of comprehending what is happening to it. Naturally, plenty of writers have investigated these processes in different ways, but unfortunately, there's always room for more investigation.

JULIA ELLIOTT's writing has appeared in *Tin House, The Georgia Review, Conjunctions,* the *New York Times,* and other publications. She has won a Rona Jaffe Foundation Writers' Award, and her stories have been anthologized in *Pushcart Prize: Best of the Small Presses* and a previous edition of *Best American Short Stories.* Her debut story collection, *The Wilds,* chosen by *Kirkus, BuzzFeed, Book Riot,* and *Electric Literature* as one of the Best Books of 2014, was a *New York Times Book Review* Editors' Choice. Her first novel, *The New and Improved Romie Futch,* arrived in 2015.

 • In a bloated early draft of my novel, *The New and Improved Romie Futch,* I got sidetracked by a digression about Romie's first erotic experience, a blissful romp with a rural third cousin during which the two prepubescent kids smear molten tar all over each other, a transcendent moment followed by a brutal reckoning. In the original flashback, Romie's grandmother catches them and cleans them up with gasoline and a hard-bristled brush, nearly flaying them, leaving them humiliated in sodden transparent clothes. Recalling badass girl cousins from my own youth, so-called tomboys who could hold their own among hellion boys, the kind of girls who could drive go-carts one-handed while taking cool puffs from stolen cigarette butts, I realized that Butter's perspective on this incident would be far more interesting than Romie's. When I took the cutting from my novel and switched the point of view, my story "Hellion" bloomed from the corpse of that killed darling.

JEFFREY EUGENIDES is the author of three novels: *The Virgin Suicides*, a twenty-fifth anniversary edition of which appeared in 2018; *Middlesex*, which won the 2003 Pulitzer Prize; and *The Marriage Plot*, which was a finalist for the National Book Critics Circle Award and was named as the best novel of 2011 by independent booksellers in the United States. *Fresh Complaint*, a collection of short stories, appeared in 2017. Eugenides is the Lewis and Loretta Glucksman Professor in American Letters at New York University. He is a member of the American Academy of Arts and Letters and the American Academy of Arts and Sciences.

• According to a file on my computer, the first impulse of the story that became "Bronze" was written on July 23, 2013. That was nine months after my novel *The Marriage Plot* had come out, at a time when I was working on a book of short stories. Clearly, I had intended for "Bronze" to be part of that collection.

It didn't work out that way. The working title of that fragment was called "Boy on Train." I knew that it involved an encounter between a college freshman and a professional actor who are forced to sit together on a crowded Amtrak train, during a trip from New York to Providence, in 1978. I knew that the point of view should shift back and forth between these two characters and that their meeting should be dramatized moment by moment. The idea was to give the story a feeling of immediacy, as if its events were happening in real time.

I made decent progress at first. The language of the story, highly inflected by the characters' personalities, felt freeing, allowing me to reproduce the way the world, or at least *my* world, had sounded back in '78. I worked on the story off and on. Sometimes I put it away for a few months to write another story, or to play around with an idea for a novel. There was a moment, early in 2017, when I felt optimistic enough about finishing the story that I told my publisher that it would be included in my forthcoming collection. In fact, a German journalist recently reminded me that an early notice for what later became *Fresh Complaint* had claimed that the collection's title would be "Bronze" and that it would contain a story about a college freshman on a train. He asked me what had happened.

I couldn't finish "Bronze," was what. I kept getting hung up by the opening. So much information had to be established that it was difficult to get it all in while keeping the story moving. Whenever I tried to simplify things by removing some aspect of the story, the story lost some of its verve and eventual payoff. So, I would put that stuff back in and quickly get tangled up again. The first page of "Bronze" still seems to me its weakest part; after that, the story gets rolling. But it's possible that I can't read the opening without remembering how much trouble it caused me.

It was only after *Fresh Complaint* had gone off to the printers that I marshaled the courage to face down "Bronze" yet again, released from any expectation that it would be included in the collection. During that final showdown, I managed to get the opening to work, and to polish the rest.

All this chaos turned out for the best, however. *The New Yorker* published "Bronze" in early 2018. In the months afterward, I began writing other stories featuring Eugene, its young hero. And so, rather than being orphaned from my previous collection, "Bronze" has begun to grow into a book of its own, the difficulty I had with the story's beginning now the beginning of something bigger.

ELLA MARTINSEN GORHAM lives in Los Angeles with her husband and children. Her writing has appeared in *ZYZZYVA* and *New England Review*. She is at work on a collection of stories, and also a novel.

• I saw that my children and their friends documented much of their lives on the screens of phones and laptops. I began to think of them as inhabiting two worlds: the touchable, physical world and the digital world. They slipped back and forth between them. This notion gave rise to the story "Protozoa."

I was interested in a girl of thirteen navigating the two worlds. I wanted to capture the moment she decides to shed her childhood self and become more provocative. The girl, Noa, transforms herself by building a new, darker online profile. She grabs the attention of an older girl, Aurora Waters, and the two fall into an intense friendship though they never meet in person. I had the idea that the physical distance between them could enable a kind of intimacy.

Noa and Aurora develop a ritual of sharing tears. I was inspired by accounts of the Japanese practice *rui-katsu*, in which groups of people convene to cry together as a therapeutic release. I wanted to know what that would look like among girls in search of an outlet for their emotions. As it turns out, the girls' motives for sharing tears in the story are mixed. The true feelings, sadness and anger, are shaded with a sense of intrigue in the act of crying for an audience.

Noa also pushes herself to hook up with a boy named Paddy, who then dubs her "Protozoa" in an online roast. While both Aurora and Paddy play a part in Noa's reinvention, I didn't know in early drafts whose influence was the more powerful. As I revised the story, it became clear that Noa's stronger drive was to impress Aurora. This led to the final scene, in which Noa posts a video of herself weeping and waits for a reaction.

NICOLE KRAUSS has been hailed by the *New York Times* as "one of America's most important novelists." She is the author of the international bestsellers *Forest Dark, Great House,* which was a finalist for the National Book Award and the Orange Prize, and *The History of Love,* which won the William Saroyan International Prize for Writing and France's Prix du Meilleur

Livre Étranger, and was short-listed for the Orange, Médicis, and Femina prizes. Her first novel, *Man Walks Into a Room*, was a finalist for the Los Angeles Times Book of the Year. In 2007 she was selected as one of *Granta*'s Best Young American Novelists, and in 2010 she was chosen by *The New Yorker* for their "Twenty Under Forty" list. Her fiction has been published in *The New Yorker*, *Harper's*, *Esquire*, and *The Best American Short Stories*, and her books have been translated into more than thirty-five languages.

• Like Romi in the story, I first saw *Taste of Cherry* in London in 1998, the year it was released. I was living in student housing near Russell Square, and the film was playing nearby at the Renoir, whose marquee advertising foreign films was dwarfed by the giant concrete Brutalist building in whose underground the cinema was housed. I went alone, which was the way I usually saw films at that time. I was already a fan of Abbas Kiarostami's films, but when Ershadi's face appeared on the screen "it did something to me," as the narrator of the story says, and what it did to me, and continued doing to me for the next twenty years, is what I tried to work out in this story. I don't have a good memory for most films: what I remember is usually atmospheric rather than details of plots or dialogue. But Ershadi's face, and scenes from *Taste of Cherry*, continued to return to me, often without having been evoked by any obvious reminder. The memory of Ershadi's face as Mr. Badii, and those dusty hills outside Tehran, seemed to have become involuntary, lodged at some mysterious juncture of synapses in my brain that was sometimes tripped, and over time he became a kind of landmark in my thoughts, one that only gained feeling the more I passed through it, or it through me.

Six years later I traveled to Japan for the first time and visited the temples of Kyoto. Did I really think that I saw Ershadi in the Zen garden of Nanzen-ji? I *remember* believing that I had seen him. But now I can't say for sure if what I am remembering is a scene I invented for this story, or something that actually happened to me. I really can't.

A moment after I wrote the last sentence I stood up to stretch my legs, wandered over to my bookshelf, and, scanning the titles of the books I've tried in the last months to cull, I pulled down *Censoring an Iranian Love Story*, by Shahriar Mandanipour. When I flipped through the pages, I found a ticket used as a bookmark: the ticket to the Zen garden of Nanzen-ji! There are the stones like leaping tigers pictured on the front of the ticket, the very place I had just been thinking about, trying to figure out whether the scene I described that took place there was imagined or recalled. I have no idea what to make of this coincidence, beyond that things that can't be explained rationally often fall to writers to investigate, because most respectable professions don't want to touch them. But all the same, they seem to promise access to regions of the mind, and being, and the world that are otherwise closed off to us.

Whether I really thought I saw Ershadi in the temple in Kyoto, or whether a scene I wrote later became conflated with actual memory over the thirteen years it took me to finally finish the story, I don't know. During those years, the story absorbed many new experiences: my time watching the Israeli dance company Batsheva rehearse, and getting to know many of its dancers; my friendship with an extraordinary Israeli actress; the arrival of my children.

More coincidences: A few days after the story was published in *The New Yorker*, I received an email from the son of Abbas Kiarostami, who lives in San Francisco. "Your story has touched so many of my friends," Ahmad Kiarostami wrote. "I received the link from at least 20 people from all over the globe, including Iran . . . It was as if I was watching a touching love story film." He offered to introduce me to Homayoun Ershadi the next time the actor was in America. I wrote back and asked whether he thought Ershadi had read the story. He replied almost immediately:

"I actually talked to Homayoun's sister, Toufan (who also helped my father for many years and was a close friend of him), and asked what Homayoun thought about the article. She said he was very emotional after reading it. She said the timing couldn't have been better. Apparently he is down these days, and your story very much helped him to feel better. She said that since it came out, he's been getting cheerful calls and texts every single day." At the end of the email, Kiarostami had attached a screenshot showing Ershadi's Facebook page, where he'd shared a link to the story.

URSULA K. LE GUIN (1929–2018) was a celebrated and beloved author of twenty-one novels, eleven volumes of short stories, four collections of essays, twelve children's books, six volumes of poetry, and four of translation. The breadth and imagination of her work earned her six Nebulas, seven Hugos, and the Science Fiction and Fantasy Writers of America's Grand Master Award, along with the PEN/Malamud and many other awards. In 2014 she was awarded the National Book Foundation Medal for Distinguished Contribution to American Letters, and in 2016 joined the short list of authors to be published in their lifetimes by the Library of America.

MANUEL MUÑOZ is the author of a novel, *What You See in the Dark*, and two short story collections, *Zigzagger* and *The Faith Healer of Olive Avenue*, which was shortlisted for the Frank O'Connor International Short Story Award. He is the recipient of fellowships from the National Endowment for the Arts and the New York Foundation for the Arts, and has been recognized with a Whiting Award and three O. Henry Awards. His most recent work has appeared in *American Short Fiction, Glimmer Train, The Southwest Review,* and *Freeman's.* He has been on the faculty of the University of Arizona's creative writing program since 2008.

· My stories are taking longer to write these days. I don't know exactly why, but the long pauses keep steering me back to story basics. I give myself more room to think about what a story's center might be and I have let go of the need to resolve every conflict that arises. I'm learning to listen to the stories as they want to tell themselves: I know that sounds odd, but it comes from years of listening to my mother's stories and only now realizing that I haven't been fully understanding them. Most of my recent fiction has come from delving again into the stories she has told me, particularly of the deportation years, as I call them, when my father was repeatedly sent back to Mexico before the 1986 Immigration Reform and Control Act changed our lives and many of those in our Central Valley town of Dinuba, California. I used to think that my parents' reunification was the only story but, as the first line proved to me, sometimes other pressures took over. When that line came to me, it snapped me out of my recurrent doubt that the "domestic" or the "realist" story can do much in a fraught and complicated world. It reminded me that the infinite ways in which we struggle to keep or make family is more than story enough.

"Anyone Can Do It" appeared in an issue titled "Restoration: Of and About the Environment," and I want to thank Laura Cogan, Oscar Villalon, and everyone at *ZYZZYVA* for thinking so generously and broadly about not only the natural world, but the lives of the people who work within it on a daily basis.

SIGRID NUNEZ'S most recent novel, *The Friend,* won the 2018 National Book Award for Fiction. She has published six other novels, including *A Feather on the Breath of God, The Last of Her Kind,* and *Salvation City.* She is also the author of *Sempre Susan: A Memoir of Susan Sontag.* Her work has appeared in several anthologies, including four Pushcart Prize volumes and four anthologies of Asian American literature. Nunez has been the recipient of a Whiting Award, a Berlin Prize fellowship, and two awards from the American Academy of Arts and Letters: the Rosenthal Family Foundation Award and the Rome Prize in Literature. She is writer in residence at Boston University.

· The first story I ever published was in *Ellery Queen's Mystery Magazine,* and though I did not go on to write fiction in that genre and am not even a big reader of such fiction, I have often found myself wanting to write about a crime. For "The Plan," I wanted to write about a certain type of criminal —violent, murderous, misogynistic—and I wanted to write from his point of view. The fierce anger and resentment that appear to consume so many men today was likely among the influences on my desire to explore this killer's vision of society and his place in it. Also, I have vivid memories of what New York City was like during the seventies, how crime-ridden and seedy and dangerous it was—a very noir place, it seemed to me—and I saw this as the ideal setting for my crime story.

MARIA REVA was born in Ukraine and grew up in Vancouver, British Columbia. Her stories have appeared in *The Atlantic, McSweeney's, Granta, The Journey Prize Stories, The Best American Short Stories 2017*, and elsewhere. Her musical collaborations include an opera libretto for Erato Ensemble, texts for Vancouver International Song Institute's Art Song Lab, and a script for City Opera Vancouver. She received her MFA from the Michener Center for Writers at the University of Texas. "Letter of Apology" is part of a linked story collection, *Good Citizens Need Not Fear*, forthcoming in spring 2020.

• A few years ago I read that the KGB had to stop arresting citizens for telling political jokes in the 1960s, due to the Khrushchev Thaw, but also because it was impossible to lock up the entire Soviet Union. Instead, officers were to engage offenders in a (re)educational conversation and have them submit a letter of apology.

Shortly after I learned this, my father told me that the KGB tried to recruit him to the Honor Guard in the 1980s. He was a model student and athlete, but the last thing he wanted was to guard Lenin's tomb. (In the end he slipped from the KGB's clutches—but that's another story.)

These two sources inspired "Letter of Apology." I'd already written a story from the perspective of a character who suspects she is being trailed by the KGB, but not one from the perspective of a KGB agent doing the trailing. I wanted to explore the loss of power a secret service agent must have felt, having to chase after citizens for a chat and letter. Finally, I wanted to examine the mechanisms of self-delusion: how does a person escape a terrible truth?

KAREN RUSSELL is the author of the novel *Swamplandia!* and three story collections, including the recently published *Orange World and Other Stories*. Born and raised in Miami, Florida, she now lives in Portland, Oregon, with her husband and son. She currently holds the Endowed Chair of Texas State University's MFA program, where she teaches as a visiting professor.

• My husband and I went to Korčula on our honeymoon, on a tiny ferry that docked at night during a tremendous storm. It seemed as if we were the only living people in the walled medieval city. "Look," my husband reassured me as we racewalked over the cobblestones, "I see some people right over there." Lightning illuminated three faceless nuns floating down a gothic staircase. Later we'd laugh about this B-horror-movie tableau, but it wasn't the nuns who frightened me that night. Something was pursuing us, I felt quietly certain. As we wandered down the silent streets, I had to consciously still my muscles to avoid breaking into a run.

In our hotel, I learned about the *vukodlak*.

Sometimes translated as "vampire" and other times as "werewolf," a *vukodlak* is a body that exhumes itself and wanders the woods after its death. According to Croatian folk belief, the dead could be protected from this fate by severing their hamstrings before burial. As recently as 1770, Dalmatian villagers requested that this "operation" be performed on a loved one's cadaver. The idea of a posthumous surgeon who operates underground came to me shortly after reading this detail in our guidebook.

I wrote the original draft of "Black Corfu" in a feverish season of hope and fear, while I was pregnant with my son and considering the unlevel landscapes that children inherit from a new vantage point. I remember working on it in the wake of the 2016 presidential election, and I'm sure this story set in a fictional 1620 Korčula was my way of grappling with the rampant injustice in our country. How many people today feel trapped in their orbits, unable to ladder out of poverty, despair? Condemned to work in the shadows while they watch others enjoy health, wealth, safety? The *vukodlak* seemed like the right vessel for a story about a father's "zombie" hopes—those undead dreams of freedom that stalk a world where they are as yet unfulfilled. In her incredible work on horror, history, and haunting, *Ghostly Matters*, Avery Gordon describes an agony that I think applies both to this imaginary Korčulan and to so many real people today: "the wear and tear of long years of struggling to survive . . . the deep pain of always having to compete in a contest you did not have any part in designing for what most matters and merits." It's the involution of hope that turns the doctor into a monster. You could say "Black Corfu" is a horror story about mobility, in a sense—*Blessed are the living*, as this subterranean doctor says, *who can move*.

SAÏD SAYRAFIEZADEH is the author of the story collection *Brief Encounters with the Enemy*, a finalist for the 2014 PEN/Robert W. Bingham Prize, and the critically acclaimed memoir *When Skateboards Will Be Free*, selected as one of the ten best books of the year by Dwight Garner of the *New York Times*. His short stories and personal essays have appeared in *The New Yorker*, *The Paris Review*, the *New York Times*, *Granta*, *McSweeney's*, *The Best American Nonrequired Reading*, and *New American Stories*, among other publications. He is the recipient of a Whiting Award for nonfiction, and a fiction fellowship from the Cullman Center for Scholars and Writers. His play, *Autobiography of a Terrorist*, was staged last year by Golden Thread Productions in San Francisco. He currently serves on the board of directors of the New York Foundation for the Arts, and teaches in the creative writing programs at Hunter College, Columbia University, and NYU, where he received an Outstanding Teaching Award.

• This piece began as nonfiction, which is to say, as the truth. I had originally intended to title it "How Cigarettes Saved My Life," because if I had not become addicted to smoking cigarettes at the age of nineteen, I would not have been self-aware enough to realize that, two years later, I was following a similar trajectory with crack cocaine. This guiding principle comprised the final four pages of the story, and the final four pages of the story were eventually, with great reluctance and remorse, completely cut. Many other facts were cut as well, and many others were bent and reshaped in the interests of make-believe. Even so, I continued to try to cleave as closely as I could to reality, perhaps as a way to make direct use of what I'd experienced, but also because I've always believed that the truth is generally more compelling than invention.

For instance, a few years ago I was riding the public bus through my hometown of Pittsburgh, where I'd gone back to visit for the weekend. At some point in the trip, an elderly black man got on and took the seat directly in front of me. He was probably about seventy years old, give or take, toothless, clearly poor, dressed in baggy, monochrome clothes. And yet, as the bus ride continued, something semiconscious began to take shape in my mind, something distressing but insistent, until I finally realized that this seventy-year-old man was not seventy years old, nor was he, in fact, a stranger to me, but rather a friend of mine: when we were in our early twenties we had worked at a restaurant together, played pickup basketball together, and, yes, smoked crack cocaine together. He'd been tall and handsome back then. He'd been a standout former high school basketball player, and a so-so former college player. I don't think he'd ever gotten his degree, which was one reason why he was living in the projects and working at a restaurant as a busboy with zero prospects for anything more. I remember that we'd spent one summer afternoon walking around Pittsburgh, off from work, nothing to do, too hot to play basketball, and both of us trying our best to avoid broaching crack. He would sometimes tell me how he'd stare in the mirror and speak to himself in the third person, almost as a mantra, with optimism and conviction. "This isn't you," he'd say. Meaning, this life of smoking crack wasn't at essence who he was, and that he could, through sheer will, surmount it.

Months later, after I'd gone and gotten professional help, and after I'd stopped associating with anyone who had had anything to do with crack, he called me one night. It was Saturday, around ten o'clock, and he needed money . . . for his brother. His brother had just gotten home from the military and he was eligible for health insurance, but he had to pay the premium now, right *now*—Saturday night at ten o'clock—and if he didn't pay it now, he'd never be able to have health insurance. Could I lend his brother forty dollars? No, I was sorry, but I could not. And that was the last I spoke to him until that bus ride in Pittsburgh, twenty-five years later, where I'd tapped him on the shoulder and we'd stood and hugged each other, and I'd tried to pretend that there was nothing remotely unsettling about his appearance. He told me he worked construction now, which I wasn't sure I believed, and I told him I lived in New York City. He wanted to know if I'd been there for 9/11. 9/11 had been fifteen years earlier. That 9/11 was his immediate association with New York City seemed to me to be a sure indication of the amount of trauma he'd been dealing with, then and now. I was very aware of that mantra he'd uttered years earlier, "This is not you," and of its brutal, unsparing conclusion.

All of this is why I wrote the story. None of it made it in.

ALEXIS SCHAITKIN'S debut novel, *Saint X*, is forthcoming in February 2020; it will be translated into French, Spanish, German, Italian, Dutch, and Hungarian. Her short stories and essays have appeared in *Ecotone, Southwest Review,* and the *Southern Review,* among other venues, and her fiction has been anthologized in *The Best American Nonrequired Reading.* She received her MFA in fiction from the University of Virginia. She lives in Williamstown, Massachusetts, with her husband, the historian Mason B. Williams, and their son.

• Jen's job writing descriptions of houses for a realtor is very similar to a job I held for a few years in graduate school. To be honest, it was a job whose potential as material I was aware of from the very beginning. Architecture is such a classic metaphor for story. And this job—stepping into someone else's home and observing, tiptoeing in the dark through a house where people are living their inimitable lives—was so *like* the writer's task.

But for years I found the work impenetrable to being written about. I was living in Charlottesville, Virginia, and like Jen in the story, I was mostly writing about houses in the city's many suburban developments. There was Avinity Estates, Redfields, Riverwood, Chesterfield Landing, Dunlora Park —all of these names that are simultaneously hyperevocative and hollow, sometimes even nonsensical. In a single spring, I wrote about six townhouses of the same model in one development—they were identical, but I needed to make each one sound unique. So the reality of the work was just pretty . . . tedious.

Then, one day, my boss gave me an address way out of town. The house was completely dazzling, and it had an observatory, just like the house in the story. After years of visiting nothing but suburban sprawl, it was surreal to step into this incredible house out in the middle of nowhere. That was the very obvious inspiration for the story.

But as the story came together, it was all of the other houses I'd visited that fueled its essential questions: what makes something authentic versus imitative or ersatz, and does this distinction even matter, and if so, how and why—in architecture, in writing, in life? One of my biggest anxieties as a writer is always "Is this good, or does it just *sound* good?" Laying that bare, exposing it through Jen's voice, was scary, but also exciting.

JIM SHEPARD has written seven novels, including *The Book of Aron*, which won the Sophie Brody Medal for excellence in Jewish literature, the Harold U. Ribalow Prize for Jewish literature, the PEN/New England Award for fiction, and the Clark Fiction Prize, and five story collections, including *Like You'd Understand, Anyway*, a finalist for the National Book Award and Story Prize winner, and most recently *The World to Come*. He's also won the Rea Award for the Short Story, the Library of Congress/Massachusetts Book Award for Fiction, the Alex Award from the American Library Association, and a Guggenheim Fellowship. He teaches at Williams College.

• I've always been interested in the Civil War—some of my earliest memories, in fact, may involve flipping fascinatedly through my older brother's Civil War cards, a staggeringly gory 1962 Topps series that uniformly horrified parents—but I've resisted for all these years writing about it because it's often seemed to me that there's something unpleasantly precious about the way the subject is often treated. So I was just doing what I usually do—reading bizarrely arcane nonfiction, in this case men's and women's Civil War letters—when I was struck by an aspect of them that seemed shockingly relevant to the unhappy position in which we find ourselves today. Even in the very last days of the war, after all of that suffering and all of those losses, letter after letter articulated its conviction that come what may, the South and the North would never reconcile their positions when it came to race, and that the abyss that had opened up in American civic life was never going to close. One Southern woman's bitter remark gave me such a jolt that it kick-started my entire story. She wrote "The breach between us is so wide that by the war's end the South can only be all Yankees or no Yankees at all."

The intensity of the sense that so many Northerners and Southerners shared that nothing had been solved, and that this problem in all likelihood never *would* be solved, was a little stunning to me. At one point in Orson Welles's *Citizen Kane*, Boss Jim Gettys, the protagonist's nemesis, tells him, "If it was anybody else, I'd say what was going to happen to you would be a lesson to you. Only you're going to need *more* than one lesson. And you're going to *get* more than one lesson." How had we managed as a country to go through five years of agony with more than three-quarters of a million casualties while still ending up having learned so little? That kind of maddeningly self-destructive mulishness has always attracted me as a subject. It's also starting to seem, dispiritingly, like one of our central characteristics as a country. There followed, then, one of my usual bathysphere descents into more focused arcane reading, after which I found myself doing what I could to imagine myself inside that recalcitrant Southerner's position.

MONA SIMPSON has published six novels and still wants to be a writer.

· In my twenties, I had two friends who studied trauma: a woman whose research centered on victims, and her fiancé, who put up flyers around campus to attract rapists, without using the word *rape*. Like many social science studies, it claimed to be about something else, perhaps male sexuality. His questionnaire used the legal definition of rape but never used the word; I remember the phrase "up to and including the use of force." Occasionally, at university events, a student play, for example, they would see a student they both knew; a favorite from one of the woman's classes turned out to be one of her fiancé's rapists. Once married, the newly minted PhDs set up practices. At one point the husband led a group of men on Rikers Island, all of whom except one had killed their mothers. The other had murdered his grandmother with an antique chair. All were victims of sexual abuse.

Until then, I'd reflexively assumed the logic of the final two lines of Auden's stanza: Those to whom evil is done / Do evil in return.

But damage, it turns out, is not always reciprocated. My friends the young therapists told me about the vast number of people, a majority, they believed, who spent their lives containing the trauma they'd endured, working not to pass it on.

My interest in the idea of this containment of destructive desire started there, with this work to which my friends have now devoted their lives.

I read research, followed online communities.

Of course, much of what I learned didn't make it into the story.

JENN ALANDY TRAHAN was born in Houston, Texas, and raised in Vallejo, California. The first in her family to go to college, she graduated from the University of California, Irvine, with a BA in English and went on to earn her MA in English and MFA in fiction from McNeese State University. It would be cool to be one of those fancy authors and write that she, her husband, her daughter, and two dogs currently divide their time between Los Altos, California, and Lake Charles, Louisiana, but that would not be true. Jenn is a Jones Lecturer at Stanford, where she was a 2016–18 Wallace Stegner Fellow in Fiction.

· Somewhere I read that Michael Phelps, the most decorated Olympian of all time, kept his headphones in to listen to music until the last possible moment before getting into the pool and did this throughout his entire career. There's that great meme of him in the midst of this prerace ritual at the 2016 Summer Olympics in Rio, getting in the zone. Now, I'm no Michael Phelps, but instead of listening to Future's "Stick Talk," I had been rereading *The Virgin Suicides* by Jeffrey Eugenides and *Then We Came to the End* by Joshua Ferris to get pumped before a graduate workshop deadline. At the time, I was reflecting on how I killed the majority of my twenties making self-destructive decisions, befriending people who didn't really care about what happened to me, and trying to impress people who would never see or value the real me. I had recently separated from my first husband and also felt ashamed for being en route to divorce, I felt ashamed for chasing my impractical dreams in graduate school, the list goes on and on. I was tired of feeling ashamed. I wanted to conjure what I had lost over the years: a sense of pride about who I am and where I come from. Out came some notes about Vallejo and a group of young women during a specific time where they felt the strongest and proudest, mainly because they were figuring out how to endure life together and play for the same team. I was still wallowing in self-doubt, however, and my classmate and homie, Sean Quinn, encouraged me to stop beating myself up in front of my laptop and to get out of the house. We ended up at a downtown Lake Charles bar, the now-defunct Dharma. This is where I met Glenn Trahan. Glenn, a Marine, had a swagger about him. His rough-around-the-edges yet good-natured vibe instantly reminded me of the Vallejo boys I grew up with even though Glenn grew up in Cameron, Louisiana. I also got the sense that Glenn wasn't interested in being anyone else but—unapologetically—himself. Suddenly I had the rest of the words and a story for that workshop deadline; Brent Zalesky materialized as the missing piece. That first draft of this story, originally titled "Take Us Back to Vinyl," wanted to explore the transportive quality of music and had a thread that constantly pitted the husbands of these women against their memories of Brent Zalesky. I would have loved to have had references to Tupac, The Conscious Daughters, Too $hort, Luniz, Mac Dre, Green Day, and the Smashing Pumpkins in it too, but it became clear that it wasn't so much about the music of my adolescence, husbands who were not Brent Zalesky, or the rediscovery of vinyl as it was about the indomitable spirit of these young women and the spirit of Brent Zalesky. To echo Violet Lucca on the *Harper's* podcast discussing "They Told Us Not to Say This," Brent Zalesky isn't so much the object of desire as the object that the "we" of the story strives to be.

The story is very much a valentine to Vallejo, a valentine to the people I grew up with at St. Basil School, and a valentine to my best friends who have stuck by my side through the years, no matter what (I'm looking at you, Marc Martello and James Cho). You could say it's also a valentine to Brent Zaleskys everywhere—people who inspire you to do things you wouldn't otherwise do, people who show up to watch you play and convince you of your strength and value when others want to insist that you are weak or that you don't belong. In this way you could say that Adrian Kneubuhl at *Harper's* is a Brent Zalesky, and I'm incredibly grateful to him for teaching me how to not only grow as a writer, but as a person. Thank you, Adrian, for encouraging me to listen to my story and my heart.

You could also say this story is a valentine to my muse and my rock, Glenn Trahan, and to my role models—the uplifting professors I've been incredibly lucky to learn from at Irvine (Alex Espinoza, Michelle Latiolais, and Lisa Alvarez), McNeese (Chris Lowe, Amy Fleury, Dr. Rita Costello, and Dr. Bärbel Czennia), and Stanford (Dr. Adam Johnson, Elizabeth Tallent, and Chang-rae Lee). I try to emulate all of them in my own classroom and strive to be a Brent Zalesky on the bleachers for my students—and for my own daughter, Teagan, though I'm fully aware that just by virtue of being her mom, alas, she will never think that I'm cool.

WEIKE WANG is the author of the novel *Chemistry*, and her work has appeared in *Glimmer Train, Ploughshares, Alaska Quarterly Review,* and *The New Yorker,* among other publications. She is the recipient of the 2018 PEN/Hemingway Award, a Whiting Award, and a National Book Foundation 5 under 35 prize. She currently lives in New York City.

• Stories come to me in waves. I will have an idea, usually a setup, and then in the months after, build out and then in (characters, conflict, place). But all of this is still in my head. For "Omakase," my husband and I had just gone out for sushi. The chef there was not the chef in this story. The "real" chef was actually perfectly sweet and normal. We made small talk. He told us about the type of fish we were eating and the kind of tools he used. We asked questions and had a good time. Yet what was odd about the meal was that for the entire night my husband and I were the only customers. I just found that setup interesting and rich. What could happen if a couple came here and the chef was slightly off—jilted, perhaps—and overshared as people do when no one is around? How intimate could a conversation get? How much do we really know about each other? And what kind of history goes into an interaction that seems fine and easy on the surface? I thought about the story for over half a year. When I sat down to write it, it was done in a week. Then edits, another week. But the core did not change. Nor did the setup.

# Other Distinguished Stories of 2018

# American and Canadian Magazines Publishing Short Stories

Able Muse
African American Review
Agni
Alaska Quarterly Review
American Short Fiction
The Antioch Review
Apalachee Review
Arkansas International
Ascent
The Atlantic
Badlands
Barrelhouse
Belmont Story Review
Big Muddy
The Bitter Oleander
Black Warrior Review
Bomb
Boulevard
Briar Cliff Review
Bridge Eight
The Carolina Quarterly
Carve
Catamaran
Catapult
The Chattahoochee Review
Chautauqua
Cherry Tree
Cimarron Review

The Cincinnati Review
The Coachella Review
Cold Mountain Review
Colorado Review
The Common
Commonweal
Conjunctions
Consequence
Copper Nickel
Craft
Crazyhorse
Cream City Review
The Dalhousie Review
December
Denver Quarterly
Descant
Ecotone
Electric Lit
Emry's Journal
Epiphany
Esquire
Event
Fairy Tale Review
Fantasy and Science Fiction
Fence
Fiction
Fiction International
Fiction River

The Fiddlehead
Fifth Wednesday
Foglifter
Folio
Free State Review
Freeman's
Gargoyle
The Georgia Review
The Gettysburg Review
Glimmer Train
Granta
Harper's
Harvard Review
Hayden's Ferry Review
Hobart
The Hopkins Review
The Hudson Review
Huizache
Hypertext Review
Image
Indiana Review
Into the Void
The Iowa Review
Iron Horse Literary Review
Jabberwock Review
Joyland
Juked
Kenyon Review
Lady Churchill's Rosebud Wristlet
Lake Effect
The Literary Review
LitMag
Longleaf Review
Longshot Island
The Louisville Review
Manoa
The Masters Review
McSweeney's
Meridian
Michigan Quarterly Review
The Missouri Review
Montana Quarterly

Narrative
Nelle
New England Review
New Letters
New Madrid
New Pop Lit
The New Yorker
Ninth Letter
Noon
Notre Dame Review
The Normal School
North American Review
North Carolina Literary Review
The Northern Virginia Review
The Offing
Okay Donkey
On the Premises
One Story
Orion
Oyster River Pages
The Pacifica Literary Review
The Paris Review
Pembroke Magazine
Pigeon Pages
Playboy
Ploughshares
Portland Review
Potomac Review
Prairie Schooner
Pulphouse Fiction Magazine
Pulp Literature
Raritan
Roanoke Review
Room
Ruminate
The Rumpus
Salamander
Salmagundi
Santa Monica Review
The Sewanee Review
Slice
Solstice
The South Carolina Review

The Southampton Review
Southern Indiana Review
The Southern Review
The Southwest Review
Split Lip
StoryQuarterly
Strange Horizons
The Sun
Superstition Review
Tahoma Literary Review
Tampa Review
Territory
Third Coast
The Threepenny Review
Tin House
The Tishman Review
Tough Crime Stories
Transition

TriQuarterly
Upstreet
Virginia Quarterly Review
Washington Square Review
Water-Stone Review
Waxwing
West Branch
Western Humanities Review
Wildness
Willow Springs
Wired
The Worcester Review
World Literature Today
The Yale Review
Yellow Medicine Review
Zone 3
Zoetrope: All-Story
ZYZZYVA

# THE BEST AMERICAN SERIES®

*FIRST, BEST, AND BEST-SELLING*

*The Best American Comics*

*The Best American Essays*

*The Best American Food Writing*

*The Best American Mystery Stories*

*The Best American Nonrequired Reading*

*The Best American Science and Nature Writing*

*The Best American Science Fiction and Fantasy*

*The Best American Short Stories*

*The Best American Sports Writing*

*The Best American Travel Writing*

Available in print and e-book wherever books are sold.

Visit our website: hmhbooks.com/series/best-american